MIX, MATCH AND MURDER

MIX, MATCH & MURDER

A Psychological Thriller

By

Raymond John

North Star Press of St. Cloud, Inc.
St. Cloud, Minnesota

ISBN-10: 0-87839-289-0
ISBN-13: 978-0-87839-289-6

First Edition: September 1, 2009

Printed in the United States of America

Published by
North Star Press of St. Cloud, Inc.
P.O. Box 451
St. Cloud, Minnesota 56302

northstarpress.com

info@northstarpress.com

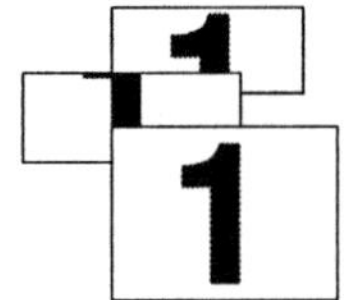

WHAT WAS THAT?

Jason quietly rolled to his back to listen.

Was there someone outside the door? As hard as the seven-year-old's ears strained to hear, the hotel room had become quiet again.

Mother didn't seem to have heard it. She still lay on the next bed facing away from him, gently snoring. Her words still kept him awake and pinned him in place like one of the orange beetles in his collection. "Go to sleep, sweetie, or I won't buy you the remote-controlled plane Grandma wanted you to have. We'll just have enough time to get it before we catch our flight."

It was a fib, of course. Like Santa Claus was a fib. Grandma couldn't have known how much he wanted a plane he could really fly. But Grandma at least was— or had been—a real person, so it was easy to believe she actually had wanted him to have a Pizazz 48" Ugly Stick with a Super P8 remote. He had seen it in *Boy's Life* and had been dreaming about it for months. He'd probably mentioned it to his parents a dozen times a day.

Tomorrow it would be his. If only he could keep still, that is.

It wasn't easy. The bed was uncomfortable, and the room reeked of cigarette smoke. Every breath made him choke. Even so, he was now so tired he could barely keep his eyes open, and he snuggled deeper into the thin pillow.

With thoughts about the Ugly Stick fading away, Jason edged toward sleep. He came to, fully alert, at a repeat of the sound he'd heard before. It wasn't a knock exactly, but more a scratching sound like Buster made when he wanted to come into the house.

Jason looked over toward his mother, wondering if she had heard it too. At first he thought she was asleep and hadn't. But she silently sat up and peered over at him. Jason pressed his eyes shut. Seconds later, she got to her feet and tiptoed to the door. It opened without a sound, letting in a flood of orange light from the hallway.

Someone stood in the doorway. It couldn't be Father. The figure outlined against the light from the hallway was taller than Father and bulky, as if he wore a winter coat, but he didn't stand like Father either. His frame looked looser than Father's ramrod posture.

Uncle Gary?

Once again, everything went dark. Seconds later the bathroom door scraped against the pile of the rug, and then scraped again as it closed.

A thread of light showed under the door. Even though Jason desperately wanted to see or hear who was with his mother, his legs remained frozen in place between the sheets.

Finally, teeth rattling more from nervousness than cold, he eased out of bed and tiptoed to the bathroom door. He pressed his ear to the thin wood.

He heard muffled sighs and kisses.

An anger he had never felt before began to well inside of him. *Whoever that is shouldn't be here!*

Jason scampered back to bed when the bathroom light went out.

Whispers.

The anger in his belly had grown, but now he felt a shiver of fear. *Who was with Mother, and why were they whispering?*

Was it Father after all?

He held his breath as Mother's bed squeaked. Someone had gotten into it. Moments later, it squeaked again.

Jason cringed at his mother's sigh.

Who's there? The words he wanted to shout froze in Jason's throat. *Who are you and what do you want?* The bedsprings creaked. Then his mother moaned.

He's hurting her! Jason nearly jumped out of bed. He might be small, but he would defend his mother.

The bedsprings groaned again, and his mother uttered a soft, almost urgent, cry.

Blood surged. Though deathly afraid, Jason knew he had to do something.

How? He had no strength against his father when he was forced to go to his room. Father would simply take his upper arm and make him move. And when he and Uncle Gary roughhoused, he never could make him stop. Then Jason remembered the woodcarving knife he had been using to work on his balsa airplane earlier that evening. It still lay on the table between the beds. Bursting with tension, he noiselessly reached for it, closed his fingers around the metal handle.

Gripping it tightly in his right hand, he flipped on the light as he jumped out of bed. "I'll help you, Mommy!" he shouted.

The figures on the bed moved together.

"No!" his mother screamed.

Head down, Jason charged. The naked man rolled off his mother. *Why was Mother naked, too?*

Barely able to see because of the tears in his eyes, Jason screamed in rage.

"Jason, stop," Mother screamed. "You don't understand."

Now as furious with his mother as he was at the intruder, he brought down the blade.

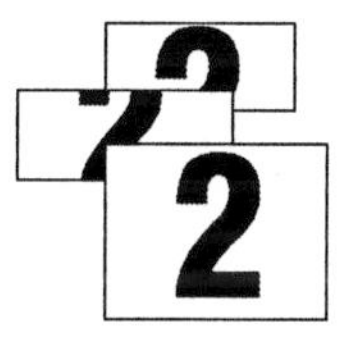

FRIDAY, MAY 21, 2008

ARRIVING AT THE LUMBER EXCHANGE parking ramp, Jennifer Cahill rotated out of her seat in the new red Audi TT Roadster to take another rueful look at the long scratch on the driver's door. Retrieving a handkerchief from her handbag, she moistened a corner and gave the mark a quick scrub. The hoped for miracle didn't happen. Wetting the hankie again, she rubbed the mark harder.

Darn. Still there. A week ago someone had let the air out of the tires and kept the caps.

Her eyes narrowed. Could it have been the same person? If so, she, unfortunately, could come up with a lengthy list of suspects. In her years as a psychologist working in the Hennepin County parole division, she'd had a large case load. Those clients had little choice in receiving her services. Many were angry and unhappy. One of them might well be acting out his or her frustration.

Or it might be one of her current clients. Adolescents could be more vindictive than adults when crossed.

With a wistful shake of the head, she started toward the stairway leading to the lobby of the Lumber Exchange.

She loved the Exchange. It was unpretentious, with small offices and little retail business. Her rental agent told her that when it was built in 1886, it was the only building outside of New York with at least twelve floors. The shiny, brass-plated entrances at street level were a continuous row of gothic arched windows and doors. Pink limestone surrounded and soared above it. The Exchange was a relic of Minneapolis' proud past. Now, while the high-powered money conducted business in the IDS Tower and Pillsbury Building, the Exchange housed working professionals of a more modest stature. Instead of Beamers and Mercedes parked between the reserved parking lines, most vehicles were fuel-efficient KIA compacts and Toyota mini-SUVs.

That made her expensive Audi stand out like a sore thumb.

Stepping through the doorway leading to the lobby, she all but ran into the security guard. "Well, good morning, Miss Cahill." His voice sounded like fingernails on a blackboard. Most of the time he was at his desk. When he was, she could ignore the obese letch leers. He also made no move to get out of her way.

"Good morning, Mr. Daniels," she replied in a frosty voice as she pushed past him and thumbed the elevator-call button.

"Heh," the man snorted, making the hairs drooping from his nose wave. "Musta got up on the wrong side of the bed this morning, huh?"

"Guess I musta," she responded, flashing a cartoonish smile. "Have a nice day."

He started to say something, but the elevator door closed, cutting him short. She dropped her smile and closed her eyes. After a leisurely ride, the door opened to the third floor. She found Eric Larson waiting outside her door.

She never liked to greet him. Merely asking him how he was could elicit a very long answer. She decided to risk it.

"I'm terrible," the teen moaned. "I haven't been able to sleep for a week."

"I'm sorry to hear that," she said in a sympathetic voice. "Come in."

He docilely followed her inside.

"Sit down and I'll be with you in a minute," she said. "Have you been taking your meds?"

"Sure," Eric said. "All the time."

Jennifer was skilled at reading tone. His wasn't truthful. "You wouldn't kid me, would you?"

Eric turned red. "Well, maybe not *all* the time. I told you the stuff gives me a stomachache. That's been really bad this week."

"Then we'll just have to get your doctor to come up with something else, won't we?" Jennifer said as she unlocked the inner door to her office. "I'll be right back."

She quickly stepped inside and shut her door. On more than one occasion, Eric had followed her in.

Taking a deep breath, she took an unhappy look at her desk. For all her wishing, the healthy stack of client files hadn't disappeared overnight. And they would still be there at that day's end. too. She had a full schedule until five o'clock that afternoon.

About to pull out Eric's file, she noticed the red light on her phone answering machine blinking. The caller's voice gave her a shock.

"Hello, Jen. It's Mike."

Her heart skipped a beat. Why was Mike calling? *Could he be in town and wanting to see me?*

"Give me a call as soon as you get this message. It's important."

She anxiously looked up the number in her Rolodex. Fingers fumbled as she dialed. She felt weak when Mike Savich answered on the third ring.

"Hello, Mike," Jennifer said, stuffing her excitement. "I got your call. What's up?"

"Actually, I've got two things to tell you. One of them involves one of my patients. He's going to show up in your office sometime late this morning. I've sent him to you, or rather he's sent himself. I think you'll be interested in his case."

She squinted. "Today? You have to be kidding. I have a full day of appointments."

"He's bringing you a thousand-dollar retaining fee. Are you sure you can't reschedule one or two of your clients?"

Jennifer grimaced as she thought about the paint job her car would need. Much as she hated it, Mammon sometimes trumped professional principles. "I suppose I could, but I still don't like it. Who is he?"

"His name's Jason Dumont. You may have heard of him."

The name meant nothing to her. "What makes you think that?"

"He was in the news several years ago. He's coming back to Minneapolis after fifteen years."

Fifteen years? Jason Dumont was no adolescent. Before she could protest, her door was flung open and a young female stormed into her office. Fuming.

"What do you think you're doing having me come in for an appointment on Monday. I'm supposed to be taking my trigonometry test," Candace Lane screeched.

"Sorry, Mike," Jennifer said, getting to her feet. "I'll be right back to you." Covering the receiver, she said. "Get out. You have no right coming into my office."

"I have every right. I asked you a question. I want an answer."

"Wait in the lobby. When I'm done with my call, I'll explain it to you."

"I'm not going anywhere," Candy snarled. "I know what you're up to. You're trying to keep me from graduating."

Seeing there was no easy way to get Candy to leave, Jennifer gave in. "I cleared everything with your teacher. He's letting you make up the test on Tuesday. Monday is the only day your mother and Doctor Lewinsky have free. Doctor Lewinsky is one of the best clinical psychologists in the country. I think she can find a way to help you stop cutting yourself."

Candy's eyes momentarily flitted away from Jennifer toward the CCTV tape recorder and quickly returned. Glaring, she said, "I don't want to see her. I'm going to take the trig test with the rest of my class."

"Sorry. Doctor Lewinsky is very interested in talking to you and your mother. She doesn't have any other free time, so you will be here. Now please leave my office."

"We'll see about that," Candy said, exhaling threateningly. Picking up one of the files, she threw it at Jennifer before turning on the rubber heels of her red Converse tennis shoes and left.

Jennifer felt the veins in her forehead throbbing. After taking a deep breath, she uncovered the phone. "Sorry, Mike. My drama queen from hell wouldn't be put off. What's this about a patient you're sending me? How old is he, anyway?"

"He's twenty-two years old and has an interesting history."

Her jaw dropped. "You have to be kidding. You know I only deal with young children and adolescents."

"I told you he has an interesting history. He may have an adult's body, but he has the emotional maturity of a seven-year-old."

Jennifer's irritation immediately began to give way to curiosity. "Really? What happened to him?"

"I'll let him give you the details. His mother was murdered in the International Hotel just around the corner from you, and Jason was present when it happened. It's a totally cold case without any physical evidence, so it'll never be solved. Jason just wants to remember what happened so he can get on with his life."

"Is he bringing his chart with him?"

"No. I'm sending it to you. I want you to come to your own conclusions about him."

"Hmm. Can't you at least tell me what you've been treating him for?"

"Selective traumatic amnesia and repressed memories. I could have sent him to some other specialist, but you're the only professional in Minneapolis I know I can trust."

Jennifer remembered Eric, who would be slouching in the waiting room. "It all sounds fascinating, Mike, but I've got another patient waiting right now. I'll do my best to fit Jason in, but I can't promise anything. Do you have any idea what time he'll be arriving?"

"Some time later this morning. He's flying from Columbus."

"Okay," Jennifer said with a sigh. "You said you had two things to tell me. What's the other?"

"Oh. I completely forgot about my big news. You remember Christine Cavendish, don't you?"

Oh, no! Jennifer thought, knowing what was coming. "Sure. She's the one who helped get you into your practice in Columbus, isn't she?"

"Yes. Well, we're getting married. We're leaving for Bangkok day after tomorrow. Our parents will be coming to join us early next week."

Jennifer swiped at the tears forming at the corners of her eyes. "That's wonderful," she said in a cheerful voice. "I wish both of you all the happiness in the world. I wish I could come to your wedding. I've always heard Thailand is beautiful."

"It is. Thanks so much in advance for working with Jason. I really appreciate it."

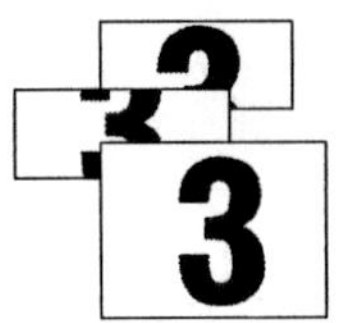

DETECTIVE-LIEUTENANT DAN ARNOLD gritted his teeth and sloshed down the last of his morning coffee.

"Bleh," he grunted, slipping the cup into the holder by the steering wheel of his 1987 Taurus. The filter in Horny Hildegard, his sensuous coffee-maker, had folded over while brewing, leaving him with weak coffee-flavored tea. After pulling into his parking spot, he dumped the rest of the cup on the ramp floor.

Taking the stairway out of the building, he crossed Fourth Street and headed for the door of the pink limestone castle known as the Old Courthouse. In former days, the building provided housing for Minneapolis' entire police department and legal system, as well as the mayor, council, and all the municipal offices. Now, nearly deserted except for the huge marble statue of the reclining Father of Waters and a few licensing departments, everything else had moved to the twin-towers of the government building across Fifth Street. Even the carillon in the belfry lay silent, and the hands on the four faces of the Big Ben clock permanently read 6:28.

Dan's footsteps rang out hollowly as he took the marble steps leading to the basement two at a time. At the bottom, the voice of Mike McNichol of Sports Radio, brayed in the hallway. A jaunt down the dimly-lit corridor brought Dan to his destination. Bill Benz slouched with his feet on his desk.

"Morning, Bill," Dan called through the wire door.

Officer Bill Benz jumped at the sound. "Jesus, Dan. Don't do that. What're you doing here this time of the morning?"

"I can't resist your ugly face," Dan growled. "Now open the door." A buzzer sounded, and Dan pulled the heavy gate open to enter the evidence room.

Inside, ten aisles with shelves extending from the floor to the fourteen-foot ceiling housed hundreds of twenty-by-twelve-by-ten-inch black boxes. Most of them contained drugs or weapons confiscated during arrests. Others had articles of clothing and non-DNA evidence from rapes and assaults. A few had the personal effects and forensic evidence from homicide investigations. Dan called it the Hall of Shame, and considered it a fitting tribute to the baseness of human nature. And the murder of Melanie Dumont had showed humanity at its very worst.

His footsteps echoed as he found the correct aisle and quickly located box 665512. The checkout card on top had dozens of entries, all but ten of which dated to more than thirteen years ago. He scratched in the date and his initials and removed the card to leave it where the box had been.

"Done so soon?" Benz asked.

"Funny," Dan said with a sour expression.

Officer Benz notated its serial number on his roster sheet. "Why don't you just keep it in your office," he said. "It'd save you a few steps."

Dan didn't answer. Tucking the box under his arm, he took the hallway to the stairway at the opposite end of the building and exited.

Wind gusted ominously as he crossed the Light Rail Transit tracks to the Government Building entrance, bringing a hint of rain. Mumbling aloud, he climbed the stairs and marched across the lobby to the elevators.

"Morning, chief," the young uniform at the info desk called out to him.

Dan ignored him. Fifteen years of frustration and defeat left him surly. Jason Dumont was returning to rub salt in old wounds by coming back.

Sometimes life really was the shits.

WITH HER EYES RIVETED to her lobby monitor, Jennifer used her peripheral vision to find her compact in her purse. By moving the mirror close to the screen, she found she could guide her fingers to smooth midnight mauve lip-gloss over neglected areas of her mouth while remaining totally focused on the overhead screen.

She wished she could see the visitor better. The light streaming into the lobby through the windows made the figure in the rattan chair shadowy. All she could clearly make out was flashes of light as he turned pages in a magazine.

Little as there was to see, she couldn't take her eyes off of the screen.

She had been on pins and needles since Mike Savich's call. A chance to treat selective traumatic amnesia was every therapist's dream.

Luckily, Jason Dumont had called just before he landed at nine o'clock. That gave her enough time to get in touch with Shelly March's mother to cancel that appointment before she left for Jennifer's office.

Smoothing her light wool skirt with a brush of her palms, Jennifer put on a professional smile and opened the door. She was greeted by blinding light, and instinctively threw her hands up in front of her face.

"Jason Dumont?"

"Yes," a youthful male voice stammered. Hurrying to pull the curtains, he said, "Sorry. It was too dark in here. I couldn't see to read."

"No harm done," Jennifer said, repairing her damaged smile. When her eyes readjusted, she discovered a sandy-haired young man staring at her. Outdoorsy in L.L. Bean cargo pants and a loose golf shirt that showed off hard pecs and brawny shoulders, and easily more than six feet tall, he looked like a model for a health club ad.

Clearing her throat, she held out her hand. "Good morning," she said. "I'm Jennifer Cahill. Please come in."

She turned to beam at him. "Did you have any trouble finding me?"

"No."

She clung to her smile but wondered if the expression hadn't become a bit lopsided for wear. Gesturing toward a couch, she said, "Have a seat."

He sat.

She shut the door and moved to a chair at the left side of her desk. It was her usual position, making sure there were no obstacles between her and the patient. The only time she sat behind the desk was when she was alone. Carefully moving a yellow legal pad next to her, she crossed her ankles and put on a studious look.

Jason responded by sitting back in the couch with jaw set and arms crossed in front of his chest.

Oh, oh. He doesn't want to be here.

Silence prevailed. Finally, she asked, "What can I do for you, Mr. Dumont?"

He didn't answer, but shifted uncomfortably in his chair and temporized by pulling up the knees of his pants. Without making eye contact, he said, "Didn't Mike Savich tell you about me?"

"Actually he didn't. On purpose. He wants me to be a fresh pair of ears."

"Oh," he said, shifting buttocks. "It's hard for me to talk about it."

Jennifer got up and stepped behind her desk. Opening a side drawer, she took out a clone of the legal pad she was using. After fishing out a pen from the center drawer, she handed them to him. "Write it then."

He pursed his lips.

"I'm serious," she said. "If it would be easier for you, write it out. Or if you would rather talk about something else, that's all right, too."

He took the pad, stared at it for a second or two, then handed it back to her. "This is stupid. All I've done is think about this for the last fifteen years. Or at least what I can remember of it, and that isn't much."

"What do you remember?"

"Damned little, actually. Mother and I came to Minneapolis on our way to Thief River Falls for Grandmother's funeral. I remember that the plane ride from Cincinnati to Minneapolis was bumpy, and I spilled chocolate milk into my lap. I also remember Mom couldn't find her luggage when we got to Minneapolis. We took a limousine to the hotel and for some reason I didn't like the room. After that, I don't remember anything that happened until I was back home and my father was telling me Mother was dead."

Jennifer gaped. So that was why Mike asked if she had ever heard of Jason Dumont. "Is there any possibility you hit your head?"

He chuckled mirthlessly. "Not according to the tests I've taken. All the MRIs, PET Scans, and EEGs have come back negative. It's definitely not physical. That only leaves one other possibility."

You lost your marbles, Jennifer thought. An unknown patient had played a prank on her by leaving a large jar of marbles on a chair in her lobby. Ever since then she often found it difficult to keep a straight face, as terrible as her client's problems were. "Actually there are several possible explanations. How much do you remember? I don't have your file, so you'll have to fill me in. Do you recall the police talking to you?"

"No, though I understand they did. All I know for sure is what they told me. I told them I couldn't remember anything about what happened. They never had anything to go on and stopped looking for the murderer about two years later. It's been a cold case ever since."

She nodded. "It's a vicious circle, isn't it? The police have been hoping you'd remember so they can find the murderer, and solve the case. You've been hoping they would solve the case so you could get your memory back."

Tears welled up in the corners of Jason's eyes, then immediately disappeared. "Yes. And I'm beginning to think neither one will ever happen. Though he's never said it, I know Lieutenant Arnold thinks I lost my memory because I killed her myself."

"Ridiculous. You were just seven years old. Little boys don't murder their mothers."

"Yeah," he said with a derisive snort. "That's what they keep telling me. But I don't believe it. According to the news, it happens all the time. I've always been sure I could have been capable of doing it."

"Usually the murders have a pretty specific reason. Were you physically abused when you were a child?"

He squinted in puzzlement. "Of course not. Why do you ask that?"

"It's one of the major reason for memory loss"

"I'm sure that's not the reason. I think it's because I killed her."

"Do you have any basis for thinking that?"

"I said I don't remember much, but I do know I was angry. Angry enough to strike out, maybe even angry enough to kill."

She watched, wondering if he wanted sympathy or intended to shock her. She decided to temporize. "How angry is that?"

"I don't know," he replied without looking at her. "I just know I was angrier at her than I had ever been in my life."

"I felt the same way about my father, but I never wanted to physically hurt him." After a pointed pause, she asked, "Did you love your mother?"

He threw her an icy glare. "Of course. I loved both my parents. I know Mother loved me more than anything else in her life. She used to hug me so hard at times it hurt."

"I don't want to state the obvious, but children who love their mothers don't kill them. Did you love your father, too?"

Angry eyes flamed brighter. "What a stupid question. Of course, I loved him. I always have and always will. I may not have been as close to him as I was to Mother, but I certainly loved him. He's always done everything he could for me. He went ballistic when Detective Arnold asked him if he thought it was possible that I killed her. I don't blame the lieutenant for being suspicious. I would be too, if I were in his position."

She nodded. In a forceful voice she said, "Isn't it much more likely that you wanted to protect her, and when you couldn't, you chose to forget everything?"

He waved his hand. "Pff. Old news. Everyone's been telling me that for years. To be truthful, I really worry what would happen if I did remember. I honestly don't know how I would react. Someone might get hurt."

"Ridiculous!" Jennifer blurted, though deep down she wondered if there could be some truth to what he said. "I'm curious. What brings you back to Minneapolis now?"

"I left something here, something related to my mother's death. I came back to find it."

She stared at him. "You expect to find something here after fifteen years?" she asked slowly.

"Yes. I think I hid it. I know this is going to sound really strange, but I found a chambered nautilus shell while I was going through a box in the basement. I suddenly had a flash of memory, and I knew it had something to do with my mother's death."

The words took her by surprise. "Hadn't you ever seen it before?"

"No. I've always been fascinated with nautiluses because their shells are an example of the Fibonacci Progression. Connecting it to Mother gave me quite a shock."

Jennifer found herself making deep eye contact, and it made her uncomfortable. "I'm not surprised," she said, shifting her position. "Something about your mother's death frightened you so badly that your unconscious mind won't even let you think about it. You somehow found one of the chinks in its armor. Your subconscious has been carrying all the weight and has got tired of the burden. It can't let go of everything directly, so it gives you hints. Do you have any recurring dreams or nightmares?"

His eyes wavered. "No."

He was lying, and Jennifer wondered why. "I'll be happy to try to help you, but I don't know how. Do you think finding what you're looking for will help you regain your memory?"

"I'm sure it will. Mike told me that retracing my steps might be the best way to do it, but he wasn't so sure it would be a good idea. He said some patients who undergo grief therapy would be better off not doing it."

"There have been some studies that suggest that," Jennifer said. "Remembering has destroyed some people."

"Father's been saying the same thing as long as I can remember, but I have to know."

"I see. Then I'll be happy to try to help you, as long as you're aware of the risks. If and when you do remember, it probably will be as clear as if it just happened."

"Really? Why?

"It's etched into your brain. It simply has a canvas over it. Brilliant colors have been protected from the light, so to speak. Do you remember what you were doing when the trade towers collapsed?"

"Sure. I was watching TV at the Ohio Union with a hundred other students."

"When you start to remember, everything will just as clear as that memory. All we have to do is take off the canvas covering."

"Great. By the way, Mike speaks very highly of you. I understand you were classmates at Northwestern."

Jennifer's lips pulled into a tight smile at the understatement. They were much more than classmates. But as always in her life, the scales didn't balance and nothing ever came of it. Looking up, she found Jason staring at her.

"Oh, yes," she said, hating herself for turning red. "Mike and I were classmates. We're still very good friends." Clearing her throat, she continued. What's your family background?"

"Father sells pharmaceuticals. Mother grew up on a farm at Thief River Falls. Dad said she always considered herself a farm girl."

"What has you life been like since your mother died?"

"Lots of psychiatrists and lots of medications. Father has been worried sick about me since mother's death, and he's kept close watch. I'm sure he has even had me followed for years. Then Grandmother Dumont died six months ago and left me some money. I decided I wanted to live my own life. He doesn't even know I've flown to Minneapolis. I just bought my plane three weeks ago."

That had to be more than just "some money." Jennifer knew plenty about overprotective parents and the responses children made to that kind of environment. "How long have you known Mike Savich?"

"Since last January. I think you know he's the lead psychologist at the OSU student health service."

"I do. How long will you be in Minneapolis?"

"Just until Sunday this trip, but I'll be coming back in a couple of weeks. I'm taking Father on a trip to the Tetons as soon as I finish my finals. I've been accepted at Harvard Medical School. He thought we should spend some time together before I left for Boston."

"That's wonderful," she said. "Just to fill me in, have you been back to the hotel where it happened yet?"

"I'm going there after I leave here. I'm also going to visit Lieutenant Arnold. Even if he still suspects me, he was nice enough when I talked to him. He said he's thought of me often and wondered what had happened to me."

"Why don't you call me after you're done," Jennifer said. "I expect it may give us a bit more to talk about."

"I'll do that. Oh," Jason took out his wallet. "Here's an advance against your fee. You can bill me for the balance."

Eyeing the thousand dollars written on the check, she again thought about her car. "Thanks. Oh, I have something for you."

She handed him a small spiral-bound notebook. "Keep that in your shirt pocket. Anytime you remember anything, no matter how insignificant it may seem, write it down. Do you need a pen?"

"No," he said. "I have one. I'll talk to you later."

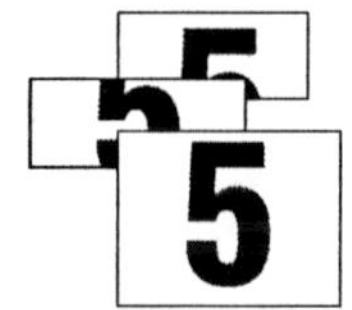

GATHERING RAIN CLOUDS splotched the bright-blue sky as Jason left the Lumber Exchange. Looking at the towering buildings down the street, he suddenly remembered the limousine ride with his mother from MSP International airport. From a distance, the city's skyscrapers had looked like fingers probing the gray late-fall overcast. The tallest looked like a middle finger, even though he had no idea of the significance at the time.

Now he realized it had been an omen, a portent of what the visit would do to his life.

Eager to follow Jennifer's instructions, he wrote down the details and his feelings in his notebook.

He walked swiftly, facing the wind that had been a mere breeze when he had arrived at Jennifer Cahill's office building. The International Hotel was only two short blocks away, between Nicollet and Hennepin avenues.

As soon as he arrived at Seventh Street, he remembered the hotel. Cold November suddenly washed over sunny May. He shivered. Jennifer was right. Even after fifteen years, the memory was strong and clear.

When he had arrived in Minneapolis that morning, he went directly to his appointment, letting the cabby drop off his bags at the hotel. Now, as he approached the building on foot, he had a clear recollection of the bay where cabs pulled in to drop off their fares and valets picked up patrons' cars. He remembered that a cold wind had torn off his baseball cap as he climbed out of the limousine. His mother saved it by scooting after it and pinning it down with her foot before it blew into the street.

Excitement rising, Jason made another note.

Triumph quickly turned to anxiety as the doorman opened the hotel door for him. Did the horror that annihilated his memory still lurk on the twentieth floor? He was sure it did, and always would until he remembered everything. Pain, terror, or whatever else lay in store for him be damned. He had to know.

Smiling bravely, he approached the desk.

"Good morning, sir. Do you have a reservation?" the desk attendant asked.

"Yes. I'm Jason Dumont."

The man's fingers flew over his keyboard. In his starched collar and bow tie, his bulbous red nose made him look like Rudolf the Red-nosed Reindeer in a tux. "Yes. Here we are. Room twenty-sixteen."

Stooping, he came up with a plastic card. "I'll make your key for you."

Jason nodded.

"I hope you had a nice flight," the clerk said cheerfully as he typed. "Your baggage is in the storage room. I'll have the bellman get it for you."

Soon, a shorter man showed up with a wheeled cart. His time-rutted face and full head of perfectly white hair suggested he was well past retirement age. Could he have been the one who had showed them to their room those many years ago?

As they crossed to the elevator, an errant wheel on the cart skidded out a noisy tattoo. "First time in Minneapolis?" the man asked in a near shout.

"No," Jason said somewhat loudly as well, figuring the man might be deaf. "I was here with my mother fifteen years ago. We were in the same room I'm in now."

"Did you enjoy your stay?"

Jason hesitated, not knowing how to answer. He didn't want the world to know, but he needed the bellman's help. "No. She was murdered there."

The cart stopped and the bellman's mouth fell open.

"Don't be concerned. I don't remember a thing about it. I'm hoping that coming back will bring back my memory."

The white-faced bellman took out the room key.

"Look," Jason said with a reassuring smile. "I'm sure everything will be fine, but I need a favor. I don't know how I'll react to coming back. If I start to . . . weird out, I want you to call this number."

As he held out the card, the bellman backed away to safety behind his cart. "I . . . I don't know, sir. This isn't . . ."

"Don't worry. I won't get violent or anything. I just would appreciate if you would stay with me for a minute or two. I know it's an imposition, and I intend to pay you for your help." He took out a fifty-dollar bill from his billfold and showed it to the bellman.

The man still looked uneasy. But, after another rheumy-eyed glance at the bank note, he said, "Well . . . I suppose . . . if you're sure you'll be all right."

Moments later, the elevator door opened and Jason's heart began to beat faster. Another deeply buried memory came to him, and as Jennifer had said, it came with amazing clarity. Twenty-sixteen was to the right from the elevator door, and on the right-hand side of the hallway.

Stepping out and taking a deep breath, Jason caught the pleasing aroma of orange-scented cleanser. They'd used pine before.

Hard on the heels of the memory, a cornucopia vase on a stand brought back another flash of recognition. As he jotted a note he wondered how many more such entries he would make before the day was through. There could be many. After fifteen years of remembering nothing, even these tiny chinks in the void's armor seemed to be major breaches. Would he run out of space in his notebook before he saw Jennifer again?

His feet felt leaden as they walked the hallway. As they arrived at the door of the fateful room, he took a deep breath.

"H-here we are," the bellman said. "Are you sure you want me to open the door?"

"Dead sure," Jason let out before he realized what he was saying. "I'll be just fine."

An unsteady hand slipped the key card into the slot, a green light lit, and Jason heard a click. With another worried look in Jason's direction, the man turned the handle and pushed the door open, ready to flee at the tiniest provocation.

Jason felt a chill as he stepped over the threshold.

Dim light revealed two double beds. The feared visions didn't materialize. In fact, Jason felt no emotion at all.

Cautiously following behind, the bellman switched on the light. "W-where do you want me to put the bag?"

"Just set it by the closet."

Obviously satisfied that his charge wasn't going to transform into a raving maniac, the old man let out a big sigh. "Are you sure you're okay?"

"I'm fine. To tell you the truth, it's just another hotel room to me. I don't remember a thing about this place." He handed the man the fifty. "But thanks. I really appreciate the help."

Bowing like an organ grinder's monkey, the bellman tipped his hat. As he turned to leave, he stopped. "When did you say this happened?"

"Fifteen years ago this November 16th. My mother and I were on our way to my Grandmother's funeral in Thief River Falls. We were supposed to catch a flight the next day."

The man stroked sallow cheeks with skeletal fingers. "I wasn't working here then, but I know someone who was. I'll ask him if he knows anything about what happened."

"Do that," Jason said, handing him a card. "He can always reach me on my cell."

The bellman slipped the card into his jacket pocket. "Gotcha. You scared me some, but I'm happy to help. No one should have to go through what you did. Oh, and here's the card with the number you wanted me to call if you was in distress."

Smiling at the man's grammar, Jason took it and slipped it into his shirt pocket. "Thanks. I'd forgotten about it."

With another tip of his cap, the man left.

Alone, Jason took a deep breath and sat on the bed closest to the door. Somehow he remembered it had been his mother's bed. Glancing about the room he felt something gnaw inside his head, but he couldn't make out what it was.

Remembering that he had an important call to make, he took out his cell phone. "Hey, Dad. How would you feel if I bought my own plane?"

Jason met with shocked silence. Finally, his father said, "I guess I couldn't stop you, but I don't like the idea."

"You know yourself flying is many times safer than driving."

"Yeah, yeah. Okay, when were you planning to start looking for a plane?"

"Actually, Dad . . . I already bought one."

"Jason—"

"And . . ."

"Jason—"

"On Mike Savich's advice, I've flown to Minneapolis."

"No. No. Jason, this is a really—"

"It's done, Dad. I think I can finally sort out what happened when mother died. I'm even staying in the same hotel room."

After a long silence, Lawrence Dumont said, "That isn't a good idea."

Jason's tone became conciliatory. "I know how you worry about me, but I'm convinced I can deal with what I find out. No matter how terrible it is."

"Dr. Kirkland, said . . ."

"I know what he said. If this doesn't work, I'll try something else. I just think it's important to make an effort. I don't want to spend the rest of my life under a cloud."

Dumont sighed. "Maybe I should come out—"

"No, Dad. Don't. Please, let me do this. Mike sent me to a counselor here, and I've already seen her. I'm not being crazy. Please, Dad. This is something I have to do."

After a long pause, where Jason could almost imagine weeping, his father said, "Melanie . . . Melanie always stayed at the International Hotel when she went to Minnesota." His voice trailed off and Jason could hear the familiar tones of guilt that crept in anytime they talked about his mother.

"Don't start that again," Jason said. "It might have happened no matter where we went. I'll be back Monday. Will you be home when I get back?"

"I may be in Chicago. I'm doing a big promo campaign for Sannat. Be sure to give me a call or leave a message if anything comes up. Okay?"

"Sure will," Jason said, and hung up.

That had gone about as well as could be expected. With a sigh, Jason kicked off his shoes and stretched out on the bed. Mother's death had been hard on him, but it had been far harder on his father. For weeks after the tragedy the man hardly ever left his room. His sister, Aunt Yvette, had come to stay with them, trying to stop Jason's incessant crying and to make sure that her brother got something to eat once or twice a day. Father finally emerged from his cave two weeks later and had devoted the rest of his life making sure that Jason had everything he needed. The burden on Jason soon became intolerable. When he recently learned that Father finally had met another woman and was considering marriage, he nearly broke out cheering.

Better days were ahead.

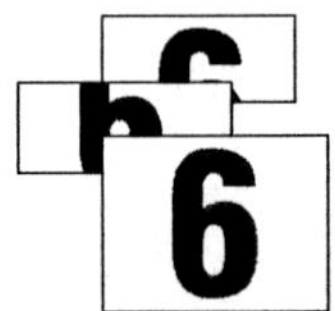

FOR THE THIRD TIME that morning, Dan Arnold read through his notes on his arrival at the Dumont crime scene. The words still hadn't changed.

When he and Carrie Flowers arrived, a crowd of blue uniforms was already there. He realized the Dumont murder wouldn't be a usual case when he saw the trail of tiny bloody footprints that led from the bathroom to one of the beds. In a surreal twist, they found an officer crouching on his hands and knees trying to lure someone, or something—it could as easily have been a cat—out from under one of the beds.

His premonition about the case turned to certainty when he peered into the bathroom. The walls themselves were bleeding! Apparently even Melanie couldn't believe it. Slouched on the commode and leaning against the sink, she stared wide-eyed in shock and horror. Dan could almost hear her words. All that blood couldn't have come from me!

Dan rubbed at his forehead.

Melanie Dumont hadn't been the only victim in the case. Dan was struck down, too. Carrie Flowers moved out the day before Christmas Eve when she realized he seriously believed Jason, a skinny seven-year-old, had done it. It was the beginning of the end of their relationship.

Maybe Jason Dumont's return would lead to a new beginning.

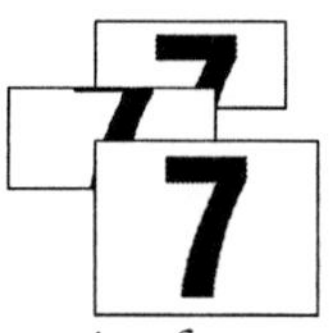

*LYING IN THE DARK, Jason cringes. He feels the tickle of many tiny feet
as spiders crawl over his nose and mouth. Once again he tries to scream, but cannot.
Somewhere, Mother begins to cry out, but that is cut short.*

*Jason jumps to his feet and lands on a wet and sticky floor. He wanders in the
dark. His foot catches onto something, and he falls. He lands upon something soft-
er and warmer than he has ever known.*

Reaching out with his hand he feels something silky. And wet.

Screaming, Jason awoke. His terror made him insensate to the pain from
knocking his head against the headboard as he sat up.

Where am I?

Furtively searching the room, recognition flooded his inflamed senses.

Yes. He was in a hotel room. *The* hotel room. He hadn't expected he would fall
asleep, but the early-morning solo flight from Columbus to Minneapolis had taken
its toll. Now he wondered if the nightmare would elicit new memories, or would it
just trigger yet more ghastly dreams? The memories were there. For a moment he
could almost see things the way they were that night. Try as he would to view them
more clearly, the shadows faded. They disappeared completely before the thumping
in his chest began to subside.

Why didn't I tell Jennifer about the dream? he wondered as his breathing finally became normal. His face pulled into a wan smile. Why would he have? He had
never told Mike Savich, either.

Glancing at his watch, he hastily swung his legs off the bed and got to his feet.
He was supposed to meet with Detective-Lieutenant Daniel Arnold in less than ten
minutes.

A light mist blew in his face as he stepped out of the hotel. Before going farther, he unfolded his visitor's map. A quick count of the streets told him the main
police station was nearly six blocks straight ahead. Should he take a cab? He would
have to run to get there in time even if the streets were dry.

"The cabs are running slow today," the door attendant said. "I haven't seen any
for a few minutes."

Not liking the sound of that, Jason took off at a fast walk. Fortunately, the sidewalks weren't slippery, and he gradually increased his speed from a walk to a jog, and finally to a trot. He was only three minutes late when the woman at the help desk pointed him to a set of elevators. After a swift ride, the doors opened on the fourth floor. In Room 406, a young, uniformed female officer opened the door for him. At his request to see Dan Arnold, she disappeared into an office and quickly returned. "Detective Arnold is expecting you," she said.

Jason took a deep breath before entering the office. Daniel Arnold was one of the officers who had come to the hotel the night of the murder. Jason sensed that whether he remembered the lieutenant or not, he wasn't going to enjoy the encounter.

The voice reassured him.

"Come in, Jason," Dan said.

Jason entered, wondering if the sight of the officer would bring up memories. All he saw was a squat man in late middle age with a round face, sideburns, and black hair flecked with gray. His muscular body looked strong. Dan smiled and offered him his hand.

"Thanks for seeing me," Jason said as he took the proffered hand, which, as he suspected, had a firm grip.

"It's my pleasure. Do you remember me?"

Jason shook his head. "Sorry. I don't."

"I guess I'm not too surprised. I don't think you were able to process much of anything by the time we arrived. I'm sure having a bunch of police officers standing around talking for so long before Officer Flowers and I arrived didn't help, either. Have you ever been able to remember anything at all about what happened that night?"

"Not really, but a few bits and pieces are coming to me now. Unfortunately, nothing that would be of much use to you, I'm afraid. Maybe things will change. I'm staying in the room where it happened."

Dan's eyes lit up. "Really? That takes guts, but it's a good idea. All the rest is here," he said, pointing at a brown folder with a large filing clip. "Here's the whole report. I got it out of the evidence box when I heard you were coming. Every year I've taken it out once or twice to go through it. Not being able to solve the case has been a thorn in my tush since it happened."

Jason detected a trace of hostility in the tone. *He still suspects me*, he thought. *Well, why shouldn't he? I probably did kill her.*

"There's some questions I want to go over with you again. Maybe they'll help to jar your memory."

"Ask away."

"First of all, do you have any idea why your footprints are the only ones leading out of the bathroom? There was a tremendous amount of blood. The murderer must have gotten it all over himself and his shoes."

Jason sighed. "Sorry. I have no idea. I've wondered about that."

"Sure," Dan said in a sympathetic tone. "We found an Exacto wood-carving kit on the cabinet next to your bed. You must have brought it with you to carve the balsa plane we returned to you with the other personal items from the crime scene. We never found the knife or the curved blade from the kit. Do you have any idea what could have happened to it?"

"No," Jason said, beginning to shake.

"We know you must have been using it in the bathroom. We found wood shavings that matched the plane on the floor. There was no blood under them, so they must have been there before your mother died."

Jason blushed. "Some kids read when they're on the toilet. I carved. Mom used to find my knives and shavings all around the house. I've always been crazy about airplanes."

Dan held out a consoling hand. In a soft voice, he said, "Sorry. I think you must know how all this looked to us."

"Of course I do," Jason retorted. "Why didn't you arrest me?"

"For one thing, we could never figure out why you would do it. But there are other things involved. For one thing, the desk clerk said Melanie had informed him her bag was lost at the airport when she checked in. Your pajamas were on the floor next to Melanie's body and she was wearing a negligee. There were no bags, but she must have had clothes with her."

"I do remember the answer to that. I had brought my pajamas with me in my backpack. I'm sure that's where I had my wood-carving kit, too. I remember the flight attendant putting the backpack and model plane in the overhead compartment."

"So your mother must have bought the negligee when she arrived here."

"I expect so."

Dan took out a new sheet of paper and made a note and dated it.

"We found a size large man's tee-shirt on Melanie's bed. We thought you or your mother may have worn it as a night shirt, but we know you both had night wear. Do you have any idea who it may have belonged to?"

Jason shook his head. "No. I just know it wasn't mine."

"That's a point in your favor."

"There are others?"

"You mother was wearing a necklace and earrings. Women generally don't wear jewelry to bed."

Jason nodded.

"We didn't find any evidence of forced entry, so it's likely that either you or your mother let someone into the room. We came to the conclusion that Melanie had a visitor," Dan said dryly.

"I find that next to impossible to believe. But if I didn't kill her, someone else did. Let me get this straight. You've put together the negligee and jewelry and lack of forced entry and come up with the idea that my mother . . . had a boyfriend."

"I'm afraid so. The night clerk said a young man dressed in a mackinac and rain hat asked him for your room number. The clerk said he was sure he had seen the guy several times before."

Jason jerked in shock. For a moment, he pressed his eyes shut, then, in a softened voice, he asked, "Was he able to give you a description?"

"Nothing useful. Tall with a light complexion is all he could come up with."

Jason nodded.

"The whole case turns on who knew you were in Minneapolis at that time. You were on your way to your grandmother's funeral, right?"

"Yes. Grandmother had died of a cerebral hemorrhage the day before. She was only fifty-two."

"Who would've known you and your mother were staying at the Internatonal?"

"Just Father and the housekeeper, Louise. Uncle Gary may have, too."

"How about people in Minnesota?"

Jason rubbed his forehead. "I'm sure Uncle Dean and Aunt Sally knew."

"Would any of them have had a motive?"

"Absolutely not," Jason shot back angrily. "Everyone loved mother."

Dan shrugged. "Then I guess there isn't much more to be said. Maybe going through the file will help bring something up."

"I sure hope so. What time did you arrive at the hotel?"

"We got the call around 11:30," Arnold said. "But we got delayed because a crew was pouring cement in the hotel parking ramp. I stopped to ask them if they had seen anyone in the ramp when they arrived, but they said they hadn't. I talked to the night manager who said someone on the twenty-first floor had called to say she heard screaming. The manager sent hotel security up to the room. No one answered the door when the security man knocked, so he let himself in. He's the one who called us."

"Do you know where I can reach him?"

"Not off hand, but his name is Jim Fitger. You'll find his name in the report. He said he saw you under the bed shivering, but when he tried to get you out, you started to scream. He left you there. You were still screaming when we arrived. In all my years I've never seen another person as afraid as you were. There you were, stark naked and shaking so hard I was sure you were going to swallow your teeth. Carolyn picked you up when we moved the bed away. She stroked your head until you stopped screaming."

Something clicked. The name was familiar but not quite right. "Carolyn? That wasn't the name. It was . . . Carrie, wasn't it?"

Dan's eyes widened in surprise. "That's right. You remember her?"

Lightening flashed in Jason's mind. "Just that you called her Carrie." he said, wide-eyed.

"Yes," Dan said. "Are you all right?"

Jason shook as his mind recalled a frighteningly vivid moment of terror. He felt his convulsing body being held against a slick blue jacket and heard a calm voice pleading, "Hush, sweetie. I've got you."

Overwhelmed, Jason called out. "I just remembered. 'Carry? Carry me.'"

"That's what you said," Dan said, excitedly. "You didn't remember that before?"

Jason shook his head.

"Carrie was a seasoned officer but she was in tears the whole time. She said she never had anyone hold onto her so tightly. Finally you stopped screaming, but she couldn't get you to stop crying. When I tried to ask you some questions, you started to scream again."

"Where is she? I want to thank her."

"She's with the Fourth Precinct in north Minneapolis now. I'm sure she'll be happy to hear from you. I know she's thought about you a lot over the years."

They looked at each other in silence. "If you don't mind, what brings to Minneapolis now? It's been a long time."

"For one thing, I took myself off my meds. I realized I had to find out what happened." He looked at the evidence box. "My psychologist at OSU thinks that reenactment is the best hope to regain my memory. If you don't mind, I think I'll take a look at what's in there," he said.

Dan Arnold nodded. "Be careful, there are some very horrible photos."

"I can handle it."

Dan slid his wastebasket toward Jason. "Don't say I didn't warn you."

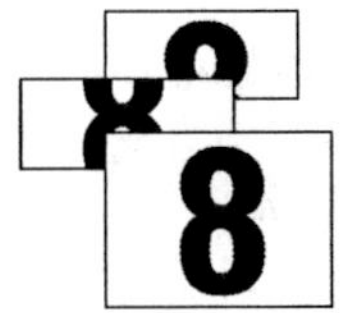

I CAN'T BELIEVE she didn't show up, Jennifer thought, taking the digital clock in her hands to make sure she was reading it right. *How can Candy dare do anything so stupid? Especially since she knows the trouble she's in.*

Jennifer shrugged. Apparently she didn't care.

Still . . .

Unwilling to trust the evidence of her own eyes, Jennifer carefully examined the image on CCTV monitor once again. She hadn't been mistaken; the lounge was empty. Candy Lane was AWOL.

She picked up her phone and pressed a button to activate the automatic voice-mail system with the digital clock timer that notated the beginning and ending times for the call, as well as the date. The court would need all the available information for documentation. She first called Candy's cell phone. When she didn't get a ring she dialed it again. Her eyes darted to the monitor as she thought she heard a sound from her lobby.

Even though it appeared empty, she opened the door and gave the lobby the once-over to be sure. "Candy, are you out here?"

Greeted with silence, she stepped back into the office to make her second call. This one to Lindsey Marshall.

"Damn," Jennifer said, as Marshall's voicemail answered.

"Lindsey, this is Jennifer Cahill. It's 2:18 in the afternoon and Candy hasn't shown up for her appointment or called to cancel. Please return my call as soon as possible."

Her statement ended with an exclamation point of thunder that shook the building. Rain began to beat against her office windows.

The developing storm matched Jennifer's mood. No one answered her call to Candy's mother. After leaving a message through gritted teeth, her phone rang.

It's about time, she thought, expecting Candy to offer some lame excuse for being late.

"Dr. Cahill?" a serious male voice asked.

"Yes."

"This is Detective-Lieutenant Arnold with the Minneapolis Police. I believe Jason Dumont is one your patients."

Jennifer's heart raced. "Yes. Has something happened to him? Is he hurt?"

"He's hurting, but the problem isn't physical. He took a look at the pictures of the crime scene and nearly passed out cold. He's still shaking pretty badly, and he asked me to call you. Is there any chance you can come here?"

"I wouldn't hesitate normally, but I'm waiting for a very difficult patient to show up. She's already twenty minutes late, but I still don't know if I should leave."

Jennifer heard Dan talking to Jason. "He says he understands."

"It sounds as if he's very frightened. Would you say this is an emergency?"

"That's what I'd call it."

She bit her lip. Even though she desperately wanted to help, she wasn't sure if she dared to leave the office during Candy Lane's scheduled time. It could be dangerous to her career.

Any patient other than Candy would call in to reschedule. Most would understand that professional time was money and missed appointments were billable. Most would not be surprised or angered to find her gone if they came late, as unusual as that would be.

Candy's mind didn't work that way. Until proven otherwise, everyone in the world was her enemy. And Jennifer was one of her worst.

She had come to Jennifer's professional attention after her fourth conviction for shoplifting. Candy first tried charm, appearing in a little- girl dress and a sad story about how the police misinterpreted her actions. Jennifer read her the police reports, then asked her about the cut marks on the underside of her forearms. Certain that Jennifer wasn't buying the misunderstood-child routine, Candy responded by declaring war on Jennifer. Still, what the teen expected would be a short campaign turned into a costly battle when she was caught lying about what happened during a therapy session. She didn't realize Jennifer had taped it. After several more defeats and another shop-lifting charge, the teenager found herself one misstep away from being sent to North Star boot camp, the most radical treatment available. She was down to her last shot. Even Jennifer feared for her being sent there. The horror stories she heard about the place frightened her.

With so much at stake, Jennifer knew she should stay in the office the entire time just to make sure the nasty little vixen didn't show up.

Still . . .

"Hold on a sec," she said. "I'll be right back."

She rushed into the lobby and turned the corner. The only place not covered by the camera was her closet.

Empty.

Candy can stew in her own juices, Jennifer decided as she hurried back to her office. Another patient needed her assistance. And from the sound of the officer's voice, quite desperately. Picking up the receiver, she said "I'll be right over."

"Thanks," Dan said, sounding genuinely relieved.

She resolutely moved to the closet. As she pulled her raincoat off of its peg, she heard an ear-shattering clap of thunder. Frightened, she picked up her umbrella.

Another explosion sent her back to her office to call for a cab. As she waited, she hastily scribbled a note to post on her door. "Candy—I waited for you twenty minutes and have to handle an emergency. Call me. You have my number."

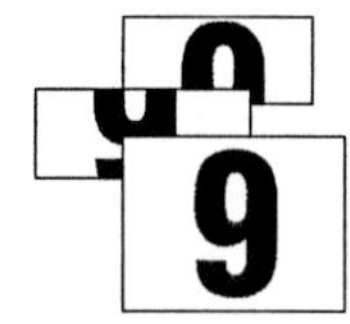

JENNIFER WAITED IN the building lobby, enduring the guard, who was obviously savoring her like a choice sirloin. Finally a cab pulled in front and stopped. Water slammed against her umbrella as she dashed for the vehicle. An ankle-deep deluge ran down the streets.

The cab crawled away. The windshield wipers were unable to keep up. "I think I'll have to pull over, Miss," the driver said.

"Please just drive slowly," Jennifer said. "Someone's waiting for me at the Government Towers, and it's urgent."

He continued at a crawl. When they finally arrived, Jennifer gave him a ten-dollar tip. As she got out of the cab, she was hit by a violent updraft that turned her umbrella inside out, and lifted her heavy skirt above her knees.

Sloshing through ankle-deep water, she high-stepped for the lobby door.

The storm frightened her, and she was as worried about Candy as she was Jason. Even though Jennifer knew she had covered all her bases, she still had a sinking feeling that leaving the office had been unwise at best, maybe even slightly dangerous.

As she climbed the stairway to the twin building's lobby, she realized she had passed the point of no return. Shrugging it off, she approached the security desk.

"The A-Building?" she asked.

The guard pointed her toward the left. "The elevators are over there," he said.

She tapped a wet toe impatiently until a door opened. Stepping in sent her on a solo rocket trip to the fourth floor.

A female officer answered her knock at Dan Arnold's office.

Jennifer was immediately assailed by the odor of vomit and floral air freshener. The female officer pointed toward an open office door and Jennifer hurried in, expecting to find her patient white-faced and shivering.

Jason was stretched out across the officer's desk with a pillow under his head. He opened his eyes. "Jennifer," he said weakly.

"Yes," she said, moving closer to him. "What happened?"

Jason swung his legs down and sat. "Everything caved in on me when I saw the photos of my mother. It was if everything I saw and felt that night hit me at the same time. It was awful. I was seven again."

"Do you remember anything about what happened?"

"No, but I still feel lousy. I'm starting to wonder if trying to remember is such a good idea."

Jennifer patted his hand. "Believe it or not, that's a good sign. Nobody said this wouldn't be painful. How do you feel now?"

"Dazed."

"Do you think you can stand?"

He got to his feet. A second later, he leaned against it for support. "I'm feeling a bit dizzy."

"Hennepin County Medical Center is only a few blocks away," Dan said. "Should I give them a call?"

"No, no. I'm sure I'll be fine. But I think I should sit down."

Dan moved the chair for him.

"Would it be all right if I took a look at the pictures," Jennifer asked.

"I guess that would be up to Jason," Dan said. "I have no objection."

"That's fine," Jason said, holding his hands up in front of his face. "Just keep them away from me."

She took a look at the first photograph and swallowed. At first it was difficult to understand what she was looking at. Captured in a small Polaroid shot, a profusion of red nearly filled the entire picture. An object near the bottom of the photograph didn't make sense at first. When she held the picture closer, she realized it was a human head resting on what may have been an arm.

With Jason's eyes locked on her face, her stomach began to roll. Quickly scanning through several more shots showing the same thing but from different angles, she came to the last and largest photo. What only showed indistinctly in the other shots now showed very clearly.

Melanie's throat was cut from ear to ear.

Jennifer gasped and handed the album back to Dan. "I certainly can see why this disturbed you so much. It really is amazing you're still alive."

"That's the key question," Dan said. "If you were in the same room with the murderer, why did he let you live?"

Seeing Jason's pained expression, Jennifer stepped in. "Maybe he was hiding, and the killer didn't realize it, or Jason was able to get away."

Arnold cleared his throat. "Maybe, but that's not what happened." He explained the trail of bloody footprints from the bathroom.

"Couldn't he have gone into the bathroom after the killer left?"

"I suppose that's possible," Dan said. "We did find Jason's blood-soaked pajamas in the bathroom."

"And me cowering under my bed. I certainly understand why you still suspect me. Anyone would."

"We don't know what happened," Jennifer said bravely, throwing a sharp look in the officer's direction. She turned to stare Jason in the eye. "What's important is that you did survive. You survived then, and you can do it again now."

Jason nodded and turned toward Dan. "I want to talk to Carrie Flowers. Do you think you could arrange that?"

"I'll be happy to try," Dan said. He dialed in five numbers. "Hey, Stan. It's Dan Arnold. Is Carrie around?" He nodded at Jason. "Great. Put her on. I have someone here who wants to talk to her."

Jason took the receiver. Seconds later, she answered. To his amazement, he immediately recognized her voice.

"Sergeant Flowers, this is Jason Dumont. Do you remember me?"

"Of course. I'll never be able to forget you. You were the most frightened little boy I've ever known. I nearly quit police work because of you. Are you in Minneapolis?"

"Yes. I have to know what happened that night. I was hoping I could talk to you."

"Any time," Flowers said. "The station is on Plymouth Avenue between Morgan and Newton Avenue North. Do you have a car?"

"No, I'll get a cab. Are you busy now?"

"Not in the least. I'd be happy to see you."

"Then I'll be there as soon I can make it."

After he hung up, Jennifer said, "You don't need to take a cab. Come back with me to my office. I don't have another appointment for forty minutes. I'll give you a lift." She threw him a concerned look. "Are you sure you're in any shape to be on your own?"

"I can't say I'm fine, but I'm able to function."

As Jason shook Dan's hand, the officer said, "Wait."

He held out a card.

"I'd like one, too," Jennifer said.

After handing one to her, Dan turned to Jason. "Call me anytime you come up with anything. It's been a cold case for more than ten years, but I'll reopen it tomorrow if there's sufficient reason. By the way, have you ever been to Thief River Falls?"

Jason shook his head. "No, but I'm flying there tomorrow. That's where mother grew up. Maybe I'll find some answers there."

"Good luck," Dan said.

The elevator door to her floor opened and Jennifer let out a little cry of surprise. Candy was sitting outside her office door. The note Jennifer had left was gone.

"You missed my appointment," the teen said with a smug smile. Other than the unnatural glitter of her eyes she looked quite normal, her thin body hidden under a bulky sweater, full skirt and colorful leggings.

"As the note said, I got called out on an emergency. You were already late. I left phone messages for you and asked Lindsey to page me if you showed up."

"Of course, I'd show up," Candy said, irritably. "You didn't think I'd give you an excuse to send me to hell, did you?" She turned to Jason. Looking him over with a hostile blue eye, she asked, "Who's this?"

"One of my patients."

"Yeah? I bet he's your boyfriend. You like them young."

"Forgive her," Jennifer said in Jason's direction. "Candy's naturally rude to people I associate with." She unlocked the office door. "Sorry I can't give you a ride, Jason, but you can ask the security guard to call a cab for you. Call me when you're done and let me know what you find out." Turning, she said, "Come into the office, Candy."

"No way. I have a job interview. It's your fault that I'm not seeing you, anyway."

"You have an interview?" Jennifer said with excitement. "That's great. Who with?"

"A cleaning service. I'll work four days a week."

"I couldn't be happier for you. What time is your interview?"

"Like fifteen minutes from now. If you came back any later, you would've made me late."

"I'll walk with you there."

"Uh-uh," Candy said in a loud voice. "I don't want everyone to know you're spying on me. And besides, I'm not walking. I'm driving."

"Then I'll ride with you. Do you have an appointment slip?"

"I don't have to show it to you."

"No. But unless you do, I'm not letting you out of the office."

With an angry *tsk*, Candy pulled a pink slip out of her purse. "Here," she said, waving it in Jennifer's face. "Why do you always have to be such a bitch?"

"That's my job," Jennifer said evenly. "I even make a little money at it."

Candy marched stiffly through the lobby with Jennifer a step behind. The guard saw them and beamed. "Good afternoon, ladies."

"Shut up, you pervert," Candy snapped.

Jennifer smiled. For the first time since they met, she agreed with something Candy said.

They took the stairs down. "This is the level where I park," Jennifer said.

"I know," Candy replied in a snide tone. "You should get that scratch on your car fixed."

A cold wave of suspicion flooded her mind. "What do you mean?"

"I saw it when I came in for my appointment. Your office room number is painted on the wall. I hate you, but you have a cool car."

Maybe Candy didn't do it.

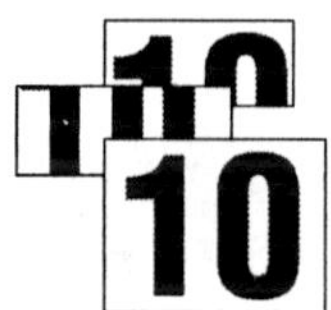

JASON LOOKED OUT of his window as the Blue-and-White cab pulled up in front of a large, town-house building. "Here we are," the cabby said. "Don't look much like a police station, does it?"

"It looks like a town house," Jason said.

"That's on purpose. The police deliberately took a low profile when they built the station in the eighties because of tension with the neighborhood. I think it looks nice."

"I do, too," Jason said, handing him a twenty-dollar bill.

He stepped out into a slow drizzle, the tail-end of the storm, and quickly found the entrance at the side of the building. Seconds after the desk clerk made a phone call, a door opened and a tall woman gestured for him to follow her.

The building reeked of cigarettes. Jason wrinkled his nose as Sergeant Carrie Flowers stretched out a delicate hand in welcome. "Jason. It's nice to see you again. I've often wondered how you were doing."

As they touched, Jason remembered the warmth of her hands.

"Remember me?" she asked.

He studied her carefully, noticing she was tall and that the trousers of her uniform—probably off the rack—didn't cover the tops of her shoes. Her dark hair had splashes of gray. Jason knew that she took care with her appearance. The creases in her uniform stood out sharply, and the sergeant stripes in her lapels shone brightly. He especially liked her compassionate eyes.

As much as he wanted to remember her, though, she was a complete stranger. Finally, he said, "Sorry. I don't. But your voice sounds familiar."

"That's a start." she gave a tinkle of laughter. "I sure remember you. Have a chair."

He did.

She looked him over with an affectionate smile. "What can I do for you?"

"For one thing, I wanted to thank you. Detective Arnold said you were the one who got me to stop screaming."

"I didn't think you ever would," she replied.

Jason caught a whiff of perfume. As he did, he shuddered at a new memory that flashed in his mind. He remembered his terror, again, and a soft hand stroking his head. A gentle voice cooed to him.

"I hurt your ears, didn't I," Jason said with a thin smile.

Carrie's eyes widened. "That's what I said when I was trying to calm you. You remembered that?"

"Just now. You wrapped me in your jacket. I was shivering."

"Yes," she said excitedly. "You were absolutely shaking."

"What happened?"

"You wouldn't let anyone touch you when you were under the bed. We had to remove it. You'd been screaming since I arrived, but when the bed was lifted away is when you really turned up the volume."

"Then what?"

"I picked you up. I must have held you for fifteen minutes before you calmed down. When I tried to talk to you, you shouted, 'Mummy, that wasn't Dad.' Were you expecting your father to come?"

"I have no idea," Jason said as he scribbled hurried note onto his pad.

"Mummy, that wasn't Dad. Are you sure that's what I said?"

"Absolutely. It's in the police report. And you were right. Your father was at a big convention in Miami."

"I can't imagine why I said that," Jason mused. "Detective Arnold said my pajamas were in the bathroom. Do you know what happened to them?"

"We bagged them for evidence. Dan probably already told you about the rest of what we found. I always wondered about the ad torn out of the yellow pages for a business that sold model airplanes we found next to your mother's table."

Jason blanched. Quaking, he said, "Did you say model airplane?"

"Yes."

"Then I know why it was there. Mom was going to buy me a model before we went on to Thief River Falls."

"We found the model you were working on, but we never found the knife you were using. Did he tell you about the man who showed up in rain gear and asked for Melanie's room number."

"Yes. That's really interesting. I never had heard about it before."

"Did he also tell you the clerk had gotten a message from Melanie to give it to him because she was expecting him?"

Jason's eyes opened wide. "No!"

Carrie reached out her hand to comfort him, but he jumped back to avoid the contact. "The clerk also said the man passed the desk an hour later as he left the hotel."

A whirl of confusing thoughts twisted through Jason's mind, and a taste of bile rose into his mouth. Whatever the seven-year-old was trying to keep submerged in his unconscious took an unsteady step toward the surface.

After an uncomfortable silence, Carrie said, "I've wondered about you through the years. Did your father ever remarry?"

"No," Jason replied, brow wrinkling. "Why do you ask that?"

"I always thought you needed a mother. Who took care of you after . . . ?"

"After mother died? Father hired live in tutors until high school. Then I went to Chapsville. It's a private school not far from Louisville. I've been attending Ohio State for the last four years. I'll be started medical school this fall."

"How wonderful. I know this must sound strange, but I would have done anything if I could have taken you home with me the night of the murder. I'm glad I didn't. I could never have given you up."

"I think Lieutenant Arnold still thinks I killed my mother."

"I know," she said, and her lips pursed. "I never could convince him how stupid an idea that was. I'm sure it was whoever asked for her room number at the front desk."

"What do you mean?"

"It's in the police report. The desk clerk said that a man wearing a rain jacket and rain hat asked for Melanie's room number. The clerk said he recognized him because he had seen him several times before. The clerk didn't want to give it to him because it was so late. The clerk said she was expecting him."

Jason closed his eyes at a confused jumble of thoughts. "I wish I had known that before."

Jason smiled. "Do cops allow kisses?"

"No," she said with a coy smile.

"Even from their sons?"

"I better shut the door."

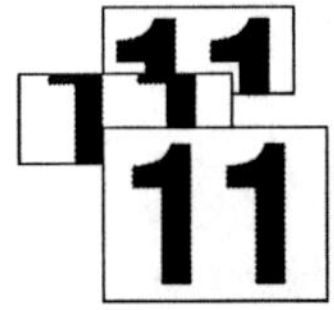

AS THE MINUTES dragged on, Jennifer finished the twisted fried-dough dessert with cinnamon and sugar that she'd bought from a corner Panaderia.

To her surprise, Candy's job interview with a temp agency on Chicago and Lake was real. Jennifer allowed her to go into the building unescorted.

Jennifer paced, eyeing the signs around her. All in Spanish. In the last ten years, this part of Chicago Avenue in the near southside had picked up the nickname Chicano Avenue, with Hispanics replacing the mostly black population that lived there before them. Even the agency Candy used was predominantly for Spanish-speaking people. Two centuries before it had been part of an Indian path from Lake Calhoun to Fort Snelling. Fifty years later, Lake Street marked the southern boundary of Minneapolis.

Try as she would to keep an eye on the agency building, buses and cars kept obstructing her view. Candy emerged as Jennifer was licking sugar off her fingers.

"How'd it go?" Jennifer asked.

"I already told you I had the job," Candy smirked. "We won't be able to meet on Friday afternoons anymore."

"That's fine. We'll switch to a different day."

"I won't have time," Candy said. "I'll be working every day. E-yew. What were you eating? You have sugar all over your face."

Unconsciously giving in to Candy's ploy to change the subject, Jennifer brushed the corners of her mouth. "Sorry, lady. Like it or not, you're going to have to keep meeting with me. If not Fridays, another day of the week. I don't think you realize how close you are to ten-mile-a-day runs. Or maybe you do. What's the name of the place where you'll be working?"

With a dramatic roll of her eyes, Candy replied, "The LaSalle Towers, not that it's any of your business. The crew leader will call home if I ever don't make it to work."

"Good," Jennifer said. "By the way, what were you doing while you were waiting outside my office?"

"Nothing," Candy said with a malevolent smile. "What would I be doing?"

Something in the treacly voice bothered Jennifer. The barely hidden sneer did, too. "How long were you there?"

"Long enough," Candy replied with eyes aglitter. Again, Jennifer felt a vague sense of foreboding. She had been sure she locked the office before going to her meeting with Jason, but now she had doubts. Even if Candy had got into the office, what mischief could she have done?

"I'm going home from here," Candy said. "I'm afraid you're going to have to find your own way to where you want to go."

Jennifer smiled sweetly. "I can do that. Congratulations again on your job, and I'm sorry I wasn't there when you came for your appointment . . . late."

Candy snorted and got into her car. Her parents had showered her with a brand new Trans-Am, and she revved it before pulling away from the curb. When Jennifer waved at her, she screeched her wheels, gunning the engine. Jennifer knew it was as close to mooning her that Candy could come while behind the wheel of a car.

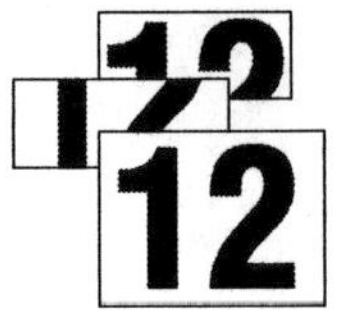

THE PHONE WAS ringing as Jennifer got back to her office. Scrambling to answer it, she found Jason Dumont on the line.

"If you're not too worried that your snotty patient might catch us," he said, "I was hoping I could meet you at Murray's. I've remembered some more things and I'd like to talk about them. It's an extra consultation, so I'll pay you for it, of course."

For a moment she wondered if she should cancel her date with Mark Driscoll for the evening, but decided against it. Even if disguised as a professional session, it would be a personal meeting. "That sounds wonderful, but I really can't."

"Fair enough," he said airily. "I realize it's short notice. I'm flying up to Thief River Falls tomorrow, as I said, and I'm leaving for home Sunday. I wasn't sure if I would have another chance to see you before I left."

She remembered he would be leaving and wasn't coming back again for several weeks after he was through with his finals. Much could be lost by then. "I'm sorry we can't get together tonight," she said, "but I don't have any plans for tomorrow. Maybe we could meet after you come back."

"Okay, but you're welcome to come with me if you want."

"To Thief River Falls?"

"Yes. There's plenty of room in the plane. Mother left some boxes of things with my aunt and uncle. I was hoping they might be useful."

That clinched it. Not only could Melanie's effects help Jason regain his memory, they might give clues to who had murdered her. It was an offer she couldn't refuse.

"Sounds good to me," she enthused. "Where are you, um, parked?"

He laughed. "At Flying Cloud airport. I'm not sure where that is, but it seemed to be a long way from the city."

"It is. I'll drive us there. What time do you want to leave?"

"It's a two-hour flight, and I want to be there before nine. So let's say six-thirty. I'll buy you breakfast when we land."

"Sounds good. I'll pick you up in front of the International at five-thirty."

After hanging up, Jennifer noticed the message light flashing on her phone. She pressed the button. Whoever called had left no message. After glancing at her watch, she took a rueful look at the stack of case histories on her desk. Two more hours to go, and she already wanted to call it a day.

Resigned to her fate, she opened the top file and searched the desktop for a yellow magic marker. Not finding one, she took out the key to the top desk drawer and was about to slip it into the lock when she stopped mid-motion.

The edge of the drawer protruded from the desk front.

Someone had unlocked it!

She yanked the drawer open and made a quick inventory of the contents. Nothing appeared to be disturbed. Unsatisfied, she pulled out the drawers and made a cursory examination of the case files.

Even though everything seemed in place, she still felt a shiver of anxiety. Her unease doubled when she opened the bottom drawer to get Candy Lane's file and it wasn't there. Now highly concerned, she went through the drawers again more carefully.

Candy's file wasn't anywhere in her desk.

Where could I have put it?

Frowning, she turned to the stack on top of her desk. Candy's file was the third from the top. Far from relieved, she got even more nervous wondering how it got there. She distinctly remembered putting the file into the desk when Jason called. Had she taken it out again without thinking?

No!

She felt a cold shock as she remembered Candy waiting outside her office. Could she have gotten in and gone through her desk? If so how? What harm could she do if she got a look at her file? Whatever she was up to, Candy would find a way to put it to its most damaging use.

It was too late now. Jennifer took out a ballpoint pen. With an unsteady hand, she began to write down the afternoon's schedule. As she did, she had a very strong feeling that a storm was brewing.

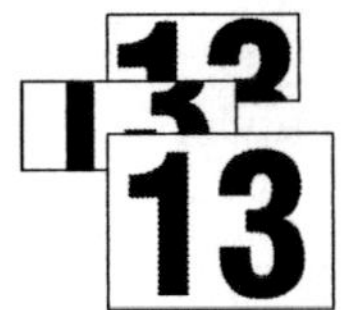

THE SKY STILL was overcast, but the rain had stopped when Jennifer stopped at the drive-through in front of the hotel door Saturday morning. The digital clock in the dash read five-thirty-two. As she stepped out, the doorman, a young man in a large gray coat, eyed her red Audi TT Roadster appreciatively. Jason emerged, waving, from the hotel.

"Nice car," he said. "It smells brand new."

"It is. I just got it a week ago. I've always wanted a red convertible."

"It's not my style, but I bet you must turn the boys' heads when you drive it."

"Maybe," she said.

She released the clutch, and the car took off. Jason grabbed for the handle on the door as she accelerated.

Leaving two other cars in the mud, she screeched across Hennepin Avenue and made a left turn on First Avenue North. She could make the trip to the Minnesota Valley blindfolded. Freeway almost the entire way. West on 394 to 169, south to 212 and 212 to Pioneer Road.

"N-nice driving," Jason stammered. "For so early in the morning, you don't seem any the worse for wear."

"Thanks to you, I got to bed at a reasonable hour last night." In truth she had been happy for an excuse to end her dinner date early. The weekend camping trip with Mark on the St. Croix River two weeks before had been a dud, and so was last night's dinner date for pastichio and retzina at It's Greek to Me.

"Have you ever been to Thief River Falls?" Jason asked.

"Once or twice, I think. I was never much of a traveler."

"It's up near the Canadian border. Detective Arnold spent a day there when he was investigating my mother's death."

"And you still have relatives there?"

"Uncle Dean Marchand, and Aunt Sally. He's going to meet us."

"How well did you know your grandmother?"

Jason shook his head. "I don't remember her at all. I was only two years old the last time I saw her. She was bed-ridden for more than twenty years before she died."

Wheels turned in Jennifer's mind. "Then I wonder why your mother brought you along to her funeral. You obviously weren't close."

"Father told me she couldn't find anyone to take care of me."

She nodded. "That sounds reasonable enough. What is it you wanted to talk to me about?"

"It's amazing, but I've been able to remember part of the night when mother died," Jason said brightly. "We arrived at the hotel after dark. It was cold and blustery—I lost my cap but Mother caught it—and I told her I wished I had stayed home. She said, 'Don't be too sure. I've got a surprise for you.' She wouldn't tell me what it was, but I remember I stopped wanting to go home. We checked into the room, and I didn't like it at all. It smelled like cigarette smoke. Smelling cigarette smoke and Carrie Flowers' perfume brought back a lot of memories."

"I'm not surprised," Jennifer said. "Smell is the oldest sense. It's part of the reptilian brain. Some scientists claim we can remember the odors of the place where we were born. What else do you remember?"

"Mother watched TV while I worked on my model airplane. A little while later she said, 'Do you want to know what your surprise is?'"

"I was hoping hard. 'I know you've wanted a remote-controlled airplane,' she said. 'Our flight doesn't leave until noon, so tomorrow we'll look for one. Grandmother wanted you to have it. But you have to get right to sleep.'"

"Did you?" Jennifer asked.

"Heck no. I was too excited. I'd wanted that model plane for a long time."

"I can believe that. What happened next?"

"I took out the yellow pages from one of the drawers and found a store that sold what I wanted. Mother said it was just a little ways from the hotel. I waited until she went into the bathroom, and I tore out the page and set it on the nightstand next to the bed, just so she'd remember. Officer Flowers found it."

"What happened then?"

"I don't know," Jason said. "I don't remember."

"Do you remember what kind of airplane you wanted?"

"It was remote control called an 'Ugly Stick.'"

Jennifer broke out laughing. "Why did they call it that?"

"Beats me," he said.

She expected him to laugh, too, but he didn't crack a smile. She glanced at him, wondering if he were completely devoid of a sense of humor. Did the poor guy ever experience joy? "How do you feel about remembering now that you've had a chance to think about it?"

"I still want to. What I can't understand is how I can remember everything in so much in detail. I appreciate that you told me to expect that. It helped."

"It's part of being shut away for all those years. Do you realize what a job your mind has had to blot these things out all this time?"

"What do you mean?" he asked.

"You said you were excited about your mother getting you an airplane. You weren't the only one who knew how much you liked them. Your father must have known, and your friends, too. Yet none of the reminders of that fact you got for fifteen years ever brought back the memory that you were working on one the night your mother died, or that she intended to buy you one. Your mind really had to work overtime to suppress that. It had to double bar the door, so to speak, so you had to have a more powerful cue to remember it."

"I see," Jason said. "Maybe one of the reasons I had trouble remembering is that Father bought me an Ugly Stick a short time after it happened."

Jennifer geared down as she approached the Highway 169 South ramp. "That's possible. How did your parents get along?"

He surprised her by responding in a sharp voice. "Why do you ask that? Why does everyone always ask me that?"

"It's an obvious question, not only for solving the murder but in trying to explain who might have shown up at the room if not your dad. Were they happy together?"

"Yes," Jason said testily. "Of course, they were happy together. Father was away a lot on business, but he called every night he was gone and spent what time he wasn't on the road with us. Every time he came back from a trip, he brought presents for us. One time he bought a diamond bracelet for Mom. He always said we were his world."

Jennifer bit her lip. She had heard similar words herself. Finally she said, "I can tell he was a very devoted father and husband, and it sounds as if he was happy. But how about your mother?"

Jason's eyes widened and his mouth opened. "What a ridiculous question," he growled. "She was happy, too. Of course she was. They both were."

"I'm sorry this upsets you, but if she were unhappy, it would go a long way to explain why she may have let someone into your room."

"Stop talking about that."

Jennifer pulled to the side of the highway. "Listen to me," she demanded. "Instead of getting angry, just stop and think. You said your father was away much of the time. Your mother could have been lonely, even if she never let on to you. You realize that children—seven-year-olds—don't know everything that goes on in the adult world."

Jason huffed and brushed at his lip, now bleeding. Not knowing what else to do, she handed him her handkerchief.

Blank-eyed, he patted his mouth and handed it back to her. "Sorry. I shouldn't have shouted at you. I know you're right. Sergeant Flowers told me that I said, 'Mummy, that wasn't Father' when I stopped screaming. I must have realized at the time that she had let someone other than my father into the room. That may have been the reason I've blotted everything out."

She patted his arm. "If it is, you'll have to come to grips with it. Did your mother stay at home with you when you were little?"

"Most of the time. She worked one day a week and volunteered another. When she was gone, either the housekeeper or Uncle Gary usually took care of me. He teaches Plant Biology at Cincinnati. Gary, Jr., is his son. He's five years younger than me. Aunt Sara died when he was born." He stopped and threw a sharp look at her. "I know what you're thinking. You think mother and Uncle Gary were involved with each other."

"It didn't even occur to me. Is that what you think?"

"I never did until now," he said, his eyes following a large moving van as it lumbered down the road.

"Is he still with the university . . . still teaching?"

"Yes. He's the main reason I got interested in science."

Satisfied that Jason was again on an even keel, Jennifer pulled back on to the road. Before long they were following city streets with an endless string of stoplights. The signs ended abruptly, and they were driving through farmland.

"I don't remember coming this way," Jason said.

"You probably didn't," Jennifer replied. "But we're almost there."

The round roof on the building to their right signaled they had reached the airport. Jennifer followed a driveway leading to a large parking lot.

"We're here!" she said. "I can hardly wait to get a look at Melanie's boxes."

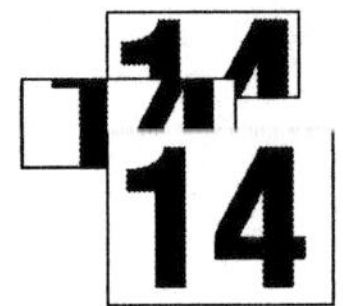

14

ENGULFED IN A light mist, the planes on the apron looked like lonely steeds waiting for their riders. As they walked, Jennifer became increasingly unhappy that she had worn open-toed shoes.

Stopping in her tracks, she said. "Why don't you go get the plane and pick me up. My feet are getting wet."

Jason broke into laughter and she joined him, even though she was half-serious. By the time they stopped next to what appeared to be an oversized swan, a squat avian creature with stubby, but proud, outstretched wings, her feet were soaking wet.

"Here she is," Jason said, proudly.

Jennifer's eyes wide. "We're going to fly to northern Minnesota in that?"

"Why not? There's more than enough room for both of us inside."

"But it's so small."

"It's more than big enough. And you know yourself, size doesn't matter."

His comment and tight smile surprised her. "For your information, that's been proven to be totally untrue," she said. She hesitated for effect and then added, "But since she's a girl, I'll give her the benefit of a doubt. Aren't you afraid to fly . . . her?"

"Never," Jason said. "She handles like a dream." Half of the right side of the chassis swung up. "Get in," he said.

"Okay," she said, taking off her shoes so she wouldn't slip as she climbed, "but I still say it looks like a Geo Metro with wings."

She easily settled into her seat. It was surprisingly comfortable, and the legroom delighted her. The smell of the leather interior reminded her of her Audi.

"Just sit tight. I'll file my flight plan."

Curious, she spent the time he was gone examining the dials and controls. When he returned, Jason adjusted his seat and rudder pedals. "Now that you two know each other better, what do you think?"

"Not bad. She looks very new."

"I just bought her eight days ago. At the beginning of the school year, Father asked me what I wanted for graduation, and I told him an airplane. I could tell he wasn't too crazy about the idea, but he said he'd think about it. Then Grandmother died and left me money. I beat Dad to the punch. He didn't realize I had already gotten my pilot's license until a couple weeks ago. The test was a snap."

"Does he buy you expensive gifts often?"

"Only when I let him," he said. "I've always made sure I really needed something before I asked him for it. He'd never turn me down for anything."

Jennifer searched Jason's face. "Do you think his generosity was related to your mother's death?"

"No. He's always been that way. He showered Mother with gifts as well."

Bribery, Jennifer decided. Her own father had used the same ploy on a smaller scale. Unsuccessfully. Jennifer had nailed him to the wall.

"I refueled when I got here, so we're ready to go," Jason said. He handed her a headset. When she had it in place, his voice asked, "Can you hear me?"

"Sure can," she said.

He hit the ignition switch, and the engine jumped to life.

She expected an overwhelming din but found instead a subdued statement of resolute power. Her estimation of the petite craft took an immediate leap.

"What do you think of her now?" Jason asked.

"I'm impressed," she said. "Where's her garage?"

He flashed a smile. *A nice smile,* she thought.

"Bolton Field. It isn't anywhere as busy as Columbus International. Now that you're not frightened for your life, let's see if we can get out of here." After adjusting the mouthpiece he said, "F-C-3-zero-1-6-niner, this is X-L-2-6-1 requesting clearance for take-off at Zero-six-twelve on runway 330. Over."

A blare of static answered him from the radio. Seconds later they were lightly skimming over the ground. Picking up speed, the craft gently lifted off. Once airborne, they quickly climbed through the overcast into a beautiful clear morning.

Jason flipped a switch. Taking his hands away from the controls for effect, he said, "Look, Ma."

Jennifer snorted derisively.

"Okay. I just turned on the GPS. There's not much to do for the next couple of hours. You can catch a little nap if you want to."

"Thanks, but I'd rather keep you company," she said. "This is exciting."

As he turned the plane's nose to the sky, the sun streamed through the windows in the roof. Jennifer put on her sunglasses. Far ahead and over them, a red-tailed Northwest Airlines jet banked to get on course for an eastern destination. The haze below them made her think she was skating on an ice rink.

"You're the first person to ride with me," he said. "Does she still seem too small to you?"

"Not at all," Jennifer said, wrinkling her nose. "But if there were as much traffic up here as there is on the ground, I wouldn't give her much of chance. Have you always been interested in flying?"

He grinned. "As long as I can remember. Mother made a videotape of me when I was about two showing me swooping around the house with toilet paper wrapped around my body and my arms outstretched. That was pretty funny, but I damned near killed myself when I was five years old. I filled up my American Flyer with rocks, put a two-by-four across it for wings, and rolled down a hill by my house. Everything was going great until I suddenly realized I couldn't stop. I barreled into the street. One of the neighbors had to slam on her brakes to keep from hitting me. I got grounded for a week."

"Served you right," Jennifer said with a smile. "Did you ever consider becoming an airline pilot?"

"Yes. But I've always been more interested in helping people. I decided to be a doctor when I was five."

"Good for you. I just wonder why you never remembered that your mother was going to buy you a remote-controlled plane until now."

"You're the shrink," Jason said with a shrug. "All I know is that smelling Carrie's perfume brought it back. The funny thing is that Mother always used to wear Patchouli, too, but I've noticed other women wearing it many times through the years."

Jennifer's heart beat faster as she saw a towering snow-covered mountainside of a cloud bank appear in front of them. "Jason," she said, pointing.

"Pretty, isn't it," he said as he passed through it. "Stratonimbus, I think. Someone's in for a storm."

She ungritted her teeth. "Where were we? Oh, yes. The perfume, right? You say you've smelled it many times, but it never made you remember."

"Yeah?"

"And you didn't recognize Carrie when you first saw her, right?"

"No, but I somehow remembered her voice. I sometimes heard it in my dreams, but I didn't recognize her until I went into her office." He inhaled noisily. "Wait a minute! Carrie had an ashtray on her desk and her office smelled like tobacco smoke. That's when I remembered."

"And you didn't like your room at the International because it smelled like tobacco, too. Do you have any idea why?"

Jason looked thoughtful. "No. I always hated the smell. Father's sister, Aunt Yvette smokes. I never liked to have her come into the house."

"Did either your father or mother smoke?"

"No. What are you thinking?"

"I'm not sure. There's some reason why the odor of smoke or Patchouli alone never triggered your memory, but putting them together and seeing Carrie Flowers did. It's like a gun with three triggers that won't fire until you pull them all at the same time."

Jason gave her a dubious look. "Are you saying it forced me to remember?"

"Exactly that. Whatever your unconscious has been forcing you to forget, another part of your mind is trying to force you to remember. It's like a jack-in-the-box with a powerful spring waiting for someone to turn the music box crank far enough. Some memories are behind doors that need more than one key to open. It makes remembering harder, but it makes things easier to accept when you finally find them."

Jason's eyes narrowed. "Are you sure you're not making all this up?"

Jennifer laughed. "I haven't published my book yet, but I'm almost certain there are other combinations that will trigger more memories. I may be able to help, but you'll have to tell me everything you know. Like the recurring dreams I asked you about and you denied having."

He blushed. "You sure are pushy."

"So sue me. Just wait until we're done with your treatment to do it."

"Okay." He told her about the spider dream. "That's all there is to it."

Jennifer's smile turned into a frown. "It's scary but I don't understand why you didn't tell me when I asked you before."

Jason looked embarrassed. "I don't know. I guess I wasn't sure if I trusted you with my whole life story. I had just met you."

"Fair enough," she said. "Dealing with a professional is a one-way street. It's the patient who's always taking the risk. I'll try to do everything I can to help you trust me."

"You're already doing a good job at that. Your coming along with me today is much more than I could have expected. I appreciate it." He paused and asked with a twinkle in his eye. "Wanna play a game?"

"Depends. You don't want to play doctor, do you?"

"No. A word game. Anagrams."

"I've never been any good at them," she said.

"It's a very useful game. Some people think you can tell something about a person or their fate by anagramming their name."

"And you believe that?"

"No, but it's fun, anyway. For example, you must have witchcraft in your background. Jennifer Cahill anagrammed is Elfin Lichen Jar."

"Cute," she said wrinkling her nose. "I'm a bit big for an elf. How about yours?"

"It looks like I had a relative at King Arthur's Court. It's 'Damn, no joust.'"

"Ha. I like that. And your father?"

"'Unlamented crow' and 'lawmen trounced.'"

"Those are good," she said with a nod. "Speaking of lawmen, how about Lieutenant Arnold?"

"The lieutenant's ancestors must go way back before we were humans. His is An Annelid Lord. He probably wouldn't like having a worm in his background, even an aristocratic one."

"I wouldn't think so," Jennifer said with a giggle.

"I told Uncle Gary his anagram, but he didn't seem to like his either. I'm not even sure how to describe it. His is Dormant Guy. I guess he thought it means all he does is sit around. I know that's not true. He's busy all the time. Do you want to try?"

"Nope," she said with a yawn. "You win. You said I could take a nap if I wanted to. I'm taking you up on your offer."

JENNIFER AWOKE FROM A LIGHT DOZE at Jason's nudge. "We're almost there," he said.

A flat black expanse with flecks of green lay below. "This used to be the lake bottom for Lake Agassiz," he said. "It went all the way up into Canada. Highway 32 is below us. We can follow it right to the airport."

Jennifer opened her bag and took out her compact. Jason laughed.

"What's so funny?"

"I was just thinking about the old joke about how women always say they're looking for honesty in men, and yet they never show their suitors what they really look like until it's too late."

"Too late?"

"I said it's an old joke," Jason said. "In the old days men and women didn't know what their partners looked like in the morning until after they were married."

"Believe it or not, there still are people like that," Jennifer said. "I'm just not one of them. I want to know what I'm getting into before things get serious."

"Good idea, but impossible. People change. The man you marry now may be an entirely different person twenty years from now."

"I believe circumstances change, not people," Jennifer said.

"You mean you actually believe that a baby picture of John Wayne Gacy would show the same person he would turn out to be thirty years later?"

Jennifer nodded. "Absolutely. He came into the world with a built-in program. The tape player may have got a few dents along the way but underneath it all, he was the same individual."

Jason frowned. "What about me?

"You're entirely different. Imagine three four-year-olds accidentally hitting their heads on a counter. The first one sits down on the floor and cries. The second one gets up and hits the counter with his fist. The third one finds a hatchet and turns the counter into splinters. It all depends on what kind of person you are."

"I think I know which one I am," Jason said in a angry voice.

"Absolutely. But I'm also sure that after you got done crying, you got up from the floor and carried on; you didn't go out and set fire to a cat. In terms of the analogy, you could say you bumped your head harder than the others and the lump's lasted a bit longer for you."

"But I know I wouldn't hesitate to grab a hatchet if I found out who killed my mother."

"That's understandable. But it's not part of the analogy. Would you hack his body up into little pieces for the fun of it and take a finger home with you for a souvenir?"

Jason grimaced. "Heck no. I wouldn't want anything more to do with the bastard," he said angrily. Pointing out the window he said, "There's the airport."

Jennifer was more than happy to change the subject. Thief River Falls Regional Airport had become visible a few miles ahead with its silver-roofed buildings east of the field with the main town further north.

"Hang on to your stomach," he said.

Against her will, she found her hands grabbing on to the sides of the seat as the runway loomed larger.

She had flown many times on commercial jets and landing was something more to be felt than seen. Now, confronted with the full view of the field, it looked as if they were intent on crashing into the tarmac at top speed.

She squealed as the wheels touched ground, cringing as they rushed forward. Her foot slammed into the floor to hit the brakes, barely missing the pedal. Then the flaps dropped and they were hit by a blast of air.

"We made it," Jason said as he cut the engine.

Jennifer found herself shaking.

Jason reached over to pat her leg and caught himself. "Are you still with me?" he asked.

"Barely. That wasn't one of the most pleasant experiences in my life."

"Relax. It's only scary the first time. When we get back to Minneapolis, landing will be much easier, I promise you. Let's meet my uncle."

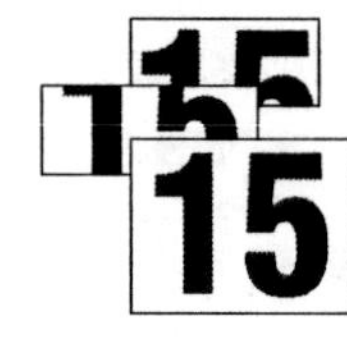

A MIDDLE-AGED MAN in a tan golf jacket holding a sign reading "JASON DUMONT" awaited them inside the building. Jennifer covered her mouth to hide a smile at the sight. How many other arrivees would there be? The man appeared to be in his early fifties, and was nearly as tall as Jason. He grinned broadly, showing off brown teeth, as Jason shook his hand. "Nice to meet you, nephew," he said.

"It's a pleasure," Jason responded. "Uncle Dean, this is Dr. Jennifer Cahill. She's a friend of mine."

"Wish I had such pretty friends," he said, offering his hand to her. "But then the missis would never allow it. Are you two hungry?"

"I don't know about Jason, but I'm starving," Jennifer said. "I left my PopTart in the toaster, so I haven't had a thing to eat."

"I had an apple from the hotel lobby," Jason said. "If I'd been thinking straight, I would have brought one for you."

"I can see both of you can use some breakfast," Dean drawled. "We're off to the Lumberjack."

Jennifer got into the back seat of the rusted blue '78 Malibu station wagon and Dean Marchand shut the door for her. Most of the vinyl in the car seat had pulverized, and bits of dingy stuffing crept out between the springs. She climbed on the tattered newspaper that served as a seat cover and hoped for the best. Behind her, an assortment of paint cans and brightly splashed tarps filled the car with the spicy odor of linseed oil. When Dean pulled away she quickly discovered that the back seat wasn't the only thing that was gone. So was the doddering Chevy's suspension system.

The ride gave the paint and her bottom a good shaking before Dean finally parked between two vintage pickups.

She appreciated Jason's helping hand as she crawled out.

The Lumberjack had a sturdy log cabin front. Inside, a deer head presided from over the door and Paul Bunyan looked out from a frescoed wall.

An aroma of frying bacon, the tinkle of silverware, and friendly conversation filled the air. Men in flannel shirts sat behind unsorted piles of empty plates, chatting or reading egg-yolk stained newspapers as they sipped from large white coffee mugs. The woman at the cash register waved at them.

"Morning, Dean," she said. "Grab yourself a table."

"Thanks, Gertie."

Jennifer giggled, thinking she had stepped back in time some seventy years. 'Gertie' was old-fashioned in the thirties.

So were the pine tables and the prices on the menu. Jennifer settled on the special: two eggs, bacon, hash browns, and orange juice for two-fifty. Only the price for coffee seemed modern. Management had grease-penciled in "75 CENTS WITH FREE REFILLS."

The special turned out to be a popular choice. "No need to come to the table for our orders, Gert," Dean called. "Three of the usual."

Jennifer and Jason exchanged smiles at the diner informality.

"I've eaten here all my life," Dean said, taking a toothpick from its dispenser and rolling it between his fingers. "Your mother liked it, too, Jason. She worked here, you know."

"I didn't," Jason said. "Was she a waitress?"

"Sometimes. Most of the time she was a cook. A danged good one at that."

"What was she like?"

"She was the sweetest and gentlest woman I ever knew. Always put others before herself. I know she would have happily stayed here and taken care of mother—your grandmother—until she died, if your father hadn't come along."

"How did they meet?"

"The way I understand it, he came here on business for the Hidden Pines Clinic," Dean said, spearing the toothpick into the space between his front teeth. "He wandered into the Lumberjack one night when Lottie was working. Before anyone knew anything about it, they were engaged."

"It must have been a real whirlwind romance," Jennifer said.

"Yeah, it was. It turned out to be a wonderful break for your grandma. Your dad owned a world class care nursing home to take care of Naomi."

"Lawrence Dumont must have been a real godsend to your family," Jennifer said.

"The Dumonts have been a godsend to the town since before the Depression."

"Oh? Why is that?" Jennifer asked.

"It's brought in people from all over the world. Billionaires, kings, bigwig corporation execs. Some of the most important people on the planet."

"Mother and Father were married here, weren't they?"

"At St. Bernard's Catholic Church on Main Avenue. Your Aunt Beth was the maid of honor. I don't rightly remember who Lawrence's best man was. From Cincinnati, I think. Lawrence flew him in special. Big fellow with a mustache and bad breath.

Jason and Jennifer traded covert smiles. "What did Grandma think of Father?" Jason asked.

"She was pleased as could be with him. Your mother was happy to take care of her, but Naomi hated being a cripple and bed-ridden. She often said she would rather be dead. She stopped complaining after we took her to Hidden Pines."

At that moment Gertie arrived with the food. "Careful. The plates are hot. Dean, are you ever gonna introduce me to your guests?"

"Sorry, Gert. This is Jason Dumont and his friend Jennifer Cahill. Jason's Lottie's boy."

"Oh," the woman said. She fumbled a plate, convincing Jennifer she was truly overcome with emotion.

After quickly setting the food on the table, Gert reached out a hand and patted Jason's shoulder. "I've worried about you ever since it happened, Jason. It's been a long time, but I've never gotten over her death. The town hasn't either, for that matter. Everybody liked her. We're still mad that the police never caught whoever did such a horrible thing. Some officer from Minneapolis came here and asked questions, and Frank Norquist investigated for a while, but nothing ever came of it. If you ask me, I still think it was that George."

"Now Gertie," Dean said, toothpick bobbing like an reprimanding finger.

"I'm not talking to you, Dean," she said, turning her back on him.

"Who's George," Jason asked in an anxious voice. Jennifer leaned closer, too.

"George Fox," Gertie said in a hoarse whisper before continuing in a normal voice. "He was dating Lottie when she was a senior in high school, and he asked her to marry him. He was mighty disappointed when she turned him down. There wasn't no way she'd leave her mother, and he didn't like it one bit."

Jason was ready with the next question almost before she finished. "Does George still live here?"

"He moved away five years ago after he got divorced," Gertie continued. "To Minneapolis. I hear the police talked to him, but nothing ever came of it."

"What does he do?"

"Computer repairman, I think. Our librarian Margie Bellamy might know. That's his ex-wife," Dean said. "We can give her a call before you go back."

"Did my mother like George?"

"Well enough, I suppose," Gertie said in a non-committal voice. "Lottie hardly ever got out of the house while her mother was sick. The only time she ever had for herself was Sunday afternoon when she used to come here before church. George was waitin' for her every week. They used to sit together over there. She'd have a chocolate soda, and he'd have a strawberry malt."

She pointed at a booth on the opposite side of the café. It was empty, but Jennifer could imagine Lottie and George sitting there. "I bet he always sat next to her, didn't he?"

"Yes. How'd you know that?"

"Intuition," she said. "Why did they break up?"

"As I said, Lottie wouldn't leave Naomi. It just didn't work out."

Jennifer nodded. She had had more than her own share of relationships that just didn't work out. The present one with Mark included. The man had the personality of a wet tennis shoe.

"Enjoy your breakfasts," Gertie said sweetly.

After she left, the trio began the serious business of eating. Jason shook hot sauce on his eggs, and Dean scooped out his yolks with a spoon and put them between slices of toast. Famished, Jennifer quickly went to work with knife and fork. Scant minutes later, she sat red-faced, nervously sipping coffee as she waited for them to catch up with her.

"Need anything else?" Dean asked. "I can get you some more toast. Eggs, too, if you want."

Jennifer frowned. She could have eaten another breakfast but didn't want to admit it. "I'm good," she said. "Do you still have any of Lottie's things around your house?"

"Most near all of them except the things she took with her when she moved to Ohio. We packed everything else up and put it up in the attic the week after the wedding. There's three boxes of stuff, if I recollect rightly. We kept mentioning them to her, but she never did anything about 'em. It was like she was starting an entirely new life or something. After she died, we just left 'em up in the attic. Anything in particular you're looking for?"

"Diaries. High school yearbooks. Just about anything that can help us find out who her friends were. I have a very strong feeling that the person who killed her came from here."

"I always wondered about that myself," Dean said, wiping his mouth and tossing his napkin on his plate. "I could never believe she would let a stranger into her room. If it wasn't someone from Cincinnati, it woulda had to be someone from here. If you're finished, we'll go to the house."

"Could we stop at the graveyard and see Grandmother's grave first?" Jason asked. "I've always been sorry I missed the funeral."

"Of course," Dean said. "I feel bad I've never been to Cincinnati to see your mother's grave. I could never take the time, and I couldn't afford it, anyway."

"I wish I knew that earlier," Jason said. "I'd have sent you plane tickets a long time ago." He paused and continued in a quieter voice. "To tell you the truth, I don't go to visit it much, either. It always gives me a stomachache."

"I better settle up," Dean said, laying a ten-dollar bill and two quarters on the table. After he got up and his back was turned, Jennifer slid another two dollars under the ten. As they left the building they turned at the sound of Gertie's voice calling out. "Why, Dean Marchand," the waitress said, holding up the dollars, "what in the world's gotten into you?"

16

AFTER ANOTHER SHORT but very uncomfortable ride, Dean Marchand pulled off the street and drove through an iron gate into a small cemetery. Jennifer knew it was Catholic by the number of angels. She hadn't seen so many since fifth grade when she attended a funeral for a schoolmate who had drowned. Even though she wasn't sure she believed in angels, she still hoped Tammie Gilliam had become one.

Jason came around to help her out of the car. She liked the strength and gentleness of his grip.

"This here is St. Bernard Cemetery. We're just a spit in the ocean compared to Greenwood. Mom's grave is over this way," Dean said, pointing to the right at a spot toward the back of the enclosure. He took the lead, and Jennifer fell in behind Jason. They walked to a small black block of granite engraved "Marchand." Two smaller stones stood in front of it. One read "François," the other, "Naomi."

Dean squatted and brushed dead grass from the headstones.

After a short silence, Jason said, "Grandpa was a lot older than Grandma, wasn't he?"

"Yes. He was forty-two when he married Mother. She was just out of high school. Everyone always claimed the only reason she married him was cuz he had a farm and she wanted the security. They were married for eighteen years. A year and a half after he died she came down with MS."

"What was her maiden name?" Jennifer asked.

"Sullivan," Dean said, pointing at another group of headstones some ten feet away. "They're over there. Us French and the Irish only make up a little more than a tenth of the population up here. That's why we have such a small cemetery. Most folks are Scandinavian or German. They end up in Greenwood."

"Were the Sullivans farmers?" she asked.

"No. Laborers. They worked in the fields and the sugar beet factories. One or two of 'em were missionaries and lived in some place in Africa. I even heard that some of 'em were Democrats." As he said it, he made a face and spat. "The Marchands were fur-trappers until François's great-great-grandfather bought a farm here. Sounds like you're interested in history."

"I am as far as Lottie is concerned," Jennifer said. "Did you and she have any other siblings?"

"There's Beth, my younger sister. She moved to Winnipeg when she got married. I told her that Jason was coming to visit, but she couldn't get away. It's too bad. We Marchands are a small family, and it woulda been nice to get together."

"How about the Sullivans?" Jennifer asked.

"Too many to count," Dean said with a laugh. He took out a can of Skoal and grabbed a pinch. "We don't socialize. You know, it's kind of a strange thing, but Mother really didn't have much to do with her own family. She'd take us to Grandmother Sullivan's for Christmas every once in a while when we were growing up, but I never was very close to any of my aunts or uncles. Cousins, either, for that matter. None of 'em were my age."

He paused and tilted his head back to drop the tobacco into his mouth. After a few chews, he pushed the wad to the corner of his cheek and continued in a hollow voice, "Lottie was a different story. She was five years younger than I was, and I know she was friends with some of the cousins in high school."

He barely got the words out before he turned his head to spit a brownish stream between the gravestones. Jennifer felt her breakfast try to escape from her stomach. Dean's stock had taken a nosedive, but at least she knew where to start when she looked through the yearbooks.

Minutes later they returned to the car. Dean headed away from the sun on a road that seemed to stretch interminably over featureless terrain. The only trace of vegetation was the low green shoots of the year's crop of sugar beets and potatoes. Another road, marked only by a mailbox, intersected. Jennifer looked in the distance for a farmhouse but couldn't see one. How could anyone stand the isolation?

At last, Dean slowed and turned on his signal, although there was no one else on the road. Like the unnecessary sign he carried at the airport, it was another earmark of the rural conservative who would have considered criticism of Ronald Reagan a mortal sin. At a crawl, he pulled into the left lane before turning. Jennifer had never seen any-one do that before.

"Sally's expecting us," Dean said, edging around a swimming-pool sized pot-hole. "She's making a roast beef for dinner. I 'spect it won't be ready for at least another three hours."

"Actually it'll be good to have a little extra time to go through Lottie's things," Jennifer replied. As she said it, she took a quick look at the farm buildings before going into the house. The once-painted barn with wooden shingles sliding down a sagging roof and disintegrating silos suggested that Dean's farm hadn't produced a crop for quite a while. The house was a small, but well maintained, two-story wood-frame with what appeared to be a brand-new roof.

"C'mon in, young lady," Dean said. "Sally's waitin' for us."

As they stepped through the door, Sally came forward to greet them wearing a red-and-black polka-dot dress and a silk scarf in her hair.

She turned down a burner and ran to Jason to give him a bear hug. Then she turned to Jennifer.

"Hello," she trilled. "Do you like your potatoes mashed or baked?"

Jennifer realized Sally was fully made up and dressed in her Sunday best. June Cleaver vintage empty nest. Though definitely in her fifties, she was still slim. "I like them either way. Do you need any help?"

As Jennifer hoped, Sally declined with thanks. "Are you Jason's girlfriend?"

"No. Therapist. I'm trying to help him remember what happened the night his mother was killed."

Sally opened an oven door to inspect a pan of parsnips bubbling in brown sauce. The lady liked to keep well ahead in her game.

"Poor Lottie," she said. "I was older than her, so I didn't know her very well, but I remember she had a sweet smile and that she was really good to her mother."

"That's what I hear. Where did she get her name? I always thought 'Lottie' was short for Charlotte," Jennifer said.

"That's what most people who didn't know her think. Dean says she couldn't pronounce her name right as a little girl so that's what everyone started to call her." She turned back to the stove to stir something in a pot. "Oh, dear. I let this go a bit too long." Turning to face Jennifer, she made a shooing gesture. "Run along and keep the men company. I'm fine here."

Sensing that Sally somehow was blaming her for the mishap, Jennifer hurried out of the kitchen. She followed the voices and found Dean and Jason conversing in a room decorated with several deer heads and antlers.

"Are you the hunter, Dean?" she asked.

"Used to be. There's a huge forest by the Indian Reservation not very far from here. I used to go every season."

"Funny thing," she said. "I used to dream about a deer with a rifle hiding in a tree waiting for a human to come by."

Dean scowled.

"Do you suppose you could find the boxes with Lottie's things?" she asked.

With a grunt, Dean got to his feet. "You don't let any grass grow under your feet, do you?"

"We don't have much time. There'll be a lot of background work to do before I go back to Minneapolis," she said.

Jason looked uncomfortable. "Um, thanks for the enthusiasm, but I don't know if I want you to put so many hours in on this, as much as I appreciate it."

"Don't be silly," she said. "This is all part of working up my case file, and it's nice to find so much material in one place. We'll need to know a lot more about your mother before we can know what really happened. Whoever killed her was really angry with her, and I think it might be an ex-boyfriend or lover. If it had happened in Cincinnati, I wouldn't have the slightest idea where to start to look. But since it was Minneapolis, I'm sure we'll find our answer here."

"Chief Norquist didn't think so," Dean said. "He hardly talked to any of Lottie's friends. You may want to talk to him yourself, sometime. I'll show you where Lottie's stuff is in the attic."

She followed him. One look at the steep steps made her want to change her mind, and the third step up, her foot slipped. She made the rest of the trip clinging to the handrail for dear life. She wasn't even sure if she could make the return trip empty-handed. Carrying anything seemed suicidal. The passageway smelled of old plaster and damp. A bare seventy-five-watt bulb provided the only lighting.

"This is all storage up here," Dean said.

He didn't need to say it.

Along with a fifties vintage Schwinn boy's bicycle and an American Flyer sled with metal runners, the rest of the floor was covered with dusty cardboard boxes with the tops interfolded. One of them, with a lion and the words Monarch Foods on the front, had brittle cardboard that looked old enough to have been put there by François's great-great-grandfather himself.

Dean tiptoed around the obstacles. "Watch your step," he said. "You don't want to fall through the ceiling."

Startled, Jennifer carefully put her foot down.

"Over here should be where I put the ones we want. Her name's on the boxes."

Squatting, he moved a few to get a better look at them. "Yup," he said. "Here's one." Jason picked it up. "And here's another. This one isn't as heavy."

Jennifer easily picked up the box. Dean grabbed the third. When she got to the stairwell she stopped. "Sorry, but I don't want to carry this down the stairway," she said.

Dean took it from here. "Don't you fret none. I'll take them down for you. I'm used to the steps. You can set your box down, too, Jason."

She watched him sidestep down the stairs and caught her breath as he seemed to lose his balance. Then, like a gyroscope, he righted himself. Minutes later three dusty boxes sat on the living room floor.

"Sally put everything away," Dean said. "I never opened any of them. Not that I wasn't tempted, but it didn't seem right, somehow. I always figured they belonged to Jason and his Dad. I offered to send them, but Lawrence said he didn't want them. She graduated with Chief Norquist."

Jennifer's ears pricked. "Did they ever date?"

"If they did, I wasn't aware of it. It would have to have been when they were in high school. Somehow I don't know if Frank would have considered Lottie his type. She wasn't a beauty queen. And Lottie was too levelheaded to be swept off her feet." He lowered his voice. "I did hear rumors he slept with the entire cheerleading team."

Jennifer made a face. "Together, or one at a time?"

Dean's shocked expression told her she had said the wrong thing. "Sorry. What's he like now?"

"Fat, and divorced. Twice."

Yay! Jennifer thought.

"Why don't you sit on the couch and be comfortable while you're working," Dean said. "You want some coffee?"

Jennifer and Jason both declined. Jennifer sat on the couch. "Come over here and sit with me," she said. "Then we can both see everything at the same time."

Jason did.

She unfolded the lid of the closest box and opened it. The first thing she noticed was a few pairs of like-new Levi 501 jeans that could help Jason pay for his first year in med school. Digging deeper she found more clothing. Eighties, middle-brow, and conservative. Lottie liked skirts. After taking out the last item, Jennifer refolded them and put them back into the box.

The second box looked more promising.

The top layer was composed of several tame Harlequin paperback romance books. Her eyes wrinkled into a knowing smile as she uncovered what lay beneath. Dozens of bodice rippers with hot pink covers lay neatly packed before her. Jennifer's mother read the same kinds of books and kept them in the basement fruit cellar to try to hide them from her just-pubescent daughter. Jennifer was too good a snoop not to find them in relatively short order. Reading the most explicit ones in a locked bathroom, Jennifer had felt some strange stirrings. Now they just seemed silly. Grown women didn't act like that. Or at least not often, anyway.

Beneath them lay four hardbound yearbooks with embossed covers, each bore the sinister name, *The Stalker*. With the modern connotation, she couldn't help but wonder why the school hadn't changed its nickname.

Her heart beat faster. Thumbing through the first, she found many of Lottie's female classmates had signed their pictures in red, green and white ink, apparently a fad at the school at the time. She had few hoped-for signatures from boys.

Paging ahead, Jennifer found Lottie's picture. Melanie Marchand had playful eyes, a big smile and perfect teeth. Though not a beauty, she was pretty enough to be able to compete with any girl for a guy who may have interested her.

"She had green eyes," Jason said.

"Really?" The yearbook was not in color. Melanie's eyes, though certainly not brown, could have been blue. "How do you remember that?"

"I don't know. It just occurred to me. Her hair was a lot longer, too." He blushed. "She sometimes had me sleep with her when Father was gone. Sometimes I'd wake up in the middle of the night and she'd be clutching me like I was her teddy bear."

Jennifer guessed he'd still make a good one. "Were you in her bed the night she died?"

Jason's eyes opened wide. "No!" he said excitedly. "I was in the one next to her. I remember I couldn't get to sleep. I kept thinking about the remote-controlled plane we were going to buy."

"Do you remember anything else?"

"No. Just what I told you."

"It's more than enough," Jennifer said with enthusiasm. "I'm excited for you."

Jason beamed as she found the yearbook index to look for other references. The only other picture showed Lottie in the girl's chorus. "Do you remember your mother singing?"

"Yes. She did all the time. We used to sing the theme from *The Dukes of Hazzard* together when we watched it."

Jennifer remembered she liked the show, too. Especially the fun-loving Luke and Beau. To a ten-year-old girl, they were the perfect older men. She turned to the "S" Section and noticed the pictures the Sullivans had signed. Andrea, Siobhan, Caitlin and Margaret. All very Irish, very trendy names. "Do you have some paper I could have?" Jennifer asked.

Dean handed her a tablet. "I'll need to know their names now," she said. "I imagine most or all of them married."

"Cousin Frances would know them. Just a second." He returned with a green phone index. "Here's her number. I run into her once in a while downtown."

She noted the information and started on the second yearbook. The pictures and the signatures were similar except for a lengthy note by Lester Bergstrom's picture saying how much he enjoyed being her Biology lab partner and how he hoped they would have classes together the next year. Jennifer wrote the name on the pad.

She put a question mark next to it when Lester's picture showed up in the next year's book unsigned. Lottie had become more active in her junior year with references to student council, girl's basketball and National Honor Society. She still had few signatures from boys. As Jennifer opened the last book, a bright green piece of paper fell out. It was an announcement for the cast of the senior class play, "The Music Man." Lottie's name appeared as Marian the librarian.

Jennifer frowned. Turning to the index she found the page she was looking for. The half-page picture showed the cast. Lottie was obvious in her librarian's costume. A tall young man stood next to her holding a baton. Jennifer's finger found the caption and the name.

Jason looked on with a quizzical expression as Jennifer flipped pages. "Here he is," she said. "Dylan Hansen."

"Mr. Hansen must have been quite a brain. President of the Science Club. Captain of the Chess Team. National Honor Society. National Science Scholar." She read the caption under his picture. "'Just call me Doc.' Do you suppose your mother and he could have been an item?"

"Why not? What difference does it make? That was while she was in high school. She hadn't even met Dad yet."

With a shrug she went back to turning pages. She stopped at the picture of Frank Norquist. Handsome, with dark features and a full head of hair. Jennifer knew the type from her class. Usually they were class president and voted most likely to succeed. His only activity was varsity football and the caption under his name read: "Most likely To."

"They sure had him pegged," Jennifer said.

"Lieutenant Arnold said Chief Norquist conducted the investigation here," Jason said. "I always wondered what he looked like."

"I'm sure all the girls had the hots for him," Jennifer said. "He wouldn't have done a thing for me."

Jason smiled at her.

"I think I'll make some calls," she said. "Do you mind if I use your phone?"

"Go right ahead," Dean replied.

Going down the list, Jennifer called each of the people, adding even more names as she went. She had just started a call on her third page when Sally appeared.

"Food's ready," she said. "Everyone go wash your hands."

After the meal, Jennifer went back to the books. She was so engrossed that she didn't realize it was after five o'clock when Jason gently reminded her they needed to start home.

Turning to Dean, she said, "I'm not nearly done. Do you suppose I can borrow the yearbooks?"

"Ask Jason. They're his. He can take all the boxes if he wants them. To tell the truth, I don't much relish draggin' 'em back up to the attic again. They'll only set there another twenty-five years if'n I do."

Jason picked one up. "I'll be glad to take them off your hands."

JENNIFER BURIED HERSELF in her notes on the return trip, looking up only when Jason turned on her compartment light. Yellow magic marker in hand, she pored through the painstakingly constructed Sullivan Family genealogy. She had five notebook sheets packed with more than twenty-five names and addresses each.

Each name had the relationship to Lottie mentioned.

Her marker made a jagged line at the sound of Jason's voice coming through her earphones. "Heads up, Sunshine. We'll be landing in less than five minutes."

She looked out the window and saw the lush green of the Minnesota River Valley. Though not nearly as large as the Mississippi, the Minnesota was once an important artery that connected the Mississippi to Mankato a hundred miles to the southwest. Now it badly needed bypass surgery.

Jason banked, and Jennifer slid toward the door. Trees, fallen and those in full spring plumage, loomed directly beneath her. So did four brown specks dashing away. She had never seen deer from a plane before.

"Hang on," Jason said.

"Talk to me again when we're on the ground," she said, eyes closed and teeth chattering.

An hour later, Jennifer stopped at her apartment door. Stacking the box she was carrying on top of Jason's, she took out her keys. He staggered comically and moaned, "I had no idea Mother's sweaters were so heavy." Even though it was a lame routine, Jennifer pretended to be amused. As much as he would hate to hear it, he had his uncle's sense of humor.

Door unlocked, she opened it. Two pairs of golden eyes glowed in the dark. "Hi, Libby; hi, Nikko." When Jason appeared, the orbs quickly disappeared.

"Where do you want me to put them?" he puffed.

"On the kitchen table will be fine," she said. As she flipped the kitchen switch, she caught sight of the blinking message light on her answering machine.

"I hope today wasn't too boring for you," Jason said.

"No. I had a wonderful time. I'm glad you invited me to come along. I've got enough material to work on for a year, and I really liked flying in your plane."

"I'm glad you came, too. It would have been a long day without you."

"Don't be so critical," she said. "Your aunt and uncle are nice people. They just come from a different background. Your mother did, too. The sad thing is, the more I learn about Lottie, the more I like her. I really wish I could have met her. What time are you planning to leave tomorrow?"

"I want to fly out at eight o'clock or so. It will be a six-hour trip and I have two finals on Monday. Did you ever hear of PChem?"

"I don't think so. What is it?"

"Physical Chemistry," he said enthusiastically. "The graveyard of aspiring chemists. It's mostly math, and I'm loving it. I doubt there are many others who have taken it as an elective. Did you know that there are some substances that are solids at one temperature and atmospheric pressure, and gases at another, each state with completely different physical characteristics?"

"Sounds like multiple personalities to me," she said.

"Good analogy. I expect there are people who are the same way."

"I'm sure there are," Jennifer said. "If you want to get the other carton, I'll make some tea for us."

"Thanks for the offer, but I've been cooped up all day, and I want to get out and walk."

"It's more than four miles to your hotel. It'll be dark by the time you get there."

"That's okay." Jason turned to start back down the stairway to the front door.

"Stick one of those junk-mail newspapers in the door so you don't lock yourself out," she called.

He didn't answer, but quickly returned with the last box. "Have fun," he said, turning to leave.

"Would you like me to drive you to the airport in the morning?"

"Thanks for the offer, but you've done enough for me already for one trip."

"It's no bother at all. Believe me. How does seven-thirty sound?"

"If you insist. But keep track of it in your hours and expenses. I won't be back for at least two weeks. Do you need any more money before I go?"

"Absolutely not. What will you be doing?"

"After finals, I've got that camping with my father in the Rockies. If you want, I'll make a stop here on the way there. It'll give you a chance to meet him."

For a moment Jennifer thought it sounded a bit like meeting the family, and realized she wasn't at all uncomfortable with the idea. That flustered her. "That's . . . that's an excellent idea," she stammered. "By then I should have had time to do some serious investigating. I'm really enjoying playing detective."

"I gathered that." He shuffled his feet. "Thanks for everything. I better be going."

"Have a nice walk," she said. "I haven't walked to work yet, but I sometimes take the bus. The parking space comes with the rent or I'd take it all the time."

"I'm sure you would," Jason said.

"Call me when you get back to the hotel. I'll worry about you otherwise."

"Okay, Mom."

"Good night," she said in a wistful voice as he stepped out into the hallway. Why did it seem so much like the end of an enjoyable date? Maybe it was because she had so few in the last few years. The elevator door opened and Jason waved. She waved back and waited until the door closed before going back to her apartment.

Then she remembered the answering machine.

"Hi, Jen. It's Mark. Sorry I missed you. I'm taking a bike ride along the Mississippi, and I wondered if you wanted to come with me."

"Sorry, Mark," she said as she hit the erase message button. "You're a great guy, but you just aren't my type."

Her impression of him had turned around completely from her first encounter at a political fund-raiser. Either she, he, or both of them, had had too much to drink, and she found him charming. The gloss began to wear thin on their first date. Beginning every sentence with, "I suppose" got old in a hurry. So did the way he constantly twitched his nose like a deranged lop-ear.

Some day, she thought. Being alone again didn't appeal to her, but it wasn't fair to keep him dangling. Maybe she would invite him to dinner and tell him then.

The message light continued to blink. She hit play and heard several hang-ups and no messages. *Rude,* she steamed.

As she was about to go to the cupboard for cat food, the phone rang. "Hello," she said. No one answered. "Hello," she repeated. "Who is this?"

She waited for three seconds and hung up. Caller ID read "unknown caller."

Darn kids.

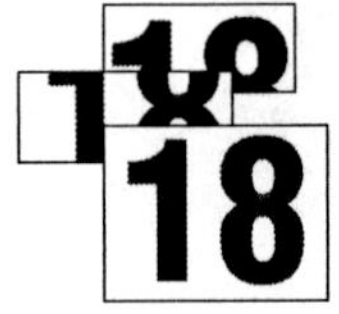

BRIGHTLY LIT MALLS and the open fields of the St. Paul campus of the University of Minnesota gave way to dark buildings. St. Paul had become Minneapolis and Larpenteur Avenue suddenly became Hennepin Avenue. As he walked on, reflections of headlights danced on the wet street. Bright lights shone from open restaurants sprinkled amid dormant industrial buildings and darkened houses.

Jason enjoyed the night. For many years, it was the only time he could escape from watchful eyes and the sense-numbing effects of the medication he was forced to take. Now, as he walked, he tasted the air, listened for the *plosh* of tires cutting through standing water, and reveled in the gentle mist caressing his cheeks and forehead.

All too soon he came to a divided four-lane suspension bridge that spanned the Mississippi. Towers and cables made it look especially strong, and he liked the architecture. He stopped midway across to gaze at the beer-cap sign of Grain Belt Beer and the distant lights of boats on the river that marked the eastern outskirts of downtown Minneapolis. Now mostly dark after being stricken by urban renewal, Minneapolis' one-time version of the Bowery, had a rowdy, boozy, history.

According to Jason's travel book, before the sixties, the Gateway was a series of bars and flophouses. Unemployed railway workers and homeless war vets could rent a room for a buck, the same price as a quart of Sneaky Pete—fusel oil and donkey piss in roughly equal parts. Piano music tinkled out of every door while feisty combatants engaged in nose-pulling contests before sleeping off their booze or fight-injuries on the street. If they didn't stir when someone stepped on them, it meant they were either passed out cold or dead. Most passersby never bothered to find out which.

Not humanity at its best, the book reckoned, but still humanity. A progressive Minneapolis council had turned it into a wasteland. Builders leveled everything—including the city's greatest architectural gem, the Metropolitan Building—and replaced them with modern buildings. A high-rise apartment building stood next to the former Federal Reserve Building. The Fed's glittering inverse arch ruled the terrain. Powerful, but cold. He quickly crossed to the other side of the street to avoid it.

North down the next street, neon lights marked a mélange of bars and shops marking the vestiges of a vanished city. He spotted the Taj Mahal Tandori restaurant.

He fancied the thought of Indian food. Drawing in a deep breath, he sucked in the yeasty aroma of naan bread and the smudgy smell of tandori. He loved them both, but tonight he wanted Indian soul food, a vindaloo hot enough to torch his esophagus.

Getting it right depended on the waiter. If he didn't believe Jason really meant spicy, he got the food back. If he got it right, he wound up with a generous tip.

The waiter led him to a darkened corner. As Jason sat, the man gently touched his shoulder.

Jason recoiled.

"I'm sorry," the waiter said in an embarrassed voice. "Anything to drink, sir?"

"Do you have Taj Mahal beer?" Jason asked in a gruff voice.

"Oh, yes, of course, sir."

"You can start with that." He wasn't a wine drinker and the twenty-ounce beer would last him through the meal.

The waiter grinned and disappeared into the darkness.

Jason laid the photo album he found in one of mother's boxes on the tabletop. It wasn't until today that he realized how little he remembered about her.

By flickering candlelight, he turned the cover. The first picture brought back memories. Once again he saw Mother's gentle smile and remembered the soft voice that tinkled like tempered glass when she laughed. Her schoolmates knew her much better than he ever did. Had one of the people pictured in *The Stalker* murdered her? If so, he hoped the school would change its nickname.

He also wondered about Jennifer and her unusual interest in his case.

He never would have imagined she would spend so much time working with him. All to the good. Her analytical skills were first rate, and she had easily convinced him that the murderer was someone from his mother's past.

He wrote "Lottie" on the napkin.

He had never heard the name before today. Father always called her Melanie, and that's what she'd called herself with Jason. Was that because of Father's wishes? If so, what other changes did he make in her life?

As he paged through the book, the clouds obscuring the memories of his mother became less impenetrable. At the same time, he got the impression he had entered a dark passage leading to something he had never dared to approach, let alone face. Worse, there was no turning back.

The waiter arrived with the beer. "Are you ready to order, sir?"

"Yes. Your shrimp vindaloo. Extra hot. You can also give me a side order of naan. I'd like dal, too, if you spice the lentils."

"Very good, sir."

"Just make sure everything is spicy hot."

The waiter nodded and left. Jason filled half of the glass with beer and went back to the photos.

One showed a school-aged Lottie with big brother, Dean, and little sister, Beth, who was several inches shorter than both of them.

Naomi must have taken the picture, Jason decided.

They didn't look very much alike. Dean had a prominent chin, Beth protruding ears, and Lottie a distinctive Roman nose. She was blonde and fair-skinned with a somewhat large mouth and expressive eyes. Beth had dark hair and complexion and seemed to be hiding from the camera, mouth closed and sad-eyed. Dean was the tallest by far, with a funny shock of light-colored hair standing straight up from the middle of his head over an easy grin. The three stood holding fishing poles. Since the picture was at the bottom right, Jason turned the page, wondering if they had caught any fish.

He didn't get an answer. The pictures on the following page were of Lottie in the *Music Man* with her long hair tied back with ribbons, wearing a cotton frill dress.

When the waiter returned, he laid three plates on the table. The steam from the vindaloo didn't burn his eyes, and he was certain he wouldn't like it. One taste was enough to confirm his suspicions.

"Take this back," he growled. "I ordered it spicy."

The waiter stared nervously at the plate. "But this is spicy, sir."

Jason lashed out in an icy voice. "I've had spicier meat loaf," he roared. "Bring me some lime pickle. I won't eat it this way."

"Yes, sir," the unfortunate waiter said, shrinking away.

Breathing heavily, Jason clenched and unclenched his fists. The anger he so hated continued to well up in him, requiring half of the beer before it began to subside.

Sweat poured from his face and he felt like a frightened child.

The waiter returned with a small bottle with the handle of a spoon peeking out from its chrome top. Gingerly laying it on the table, he attempted to beat a hasty retreat. Jason stopped him.

"Sorry," he said. "The food isn't your fault."

"Thank you, sir," the man said in an unconvincing voice before quickly disappearing around the corner. Once again Jason wondered if his own anger was what lay in the heart of darkness buried so deeply inside of him.

Finished, and with stomach pleasantly aglow, Jason strolled back to his hotel.

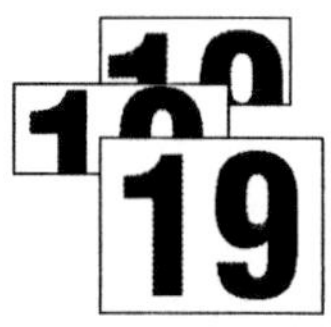

LIBBY AND NIKKO rested in their accustomed places on either side of Jennifer as the alarm went off at six on Sunday morning.

They barely moved as she got up. When the weather was cold, they snuggled up to her to keep warm. Now, with spring well along, they posed in regal isolation like the lions at the entrance of the New York Public Library.

Nikko blinked her orange tiger-eyes when Jennifer bent over to pet her. After accepting a few strokes, she licked Jennifer's hand with a long, scratchy tongue. It was her own quixotic way of showing affection because she never purred. Feeling left out,

Libby arched her back and rubbed her spine under Jennifer's chin. "E-yuh," the animal complained.

Jennifer scratched Libby's head. "Sorry, but I have to drive Jason to the airport," she said.

Hoping for more attention, Libby followed Jennifer into the bathroom, jumping on the toilet seat cover just as her human laid her robe on it.

An angry lump moved under the terry cloth and claws appeared through the fabric. The animal didn't move until Jennifer finished her shower and put the robe back on. It promptly grabbed Jennifer's hand with its claws and bit.

"Out," Jennifer shouted, giving the cat a light kick with the side of her foot. With a growl, it scampered away.

As she stood by the mirror she wondered how much she had changed in the nine years since she had graduated from college. More subtle lines and crowsfeet, certainly. But only a photographer would notice. Maybe a little heavier, too.

She stepped away. Looking over her shoulder, she wondered if her bottom had gotten larger. She considered it roomy and was as comfortable with it as she was with the rest of her body. The select few men she had allowed to become familiar with it never complained, either.

Turning back, she threw herself a suspicious frown in the mirror. Had she suddenly become aware of the effects of aging, or did something else raise the questions?

She half suspected it was Jason Dumont.

"No," she said aloud. "I'm not going there."

To demonstrate her determination, Jennifer slammed the plastic eye shadow container down on the right corner of the sink. Thankfully, Jason hadn't shown the slightest interest in her other than as a patient and partner in investigation.

She took out her make-up kit from its bag. Beginning with the eye shadow, she intended to work with beige, but her eyes fell on bronze and it appealed to her. After finishing one eye, she liked it even better. It made her look like a dangerous cat. A few strokes with the mascara brush finished the eyes and a pat of blush on each cheek the rest of her face. That only left the lip-gloss, and she decided on peach.

Nikko suddenly appeared on the sink. Before Jennifer could move her away, the cat took one startled look at her, pulled back her ears and high-tailed it out of the bathroom.

My God. I scared her away. What was I thinking of?

She was about to reach for the cold cream when she looked at her watch.

No time. In a panic she rummaged through her closet and came up with a green two piece suit. Her last remaining pair of clean pantihose went with the outfit and so did the golden pumps.

I'll scare him, too, she thought as she grabbed her purse and hurried out of the room.

Jason and his bag were waiting for her. "Hi," she said. "I hope I'm not late."

"We have plenty of time." After dumping his bag into the trunk, he stood looking at her.

Oh, no, she thought, wishing she could crawl under the car. To her surprise, he swallowed awkwardly. "My goodness, I . . ." He stopped. "You look . . . lovely." Then he quickly added. "I hope you don't mind my saying so."

"I don't mind at all. I'm flattered."

"I've got something for you," he said. "Hold out your hand, palm up."

She did and he laid a shiny Red Delicious in her hand. "I thought you may have forgotten breakfast again," he said.

She felt curiously touched. "How sweet of you. And you're right. I did forget."

He swung himself in.

As they drove, she glanced over at him and felt uneasy as she realized how much she would miss him. His departure was all for the best. She needed the separation to regain her objectivity.

"When we get to the airfield, I'll give you my card with all the numbers and addresses where you can reach me," she said.

"I'll give you one of mine, too." He paused. "To tell you the truth, I wish you were flying back to Ohio with me. Do you like lobster?"

"Of course. Why?"

"You could be my date for the wienie roast. You could even get some champagne to go with it."

"Sounds like fun, but I don't date clients."

"I should hope not," Jason said. "They're mostly under eighteen aren't they?"

"Yes," she said, having a difficult time keeping a straight face. "A good portion under ten. But even if they were adults, I couldn't get involved. It wouldn't be ethical . . ."

She caught the look on Jason's face. "But if you ever need to talk, just call me. No matter what time it is." She paused. "Do you have anyone else to talk to?" Another pause. "Like a girlfriend?"

"No. I haven't even dated that often. Women haven't interested me that much." Blushing, he quickly added, "Oh, don't misunderstand. I don't have any interest in men."

"Do you think that that might be related to what happened to your mother?"

"Maybe. Why aren't you married?"

She colored. "For the obvious reason. Anyway, I've got my cats to keep me company."

"Just the cats?"

"For the moment," she said primly. She turned on to Highway 169 and headed south. All three lanes were blocked, and she began to wonder how long it would take to get to the airfield.

Jason seemed unconcerned, and before long, they were at the 212 turnoff.

As they drove in silence she wondered, what would it be like to go with him? The idea appealed to her because it'd be so unlike her. More than once she had wondered if her inability to find a partner stemmed from the tight control she kept on her life. Being trained to recognize the mistakes others made, she was determined not to make them herself.

Wise, but often boring.

Jennifer pulled into the parking lot. Jason got out and retrieved his bags from the trunk. She got out of the car. "Good luck on your exams," she said.

"Thanks. You didn't eat your apple."

"I didn't get a chance," she said. "I will before I start back."

He surprised her with a hug. "I'm sure glad you're on my side," he said.

She liked the feeling of his arms around her. Too much. "I am, too," she said.

AFTER FINISHING HIS ham-and-cheese breakfast bagel and large Cocoa-Loco at the Cuppa Java Coffee Shop on Penn and Cedar Lake Road, Dan stood on the corner trying to decide whether to wait for the bus or walk. A whiff of the fresh breeze and a glance at the sun shining through the partial overcast made up his mind for him. He desperately needed some exercise.

He also needed something to take his mind off of Jason Dumont's return. The greatest affront Dan had suffered in his professional life was about to be remedied, or . . . he didn't even want to think about the alternative.

Though not deeply religious, Dan sincerely believed that everything, animate and inanimate, had a purpose. For whatever reason, they were placed on Earth to fulfill a role or a destiny. Once fulfilled, they returned to whence they came. Their duration depended on their particular fate, and fate could provide many different outcomes. For living beings, some remained on earth until their bodies gave up on them. For others, accidents and disease gave them but few hours to do what was required of them. Either alternative was as it should be, their destinies were fulfilled and their deaths an acceptable part of the grand scheme of life.

Suicide and murder were different. Both ended their destiny by an act of will.

Suicide was an act of choice. Murder was not. Murder tore the fabric. When Cain killed Abel, he didn't just kill one man, he eliminated millennia of Abel's descendants as well. Original sin didn't begin when Eve took a bite out of the apple, it began when God made Cain the father of modern civilization. That was the main reason Dan didn't go to church.

A light drizzle dampened Dan's hair and shoulders as he arrived at the Government Building. The guard nodded as Dan flashed his badge. Somewhere a bird chirped as Dan waited for an elevator in the nearly deserted lobby. Sparrows often flew in through open doors, especially in the winter. They white-washed the window sills, feasted on the muffin crumbs from the indoor deli and left when they wanted or were able.

Dan often thought it was the perfect life.

The door opened to the twelfth floor and he got out into a darkened hallway. He knew he wouldn't have to put up with interruptions or harassment from the troops.

Other than Chief Nelson. He could show up at any hour of the day or night. Two young rookies had found that out to their embarrassment when he wandered in on them in the supply office at three o'clock on a Sunday morning. The story quickly made its way around the department, and the couple was still fielding jokes about protection and night sticks three years after they were married.

Funny how some people still had the idea that cops didn't have a sense of humor. Or a life.

As he opened his office door, he immediately began the game he had begun to play with himself since he had become a policeman. He assumed his own office was a crime scene. What evidence could he gather from it?

On this particular Sunday, not much. His neatly arranged desktop and the ceramic coffee cup sitting on his file cabinet without any unsightly stains said nothing about the occupant or recent activities. The evidence box sat at the corner of his table and his wastebasket stood empty, with a clean plastic liner. The dark-brown stain underneath his chair might be worth a shot of luminal to test for blood, but Dan knew it was just coffee.

The sound of his phone ended the game.

Who the hell would be calling on a Sunday?

He let it ring two more times before answering. "Arnold."

"Hello, Lieutenant," Jennifer Cahill stuttered. "I didn't expect you to be there. I just wanted to tell you I was sending you a fax."

"What about?"

"Jason and I flew up to Thief River Falls yesterday. Jason was hoping he'd learn something that would help him remember."

"Did it work?"

"Not yet, anyway. Melanie's brother didn't remember much about her. We did find out she had left three boxes of her things in the attic at the Marchand farm."

Dan squinted. Sheriff Norquist never mentioned anything about them. "Have you had a chance to go through them, yet?"

"Just the one box. It seems to be things from her high-school days. Her brother said Melanie left them there when she got married. The reason I called is I came up with something in one of her yearbooks that might interest you."

Dan tensed in interest. "Yeah? What's that?"

"Lottie's class put on *The Music Man*. Lottie was Marian. Her leading man was Dylan Hansen."

"I don't recognize the name."

"It was in her graduation yearbook. There's probably nothing to this, but it occurred to me that if Melanie knew the person who murdered her, it could easily have been an old boyfriend. She and Dylan Hansen must have spent a lot of time together when they were rehearsing."

Dan's face lit in excitement." Good thought! "Do you have the yearbook now?"

"Yes. I'll scan the pages and send them to you. Will you need the boxes as evidence?"

"I don't think so, but it sounds like it might be a good idea for me to take a look through them some time. Did you learn anything else?"

"Lottie must have more than a hundred cousins. I'm putting a list together. I'll send a copy along with the scans if you'd like."

"I sure would," Dan said. Along with his excitement he was beginning to feel the stirrings of anger at Sheriff Norquist's investigation. "Thanks for the help."

After hanging up, Lieutenant Arnold opened up the bottom drawer of his desk and took out his valise. Once again he paged through his official report. He had covered most of the evidence with Jason, but there were a few more notes at the end of the report.

Other than more blood spatter by the closest bed, a rudimentary examination of the rest of the room had turned up little.

The hallway didn't help much, either. Just a few spatters of blood directly outside the hotel room door. The stairway was kitty-corner three doors away. No blood traces. When Dan took the elevator to the basement, he found two doors, one leading to the stairway, the other to the hotel garage. The garage door was locked from the inside.

The last note read, "Everyone in the entire hotel had to come in through the lobby or had a room key to enter through the garage."

Finished, Dan looked up from his reading and startled. Chief Lance Davis stood in front of his desk.

"Sorry, Dan. I didn't mean to spook you."

"No problem. Good to see you, Lance. What are you doing here?"

"Just out for a stroll. How about you?"

"I'm taking another look at the Dumont case."

Davis nodded. "I heard that the boy's in town. Does he have anything new?"

"No. But he remembered Carrie. He's hoping he'll get his memory back. I think he may have a chance."

Davis's eyebrows rose. "Why's that?"

"He's working with some young psychologist. She seems pretty sharp. In fact she may even have turned up a possible suspect for me."

Davis shifted his spare behind onto the edge of Dan's desk. "Sit down, Dan. What're you trying to tell me?"

Dan sat, then recounted Jennifer's phone call. When he was done, Davis shook his head. "It sounds pretty far-fetched to me."

"Why?" Dan demanded. "We found no sign of forced entry, and she was wearing makeup, a negligee, and jewelry when we found her. She must have been waiting for someone. I never heard of Dylan Hansen before, but I say he sounds like as likely a candidate for a possible boyfriend as any."

"Okay. Go for it, Dan. You know I want to catch the sonabitch who did this as much as you do. Find this Dylan Hansen and interrogate him."

"I intend to. I'm also going to alert the media about reopening the case. No one responded with information when I tried it fifteen years ago, but someone may remember seeing or hearing something now."

"Not a bad idea."

"I even want to go one step further. I want to make a trip to Cincinnati and have another talk with Jason's father. I have a few more questions I need answered."

Davis scowled. "Why can't Trent North talk to him?"

Dan's mouth pulled into a faint smile at the name. Trent North was the sheriff of Indian Hill and had done most of the legwork with the Dumont family. The one-hundred-page report he sent at the end of the investigation was meticulous. The end-of-action sent by Sheriff Frank Norquist of Thief River Falls took less than five and could have been boiled down to a single paragraph. "Nothing to report."

"Well?" Davis said.

"Sorry. I'm sure he could, but I want another crack at Lawrence Dumont myself."

"Negative, Dan. If the father had anything to do with Melanie Dumont's death, Jason would have been killed off years ago."

"I realize that," Dan mumbled, "but I still want to talk to him. If I have to, I'll do it on my own time. I haven't taken time off for six months."

"Tell you what. I'll give you the time, but you have to pay your own expenses."

"Fair enough. I have a free flight voucher I can cash in."

"Fine with me." Davis stopped and looked around. "Why isn't your coffee-maker on?"

"I didn't think of it. I have some good Jamaican Teaberry. Come back in half an hour and I'll give you a cup."

Davis left and Dan opened his miniature refrigerator to take out a bag of coffee beans. He poured three spoonsful into his miniature grinder. A few minutes later, his coffee-maker began to spout.

The chief had a good nose and would show up soon. Dan wanted to have his prospective travel itinerary ready.

Davis returned with mug in hand twenty minutes later. As Dan filled his boss' cup he said, "I caught a break. I found a flight tomorrow afternoon and coming back Tuesday night. I'll only miss one day at the office."

The right hand column of Jennifer's yellow legal pad was filled with check marks by the time Jennifer called Siobhan Sullivan.

"Hello," a timid voice said.

"Good afternoon. This is Jennifer Cahill. Melanie Marchand's son is my patient and I'm calling people who may have known her. Were you good friends?"

"Probably her best. We graduated together and used to hang out when she wasn't with her mother."

"You're just the person I want to talk to!" Jennifer said with enthusiasm. "Do you know if she had any boyfriends?"

"Other than George Fox, you mean?"

"Yes."

After a puzzling silence, Siobhan answered. "I don't know if you would exactly call him a boyfriend, but Lottie really liked Frank Norquist for a while."

Remembering Dean Marchand's description of the womanizing sheriff, Jennifer scowled. Lottie couldn't have been taken in by him, too. "When was this?"

"In her senior year," Sullivan said. "She even drove to Grand Forks to see him play football. She told her mother I was going with her, but she actually went alone. The game was Friday night, and she didn't come back until the next afternoon."

Jennifer's frown deepened. "I'll admit I don't know very much about her, but what little I do, that doesn't sound like her. Do you think there's any chance she continued the relationship?"

"I don't know. We never talked about him."

"Did Chief Norquist ever question you after Lottie's murder?"

"No. As far as I know, the only person he talked to was George Fox."

"I see," Jennifer said. As much as she disliked the thought that Lottie and Norquist may have been lovers, Norquist's own guilt might explain his slipshod investigation. "Did she ever say anything about George?"

"Just that she enjoyed his company. I'm almost certain she wasn't very serious about him."

"Did you ever think he could have been the one who murdered Lottie?"

Siobhan laughed. "Sorry. It isn't funny, but the only way he could have killed her would have been by choking her to death with marijuana smoke. He's a tick."

Jennifer had never heard the expression, but she guessed it meant harmless loser. "Let's try someone else," she said. "How about Dylan Hansen?"

After another pause, Siobhan said, "Well, I just don't know. They sure spent enough time together practicing for the play, and they made a very cute couple in the musical. Lottie didn't talk much about her love life, but Dylan would have been a good catch. He was extremely bright. He turned out to be a doctor, you know."

"That's what I hear. I'm trying to get in touch with him. Do you know where he is?"

"Kaw. It's some place in French Guiana. No one has heard from him since his mother died."

"Did Lottie have any other close friends?"

"Not that I'm aware of. I think she considered me to be her closest."

"If you think of anything, let me know," Jennifer said. After giving her office number, Jennifer hung up. Why did she get a distinct feeling that Siobhan was lying?

JASON ARRIVED AT BOLTON Airport at 16:20 p.m. EDT. After stopping to refuel at Rockford, Illinois, he had flown the rest of the way non-stop.

Now he felt like road kill.

He perked up when he found Roger Holmes, his PChem lab partner, waiting for him at the airport. They studied together for the rest of the afternoon except for the session with the anchovy-and-jalapeno pizza they ordered. When they separated at 8:30 Jason fell fast asleep on his couch until the sound of his cell phone woke him.

"Hi, Dad. Where are you?"

"Chicago. I've got an early morning meeting. How are things going?"

"Great. Jennifer and I flew up to Thief River Falls over the weekend. We brought the boxes with mother's things back with us. Did you know she was the star in her high school musical?"

"No. How do you know that?"

"It was in her yearbook. She was Marian the librarian in the *Music Man.* Someone named Dylan Hansen played Harold Hill."

"Hmm. You didn't know about your mother's talents, did you? Have you been able to remember any more?"

"Just bits and pieces—most of them are disconnected, and I can't put much together—but quite a bit actually. Jennifer is pretty sure I'll remember everything, sooner or later."

"Be sure you let me know when you do," Lawrence said, his voice cold. "I've been waiting a long time to settle a score."

"I'm flying back to Minneapolis tomorrow afternoon when I'm done with my finals. Why don't you come and meet me there?"

"I'd really like to, but I have some important meetings set up for the home office. Maybe after that. Sorry to cut you off, but I've got to run. Call me if you have anything to report."

"Sure, Dad," Jason said.

With her printer humming merrily as background music, Jennifer moved the cursor to the next listing, nearly upsetting a paper cup of cold triple espresso sitting next to the mouse pad in the process.

The printer fell silent, and she removed the still-warm page from the baler. Using a yellow marker, she highlighted 594, the telephone country code for French Guiana. The *Underground Tourist* also noted that officials in French Guiana rarely checked visas, which could explain how Dylan Hansen had been able to stay away from the U.S. so long. Unfortunately, the on-line tour book didn't have any telephone numbers for Kaw.

She sat back, happy for the support in her lower back. The chair was one of the two great pleasures of her office. The second was the antique Black Forest clock hanging on the wall opposite her. Two wooden sawyers endlessly toiled on a log to the steady beat of the clock's pendulum. She especially liked their blue flannel shirts and red suspenders. The sawyers seemed to be symbols of irrepressible energy, and joy in occupation. The only time they rested was when she forgot to raise the weights. If she ever needed inspiration, all she had to do was take a look at them.

Okay, guys. How do I locate Dylan?

The answer came in a flash. It was so simple she wondered how she could have overlooked it. Nearly knocking over the coffee cup again in her haste, she grabbed for the telephone. "International operator, please. French Guiana."

"Please hold."

With *"Fur Elise"* tinkling in the background, she impatiently drummed her fingers waiting for an answer.

"Puis-je vous aidez?" a male voice asked.

Jennifer hesitated, then answered. "The number for the Kaw police station, please."

At first she wasn't sure he understood, but she heard clicking in the background. "There is no listing for that. Emergencies are handled by the police in Cayenne."

"Would you connect me please?"

"Of course. The number is 51194.

Holding her breath, she heard the distinctive *reen-reen* of a European phone system. The sound brought a smile. When she was eight, her parents had spent several weeks in London visiting a terminally-ill relative. They didn't wanted to take Jennifer out of school, so they left her with an aunt. The compromise was that she could call once a day to talk to them. She quickly came to associate the ring with their voices, and the taste of Aunt Tina's oatmeal cookies that were always close at hand.

The smile faded as the phone continued to ring. Wasn't anyone around?

"Commisariat."

"Allo," Jennifer said. *"Parlez-vous Anglais?"*

"Yes. How may I help you?"

Gasping at her success, she grabbed for her legal pad and pen, ready to write. "I'm trying to locate an American doctor who's supposed to be working in Kaw."

"Kaw is just a village, and we don't really have anyone stationed there. This is Cayenne. It's forty miles away," the gendarme replied in a smoky voice.

"Is there any way to contact someone there other than by mail? It's very important."

"Some residents have short-wave radios. Whom do you wish to reach."

"A doctor named Dylan Hansen."

"Hmm," the man said. "I don't know the name."

"He's working in one of the missions," Jennifer pleaded, frustration rising.

"The only mission near there that I'm familiar with is Ste. Margarethe, but I've never heard of Dylan Hansen before."

"Damn!" Jennifer said. "He has a post office box in Kaw. Is there any way to trace him that way?"

"Yes, but you would have to go through the department's administration in Paris after you obtain a court order. I regret to say that it may be a long process. It was once said that escaping from Devil's Island was easier."

Though frustrated, Jennifer chuckled at the humor and touch of sympathy in the gendarme's voice. "I don't have that much time. Do you know of anyone in Kaw who works as a private investigator?"

"Marcel Digus may qualify," the man said with a laugh. "He's a native Maron Indian and his tribe owns the land with our game reserve. He acts as their attorney. I expect he could be persuaded to assist you."

The words brought a flush of optimism. "Could you reach him for me? I really need his help?"

"Do you have a short-wave radio?"

"No. Does Mssr. Digus ever come to Cayenne?"

"*Oui. Assidument.* At least once or twice a week. As a matter fact, I expect he will be in tomorrow. If you will give me your name and the number where he can reach you, I will happily pass it on to him."

Excited, Jennifer quickly gave it to him.

"May he call you collect?"

"*Mais oui,*" Jennifer said. "*Merci beaucoup.*"

"*Enchante,*" the officer said.

AT EIGHT O'CLOCK Monday morning, Marcel Digus parked his Vespa motorbike outside the tiny thatch-roofed building that served as his office in Kaw and ran inside.

Someone would be hungry.

"Allo, Anjol," he said as he opened a small candy tin sitting next to the cage. The baby cayman blinked at him as he took a pencil from his desk. "*Comment ca va?*"

The reptile blinked again.

"So happy to see me you're speechless, *ne c'est pas?*"

Wetting the eraser end, he dipped the pencil into the tin.

"Here you are."

The tiny alligator eagerly snapped up the fly at the end of the eraser. Marcel had found Anjol trapped inside a plastic cup along the Approque River, unable to escape. Fly disposed of, the infant reptile, named for Angelina Jolie, nudged the pencil for more.

"That's all for now," the Indian said in French. "I catch you another later."

The irony struck Marcel with hammer-blow force, and he laughed aloud. If business didn't improve, he could be spending whole days catching flies.

Perhaps even eating a few himself.

With a wistful sigh, he tossed his hat on top of his file cabinet and took a moment to comb his shoulder-length hair with the tortoise-shell comb sitting on top of his file cabinet. Finished, he examined himself in the full-length mirror on the opposite wall. Most of the time he wore a black and white hound's tooth sports jacket over open-neck tee shirts and a green cravat. Today he settled for a white polo shirt and khaki slacks.

Depression did that to him. Most of the time he enjoyed amusing and shocking people by his appearance. Now, in a funk, he dressed conservatively. Mail for his three businesses still sat unopened on top of his desk from the day before. His trip up the Approque to pick up documents for his tribe's lawsuit against the French government had been a complete bust. The tribal curator couldn't find two of the most important ones—and the trip back took much longer than anticipated, so he never even went back to the office. He didn't want to read his mail, anyway. Most were bills. The rest were for his work for his tribe. Pro bono work, at that.

At least now he had a client. If nothing else, it gave him something to do.

AT EIGHT O'CLOCK in the morning, Sheriff Frank Norquist arrived at his office balancing his usual breakfast, ham and egg on bagel, against a large cup of black coffee. After depositing his load on his desk, he hung up his jacket and unfolded a napkin. As he squeezed into his chair, he silently kvetched about how it seemed to have so much less room in it than it did before.

Damned lovehandles.

He had just taken his first bite when his phone rang. Quickly bolting down the mouthful, he picked up his receiver as the answering machine came on. "This is Sheriff Norquist," he said.

His eyebrows rose. "Good morning, Lieutenant. It's been a long time."

"Fourteen years, six months, and three days, to be exact. I was just going through the Melanie Dumont case file, and that was the date of our last contact."

"I'll take your word for it," Norquist said, worrying out a piece of ham stuck between his teeth with a fingernail. "What can I do for you?"

"Jason Dumont came in to see me Friday."

Norquist's eyebrows lowered. "Melanie's boy? What brought him back after all these years?"

"He's working with a local psychologist to try to regain his memory."

"Yeah?" Norquist said, his heart beating faster. "Any luck?"

"I don't know how much she's been able to help him with his memory, but she's doing one helluva fine job of coming up with names of people we didn't contact during the investigation. I never realized that Melanie had so many cousins."

"I talked to all of them," Norquist said, not liking the direction the conversation was moving. "None of them had anything to add to the case. As far as I was able to find out from my investigation, George Fox was the only person who was romantically involved with her. I questioned him, and he had an alibi for the night she was killed."

"It isn't George Fox I'm concerned about, partner. Jason and his psychologist have been going through Melanie's effects from when she was living on the Marchand farm. The shrink's name is Jennifer Cahill, and she seems pretty sharp. She turned up a name that sounds promising. What can you tell me about Dylan Hansen?"

Norquist's heart skipped a beat. "Einstein? Wherever did you hear about him?"

"Miss Cahill found his name in the yearbook. He was the lead in The Music Man with Melanie. Were there ever any rumors that he was anything more than that to her?"

"Shit no. He was a monk as far as I knew. What do you want with him?"

"I just want to ask him a few questions," Arnold replied. "Why'd you called him 'Einstein?'"

"Because he was the smartest person that ever came from around here by a country mile. He was offered a full scholarship to Harvard Medical School and was unanimously elected 'most likely to succeed.'"

"Why did you say he could have been a monk?"

"He never came to any of the class doings, and he never seemed to be interested in anyone, male or female. Everyone considered him to be a geek."

"Then you must have been surprised when he got the lead in *The Music Man*."

"It surprised everyone," Hansen said. "He actually had a pretty good voice."

"If he and Melanie were the leads, they must have spent quite a bit of time rehearsing together."

"That's true. Sometimes I'd come back from baseball practice and I'd find them singing together in the auditorium. Lottie . . . Melanie . . . had a beautiful voice. But as far as them being lovers, it seems too far-fetched for me. And even if they had been, the play was ten years before Melanie was murdered."

Arnold sighed. "Yeah, I suppose. What did Melanie do after she graduated?"

"She took LPN training and stayed home to take care of her mother. Naomi couldn't do anything for herself, and Melanie was the only one in the family who spent any time with her. Dean was courting Sally, and he wasn't home that much. Then Beth, the other daughter, moved to Minneapolis to go to school."

"Leaving Melanie to take care of Naomi," Dan said in thoughtful voice.

Norquist rolled his eyes. *Brilliant deduction, Sherlock,* he thought, taking a mournful look at his sandwich.

"Just because she was taking care of her doesn't mean she was a nun," Dan continued. "She could've been going out at night after her mother went to sleep."

"Yeah. Or someone could have been visiting her at her house. Not likely, though. This isn't New York City. There would have been rumors, and I never heard a peep. Melanie seemed to be willing to do just about anything to see her mother got the care she needed. Heck, if Lawrence Dumont hadn't come along, I don't know if she ever would've gotten married. He had money. When he showed up, lo and behold, Lottie married him. I can't say I blame her."

"So you think it was a marriage of convenience?"

"I didn't say that. Let's just say that I don't think she had too many other hot prospects."

"Did Melanie come back to visit her mother often after she got married?"

"Every other weekend, at least for the first year. She must have spent a fortune on airfares, even with frequent-flyer miles. Luckily, Dumont could afford it." He took a deep breath. "I don't want to hurt your feelings, Dan, but you're barking up the wrong tree."

"Maybe, but I still want to locate Dylan Hansen."

Norquist flinched. Looking at his cold sandwich, he tossed it into the wastebasket. The conversation had taken away his appetite. "I'll see what I can do."

JENNIFER ARRIVED AT her office just in time to hear her phone ring. She almost jumped with excitement when the caller identified himself.

"*Bon jour, M'sieur Digus,*" Jennifer said with enthusiasm. "*Parlez-vous Anglais?*"

"Oh yes," he said in his most urbane voice. "English, French, Taki-Taki, Marone Boni. Even a little Dutch."

Jennifer laughed. "Where are you calling from?"

"Cayenne. Like the pepper. The chief of police called me last night on my radio, and I biked here this morning."

"I'm glad you called. I understand you do investigative work."

"The best you can find outside of Georgetown," said Marcel in a crisp voice.

"I also understand you're a native South American Indian."

"*Bien sur.* Boni. We are distant relatives of your Navahos." He paused and chuckled. "I wish we were speaking on photographic cell phones."

"Why is that?" Jennifer asked. She found herself liking the man and wished she could see him.

"I'd show you my grandfather's head. I have it suspended on a string over my desk."

Jennifer burst into laughter. "I think we had better get down to business. You're the one paying for the call."

"*C'est vrai.* How may I help you?"

"I need to locate someone. All I have is a post office box address in Kaw. Do you think you could help me?"

"*Mais oui,* Mam'selle, I know all the residents well. When was the last time this person wrote from Kaw?"

Biting her lip, she said, "I don't know. He sent postcards to his mother until she died. That was more than ten years ago."

"Um, that would seem to leave a rather cold trail."

"I know, but he's a doctor working at a mission. His name is Dylan Hansen. The man I talked to with the police said he thought that would be Ste.. Margarethe."

"Ah," Marcel sighed. "*Oui.* I have been there. That would be the place to start."

"I don't expect they have a telephone."

"No telephone, no radio. They are but a room with path."

Jennifer giggled at the pun, but she quickly turned back to business. "Is it far away from you," she asked in a worried voice.

"Twenty miles. An hour's ride both ways."

"It's very important that I reach him. I would like to hire you to find him. How much would it cost?"

"I charge one hundred Euros a day plus expenses," Marcel said crisply. "However, I can also arrange an hourly rate."

"No, no," Jennifer said quickly. "One hundred Euros is fine. I'm just worried about being able to contact you."

"I quite understand. How would it be if I charged you a flat rate of three hundred Euros to find him? Then we won't need to communicate so often."

Jennifer could barely believe her ears. "Deal. Give me your address, and I'll send an international money order to you today."

"*Tres bien,*" Marcel Digus replied. "I will get back to you when I have found him."

"*Formidable,*" Jennifer said. "*Au revoir.*"

HALF AN HOUR later, Jennifer glanced up at the CCTV monitor. In the lobby, Galen Parks stood earnestly playing with the How-Do-I-Feel-Today chart on her wall. She got it as an office-warming present and soon discovered it was a great weather-predictor of what to expect in her session. The chart's pieces showed surprise, anger, fear and other emotions. Each piece was divided in two to move independently. Park's creation showed half of a face with large eyes and dash-eyebrows high above them; the bottom, a down-turned mouth.

As usual, Galen wasn't quite sure how he felt.

He had come to her for treatment for obsessive-compulsive disorder. Unable to throw anything away, he had filled his bedroom to overflowing with shoeboxes. He kept every piece of paper he handled in the last five years, including expired pizza coupons, bus transfers and a complete run of newspapers for the last seven years neatly bound together in consecutive order. While under the care of a psychiatrist, he had been assigned to Jennifer for a behavioral modification program. His routine never varied. After setting his medication on the desk in front of him, he sat stiffly gripping his Minnesota Twins baseball cap in his lap unless compelled to move. He never spoke except when spoken to. Jennifer had never seen him without a frightened expression.

As often happened, he had left his Melladril on her desk the previous session.

Feeling a bit nervous, she opened the drawer.

Her heart skipped a beat when she realized the bottle wasn't there.

It skipped another when she realized what must have happened to it. *Ohmygod! Candy!*

Hands shaking, she snatched up the phone with her left and used the right to flip through her Rolodex. At last she found the number for Candy's school counselor. She got Alice Taylor's voice mail. "This is Jennifer Cahill, Candy Lane's psychologist. Candy may have taken Melladril. Please call me as soon as you get this message."

A feeling of dread descended on Jennifer as she took down her copy of the *Physician's Desk Reference*, the pharmaceutical bible, and found the thumbnail with the letter M. A few pages later she found her answer. Melladril—an antidepressant used for short-term treatment of high-moderate to severe depression. The psychiatrist prescribed it because Galen often broke out in cold sweats and muscular spasms when forced to discard any of his shoeboxes.

Unable to sit, she paced the floor waiting for Taylor to return her call. She gave up and opened the door to the lobby. Besides Galen, she found Candy Lane waiting.

"My mother will be coming to see you," Candy said in a slurred voice. "You're in trouble, and she's mad at you."

Jennifer cringed at the teen's dilated pupils. "What did you do with the medicine you took from my desk?" she demanded.

"I brought it home with me. You left your office and desk unlocked, you know."

"Where's the bottle now?"

She took a container out of her backpack. To Jennifer's horror, it was the Melladril. "There're only a couple of pills left. I don't like them. They're making me sleepy."

Jennifer the pill bottle out of her hand, then took her by the wrists and shook her. "How many pills did you take?"

Candy limply resisted. "Stop that."

"I want an answer," Jennifer demanded.

"Not more than ten or eleven."

"Do you realize they can kill you? When did you take them?"

"This morning. After breakfast."

"How long ago was that?"

The logy teen struggled to get free. "I don't know. Maybe an hour. Take your hands off of me."

Candy's head snapped back as Jennifer pulled her to her feet.

"Hey," Candy shouted, "let me go."

"Not on your life," Jennifer said, pushing her toward her private office. Then, realizing the damage she could do there, she shoved her patient into the closet and moved a chair in front of the door.

"What are you doing?" Candy screamed.

"Calling 9-1-1. You're going to the hospital."

"No, I'm not," Candy said, beating on the door. "Let me out."

Jennifer continued to dial. "Sorry, dear," she said. "You can gloat all you want about getting me into trouble, but it's going to cost you. You're getting your stomach pumped, and it won't be fun."

The hammering got louder, combined with screams, then finally subsided. Minutes later, three emergency techs arrived with a stretcher. "She's in there," Jennifer said. She stepped back as they moved the chair away from the door.

One of the medics opened it. "Oh, my God," he said.

"What's the matter?" Jennifer cried.

Looking into the closet, she saw Candy slumped against the wall with blood streaming from her head. Jennifer reeled backwards as she realized that her malevolent patient had found the perfect way to retaliate. By beating against the door with her head, Candy had made Jennifer appear doubly negligent. Not only had she, the attending psychologist, been careless by leaving drugs unprotected, but she had also exhibited extremely poor judgment when she locked her patient in the closet in an attempt to restrain her. Jennifer knew what words would come next. Shouldn't any competent professional be able to envision the possibility that a patient under the influence of drugs might do herself harm?

As the medics carried Candy from the room, Jennifer was sure she saw a smirk on her enemy's face.

Congratulations, Jennifer thought with a wan smile. Even unconscious, you're holding the winning hand.

UNABLE TO CONCENTRATE, Dan splashed his face with cold water in the men's room. Then, deciding he needed a break, he took the elevator to the basement.

The aroma of coffee from the deli hit him as he got out. Pure ambrosia.

Ben Morris from Burglary gave him a wave. Dan was glad to run into him. Friendly faces on Monday mornings were few and far between.

The counter attendant set Ben's coffee on the counter, and the officer slipped the cup through a paper collar. Wiping at his perpetually beefy brow with a shirt-sleeve, he asked, "Who's the greatest inventor of all time, Dan?"

Dan shrugged. Morris was the only person he knew who would look overheated standing naked in the middle of a blizzard. "I don't know. Edison, I suppose."

"Nah. It's gotta be the guy who invented these coffee cup collars. What would America do without them? Think of all the Starbuck's and Caribou customers who can carry their coffee around without getting their fingers burned because of him. The man deserves a monument."

"By golly you're right," Dan said in a distracted voice. "But what if it was invented by a woman?" His eyes passed over the gigantic bear claw pastry he had been examining and settled on a glazed doughnut.

Morris paid for his coffee and stepped aside. "Heard a really funny one from Sandy Schultz. Schultzie and Perry were cruising up on Penn Avenue and Broadway, and all of a sudden this black Acura starts speeding away. Sandy chases him down. Guess what the three letters in the license plate were?"

"No idea."

"It's the same as his occupation."

"I give up."

"PMP! The guy was a pimp."

"Hilarious," Dan said without laughing.

Morris' grin faded. "I thought it was funny. Hey, I hear you want to reopen the Melanie Dumont case."

"Word gets around."

Morris nodded. "I saw Carrie last Thursday. She asked about you."

"Yeah?" Dan said, waving off the fifty cents change from his purchase. "What'd she say? "

"Not much. She just asked how you were."

"She didn't realize Little Boy Blue was coming back to town. He came into my office on Friday."

"Jason Dumont? He must be in high school now."

"Just finishing pre-med in college. He says he's trying to remember."

"Do you think he will?"

"Maybe, but I don't want to get my hopes up too high."

Jennifer sat in the overstuffed chair outside the emergency room with a copy of *Cosmopolitan* in her hand. Even reading "Drive Him Crazy! Find His G-Spot!" couldn't hold her attention. All she could see was the double doors to the emergency room and the uniformed guard who opened them to let people in.

Stephanie Lane, Candy's mother, had arrived fifteen minutes previous and gone in without a word to Jennifer on the way. Steaming.

A man in a dark blue suit saw Jennifer and came over to her. Regarding her from under bushy eyebrows, he asked, "Are you Jennifer Cahill?"

"Yes," she said in a tone that clearly wanted to know who was asking.

"I'm Lieutenant Tim Vincent," he said. "I wonder if I could ask you a few questions."

"Of course, but you have to do something for me first," Jennifer said.

"What's that?"

"Find out how Candy's doing."

His expression softened. "I'll see what I can do," he said.

Vincent walked to the guard and spoke with him. The guard hit a buzzer and the officer passed through the door. Jennifer watched him. She guessed he was in his mid-thirties. He had the fitness of someone who worked out regularly. Quite good-looking, in a craggy sort of way.

Minutes later he came back out and sat down next to Jennifer. "They've emptied her stomach," he said, "but they don't know how much got into her system. It'll be another hour or two before she's out of the woods. Would you like to tell me what happened?"

Jennifer sighed. "I've been treating Candy for about four months, and she's been resisting me. Now, I'm her number one enemy. Apparently she discovered a way to get into my office and found some medicine that belonged to another of my patients."

Vincent gave her a sharp look. "How'd she do that?"

Jennifer steeled herself. "I have no idea. She had an appointment with me last Friday. She was twenty minutes late. While I was waiting for her, I got an emergency call from another patient. I tried to call Candy's counselor and her mother, then I left a message on Candy's cell. When I got back she was waiting in the hallway."

"Did you leave the door to your office open?"

She wondered how many more times she would have to answer that question. "No. I never checked it before I left. I know it was locked."

Vincent took out a notepad and made a note. "Where was the medicine?"

"Locked in the top drawer of my desk."

The officer regarded her with a puzzled look. "Candy Lane broke into your locked office and stole the medicine out of a locked desk?"

Jennifer rolled her eyes. "Look, I know how all this must sound, but it's the absolute truth."

"Why did you lock her in your closet?"

She felt her face color. Taking a deep breath, she replied, "I didn't feel I had a choice. I was sure she was going to run. Melladril is a dangerous drug, and she had overdosed on it. It could have killed her."

Vincent scowled. "If it's so dangerous, why was it in your office?"

Now struggling to keep control, she continued in an even voice. "One of my patients left it there. When Candy showed up this morning and told me she had taken the pills, I knew I had to detain her until emergency help arrived. I had no idea she would intentionally hurt herself the way she did."

He searched her face for several seconds before continuing. Jennifer felt no hostility, but she could sense his skepticism.

"If your door was locked, she either must have found a way to open it or there's another way into your office. Is there a fire escape?"

"No. The hall door is the only entrance. I have no idea how she got in."

"I'm afraid most people would question your story, but I believe you. I have a troubled niece. Shelly ran away from home and would have died of starvation on the streets if my brother hadn't found her. Someone's had to watch her every second since then."

"That could be Candy," Jennifer said with a sigh. "I have no idea where this is all going to end."

"I think you do," the officer said evenly. "At the very least you can probably expect a civil suit from the family. Even if you win, it won't do your professional reputation any good."

"I just hope it doesn't cost me my license," Jennifer said. "I don't have the slightest idea how to prove I'm not at fault."

"Find out how she got in."

It's so simple, she thought, forcing a tight smile. "That's easier said than done."

"I may be able to help you."

The idea intrigued her. "How?"

He shrugged and gave her a small smile. "I'm a cop, aren't I?"

Jennifer's smile turned into a grin. "Yes. I guess you are."

WHEN JASON'S PHONE rang at 10:30, he was happy to hear Jennifer's voice, even though his first final was just a half hour away.

"Hi. I'm glad you had a safe trip," she said in a somber voice.

"Thanks," Jason said. "You sound unhappy. Is anything wrong?"

"I'm at Hennepin County Medical Center. The girl who was waiting for us when we got back to my office ODed on some dangerous pills a patient left in my office."

Jason's frown deepened into a scowl as Jennifer related the rest of her morning adventure. "That's terrible. Can I help?"

"There's nothing you can do, but thanks for the offer. I'm going to have to prove I wasn't negligent by leaving the meds where she could get at them. A police officer is trying to help me find out how she got into my inner office. I have no idea unless she picked the lock, but I wouldn't put it past her if she did."

"Hang in there."

"I will. But I may not have as much time to spend on your case as I hoped."

"Ah," Jason said, his heart sinking.

"Don't worry. I sent a list of names from our trip to Detective Arnold. I'm sure he'll turn up something new."

"Right," Jason said in a dejected voice.

"What's the matter?" Jennifer asked.

"It sounds like you're giving up on me."

"No way," she quickly returned. "As soon as you get back, we'll straighten everything out together. I promise. Just do a good job on your finals."

"I will. Thanks. Good-bye."

Jennifer sat with her cellphone in hand. Calling Jason had been a mistake. He sounded desolate. To make matters worse, she also realized that, whether or not it was her intention, her call to him was a form of blackmail to get him to come back.

She smiled ruefully. Surprise, surprise. Who could be better at mind games than a psychologist?

Candy, maybe. She was a grand master.

In fact Jennifer had never met anyone better, and she had known some real pros.

In her first job, with state corrections, Jennifer encountered many hard cases, especially drug dealers, gang-bangers, and Level 3 sex offenders. All were street smart and cunning, able to put on a façade of harmlessness that pleaded, "Just look at me. Can't you tell people are wrong about me? I'm really not that way at all." Invariably, the façade crumbled when it became clear she wasn't buying it. Then the smiles turned to glares, and sweet words to "bitch." The worst came from a pleasant-looking young man who had raped an eight-year-old girl. When Jennifer let him know that she wasn't impressed, he gave her a Jack Nicholson smile and said, "I can hardly wait to get out so I can come and visit you." Another was a pedophile who dressed as a clown, like Stephen King's It, and enticed children into his ice cream wagon. When questioned, he giggled, clownlike, and said he really loved them and never hurt them. He had been getting away with his activities for years because of children's love of keeping secrets.

Both men scared her silly and she still worried about them. But Candy frightened her more. She was as cynical, street wise, and manipulative as any hardened criminal she had ever met. Perhaps even more so. Worst of all, as a teen-ager she was protected by the system, even though the system clearly needed protection from her.

As her Monday wore on, Jennifer met with each of her appointments. Twelve o'clock came and went with her still in her office, intently going through the pages of notes she had compiled about Melanie Dumont's relatives and friends.

A knock at her door interrupted her thoughts. Looking up at the monitor she saw Tim Vincent in the hallway. "Come in," she said, standing aside.

"I've taken a look at the lock on your office door," he said, handing the spare key ring with three keys to her. "There are some suspicious scratches by the keyhole, but I can't tell anything for sure. I didn't notice any marks on the lock on the desk."

"Have you heard anything more about Candy?"

"She's fine. She's being released tomorrow. Apparently she has no idea how close she came to killing herself."

"On the contrary," Jennifer said firmly, "I think she knew full well. Her timing was perfect to make sure she would get attention in time. Is there anything else I can do to find out how Candy got into my office?"

"Yes. Lie low for a while. I'll check on some of her friends. Maybe one of them is a cat-burglar."

"KSTP found out about what happened. One of their reporters has been trying to contact me all morning."

"My recommendation is don't talk to anyone," Vincent said. "Have you heard anything from Candy's family?"

"Not yet, but I'm sure I will. I know they've hired an attorney. I'm going to contact the American Psychological Association tomorrow morning. They may be able to help me find legal resources to defend myself."

"Candy's mother tells me you're treating Candy for being a cutter. My niece is one, too. What's with them, anyway?"

She threw him an arch smile. "Do you want to know what I think, or do you want the DSM definition?"

"What's a DSM?"

"The *Diagnostic and Statistical Manual of Mental Disorders*. It's the bible."

"Give me your definition."

"Okay. To begin with, the condition is called Deliberate Self-Harm Syndrome or DSS. Most cutters are teenagers, so they have adolescent issues to begin with. Many of them have deep-seated guilt and many are also extremely paranoid. Most of the time they're passive-aggressive and try to con people by promising to quit. Usually they just try to find a less noticeable spot on their bodies. Sooner or later they get caught and when you confront them, they attack."

Vincent nodded. "So you confronted her?"

"More than once. I wouldn't let her get away with anything. Even worse, I was threatening to send her to a program that's tough on acting-out kids. The leaders are in your face every second and they also make you have to depend on someone else to survive. Having to depend on someone else is the worst thing Candy could have to face. In her world, everything is about her."

"That sounds like Gayle, too," Vincent said. "But it also sounds like most drug addicts I've run into."

"It's not a coincidence. They're similar, because self-mutilation is a form of addiction."

"Interesting," Vincent said, getting to his feet. "Thanks for the lowdown."

Jennifer stood, too. "Are you leaving?"

"I have another appointment, but I'll give you a call tomorrow."

"Do that," Jennifer said, seeing him out the door. She walked with him to the elevator and waited with him until the elevator showed up. As the door closed, she thought that Tim Vincent might be just the right person to take her mind off of Jason Dumont and Candy Lane.

IT WAS ONE O'CLOCK and the Kennedy Commons coffee shop, despite its festive scarlet and gray bunting, had begun its end-of-classes slump. Jason bought a crumbly cinnamon roll and a cup of coffee and chose a place to sit. He picked a spot at a distance from a table of boisterous revelers quizzing each other about answers to the Inorganic Chem final.

Being the second person in the class to finish the PChem final gave him a few extra minutes before his next exam. Totally out of the blue, while working a problem, he remembered a long-forgotten name his mother had called him. "Decklin Hi," and he wanted to tell Jennifer about it.

He had no idea what it meant or why he remembered it. The only other memory associated with it was that she had said it with a smile, so it wasn't meant to be a negative term. Best of all it gave him an excuse to talk to Jennifer. He worried about her.

Three punches on his cell phone brought up her number, and she answered on the first ring.

"Hi," Jason said. "Sorry for calling back so soon, but I was worried about you. Anything new?"

"Candy's parents have hired a lawyer," Jennifer said in a subdued voice. "How about you? Have you taken any of your exams yet?"

"I just finished PChem. I thought it was fairly easy. A funny thing happened while I was taking it. I remembered something my mother called me when I was really little. 'Decklin Hi.' What do you make of that?"

"I have no idea," Jennifer said. "What do you make of it?"

"All I remember was that she laughed when she said it. You gonna put that in my file?"

"I sure will," she said with a laugh. "Do you recall what you were doing when you remembered it?"

"I was working an enthalpy of vaporization of a liquid problem using the Clausius-Claperon Equation."

"Oh," Jennifer replied. "Then I can certainly see why that would remind you of something your mother called you." She laughed, and then continued, "When did you say you were planning on coming back?"

Her tone worried him. "I'll be done with my exams late tomorrow morning. I can fly to Minneapolis then and help you with your patient."

"That's really sweet of you to offer, and I really would like you here, but I don't know what you can do for me. Candy's case is stronger than mine is. I can't prove I locked my office door. My best hope is that Tim can find a way to prove she picked my lock."

"Tim?"

His tone of voice made her realize she had made a mistake. "Lieutenant Vincent from the police. He spoke to me at the hospital and believes I'm being set up. He says my best hope is that Candy bragged to some of her friends that she was going to me in get in trouble."

"Have the police asked her how she got into your office?"

"She claims the door was unlocked, and she just walked in."

"And how did she get into your desk?"

"According to her, I left the keys to the desk sitting out. That much may be true. I have an extra set for the desk she may have found."

"Have you ever left your office unlocked before?"

Jennifer snorted. "Please. I used to work with prisoners."

"Sorry," Jason said. "Wait. Your office has two doors, doesn't it? One from the hallway to your waiting room, and one that actually leads into your interviewing room."

"That's right. Is there some significance to that?"

"Maybe. Do you always keep the door between your office and waiting room locked?"

"I don't know, I've never really checked it. I just open it to let my patients in or out. Why?"

"It could be important. Why don't you check and see?"

He heard her set the receiver down. Seconds later she said, "You're right. It is unlocked."

"That's good. If Candy got into your waiting room, she could have walked right into your inner office."

"Yes," Jennifer said. "But that still doesn't answer how she got into the waiting room. I know for a fact that the hall door was locked."

"Not to worry," Jason said with mounting enthusiasm. "We have now reduced the problem to its essential elements. As I see it, there are only two possible explanations. Either she picked the lock or she was hiding in the waiting room and entered your office after you left."

"She may have picked the lock, but she wasn't in the waiting room. I know it was empty because there's no place to hide."

"Are you sure about that?"

"Absolutely. What's more, I regularly checked the CCTV monitor when Candy didn't show up on time. What you're suggesting is impossible."

"Maybe not," Jason said. "Does your camera take in the entire outer office?"

"Everything but the closet. I know she wasn't there because I got my coat from it before I left."

"Is your camera attached to a video recorder?"

"Yes, but I don't keep tape in it. I'm not worried about security. I just want to be able to tell when my patients arrive."

"Too bad. I'm willing to bet the camera picked Candy up sometime that morning. Do you pay any attention to the monitor when you don't have patients scheduled?"

"No," she said, in a thoughtful voice. "But I see what you're getting at. If she came in early, I may not have noticed."

Jennifer remembered a visit some weeks ago when she found Candy making disdainful gestures into the camera while she was waiting in the lobby. Candy asked to see herself on tape. Jennifer hadn't paid much attention at the time, but Candy seemed to be very interested to learn that Jennifer didn't keep film in the recorder.

"I don't know how else it could have happened," Jason said.

"Just a minute. Even if she had come into the office when I wasn't watching, how could she have hidden so I didn't see her?"

"Maybe she hid behind the curtains."

Jennifer sighed. "Nice try, but they're so thin you can see right through them. And even if she had found a way, to hide in the lobby, she certainly couldn't have known you would call and I'd so obligingly leave the office for her." She paused and sighed again. "I'm afraid my best hope is that Tim—Officer Vincent—can prove that Candy has a locksmith boyfriend."

"I suppose you're right," Jason muttered. "I know it's none of my business but do you normally refer to police officers by their first names?"

"No, but Officer Vincent is being very supportive. He has a troubled niece himself who cuts herself, so he knows how difficult kids like that can be. When's your next final?"

"An hour and a half from now. I came in to catch some grub before I take it. Bio-Statistics is a bore. I learned all I needed to about regressions and dispersal algorithms my freshman year."

"Good luck," Jennifer said. "Are you still serious about coming here after you're done with your finals?"

"I sure am."

"Will your father be with you? I'd like to meet him. And I have some questions I'd like to ask him."

"He's away at some conference, but I'm sure he'd be glad to answer any of them," Jason said. "I'll call him and see what he says."

"Thanks. Good luck till then."

"You too," Jason said. "Thank Tim for me for helping you."

After a short pause, Jennifer said, "I'll do that."

MARGERY BELLAMY FINISHED making her cuttings from the *Thief River Falls Times* and got to her feet. When she looked out through the window to the children's room, she let out a shriek.

The room was a pig sty. Again.

Helen Montgomery's third graders had left every middle-grade children's book on the floor or reading table. Several lay open with spines up or covers bent backward. Did that woman leave her own classroom looking like that? If so, how did Principal Green put up with her?

With a growl, she got down on her hands and knees to start picking up books.

Having to take time to clean up after someone else always irked her. Today, the time lost was intolerable. Year-ending inventory was already more than a week late and she still needed to order Native American materials to go with the frieze in the main lobby that depicted the final battle between the Ojibway and the Sioux.

She looked over her shoulder at the sound of a door opening and her eyes narrowed at the sight of Frank Norquist.

Oh shit! What brings his fat ass here?

The thought reminded her of the prominent position of her own derriere. Since he was the last person she wanted to get a look at it, she quickly got to her feet. As she did, she caught a look at her reflection in the window. Her bright red lipstick looked all right, and she was glad she had plucked her eyebrows that morning. But she didn't like how her hair lay flat against her head.

You'd think I was in love with the bastard!

After shelving the last of the books at a deliberate pace, she turned to face him. His grin turned her stomach.

"What do you want, Frank?" she asked.

"My, my. Don't I even get a 'hi'?"

She cringed. "Yes, and that's all you're going to get."

When he didn't reply, she said, "Okay. Hi, Frank. Now what do you want?"

"I'm sure you were hoping I'd ask you to spend the weekend with me in Minneapolis, but I'm here on official business. Do you have Dylan Hansen's address?"

Her eyes widened at the name. Dylan Hansen? What would Frank Norquist want with him? "I don't think so. What do you want that for?"

"The officer who re-opened Lottie's case asked for it."

"Sorry."

She felt a chill as she realized he was looking at her with the same expression he had on his face the winter day he had caught her coming out of the gymnasium so many years ago. The mild crush she had on him ended abruptly when he forced her against a locker and began to kiss her. When he put his hand between her legs, she bit him on the arm to free herself. He backed away in amazement. He was about to slap her when the wrestling coach appeared. That put an end to a continued attack.

Norquist still wore the scar on his ego, now decades after all traces of the bite had disappeared. No one had ever refused the star athlete, the most popular boy in the senior class. At the time she didn't realize he had committed sexual assault, and she never pressed charges, but she hated the man passionately ever since.

"Anything else you need, Frank?"

"I guess not. It appears to me there's no way to track him."

"Sorry I couldn't be more helpful, Sheriff," she said, dripping sarcasm. "Maybe you'll have better luck next time, though I doubt it."

The infuriating grin appeared again. "Maybe you'll have better luck then too. I might ask you out."

She gave him the finger when his back was turned.

After he left, she moved to the circulation desk and picked up the telephone. "Hi, Judy. It's Marge. Who chaired the committee for the sixth class reunion? . . . Gayle Schwartz? Thanks."

JASON DESCENDED THE STEEP amphitheater steps to turn in his Biostatistics exam book. Pete Wilson, the class teaching assistant and former president of the Premed American Medical Student Association, added the booklet to the stack. "Why so glum, Bud?" he asked. "I thought this would be a snap for you."

"It was easy enough. I guess I must have got distracted."

Wilson nodded sympathetically. "Happens. I hear you got exempted from the Neur-D Biology written final. Congratulations. That doesn't happen very often."

Jason smiled at Wilson's term for Neurological and Developmental Biology. "That's what they tell me. I'm glad I don't have to take it. After the lab finals tomorrow, I'm out of here."

"You're coming back for the Wienie Roast on Friday, aren't you?"

Jason smiled. The so-named annual pre-med graduation bash probably had everything but wienies. It was an annual bacchanalia for graduating seniors paid for by shamelessly extorting money from incoming members of AMSA. He had laid out the hundred and fifty-dollar mandatory "donation" himself when he joined the organization. "Actually I won't. Much as I hate to miss it, I'm flying to Minneapolis after my last test."

"Hot date?"

"Not exactly. A friend needs me."

"Too bad. We're having lobster. Nova Scotian, no less. Tell you what, I'll save you one and FedEx it to you. You can toss it in a pot yourself." Bending across the table he whispered, "I'll even see if I can sneak a bottle of Dom Perignon to go with it. You paid for it, after all."

Jason choked. "That's very thoughtful. Have a great time. I'll give you a call."

As he turned, he met Linda Hayworth on her way to hand in her exam. He had known the woman, a double for Mary Ann on the Gilligan's Island television series, since high school. She beamed at him. "Hi, Jason. Can I buy you a cup of coffee?"

"Sure," he said.

She handed her paper to Pete Wilson and skipped over to take Jason's arm. Outside, students lounged on the grass. Some were asleep, others reading. Two men tossed a psychedelic green Frisbee over each other's heads.

"I'm surprised you're still here," she said, giving his arm a squeeze. "I usually don't get done until half an hour after you've left."

"I couldn't seem to focus. How do you think you did?"

"I'm sure I passed. But barely. I'm already toast, and I still have three more exams left. I can hardly wait for the Wienie Roast. Are you taking anyone?"

"I won't be there. I'm leaving right after my last exam."

"Oh no!" she said, stopping in her tracks. "You have to come. Someone you know will be happy to do whatever it takes to make it worth your while."

Jason blushed at the words and Linda's puckish smile. "Really. Who's that?"

"One of the female AMSAns. We've had a pool for two years to see which one you would ask out first. I even threw in a dollar myself."

The light dawned, and he flushed. "I'm really sorry, Linda. I had no idea. I like you, but I already have a girlfriend."

She let go of his arm. "Oh, no."

"Do you still want to go for coffee?"

"No," she sighed. "Let's go to O'Shaughnessy's. I need a real drink."

UNABLE TO THINK straight, Jennifer closed Candy Lane's file and stood. Happy to be on her feet, she stretched and took her watering can down from its shelf. On the way to the rest room to fill it, she once again halted in the waiting room.

Could Candy have been hiding here?

She looked into the camera and imagined it looking back at her. The inquisitive electronic eye constantly took in a panoramic view of the entire waiting room.

The view hadn't changed since Candy had broken in to Jennifer's office. The closet in the tiny alcove at the left of the hall door was still the only place Candy could have hidden not covered by the camera's all-seeing eye. Even if she had slipped in unnoticed, she had nowhere else to hide.

Fighting back tears, Jennifer straightened the magazines on the coffee table in the middle of the room before continuing on her way with the watering can.

In the lady's room, she turned on the cold water tap and looked at herself in the mirror. Not happy with what she saw, she forced a smile. Cold water spilled over the top of the sprinkling can and ran across her wrists. It felt so good she cupped her hands and splashed her face.

Her spirits revived. She smiled again, this one genuine, and straightened her blouse. *Okay world. Here I come.*

At four-thirty, Madison Devereaux appeared in the Thief River Falls Library, for her shift as library aide, her freckles pulsing and carrot-red hair ablaze from exertion. Margery had hired her because she liked the offbeat pairing of a hypermodern first name with a classic literary surname. Who could forget Blanche Deverieux in *A Streetcar Named Desire?*

"You're late."

Panting, Madison said, "Sorry. I had to drop my brother off at the ball park, and I couldn't find the coach. What do you want me to do?"

"I'm way behind on my shelving." Margery said, pointing at an overloaded cart. "You can start with that. After that, I need something from the basement."

Madison made a face. "Do I have to?"

"I know you don't like going down there, but I need one of the scrapbooks."

"Okay," the girl said in a resigned voice. "But the shelving will probably take awhile."

"That's all right," Margery said sweetly, "I can wait."

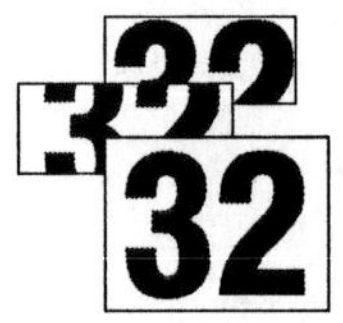

NERVOUSLY COUNTING THE seconds until take-off, Dan Arnold laid his bag on the inspection conveyor. "Remove your shoes, belt, and coat, please," the guard said.

"I'm a cop," Arnold said, surreptitiously flashing his badge.

The guard glanced at it and nodded. "Why didn't you say so sooner?" he asked. Taking Dan by the arm, he escorted him through the outcoming-passengers passageway. "Where you going?"

"Cincinnati."

The guard took a look at the ticket. "Concourse Three is that way. You'll have to hurry to catch your flight."

Dan took off at a canter. He reached the concourse panting. By the time he reached Gate Ten, he was gasping. He squirmed, absolutely mortified when the frightened attendant at the gate offered him in a wheelchair to help him to his seat.

"I can walk, thank you," he puffed.

His heart still beat wildly at takeoff. As it gradually returned to a normal rhythm he desperately hoped that the money he was spending on the trip wouldn't be wasted. He didn't need any more frustration from the Dumont murder case.

At least the transportation to and from Covington airport would be free. Sheriff Trent North would meet him when he arrived at CVG International airport and give him a ride back when he returned. That'd save cab fare. North had been the investigating officer in Indian Hill, Ohio, where Melanie Dumont lived. Now just a year from retirement, would he still have the fire in the belly to reopen such a frigid investigation?

But Trent responded enthusiastically. The case still bothered him, too. It was only the second murder case he knew about that involved someone from Indian Hill. Dan liked him immediately. The man could do a perfect Donald Duck.

The fasten seatbelts lights turned off, and Dan reached under the seat ahead of him for his briefcase. The scans of the report Trent had sent him lay on top. Even though Trent had considerably less to work with than Frank Norquist, he managed to fill more than twenty pages of notes. The first three dealt with the results of the physical investigation of the Dumont residence.

As Dan skimmed through them, North's crabbed handwriting recounted the findings. The police search of Melanie's and Jason's rooms in the Dumont mansion turned up nothing significant.

Jason remained a strong suspect, even though he was only seven years old when it happened. More and more children were murdering their parents all the time. Even very young children sometimes struck out in anger. But a seven-year-old cutting his own mother's throat? Not even Michael Meyers from the Halloween movies had done that.

Dan was about to go on to the next page when a flight attendant came with the refreshment cart. "Juice or coffee?" the man asked.

With unintended irony, Dan replied, "Bloody Mary."

YAWNING, MARGERY BELLAMY shelved the last of the children's book, a copy of *The Secret Garden*, then turned off the light and started back to her office.

On the way she stopped to admire the just-completed 1868 Chippewa/Sioux battle frieze. The State Historical Society's suggestion to use a blue-tinted mirror to represent Thief River worked perfectly. The water now looked far more realistic than her paint-on-plywood version. Using bits of sponge and sawdust mixed in with green paint for the grass and foliage worked well, too. The frieze stood next to the statue of Pierre Bottineau, the Kit Carson of the Northwest and one of her favorite characters.

Though born a Meti, or half-breed, Bottineau gained respect from whites and Indians alike. Known as the walking peace pipe, he helped to settle the war between the Chippewa and the Sioux in 1870. Margery took a last admiring look in his direction. With a satisfied nod at her handiwork, she continued toward her open door.

It had turned out to be a very good day. Even if bittersweet. Relearning Dylan Hansen's address pleased her. Keeping it from Frank Norquist pleased her even more. The worm could do his own legwork. The fact that she would be withholding evidence allowed her a little shiver of pleasure, too.

As much as she had wanted Dylan, her pursuit of him seemed doomed from the start. He seemed oblivious to her flirting, and everything ended with a crash when Marsha Davidson, the drama teacher, chose Lottie to be Marian the librarian in the class play instead of her.

Even though everyone else in town considered him to be a geek, Margery recognized him for what he was: a warm and compassionate human being too good for the people he was forced to associate with. They looked down on him and ignored him or giggled at him behind his back. Maybe that was why he'd an air of mystery about him, a hint at a dark side that appealed to her. Always super-polite at the surface, anger sometimes simmered deep in his eyes. Especially when someone teased him about his mother.

It wasn't easy being the fatherless son of a drug addict.

Why did people ridicule him? Because he was smart? He was born that way, just as Frank Norquist was born with his physical talents, and no one ridiculed him for being an All-Star athlete, or put him down for showing off. Dylan was exactly the opposite. Until you talked to him or heard about his reputation, you would never have suspected how intelligent he was. So why did people fawn over Frank and make fun of Dylan behind his back? It didn't make sense.

And it wasn't fair.

As Margery thought about it, her eyes opened in a moment of understanding. Was that why he never responded to her letter? Did he think she was making fun of him, too? If so, it was time to put him right. And she knew just how to do it.

SHERIFF TRENT NORTH turned off Highway I-71 and soon halted in a parking lot with a large sign that read "Bearcat Inn." It looked rustic, surrounded by a barberry fence and covered with wooden shakes. The wisp of smoke from the chimney added to the illusion. As Dan stepped out of the car, the noise coming from within sent the impression tumbling.

"It's a bit noisy," North said in classic understatement. "But we can talk here."

Wanna bet? Dan thought as he nodded. He wished he hadn't agreed the moment he passed through the door. The immense jukebox thirty feet away blaring the plaintive wails of some country singer named Randy sounded like someone had stuck a megaphone against his ear and shouted. How anyone could hear at all was beyond him.

A waitress, dressed like a fifties carhop without roller-skates, shouted out a greeting. Her nametag, surrounded by tiny flashing lights, read "Mickie." Trent shouted something into her ear and she led them to a corner booth that may have been the quietest spot in the building.

Amazingly, the jukebox quit as they sat. "You want anything from the kitchen?" Mickie asked, punctuating the question with a snap of her gum.

Before Dan could speak, Trent ordered one super-sized order of blazing hot Buffalo wings for the two of them, and a root beer for himself. "You'll like the wings," he said. "They're really great."

Dan nodded and ordered water.

"Sure," the waitress said. After snapping her gum and shrugging her black bra strap back under her blouse, she headed toward the bar, leaving a scent of green apple bubble gum in her wake.

"Got something for you to look at," Trent said. Undoing the leather thongs on his briefcase, he reached in and pulled out a five-by-eight photo. He slid a water glass out of the way, and laid it on Dan's placemat.

Dan dug out his glasses.

"That's the whole Dumont gang," Trent said, pointing. "Husband Lawrence, wife Melanie, Uncle Gary, Jason, and Aunt Yvette Dumont Gilbert holding Gary, Junior."

Dan turned the photo over and noted the handwritten date. "So this was taken about two years before the murder. I never saw it before." He looked up at the sound of cheering. The brace of television sets stretching the length of the bar showed a baseball player wearing red stockings trotting around the bases. "Someone musta hit a home run," he muttered.

North glanced up. "It's about time. No one on the Reds has hit one for a week." He looked over at Dan. "Do you still think Lawrence Dumont is our killer?"

"From the very beginning. You know the spouse is always the most likely suspect."

"Sure. Only he didn't have motive or opportunity," Trent said. He paused and continued in a voice dripping with irony. "Even Jason would be a more likely suspect."

Before Dan could answer, the jukebox started another barrage. He hadn't heard "Stand By Your Man" for years.

"All right. Rub it in," he shouted. "I'll admit I'm still mad at him for not remembering. Getting back to Lawrence—he tries to come off as a southern gentleman. He just seems oily to me."

Trent nodded sympathetically. "I agree. He may be hiding something, but I still don't know how he could have murdered Melanie. I checked all the airlines and independents. As far as I could tell, he wasn't on any of them."

"Couldn't he have been traveling under an assumed name?"

"Possible, but not likely. There weren't many flights to Minneapolis that late at night. I ran down all the passengers. Their IDs all checked out."

"Yeah, damn it. I know."

After Tammy Wynette finished standing by her man, Dan realized he didn't need to shout.

"Give it up, Dan. Dumont was in Miami at the time the murder was committed. He and Bill Connell had adjoining rooms at the hotel. Connell said Lawrence never left his room.

"Yeah. I know," Dan said. "Same old, same old."

A heaping basket of buffalo wings and Trent's root beer appeared before them. Dan's eyes began to water.

"Something wrong with the jukebox?" he asked the waitress. "It hasn't been playing for all of three minutes."

"I'll go see," the waitress said as she disappeared into the woodwork with another crack of her gum.

"Dig in," North said.

Dan sniggled a small one. Taking one bite, he pushed the basket away. "I sure hope you can eat all of these yourself. I won't be able to help."

"They're good reheated," North said, laying a double-bone on the oversized plate next to the basket. "Sorry. I should have asked before ordering. You want something else to eat? My treat."

"No, thanks. I had a ham sandwich during the flight. "

"Suit yourself. Getting back to Lawrence Dumont, even if he found a way to do it, there's still the question of why Jason Dumont is still alive. The kid has had amnesia, but for all Lawrence knew, Jason could have come out of it at any time. And the kid may have seen the whole thing."

"I know," Dan got out before the jukebox let out another sonic blast.

Me and my big mouth, Dan thought. "Speaking of Jason Dumont, I've been asking the same questions about him for fifteen years."

"You still think there's a chance he did it?"

"Absolutely. He's always been my number two suspect, even though thinking so cost me the only woman I've ever loved."

"He was seven, Dan. I read the reports. The poor kid was scared to death."

"I know, I was there. But as far as we know, he was the only one on the scene at the time the murder took place."

"It happened after eleven o'clock. He probably would have been asleep at the time. She may have been, too. Kids don't premeditate violence, they strike out during an argument."

Dan's mouth twisted. "Tell me something I don't know," he groused.

"Have you ever come up with any other suspects?"

"Nothing substantive, but Jason said he had only been to visit Melanie's mother once before she died. Chief Norquist told me Melanie visited Naomi once or twice a month the whole time she was married." He paused dramatically, waving his improvised baton for emphasis. "You can draw your own conclusions."

"It's a start. Why the hell didn't I ever hear about that before?"

"I didn't know it myself until a few hours ago. Norquist just let it slip when I was talking to him."

Trent's eyes narrowed. "Do you think the guy could be dirty?"

"It's occurred to me. I do know he did one hell of a half-assed investigation, if that good. Did you bring your write-up of Lawrence Dumont's actions?"

Trent reached into his briefcase and pulled out a bulging manila folder. After leaving a greasy red fingerprint on the flap, he remembered his fingers and licked them. "I made copies of all his receipts, and he can account for just about every minute of the time he was in Miami."

"You think there's any chance his friend Connell could be lying?"

"It's possible, but I really can't imagine why he would."

Dan raised his eyebrows. "Blackmail, maybe?"

Trent threw him a reproachful smile and pulled the straw out of his root beer and offered it to Dan.

"Funny," Dan said with a pugnacious yawn. "You're right. I am grasping for straws. While I'm looking at your file, you can take a peek at these. They're copies of the hotel records of the guests the night Melanie was murdered."

"I remember you mentioning you had researched it. How many paid with cash?"

"I came up with a dozen or so for the whole hotel. Just one on the twenty-second floor. Janet Williams. I interviewed her, and she did seem awfully nervous. She claims she was in town for her best friend's wedding. The kicker is she said she was away from her room until after three in the morning. Some sort of party for the bride."

"Really! Did her story check out?"

"Yeah. I talked to the bride the next day."

"I expect you didn't find anyone else you considered to be a likely suspect."

"No. I just brought it along because I thought it might come in handy." He yawned again, gaping wider than before. "Sorry, bud. I'm really getting tired. Would you mind if we adjourn until tomorrow."

"My pleasure," North replied, holding up a finger to summon the waitress. "I'll let you sleep in a bit. We can visit Dumont's house around ten. We're only a few miles away."

35

TUESDAY MORNING, JENNIFER arrived at the Lumber Exchange at 8:22. In order to look professional when Candy's lawyers came calling, she deliberately chose an enormous floor length Tartan wool skirt and plain white blouse. To further the image, she hadn't worn make-up. Her kit was in her bag.

Opening her office door, she found a messy stack of letters lying on the floor. Mail was early today.

She sorted through them as she trekked through the anteroom to her office. Most were bills; the hand-addressed ones, payments. One crisp, heavy bond business envelope with the return address of Paxton, Miller and Crown, Law Offices made her stomach turn. Jerome Paxton requested a time to take a deposition. That didn't help.

Remembering that the attorneys would be in to take photos, she made a bee-line for her Rolodex. Like it or not, a call to Mark Driscoll had become mandatory.

But what would she say, and how could she make it clear that she only wanted his professional services?

Fingers shaking, she called his number. She heard his voice and swallowed.

"Hi, Mark," she said brightly. His voice continued, and Jennifer sighed in relief. At the beep, she said, "Hi, Mark. It's Jennifer. I need a lawyer."

She hung up, then jumped as the phone rang immediately. *Mark?*

"Hello, Jennifer. It's Jason."

He needn't have identified himself. She already knew his voice. She was a bit surprised at how happy she was to hear it. "Good morning. How are your tests coming?"

"I'll be done this morning and will be flying directly to Minneapolis. I should arrive some time around seven tonight."

She had to struggle to keep the excitement out of her voice. "Aren't you going with your father to the Tetons?"

"Plans have changed. I called the night before yesterday and told him about our progress. He's out of town and okay with waiting for a while."

"Great. Will you be coming into Flying Cloud again?"

"Yes."

"Then I'll pick you up."

"Thanks," Jason said. "The real reason I called is I've been thinking . . ."

No surprise that, Jennifer thought.

"Let's just suppose I'm right and someone was hiding behind the drapes. It was raining. There must be some signs someone was there."

"You're probably right," she said. "Could you call me back on my cell phone?"

Seconds later he did.

"I'll take a look behind the windows nearest my office." Nothing but dust, dead flies and a Tootsie Pop wrapper someone had stashed there. "I'll try the other one."

Pulling the right-hand drape back, she could see no signs of disturbance. Mouthing a silent prayer, she opened the left.

At first she couldn't see any difference, but taking a step backwards to catch the sunlight, she saw one clearly discernible footprint in the dust.

Squeaking in excitement, she said, "You're right. Someone was standing there. There's even a footprint."

"Great," Jason exclaimed. "Get your police officer friend to take an impression."

The words made a strange impression on her. "I will. I still can't imagine how she got in without my seeing her, let alone why I didn't see her standing behind the drapes."

"The next time it rains, you should be able to find out."

"I'll be waiting for you at the airport. In the meantime, I'll have someone from the police come over and check out the footprints. I don't know how much good it's going to do me now. The police probably will think I put them there myself."

"Maybe," he said with a sigh. "At least we'll know how she did it. Things will work out for you. I'm sure of it."

The words brought the first smile of the morning. "Thanks. Bye"

She hung up and the phone immediately rang.

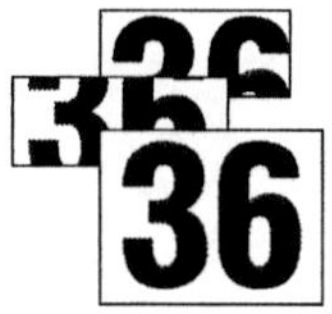

"YOU SHOULD HAVE WORN your tux," Trent North said as Dan climbed into his car.

Having spent a restless night, Dan was in no mood for levity. "Excuse me?"

"You ever been to Indian Hill before?"

Dan scowled. "No. Why?"

"We're visiting the high rent district. Nothing but verandas and ten bedrooms, and there're probably more horses than people around here. Some of the grounds are even big enough to race them. You eaten yet?"

"No," Dan said. He hadn't wanted the continental breakfast the motel provided, and now he was feeling hunger pangs. "Any chance we'll find a Mac and Don's close by?"

"There's one on Wooster's Pike. It isn't too far from here. On a budget?"

Dan told him about his deal with the chief. Before he could offer sympathy or a breakfast sandwich and cup of coffee, Dan said, "Don't worry. This is the best money I've spent in a long time. Some wounds don't heal until you open them up again."

Trent nodded. "Yeah. I know what you mean. Hey, I just remembered . . ." He pulled down the windshield shade and took a piece of paper out of the elastic band. "If you want to try Perkins, I have a two-for-one coupon. The darn thing's been riding around with me for a month and it's about to expire."

"It sounds like a winner to me. We can split the bill."

Jason sat forward as the next slide appeared on the amphitheater screen. The enlarged image showed a tiny white thread.

"All you guys out there should get this one," the grad student who was operating the slide projector said with a leer. "You girls, too."

Several males began to laugh. Some girls giggled in embarrassment. Jason Dumont merely snorted as he wrote "vas deferens" on his answer sheet. The excursion through the cadaver's body, which had begun in the head, had now worked its way through the thorax to the abdomen and now had begun to explore the reproductive system. Some wag, maybe Vesalius himself, had coined the quip: "There's a vas deferens between your epidydemis and your urethra." The vas deferens and vas efferens connected the testes to the urethra.

Jason yawned.

The exam was boring in its simplicity, though Linda, sitting two seats away, seemed to be wearing a perpetual frown. It disappeared as she looked over at him and flashed a wistful smile.

Jason sent a similar one back. He had been unhappy for her since he learned of her feelings for him. What do you do when there's no way to let someone down easily?

Would he have felt differently if he hadn't met Jennifer? Probably not. He had known Linda for more than ten years and had never considered her to be anything other than a friend. He had only known Jennifer for a few hours, and she had occupied nearly all of his thoughts since he met her.

Jason shifted uncomfortably in his seat as he remembered Jennifer's reference to "Tim." Emotion began to boil in his mind. He hadn't been jealous since . . .

Since his mother was alive? He shivered as he caught a glimpse of himself lying on his bed in the hotel room, realizing someone was with his mother. Everything went red. He shivered again as his seven-year-old mind shouted, "It's bad enough you sleep with father. I'm not going to let you sleep with a stranger."

I must have killed her! How many times had he had the thought through the years? How many times had he been reassured he couldn't have?

He looked over and saw Linda watching him with a concerned look. Forcing a smile, he pointed at the screen.

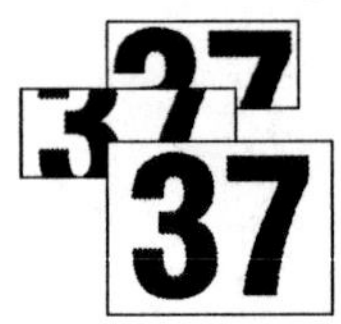

"JEEZ," DAN SAID, looking up to the top of the hill where a white southern mansion stood amidst a grove of mature oak trees. "I didn't know Dumont was a Rockefeller."

Trent laughed. "I told you what to expect. All the houses around here are like this. You ready for a walk?"

Casting a rueful look at the "PRIVATE DRIVEWAY. DO NOT ENTER" sign, he grunted, "I suppose so. It doesn't look as if it's too far away."

Trent laughed again. "You may be surprised."

He was. The road, which at first looked like a straight path up the hill, suddenly leveled off and meandered to the right as if on its way to the next county.

Trent answered Dan's groan with a none-too-generous "I told you so."

Dan halted in his tracks. His handkerchief, already saturated from his sweat, simply added more moisture to his face and dark crown. Looking around he asked, "Where the heck did the house go?"

"Just keep walking," Trent said with a chuckle. "You'll see."

Sycamores and a variety of oaks grew from the wide expanse of manicured bluegrass to their left. A suffocating haze hung over the landscape. "Who the heck mows the lawn?" Dan puffed.

Trent shrugged. "I have no idea. They have a gardener."

"He must use a baling machine."

The road finally banked back to the left. Heat waves rippled from the asphalt. When Dan was sure he couldn't go any farther, he saw an enormous ancient red oak to the left of the road.

Both men were happy for the shade. Unable to stand, Dan squatted and took several deep breaths. Finally able to speak, he gasped, "How can you stand this heat?"

"You get used to it," Trent said without effort. "I usually save my walking for when the sun goes down."

"You say this is one of the smaller houses?"

Trent chuckled. "I was pulling your leg. Indian Hill goes back to Revolutionary War days. An Indian killed some white settlers and got hanged for it. Except for actual farm country, it's the least densely populated area in the Cincinnati area. Families that live here are old rich. Some go back to the original settlers."

"How about the Dumonts?"

"Carpetbaggers. They've only been here two hundred and fifty years. You remember hearing about Dumont televisions?"

"I didn't just hear about them, I saw one in an antique shop," Dan replied. Seeing a swallow-tailed bird land in the tree above him, he took a cautious step backward. "The dealer was asking as much for it now as it cost when it came out. Fifteen hundred dollars? That's ridiculous."

"Yeah. Well, the Indian Hill Dumonts are related. Cousins, I think. Great-great-granddad Dumont made rifles during the Civil War."

"What did they do after that?"

"I'm not entirely sure. I know they tried their luck making automobiles around the turn of the twentieth century and gave it up when the World War I started. Going back to making rifles was more profitable. I hear they made a lot of money during the Depression. No one I know has ever been able to tell me where it came from. But you know what Honore Balzac said, don't you?"

"No," Dan said, impressed. "What's that?"

"Behind every great fortune lies a great crime. Recovered enough to go on, or do you need a hand?"

Dan snorted. "Race you to the door."

At last they came to the end of the driveway and started up the sidewalk to the front door. Chime music resembling the hallelujah chorus rang out inside the house when Trent pushed the doorbell.

A squawky voice from above their heads answered. "Yes."

"Police," Trent said. "I'm Deputy North. Lieutenant Arnold of the Minneapolis police is with me. Mr. Dumont is expecting us."

"He's not here yet."

"We don't want to have to come back and we're on a tight schedule."

Seconds later, a woman in a housekeeper's uniform answered the door. She squinted at their badges, but shook her head. "I'm sorry, but you'll have to wait until he comes. It shouldn't be more than an hour from now."

Seeing it would do no good to argue, Dan said. "Okay. We'll come back then."

As they started back down the hill, Trent asked, "What do we do now?"

"We might as well pay a call on Uncle Gary."

JASON DUMONT EASILY found a chair in front of a screen and keyboard in a nearly deserted Ackerman library. He remembered the last time he had visited. All the seats were filled and he had to wait more than half an hour to get on a machine. Today, all but two were available. Everyone else was either on their way home or waiting to go out and get sloshed, happily or unhappily, at the Bier Stube.

He typed in his student name and password. After what seemed like an eternity, another screen appeared demanding his ID number. Students in the pre-med program had to clear two hurdles. The information he needed couldn't be found on Google, or if it was, he couldn't access it from his personal laptop. His pre-med enrollment and personal password opened doors in professional sites unavailable to ordinary Web surfers.

Anxious as he was to begin his trip to Minneapolis, his renewed remembrance of his anger at his mother frightened him, and he wanted more information.

At long last the page for the American Psychiatric Association appeared on the screen. Taking a deep breath he typed in "Juvenile matricide." It brought up more than twenty pages of hits.

With a sigh, he began to scroll through the references. The first page dealt with teen-agers. Most mentioned abuse in the case histories. He stopped to read the account of a ten-year-old girl who killed her mother while she slept after the woman had scalded the girl with boiling water for wetting her pants. Two boys, one ten and one twelve, had killed after being sexually abused by their mothers.

Jason jumped at the sound of footsteps behind him. For a second he felt as guilty as a teen caught at a porno site. The footsteps passed on without a pause and he turned back to the screen.

Scrolling through three more pages, his mouth tightened in frustration. He couldn't find any references to seven-year-old children committing acts of murder. After scanning two more pages, he returned to the browser area and typed in "Matricide by seven-year-old males." To his amazement, two hits appeared on the screen.

The first was about a California boy who killed his mother when she had refused to buy him an X-box. The father had left a gun handy and the boy used it. Still holding the gun when the police arrived, he had no memory of having shot his mother. The official diagnosis: amnesia due to post traumatic stress syndrome.

Jason felt a chill. *That's me all right.* In the grips of fear, he opened the second reference.

The story chilled him even more deeply. Thomas Middleton of Terre Haute, Indiana, had come home early from school and found his mother in bed with a man.

Both were asleep. Thomas had gone to the kitchen and returned with a butcher knife, stabbing each of them as they slept. In this case, Thomas had a clear recollection of everything he had done. They boy had been overjoyed when his mother had made his father leave the house. He became enraged to find mom in bed with another man. Testimony in what became a groundbreaking case indicated that while most seven-year-olds had no inkling what sex meant, Thomas had a very clear idea and had even experienced erections. Prosecutors provided a host of psychological and medical authorities to dispute the fact, saying such physical precocity was impossible. The defense rebutted by providing proof in a hospital setting using adult magazines.

Jason wiped tears from his eyes as he logged off. Had he had such feelings for his mother? He didn't think so, but he couldn't remember. All he knew was that he was in for a long flight to Minneapolis.

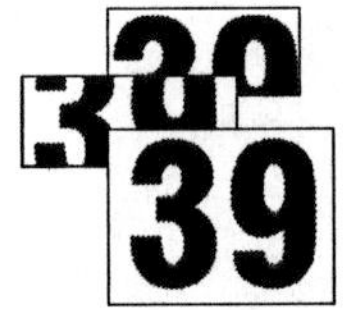

PROFESSOR GARY DUMONT lived on Marshall Avenue in a wooded area near the University of Cincinnati. As instructed, Trent parked on the street. Walking around the side of the house, they came to a sizable glass structure in the rear. A lanky figure in a long white coat emerged from the fog inside to answer the door.

"Good afternoon, gentlemen. I'm pleased you found your way."

"Getting off I-75 was the hardest part," Trent said. After wiping the condensation off his sunglasses, he slipped them into his shirt pocket. "This is Lieutenant Detective Arnold with the Minneapolis police."

After shaking hands, Dan inhaled deeply. "You must love working in here."

Looking around, he noticed a large table covered with brightly decaled flower pots and oversized sprinkling cans toward the back of the greenhouse. A large corkboard had pictures of children dressed as flowers or working with plants. "What kind of research are you involved in?"

Gary gleefully pounced. "I'm comparing DNA from tropical plants from Africa to similar species found in South America," he said, beaming. "I'm on sabbatical and spending half of my time here, and half at the university's botanical lab."

"It looks as if you spend some time with children, too."

"That's so much fun. Once a week I teach a gardening class to kids at the local grade school, and they come here on Saturdays. I want to get them involved with plants at any early age. As I'm sure you know, plants are getting more important all the time. If you're interested, I'll show you my research."

He proudly led them to several trays containing plants with long graceful curved stems growing from what appeared to be mint leaves. "These are Boraginales. The common name is heliotropes. Plants on this table are from Africa; the others are from South America. They're so similar that there used to be a big argument if it was due to plate tectonics or endozoochoria. I'm checking DNA markers to see if the African plants are parents or siblings to the South American varieties because I'm convinced that birds carried the seeds from Africa. Otherwise it would be as if plant biologists of a million years from now concluding that Oregon and China were connected at one time because they could find similar bamboo species in both places."

"But all the continents were connected at one time, weren't they?" Dan said. "At least they were a few million years ago, anyway."

"Oh, you mean Pangaea. Yes. They would have fit together quite well."

"I have a few heliotropes in my garden. They've been fairly easy to grow after I moved them into the sun."

Gary Dumont nodded appreciatively. "Always a pleasure to meet someone with an interest in plants. What can I do for you?"

Before answering, Dan took a closer look at Lawrence Dumont's brother.

He remembered Trent's description, and the photograph he showed him in the bar. The only real family resemblance he could envision was the large jaw and curly black hair. The biggest difference was the stature. Lawrence was athletic, Gary slight, but wiry. If Lawrence was slick, Gary was nearly transparent. Dan liked him.

"I needed to ask you a few more questions about Melanie's death."

"Come into the house where we can sit and have some ice tea."

"I'd like to stay here, if you two don't mind," Dan said, glancing at Trent.

Trent shrugged.

Dan drew in a breath. "This place is like an oxygen tent. I'd live here if I could."

"I spend as much time here as I can, too," Gary Dumont answered with a pleased look. Finding a seat on the edge of one of the heavy metal plant holders, he gestured for Dan and Trent to follow suit. "What did you want to ask me?"

"I'm trying to get a picture of what happened before Melanie left for Minneapolis. Did you know anything about it?"

"Yes," Gary said, slipping off his dirt-stained gloves to wipe his face with a handkerchief. "She called and asked me if I could take care of Jason."

Dan's mouth opened in surprise. "I didn't know that. I always assumed she intended to take him with her."

"I was a little surprised myself, but I'd already committed to being a speaker at the Horticultural Society's convention in Dayton, so I couldn't. Yvette was busy, too. Melanie decided to take Jason with her. Sadly, I fell ill and had to cancel the engagement. He could have stayed with me after all. I've felt bad about what happened for years. Jason would be an entirely different person today if he hadn't gone to Minneapolis."

"He isn't the only one," Dan said dryly,

A wistful look came into Gary Dumont's eyes. "I always liked Lottie. She had a great sense of humor and was playful. No one could have asked for a better mother. She adored Jason and did everything she could to be a good wife to Lawrence. Jason always was a lot quieter. You probably already know he's a genius. I've never known anyone as smart as he is. He was talking in sentences at fourteen months. We were best of friends. I took care of him every chance I could. He and my son were like brothers."

"Who took over raising Jason after Melanie died?"

"I suppose you could say the housekeeper and I did . . . maybe his bodyguards, too," he added with a chuckle.

"Bodyguards?"

"Yes. Jason had someone with him just about all the time."

"You mentioned the housekeeper. What about her?"

"She stayed with him, even when he was hospitalized with his anxiety attacks."

Dan sat up straight. "When did they start?"

"Almost immediately after Melanie's death. Lawrence was able to get Fluvoxamine from Switzerland and it helped a little bit when Jason was young, but the attacks got worse as he got older. He needed to be hospitalized three times as a teenager."

"What's Fluvoxamine?"

"It's an anti-anxiety drug that's a cousin to Prozac. Lawrence knew about it through the trade. You knew that our family has a big manufacturer in Canada, didn't you? It's called Maple Leaf Pharmaceuticals."

Wheels turned in Dan's head, but they seemed rusty. "Yes. It's in my notes. It's one of the biggest pharmaceutical producers in the world, if I remember correctly. Can you tell me when was the first and last times Jason was hospitalized?"

"Fourteen was the first. He had just graduated from high school the last time."

"The poor kid. How often did you babysit him."

"Usually at least once a week. Lawrence was gone as much as he was at home. Grace, my mother, made me promise to do whatever I could to take care of him, so he was here a lot of the time. Grace liked Lottie and really loved Jason. She didn't approve of Lawrence spending so much time away from home."

"Was she on the outs with him?"

"Oh, no. It just was Mother's way of letting him know that she expected him to live up to his responsibilities. She wasn't crazy about all the trips Melanie made to Minnesota, either, but she understood the reason for them. Lawrence was a different story. I heard her tell him a number of times he could send someone else, but Lawrence has always insisted on running the entire show himself. Grace worried about Jason's depression and anxiety."

"Was he ever suicidal?"

"He could have been. He used to get dangerously angry at times. Most of the time it was directed at himself."

"I suppose that's the reason Lawrence used bodyguards."

"Maybe. All I know is Jason always had company when he visited me."

"Are they still watching him?"

"I'm sure they are, but he's not as easy to control, now. Mother died four months ago. She had quite a bit of money that wasn't part of the family estate. She gave Yvette and me tidy sums, but she left Jason two-and-a-half million dollars. The first thing he did was start taking pilot lessons, and now I understand he's purchased an airplane. The second was to throw away his medications and start seeing a new therapist at OSU. Lawrence was furious. He was desperate to make sure nothing ever happened to Jason."

"What does he think about Jason flying?"

"He was furious when he found out about the lessons. I'm not sure he knows about the plane yet. I didn't either until Jason called me and said he was flying to Minneapolis after his finals. Lawrence is sure to go ballistic. He thinks that's way too dangerous. Seems like a strange idea for someone who took flying lessons himself, wouldn't you say? He knows flying is loads safer than driving a car. Especially on today's highways."

The words struck like a icy dagger. "Does his company have its own aircraft?"

"It did. A Learjet," Trent said. "They sold it about five years ago. It's in my notes. The log says it wasn't flown the night Melanie died."

"Why did your mother give Jason the money?"

"She never liked the way Lawrence tried to run Jason's life. I think she wanted him to be able to decide for himself about whether he wanted to take over the business as the eldest son and heir. I know he doesn't. He's set on being a doctor. I also know why Lawrence is so adamant. He intends for Jason to become his clone. It's not going to happen. Jason's idea for the company is closer to mine."

"What do you mean?"

"Lawrence wants to keep a tight hold on the pharmaceuticals he invents. I want them to be easily available to everyone in the world. We've been having discussions about that for years."

"Most of the products are pain-killers, aren't they? That could cause a big headache for the drug enforcers."

Gary laughed. "You could say that. The company has many other products. A lot of them are new botanicals I discovered. I've been to every rainforest in the world for my specimens. One of my discoveries works well with Interferon."

Dan nodded and made a note in his notebook. "That does sound important. Were you close friends with Melanie."

"Best. We worked in each other's gardens. She had some wonderful exotics and could have had a real prize-winning display some day if she'd lived."

Dan nodded. Taking another deep, exhilarating breath he said, "I know this is awkward, but did you ever have any suspicions that Melanie may have been involved with anyone other than her husband?"

The question seemed to take Gary by surprise, and he hesitated before answering. "No. But I know she was lonely and really missed her mother. You knew she flew to Minnesota at least once a month, didn't you? She usually left Jason with me."

"I didn't," Dan lied. After a short pause he said, "Sorry to have to ask you this, but how did she get along with Lawrence?"

"She was devoted to him, probably more in love with him than he was with her."

"What makes you say that?" Dan said, eyes narrowing.

"For one thing, she bragged about him to Jason all the time. I already mentioned she was spontaneous. Lawrence has always been more detached. He always planned everything out to the tiniest detail and has always wanted to head off problems before they developed. She liked to do things on the spur of the moment. I always thought Lawrence was missing out on a good thing with her when he was gone so much. With Jason, as well."

"If Lawrence has a business in Thief River Falls, he must have had to go there fairly regularly. Did Melanie ever go with him?"

"Just once, when they were first married. Otherwise he wanted Lottie to have her time alone with Naomi."

"Hmm," Dan said. Taking a deep breath he asked, "Could he have been involved with another woman?"

"Hardly likely. He moved around too much. He would have been too afraid of scandal, anyway. Image is everything with my dear brother."

"I see. How about Melanie? Could she have been interested in someone else? Someone from Minnesota perhaps?"

Gary frowned. "From the way the murder happened, it sure seems possible, doesn't it? I had a hard time believing she would cheat on Lawrence, but she certainly made a lot of trips back to see her mother. It would have given her plenty of opportunity. Didn't you find her diary?"

The words struck with lightning force. "Diary? No. Did she keep one?"

"One afternoon about a year before she died, I went over to work in her garden. Lawrence was out of town, and the housekeeper let me in. I found her sitting on her bed and writing in a little book. When she noticed me, she got very flustered and stuck it under her pillow." He stopped and resumed with an embarrassed smile. "I'm no psychologist, but I've read that when women write about someone they're romantically involved with, they generally do it on their beds."

Dan remembered that Carrie once had told him the same thing. She also said they also often kept their diaries and love letters in their underwear drawers. Trent had gone through all her belongings carefully and didn't find anything unusual. "Do you have any idea where she kept it?" he asked in excitement.

"None whatsoever."

"Would your brother know?"

Gary Dumont tossed his head. "Probably not. If she was so embarrassed about my finding out, she probably hid it from Lawrence, too. I expect she kept it in a safe and very secret place."

Dan and Trent North stared at each other. "If it's still around, we have to find it."

"I hope you do," Gary said, putting on his gardening gloves. "I'm sure it'll be a big help to Jason, too."

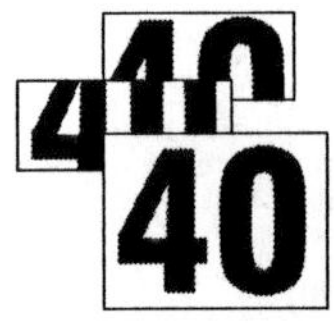

OFFICER TIM VINCENT laid a piece of transparent plastic with white inch markings next to the footprint in the dust. "Fingerprint lift should work to pull up the print, but if it doesn't, we'll still have a photograph. The shoe looks to be about size eight."

"That's my size," Jennifer said. "But even if it's Candy's size, too, she can always say I planted the shoeprints myself. There's no way to prove when they got there."

Vincent snapped a picture with a digital camera and put it back into his valise, taking out a ten-by-ten-inch piece of clear plastic in the process.

"No. But the smears certainly would indicate that the shoes that left the prints were wet, and it was raining the day she would have broken into your office. The clear print probably was left after her shoes had a chance to dry a bit."

He pulled off the backing from the plastic. "Here goes." Stretching the sheet tight, he carefully laid it on the window sill and flattened it with a rubber roller. "Let's see what we have here."

Grabbing the plastic by two corners, he slowly pulled the plastic from the stone. "Voila."

He held it up for her to see. A clear impression of a shoe print showed through the transparent surface.

Jennifer applauded.

"By the way," Vincent said, "Whoever wore this shoe tended to walk heel to toe. The print is from the left foot. See how the tread is worn on the left side toward the toe. There's also a nice cut in the tread where the little toe would be. If we ever find the shoe, it should be a snap to positively identify. Want to try an experiment?"

"Why not?" Jennifer said.

"Do you have an old pair of shoes around your office?"

"I think I can find some," Jennifer said as she walked to the closet. She returned with a pair of dusky sneakers with worn soles. "I only wear these if I get wet feet on the way to work."

Vincent examined the soles. "Great. I can already tell you didn't leave the prints. Your foot isn't nearly as narrow."

Jennifer's nose wrinkled. That sounded vaguely insulting.

He pointed at the wear toward the front of the shoe. "And you walk on your toes and the balls of your feet, like a ballerina."

"A very clumsy one. I hated ballet class. Is there any chance this could help my case?"

"It can't hurt. Too bad this isn't a criminal case. If we had probable cause, we could get a warrant to search Candace's closet to find a match. Since it isn't, her lawyer would never allow that. The rules of evidence aren't quite as stringent in a civil case. Do you mind if I take the left shoe with me?"

"Foot fetishist?" Jennifer asked with a puckish smile.

"How'd you know?" Vincent said, grinning back. "Actually I took a crash course in forensic podiatry at Quantico. I need to make an impression with black ink. After I give it back to you, you may not want to show off the bottoms of your shoes for a while. By the way, showing off your soles is a sign of disrespect in Japan."

"I'll remember that when I go there." Jennifer said. Her smile disappeared. "Would you be a witness for me?"

He grinned back. "Of course. Character or material?"

"Material, of course. You don't know anything about my character."

"Not true," he said. "I know your reputation with the drug enforcement and sexual offenders program well. You were every bad-guy's nightmare."

Jennifer put her hands on her hips. "And just how do you know that?"

"I looked at your files."

Not knowing whether to be flattered or angry, she replied, "And why did you do that?"

"Merely part of my investigation," he said in a breezy tone. "How do you know when someone's smoking crack?"

Surprised by the question, she caught her breath before answering. "By the burn marks on the lips. The pipe is hot."

"Right. How about using Skunk?"

She smiled at the street reference to Heroin. "Watery eyes. Everyone knows that."

"Red Gold?"

"Butyl Nitrate? Slurred speech. Coughing. Sores on the nose and mouth."

"Excellent. What are the standard treatments for sex offenders?"

"Shock treatment, behavior modification, psychotherapy, and drugs to lower the sex drive. None of them work because you can't change people's sexual preferences. Why are you asking me all these questions."

Vincent stepped closer to her and stared her in her eyes. "Because I know that anyone as professional as you would never leave her door unlocked. All we have to do is prove it."

"Th-thanks," she said, unconsciously taking a step backward. "We better wrap this up. I've got a client coming in ten minutes."

"That's a long time," Vincent said. She shivered as he moved closer.

"Are-aren't you supposed to be on duty?"

"It's my day off," Vincent said.

"Well it isn't mine," she said in a firm voice.

The officer stopped in his tracks with a surprised look. "When's your last appointment?" he asked.

"Four o'clock."

"How about if I pick you up then, and we can have an early dinner?"

"Maybe some other time."

Vincent winced. "Boyfriend?"

"Patient."

"Tomorrow night, then? How does dinner at the Nicollet Island Inn sound?"

"Far too romantic for a first date."

"Darn. If you like Italian food, the Amove Victoria on Lake Street is one of my favorites. Their homemade bread is to die for."

"I've never been there, but it sounds good. Maybe we can go there some time."

"You surprise me. I got the distinct impression we could be very good friends."

"You're moving too fast," she said, regretting her flirtation. "I hardly know you."

"Okay. Would a hug fit into your timetable?"

"I may be able to squeeze it in," she said, smiling at the pun as she moved into his outstretched arms.

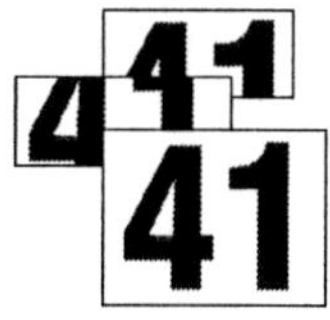

AFTER SURVIVING A second grueling trek up the Dumont driveway, Dan again pushed the call button. The Hallelujah Chorus drowned out the endless whir of cicadas that filled the trees. As he waited, he glanced up at the soaring Greek arches of the veranda. *What kind of idiot would design a portico that provided no shade?*

Finally the voice of the housekeeper squawked through the speaker above the door, and Dan identified himself.

"Sorry. Mr. Dumont hasn't arrived yet," she replied.

"Would you please let us in anyway?" he said, gasping for breath. "We're about to fall over from the heat."

After a short pause, the voice said, "I'll be right there."

The door opened. "So sorry. Do come in. I can't have you dying on my doorstep. Please take your shoes off."

"Thanks," Dan said. Stepping in, he got a cold blast of air as shocking as a dip in ice water. He pulled off his loaners and set them on the mat near the door. Taking a deep breath, he took in as much of the house as he could see from the hallway. Oak floors with twenty-foot boards, billowing Burgundy brocade curtains, and a Federal Era hall cabinet with wood burnished to a cherry-wood glow was all he needed to see to realize he had entered another world.

"Where would you like us to wait?" he asked.

"Since you're investigating Ms. Dumont's murder, I'll show you to her room."

Unable to believe his ears, Dan grinned at Trent. "Lead the way."

They fell in behind her. Her footsteps rang loudly on the marble spiral staircase. "Is Jason's room up here, too?" he asked, voice echoing.

"It's right next door to hers."

After a short right turn at the top of the stairway, she gestured. "Here we are."

She opened a wide door and turned on a light.

Dan was overwhelmed. At first he thought he had stepped into an expansive living room furnished with antique settees and overstuffed chairs. Rounding the corner he saw the bed, queen-sized with a crazy-quilt cover, and a spartan hautboy and dressing table. He guessed that the half-opened door to the left led to a bathroom.

"Did Mr. Dumont sleep here, too."

"No. His bedroom is at the end of the hall."

Dan wondered about the separate bedroom, but decided to not ask the housekeeper.

"The room is exactly the way it was the day Mrs. Dumont flew to Minneapolis," the housekeeper said. "Jason insisted I keep it that way, and Mr. Dumont didn't mind."

"Nice," Dan said, catching the sachet of lavender in the air. A tall rabbit doll reclined on the queen-sized bed. Dressed in denim overalls with one ear erect and the other lopped over, it was as down to earth as the bed's duvet. Dan straightened the sagging ear before moving his attention to the cabinets, dressing table, and chair. Bright yellow floral wallpaper gave the room a feeling of airiness and underscored the simplicity of the trappings. Whatever lifestyle the rest of the family practiced, Melanie had stuck to her simple beginnings.

The housekeeper pointed at the chairs. "Have a seat, and I'll bring you some lemonade."

Dan sat, itching for her to leave the room. When she did, both men sprang to their feet in unison.

"I don't know what's going on, but we better move fast," Dan said. "We only have a couple of minutes. Where would Melanie have hidden her diary?"

"Beats me," Trent replied.

A weathered bible and several paperbacks lay on the end table. Melanie Dumont liked romances and trashy novels. A crocheted bookmark halfway between the covers marked her progress in Judith Krantz's *Till We Meet Again*. A quick glance inside the table drawer revealed nothing.

Too obvious.

After moving aside the bottle of Ciara perfume, he opened the jewelry box. Neatly arranged earring and necklace ensembles resting on red velvet filled most of the top tray. As he pulled the top back farther, a similar compartment of pins came into view. Below that, Melanie kept an assortment of cocktail rings, some with stones of at least three full carats. In one corner, plain pearl earrings and gold amulet on a delicate chain lay where they had been carelessly thrown into the box. Dan threw an anxious look over his shoulder. "You finding anything?" he asked.

Trent pushed a drawer back into the dresser. "No. You?"

"Not really," Dan said, as he untangled the delicate chain to look at the amulet. It was charm-bracelet-sized gold book.

He felt a shock of recognition. It was the necklace and earrings the coroner removed from Melanie's body before the autopsy. After cleaning them, Dan personally boxed them with the rest of her effects. A glance at the rest of the jewelry brought another observation. The chain and amulet were yellow. Everything else was white gold.

About to set the necklace back into the jewelry box, he stopped, intrigued, as he noticed something on the earrings caught by the morning sun. Taking out a small magnifying glass, he examined the earrings carefully. The carving on the pearls should have been visible to the naked eye. Each one had a tiny heart scratched on the surface.

"Come over here when you're done," Trent said. "There's a shelf in the closet, but it's too high to see what's on it."

Dan closed the box. With a glance at one of the overstuffed chairs, he fairly ran to push it next to the closet door.

Trent held out his hand, and Dan climbed onto the cushion. "There's a box up here," he said, jumping down. "We'll have to move the chair."

Both men furtively looked toward the door, as Dan stretched on his toes. Moving the box brought a cloud of dust down on his head. "There's a newspaper here, too," he said, handing Trent the box. "I can just reach it."

Dan climbed down and they moved the chair back into place. Expectant eyes strained as Dan pulled the cover off the box.

Inside was a lovely knitted hat.

Though too small to hide a diary, he still gave it a shake. He quickly dropped it back in the box at sound of footsteps ringing on the stairway. Tossing the hatbox, he dashed back for his chair, nearly tipping it over backward in his haste.

The ringing of the footsteps ended, and the housekeeper entered the room carrying a silver tray with two large tumblers and a pitcher of lemonade. "Sorry I took so long."

Dan shifted in his chair. "Oh, that's all right. The view is nice up here."

As she gave Trent his glass, Dan noticed the newspaper on the floor beneath his feet and quickly snared it to jam it under his coat.

Turning toward Dan, she glanced over toward the jewelry box. He winced as he saw he had not put the perfume bottle back in its proper place.

Would she notice?

He was sure she did when she gave him a strange expression. Looking down, he noticed the dust on his jacket. He knew he had it on his hair, too.

With a faint smile, she handed the glass to him. "I think you should drink your lemonade downstairs. Mr. Dumont would get upset if you spilled on the floor."

"Good idea," said Dan.

As they fell in behind her, Dan and Trent traded glances.

She wanted us to snoop!

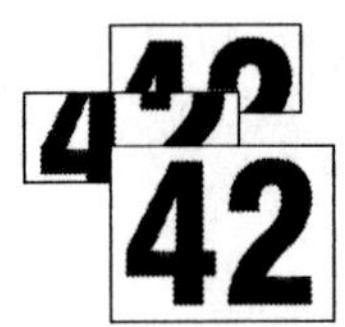

A HOT BREEZE rattled the giant palm fronds guarding the road as Marcel Digus drove his motorbike along the seldom-used path leading to Ste.. Margarethe Mission.

Kaw was on an island, the mission in the mountains. As always, living only 300 miles from the equator in a tropical rain forest, he had a light mist in his face. Sometimes it annoyed him; today he loved it. The gentle brush of the vegetation against his hands and arms, the insect-like buzz of the scooter's motor as it answered the call of brightly-colored birds, and the heady smell of rich damp soil exhilarated him.

It was a glorious day, thanks again to the benevolent neglect of L'Etat Française, and the phone call to Jennifer Cahill.

Through the years, Marcel had many issues with the French government. Most involved the withholding of departmental funds and the lack of human services to the native tribes, but never over its land-use policy of the Guianian interior. The country still remained a treasure chest of wildlife and natural resources, untouched except by poachers. And his people had learned how to keep even them in check. Ambush worked as effectively against the law-breakers as it did for the poachers themselves.

Marcel was determined to make sure the treasure chest remained closed.

Or at least to insure his tribe held the key. The French bureaucratic system helped tremendously. So far, developers of every ilk had gotten flat refusals or were unceremoniously referred to the labyrinthine permit section. He had heard that some of the applications were more than thirty-five years old, and others older still, but vacated when companies lost interest, or went out of business. Only one of the few permits that emerged affected the Marone tribes. The commissary in Kaw bought tribal vegetables and fish and sold imported foods and drinks.

A tiny clearing wriggled off to the right, and Marcel made the turn. Well-hidden in the forest, Ste.. Margarethe had one of the earliest programs in the world for AIDS victims. Even so, more howler monkeys visited the enclave than human patients. He had only been there thrice, and that made him a frequent visitor. A friend who had contracted AIDS from a tainted blood transfusion spent his last days with the sisters. That had been more than fifteen years ago.

The sight of the middle section of a twenty-foot anaconda crossing the road brought him to a halt. It was one of the few predators in an unspoiled Eden of birds, plants and animal life, and he didn't want to run over it, though he was sure it wouldn't hurt the snake if he did.

The smell of smoke told him that the mission was not far ahead. Would he find Jennifer Cahill's doctor there?

He would soon find out.

Unable to concentrate, Jennifer turned off her computer screen. Between her encounter with Tim Vincent, the imminent visit of Candy's lawyers, and the prospect of seeing Jason again, she felt exhausted. And the day wasn't even half over. She would have to face Mark, too. He agreed to be around when Candy's lawyers came to take pictures.

Sighing, she looked down toward her desk. Her eyes fell on the legal pad she had been working on. Along with her margin curlicues, flowers, and other doodles she had written the words "symbiotic relationship" with a question mark behind it.

Although not a common disorder, it did occur with some regularity. The term referred to a situation where a mother becomes so attached to her baby that the two actually became more like a single entity. Any attempt to break the bond or separate them was viewed as life-threatening by both the parent and child. Jason seemed to fit the characteristics. If he were a symbiote, how would he react to his mother's infidelity? Such an extreme attachment might well trigger extreme actions.

Returning to her computer she entered, "psychological symbiotic relationship," into the American Psychological Association's search engine. Carl Jung's theory of symbiosis came up first. As she read, she remembered the reason it occurred.

Children, usually up until they reach the age of about ten, have no sense of ego or selfhood. They identify themselves almost totally with their parents. The lack of a sense of ego was one of the main reasons that children usually didn't report abuse. Essentially, they didn't know any better and were unaware they should defend themselves or tell another adult when someone was hurting them. With symbiosis, the child becomes totally attached to a parent, usually the mother, and vice-versa.

She felt a chill. The more she investigated, the more plausible it seemed that Jason could have murdered Melanie. The unthinkable could no longer be ignored.

"I SEE WE have guests," Lawrence Dumont said in an urbane voice as he gestured in Dan's direction. Though the voice was pleasant, Dan also detected a well-disguised note of displeasure.

He set his tumbler on the wicker table and got to his feet.

A man dressed in a meticulously tailored Italian silk suit and sport shirt open at the neck stood a short distance away.

"I'm Dan Arnold with the Minneapolis police. I was the lead investigator on your wife's case. I think you know Deputy North."

"I remember him," Dumont said, a polite nod to Trent. "How may I help you?"

Dan threw him a broad smile. "You'll be happy to know we're reopening Melanie's case. I remember how upset you were that we hadn't been able to find out who did it. I didn't think you'd ever would stop calling."

Dumont nodded. With what came close to being a sheepish look, he said, "Only out of concern for Jason. I loved Melanie very much, but she only suffered for a short time. Jason has had to endure fifteen years of misery. But why are you reopening the case now? Have you found new evidence?"

"New leads, actually. Jason's therapist brought them to me after she went to Thief River Falls with your son. She's a very sharp investigator."

"That's what Jason says, too. What's her background?"

"She worked for Hennepin County as a drug and sexual violence counselor for three years while she was getting her master's. Now she has a private practice as a child psychologist. Hennepin County and the local school districts send her a lot of business."

Dumont shook his head. "I don't want to sound unkind, but referring Jason to a child psychologist sounds exactly like something Mike Savich would do. That man should have had his license pulled years ago. I've spent thousands of dollars on psychiatric treatment for Jason, and Savich undid all their work in less than a month. Jason stopped taking his meds and refused to see the doctors entirely. Now that he's inherited some money, he'll never go back. My son's completely out of control right now. He even bought an airplane."

"Hmm," Dan said. Glancing at the housekeeper he found her scowling. It intrigued him. "What kinds of meds?"

"Anti-depressants, mostly. The doctors worked out a regimen for him, and it was working well by the time Jason started Ohio State. He was a straight-A student in pre-med, and he had absolutely no reason to stop taking them."

"Maybe he doesn't believe in drugs," Dan said.

"Well I do. We're in the top ten manufacturers in the world, and we turn out new life-saving drugs every month. I'm proud of that."

"I'm sure you should be. But, as I said, not everyone believes in drugs."

"To be truthful, we use a variety of techniques besides medication to treat our patients at Hidden Pines. That's our clinic up in northern Minnesota. But if you ask me, acupuncture and biofeedback and all the other homeopathic quackery can't compare to carefully prescribed pharmaceuticals. As far as I'm concerned, people who use alternatives just *think* they're getting better."

Dan could understand how someone with a pharmaceutical company might have that point of view. "Jason told me he's been feeling fine and is starting to remember."

"That could be dangerous for him. What if he actually remembers killing her? He could spend the rest of his life in a mental institution. I've read some studies . . ."

As Lawrence Dumont spoke, Dan's eyes again flitted toward the housekeeper. Why did she look so angry? "From what Jason told me, he understands the risks, but he's intent on finding out what happened to Melanie."

Dumont's polite façade cracked. "Is that why you showed him the pictures of Melanie's body?" he asked in a hostile voice. "He said it made him sick."

"I warned him."

"You should have done more than that. It was his mother, for God's sake."

Dan shrugged to control his own rising anger. "Exactly what should I have done? He's not a minor. I couldn't really stop him without a restraining order. It's still technically an open case, and he was a material witness. The only one, I might add."

Lawrence uncoiled. "I suppose that's true. Louise, would you make some coffee, please." He waited until the woman left the room before continuing. "What new information have you discovered?"

"I can't tell go into it now, but there's good reason to suspect that whoever killed Melanie may have been someone she knew when she lived in Thief River Falls."

"Really. That never even occurred to me. I do know that the sheriff there suspected someone named George."

"George Fox has an ironclad alibi. Any other ideas?"

After a thoughtful look, Dumont shrugged. "Sorry. Not a clue."

Dan nodded. So far so good. The tough questions would come later. Maybe Louise could even help answer them.

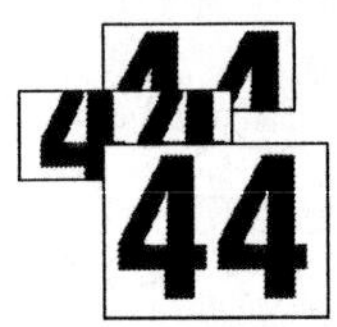

HEARING THE SOUND of her phone ringing sent Jennifer on a mad dash to her office. She should have known that would happen. Step out to the lady's room and the phone always rang.

She picked up the receiver just before it switched to voice mail.

"This is the international operator. Will you accept a collect call from Marcel Digus in Cayenne, French Guiana?"

"Of course," she panted.

"*Bon jour,*" Digus said in a not-too-cheerful voice. "I hope I didn't catch you at an inconvenient time."

Noting the tone, Jennifer braced for bad news. "No. Did you learn anything?"

"Yes, but not what you hoped. I visited Sainte Margarethe mission *ce matin* and spoke to Mere Adrienne. *Tristement.* No American doctor has ever worked with them."

Jennifer's heart fell.

"But do not despair. All is not lost. She says she knows of another mission in the savanna, and he could be working there. Lamentably, she doesn't know its exact location, and I've never heard anything about it."

"Oh," Jennifer said, feeling the sawyers on the clock cutting into her skull.

His tone brightened. "Now for the good news. I know the Kaw postmaster well, and spoke to him. I tricked him into admitting Dr. Hansen has a postal box."

"Tell me more!" she said excitedly.

"*Le docteur* has been renewing the rental for many years, but he has never received any mail in the five years René has been postmaster."

It all fit, Jennifer thought. "That is good news. Does Dr. Hansen come in regularly to find out if he has any mail?"

"*Je ne sais pas. Et malheureusement,* René refuses to tell me.

Jennifer bit her lip in frustration. "We really need to find Dr. Hansen. Is there any other way to locate him other than camping out at the post office?"

"Possible. But even if there were, I couldn't spend that much time away from my office." He paused. "*Attendez! Peut'etre* I may know of a way. Louis always sends his son to me to let me know when I receive registered mail from France. I would be very surprised if he didn't do the same for any other important mail that comes to his office. He is always deathly afraid when it comes, so he makes sure it is picked up as soon as possible. He knows if it should become misplaced, he could lose his position."

The words brought a surge of hope. "How long would it take for a registered letter to arrive in Kaw?"

"*Eh bien*, perhaps a week."

"That's way too long. Does Kaw have international express mail?"

"No. But Cayenne does. Mail to Kaw would be dispatched by courier. It would be very expensive to do this."

Genuinely excited, Jennifer said, "Expense isn't an issue. I'll send a parcel to Dr. Hansen by Express Mail. Be sure you're at the post office when it arrives for him."

"*Mais certainement, Ma'mselle.* I will be most happy to oblige."

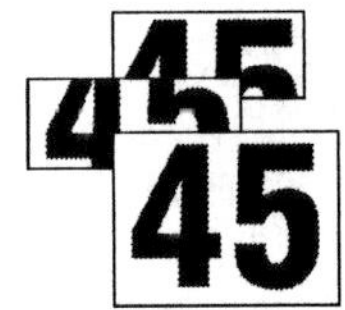

45

THE HAZY OUTLINE OF OHIO'S capital city, some ten miles away, appeared to sprout out of the top of Jason's Liberty XL-2. *Good-bye Columbus,* Jason thought. It probably would be one of the last views of it.

The yellow-clad Bolton Field attendant turned off the powerful pump. "Good morning. I put in seventy-five gallons for a full tank. How far are you flying?"

"Minneapolis."

"Then you'll have to stop at Green Bay."

"Thanks," Jason replied. As he swung open the door to get into the plane, he got a whiff of aviation fuel. "Smells like you must have spilled something."

"I don't think so," the attendant said with a shrug. "But I can't tell anymore. Have a safe flight."

Jason climbed into the plane. After checking his gauges, he called the control tower. Getting cleared for a take-off, he asked, "How's the weather along my route?"

"Bright and sunny until you reach Eau Claire. You may have to put down there. Minneapolis is having a heavy rainstorm."

The lobby buzzer sounded. Jennifer winced as she looked into the CCTV monitor. "They're here," she mumbled.

Mark Driscoll, wearing a custom-sewn black suit, got to his feet. Flashing a cheerful smile, he said, "Let's go meet them."

An austerely lengthy man who looked like an undertaker set his valise on the floor and took off his hat and raincoat. After setting them on the rack, he held out his hand to Jennifer. "Good afternoon, Miss Cahill." His voice was crisp. "I'm Kenneth Paxton, the Lane family's attorney. We're here to take pictures."

"I have no objections. Do you know Mark Driscoll? He's representing me."

Nodding, Paxton said, "Where's the closet where you locked Miss Lane?"

Though surprised by the directness, Jennifer led him to the closet. The blood stains inside the foldaway door looked like the Exxon Valdez oil spill. She took a nervous step to the side to let the photographer get closer.

"I see you haven't tried to clean since the incident."

"No. But even if I did, the police took their own photographs."

The man took a picture of the opened doors, then closed them to take another. Jennifer sighed in relief when he didn't take any close-ups.

"Now would you please show me where Miss Lane found the Melladril?"

She led the parade into her office. "Top middle drawer of my desk."

The photographer took a picture of the desk. "Would you please open the drawer?"

Her fingers shook slightly as she unlocked it. The photographer took another shot after she pulled it open.

"Thank you," Paxton said. "That should do it. I just have a few questions I'd like to ask. I'll be back at a later date to take a deposition."

Mark stepped in. "She'll answer all questions at the deposition."

"I see." Paxton set his valise on the desk and opened it. He took out a manila envelop and handed it to Jennifer. "Then we'll be leaving." He gathered up his briefcase. "Oh. I have something to show you. This is a picture of Candace when she arrived at HCMC."

As hard as she tried, she couldn't prevent her hand from shaking when she took the photo from him. Candy's eyes were open and staring, several rivulets of blood striped her forehead. "I'm very sorry that she hurt herself," Jennifer said in a soft voice.

"So am I," Paxton said. "I'll be talking to you further in a few days."

"How's Candy doing?"

"She's home. Her parents are going to send her back to school tomorrow."

As she followed them to the office door Jennifer felt a sense of foreboding that left her shivering.

She watched them get on the elevator, then turned to Mark. "I'm going to lose my license."

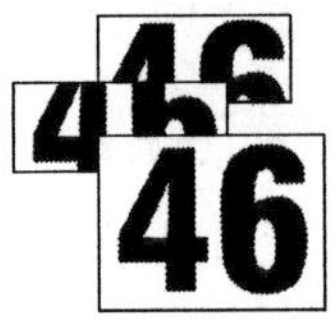

IN THE POND outside Lawrence Dumont's living room window, two well-fed Mallard ducks dipped their heads into murky water. The ducks were just barely wild; the pond didn't come close. It could as well have been a swimming pool. Dan watched them as he sipped the best coffee he had ever tasted. Where did the richness and caramel taste come from? "This is wonderful. What is it?"

Dumont smiled. "Kopi Luwak. I have it specially imported. It's the only one I'm aware of that comes from beans passed through an animal's alimentary tract."

"I've heard about it. It's terribly expensive, isn't it?"

"I suppose," Dumont said airily. "Some people like to spend their money on alcohol. I prefer to spend mine on my coffee. Please have some more."

Dan didn't need to be asked twice. He watched greedily as Louise refilled his wafer-thin cup. Seeing some spill over into his saucer made him wince. When she was finished, he carefully poured the spillage back, and would have licked the saucer if he thought he could have gotten away with it. He winced again as the housekeeper took Dumont's half-empty cup to the kitchen.

"You asked if there were any people around here Melanie was close to," Dumont said. "She spent quite a few afternoons with the next door neighbor. Unfortunately the Kennedys moved away a few years ago, and I don't know where they went."

"If you give me their names, I'll research them."

"Don and Meredith. Like the quarterback."

"Anyone else?"

"Melanie worked in an evangelism committee at the church. I gave Sheriff North the information at the time."

Trent nodded.

"How did she get along with your family?"

"Everyone liked her. Gary used to spend hours with her in the garden. You can still see what's left of it."

Dan looked where Dumont pointed. Next to the duck pond, a few lonely irises and poppies still sprouted amidst rampant ground cover.

"You must be proud of Gary. I'll bet he's a fine botanist, and I saw the little workroom he set up for children."

"He's been surrounded by kids all his life. They seem to naturally flock to him. He's an excellent botanist, too. He's come up with biomatter ingredients for several of our products. He's my brother and I love him, but he's too god-damned fuzzy-headed and liberal for my taste. Holistic medicine is a joke."

Dan's mouth wrinkled into a faint smile. "Did Melanie get along with Yvette?"

"She didn't see as much of her, but Melanie loved to hear her play the violin. They always laughed a lot when they were together. Melanie and Mother were very close, too. They had a once-a-week Scrabble match. Melanie was the first woman Grace ever approved of. I was a bit surprised. I thought she would have considered her to be below our class."

Just one big happy family, Dan mused as he started on his third page of notes. "Excuse me a second."

He opened his briefcase. Louise had returned from the kitchen and now stood in implacable silence a short distance away. As he took out the transcript of his case notes and laid them on the table, Dan watched her out of the corner of his eye. "I know this was a long time ago, but I need to go through some particulars again. First of all, how did Melanie find out Naomi had died?"

"She got a phone call from her brother, Dean, late in the afternoon. Apparently Naomi passed away at Hidden Pines the night before."

"You knew she was going to the funeral, but you had no idea Melanie had taken Jason with her, did you?"

"No," Dumont snapped. "My understanding is he was staying with Gary. I asked Gary about that, and he said he told Melanie he couldn't because he had some kind of horticultural meeting the next day."

"It sounds as if someone wasn't telling the truth. Did Melanie directly say your brother was taking care of him."

"What she said is, 'I just talked to your brother. You don't have to worry about baby-sitting for Jason.' I assumed that meant he would be staying with Gary."

"Would you have let him go if you knew Melanie was planning to take him?"

Louise smiled faintly. Finally Dumont answered. "I don't know. I've never thought about that. I certainly wish she hadn't."

"We couldn't reach the housekeeper, so we didn't find out where you were until the next morning when we called your office. We called the convention center at nine-thirty your time and left a message. You didn't return the call until one-thirty."

139

Dumont's jaw worked. "I was involved in presentations. I couldn't get away."

Louise's eyes now flamed. Raising his cup, Dan finished the last dregs of the coffee before continuing. *Let him stew in his own juices.*

Dumont noticed. "I can have Louise make more coffee, if you'd like."

Far too tempting, but Dan didn't want Louise to disappear again. "Thanks, but I'm good. When you called, the first thing you asked me was if Jason had seen who had done it. Weren't you at all concerned that your wife had been killed?"

"Of course. I was heartbroken, but she was dead, and I couldn't do anything for her. Jason was still alive. He's the one I needed to worry about."

"Sure," Dan said. "But why did you ask if Jason had seen the murderer?"

"I was furious. If he had, I would have found the bastard and killed him myself."

"We found two different blood types at the scene. Type B and Type O. Melanie was a Type B. What's yours?"

"A."

"Melanie and Jason were Type B," Dan said. "What happened in Miami?"

The housekeeper's eyes turned attentive.

"It was a national pharmaceuticals convention as well as a sales recognition meeting for our company to celebrate the unveiling of Crystoft. We had just gotten FDA approval the week before. It's an important new cancer medicine that slows metastasis. We were sure it would be a breakthrough drug. I wanted to reward my staff."

Seeing no reaction on the woman's face, Dan asked, "Tell me again what you were doing on the night Melanie was murdered."

"Bill Connell and I had adjoining rooms. We ate an early supper, went up to our rooms, had a few bumps from the honor bar and watched some silly adult movie. We were both tired and turned in early."

At the words, Louise turned and left for the kitchen with unmistakable anger in her eyes.

Puzzled, Dan paused before asking he next question. "What time was that?"

"Around nine o'clock."

"What time did you get up?"

"Seven. We had breakfast and were on the convention floor by eight-thirty."

"Is there anything else you recalled since then?"

"Nothing. I still ache from Melanie's death and want her murderer to be brought to justice, but not at Jason's expense. He's been through enough."

Dan nodded. "I agree."

"Melanie's death really destroyed him. As much as I have always loved him, I knew he could never love me as much as he loved her. They were inseparable from the time he was born. She stayed in his room until he was asleep every night for the first two years. It wouldn't surprise me if she was breast-feeding him all the while. I accepted their closeness. In a way, Jason was all she had because I was away so much. He deserved all the attention he got."

"I understand you've kept him on a short leash since. Gary says it's been as if Jason was in prison."

"As usual, he's exaggerating. I will admit I've always worried about his safety. I used to be convinced that Jason lost his memory because he knew who killed Melanie, and the murderer would some day try to end the threat. I was even more certain after the near-accident."

Dan tensed at the words. "Near-accident? I never heard anything about that."

"It happened about six months after Melanie's death. He was nearly run over when he and Louise were crossing the street in front of the house. The car was speeding, and she barely pulled him back in time."

"That doesn't sound like an accident to me."

"I don't think so, either. I just made sure Jason was safe after that."

"I'm sure you did," Dan mumbled. "Oh. There was another thing I wanted to ask you. Melanie was wearing a necklace and earrings when she was murdered. Do you remember them?"

"Vaguely. What about them?"

"Did you buy them for her?"

"I'm sure I did. I think they were a Valentine's Day present. Nearly all of her other jewelry was white gold. She was allergic to yellow gold unless it was 24 caret."

Dan made notes. "Tell me more about Hidden Pines."

Lawrence Dumont's eyes narrowed for an instant. "What do you want to know? My grandfather built it after he got out of the munitions business. He fell in love with northern Minnesota while he was there on a fishing trip because it's wild and beautiful. He built a big pharmaceutical plant in Winnipeg in 1922, and wanted the facility to be near it. Thief River Falls turned out to be the perfect location."

"Why did he switch to pharmaceuticals from munitions?"

"Penance," Dumont said in a soft voice. "Grandfather was overcome with guilt for all the people who died because of his weapons. Mrs. Winchester built a mystery house; Samuel decided to dedicate himself to making medicines to save lives."

"Very noble. What kind of clinic is it?"

"We treat chronic pain. I think you know Melanie's mother had severe MS."

"I had heard that. You must use a lot of Class One Drugs."

"Certainly."

"Who was her physician?"

"Art Peterson. He runs the clinic and arranges testing for new products."

"Did he try out any of these new products on patients?" Dan asked without smiling.

Lawrence Dumont's eyes narrowed briefly, then relaxed into a smile. "I'll take that as an attempt at humor. Of course, he didn't, but what if he actually did? Opiates are far easier on the body than the over-the-counter painkillers that don't work and end up messing up your liver. Some of our patients have been in constant agony for years. We have people in our hospice unit who have but hours to live. I'm sure you must know that all the best pain-killers are controlled, so what are sufferers supposed to do? Father told me that one of his uncles endured months of agony from colon cancer because his doctor refused to prescribe morphine for him. He said it was addictive. Apparently the man had some crackpot religious view that suffering was ennobling. Even if it is, he could have left it up to Great-Uncle Melvin to make up his own mind about its virtues. If Melvin chose painkillers, where was the danger if a man with a month to live became an addict?"

"Morphine was illegal," Dan said with a shrug.

"Illegal without a doctor's prescription. Any reputable physician who wasn't a religious fanatic would have prescribed it. Did you ever hear of a Brompton's Cocktail?"

"No."

"It's what's called an entheogen. Indian shamans used drugs with similar effects for centuries before we discovered effective painkillers. British hospices used Brompton's Cocktails because they include cocaine and heroin. It's one of the most potent painkillers ever known. Some of the users said it gave them a glimpse into the afterlife."

Dan threw him a stern look. "Heroin and cocaine are illegal, no matter how sick you are or how well it works."

"That's what the police and medical authorities in Britain decided, too," said Dumont with a patronizing smile. "I'm certainly not trying to convert you, and I'm no apologist for the illegal drug trade. To my way of thinking, all drugs should be legal. They are in the Netherlands, and they don't have anywhere near as many addicts as we have here. I also want to assure you we don't do any testing at Hidden Pines. We hire medical research firms to do that. As I mentioned, drugs isn't our only treatment plan. We even have a yogi who teaches transcendental meditation."

"Interesting. Is there any chance you still have Naomi Marchand's file?"

Lawrence squinted. "No facility keeps records indefinitely. The Pennington County coroner did an investigation and determined Naomi died of advanced MS. Why would you . . . why would anyone be interested in her records after that?"

"Good question," Dan said in an angry voice. "And I'll tell you why. From the time I entered your wife's hotel room fifteen years ago, I followed police protocols on obtaining records and collecting physical evidence to the letter. Despite that, we've never found the slightest clue to the identity of the perpetrator, and the only person who might have known what actually happened can't remember a thing. The only way this case will ever be solved is to follow every lead to the limit."

"I share your frustration," Lawrence said. "Jason does too. But I still don't understand why you're asking me about Naomi. She has absolutely no connection to the case."

"Maybe not the murder itself, but her death was the reason Melanie was in Minnesota. I'm ashamed to say I've never investigated her background. Thanks to Miss Cahill, I'm beginning to realize how much I don't know. From this point on, I want to know everything about Melanie's family and history I can come up with."

"I'll help you any way I can as long as it doesn't directly involve Jason."

"Fair enough. Is there anything you remember about her treatment you can tell me?"

"Just that she was receiving large doses of Senecal," Dumont said with a thoughtful frown. "It's a drug we developed. It's perfectly legal, and much more powerful than morphine. About a week before she died, she didn't seem to need it anymore and we began to treat her with acupuncture."

"You must have known quite a bit about her treatment plan. Did Melanie ever question the clinic about Naomi's condition?"

"I know she did, but I kept closer tabs on Mrs. Marchard because I wanted to know the efficacy of Senecal. It seemed to work well with all our patients. It certainly helped her."

Dan opened his mouth to ask another question, then quickly closed it. Gathering up the transcript and his notes he said, "Thanks. Do you suppose we could take a look at Jason's room?"

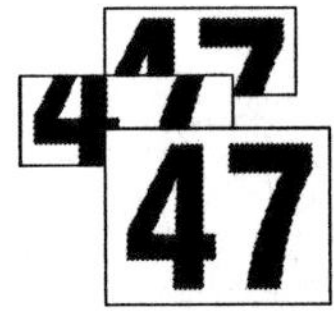

THE SKY OUTSIDE Jennifer Cahill's office lit up like an Arthur Stieglitz image. Another brilliant flash flared and an enormous thunderclap less than a second later.

That was close, she thought with a shiver as midday darkness returned to await another bolt.

She took one look at the curtains and hurried to the office next door. Marilyn Reid, busily typing on a keyboard, looked up in surprise as she found Jennifer standing in front of her desk.

"Can you get away for a minute?" Jennifer asked.

"Sure. What's going on?"

"I need your help to do an experiment."

Marilyn threw Jennifer a puzzled look. "What do you want me to do?" she asked.

"Stand behind the curtains in my waiting room."

Marilyn's expression almost made Jennifer giggle. But she followed Jennifer back to her office and climbed up onto the window sill.

"Like this?"

"Move to the other side. There." She clapped her hands in delight. "Jason's right. You can't see through the curtains with the office lights on. One mystery solved."

Marilyn stepped down from the window sill. "There's more?"

"Yes. I want to know how Candy got in here without my noticing. I know Candy knew about the CCTV because she'd make faces at me in it."

"Hmm," Marilyn said. "Good question. I'll go back to the office and tell the boys I'm taking a coffee break. Be right back."

"Thanks a mill, girlfriend."

Marilyn returned seconds later. "Now, where were we?"

"We're trying to figure out why Candy was so bold. She couldn't have known I wasn't watching the lobby."

"Let's go into your office."

Jennifer grinned in embarrassment at the untidy stack of patient's files on her desk, but Marilyn didn't seem to notice. "The monitor is over your door," Marilyn said, pointing up at it. She moved behind the desk and sat in Jennifer's chair.

"Okay. From here you have a clear view of the screen." She paused. "Wait! Your phone is on the other side of your desk. If you answer it, you could be looking away from the monitor. Your memo pads are there, too."

"You're right," Jennifer said, pleased by Marilyn's insights. "If I answer the phone, I'm not looking at the monitor."

"Then that's your answer. Do you remember getting any phone calls at the time you were waiting for Candy to show up?"

Jennifer scowled. "Yes. Actually I did get one. I remember thinking that Candy was calling to cancel or change the appointment. No one was there when I answered."

"Did you check the caller ID?"

"No, but the number is in my top desk drawer . . ." Marilyn stood aside and Jennifer retrieve the dog-eared pink slip.

". . . And I think I know just the person who can trace it for me." Jennifer continued. She was sure Tim Vincent would be happy to spend another few minutes of his day off to help her.

Marilyn moved back to view the screen and the black cords leading from it to a rectangular metal box on a middle shelf of a bookcase. "You don't have a tape in the recorder, do you?"

"You're right. How do you know that?"

Marilyn pointed at the flashing green "12:00" on the LED screen. "Either you've never set it up, or the power went out."

"I've never used the recorder," Jennifer mumbled.

Marilyn brushed her hands together. "Candy would have noticed for sure. Any other questions, lady?"

"Yes. Why aren't you with the police?"

"I was. I couldn't stand the job."

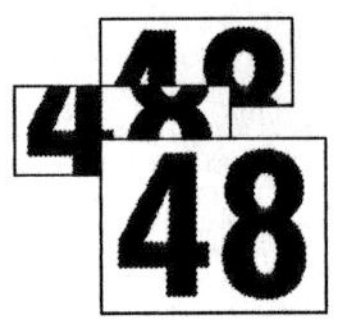

DAN STOPPED IN the hallway and waited for Lawrence Dumont to open the door. As always, he took pains to view the entire room before entering it. It had become second nature to him.

What he found surprised him.

While at home, Jason slept in a bunk bed next to a floor-to-ceiling poster showing Albert Einstein sticking out his tongue. R2-D2 and C-3PO replicated themselves repeatedly on the wallpaper, along with Luke Skywalker and Darth Vader.

The first thing Dan noticed was another poster—James Watson. "Who's this guy?"

"One of the discoverers of the human genome," Dumont said. "He's one of Jason's heroes."

Dan frowned and looked around the room. Though obviously a child's room, there were only two indications that Jason Dumont had any common interests with other boys. The first was the sizable collection of model airplanes hanging from the ceiling and lying on all available flat surfaces. The other, the computer sitting on a desk in the corner.

"Does Jason really sleep in this bed?"

"Yes," Dumont said. "On the top bunk. He says it makes him feel more secure."

Dan smiled and opened the clothes closet door. Maybe he wouldn't find anything, but he doubted Trent North or any of the other investigators had looked there very carefully. The racks were jammed tight with pants and shirts of all sizes. Many reeked of mothballs and looked as if they never had been worn.

There's enough clothes here to outfit a family of eight, he mused.

Stepping inside, he ducked under shirts and worked his way to one corner and started back. As he suspected, many of the clothes still had price tags on them. Sorting his way to the opposite end of the closet, he found a small suit jacket. His grandmother would have called it "Sunday Best." Made from good-quality tweed, it would be a perfect fit for a young boy. He also noted a dress shirt inside of it. As he took a closer look he saw what appeared to be two long gashes on the shirt-front.

Intrigued, he took it off the rack and inched his way back out the closet.

"Find something?" Trent asked.

"I don't know," Dan said. He held it up for Lawrence. "Did Jason wear this to Minneapolis?"

"No. He wore it to Melanie's funeral. He looked just like John-John Kennedy at President Kennedy's funeral. It broke my heart."

Dan removed the coat from the hanger. The dress shirt had two distinct slits cut in the fabric. Turning the shirt around, his mouth dropped open in surprise. There, in large capital letters drawn by a felt-tip pen, were the words: "I hate you."

Dumont took the shirt. "I never saw this before," he said in a worried voice. "He must have been out of his mind with grief."

"Do you have any idea who the 'you' refers to?"

"None whatsoever."

"Maybe he was referring to himself," Trent mumbled.

Dumont shook his head. "I'll ask him, but I'm worried about what it may do to him."

"Would you mind turning on his computer?" Dan said, pointing.

"Yes, I would."

"I don't intend to look into his private documents; I'd just like to see what kind of files he has in it."

Lawrence Dumont scowled. "Let me take a look first."

Dan stood aside. Seconds later the console chimed. Finally, Lawrence called him over. "There isn't much there."

Dan peered at the screen. One icon was for an on-line medical dictionary. Another, Ohio State's Research Guides and Tools. The most interesting seemed to be three Flight-Simulation programs. "Your son must be really interested in flying."

"Yes," Dumont said with a sour expression.

"This computer looks pretty new. Did Jason have one when he was young?"

"Since he was five years old. He told me he had to have one, and I listened."

"This isn't it, is it?"

"No. It was a Mac Apple Plus."

"Do you still have it?"

"It's in the basement."

"See if you can find it for us after we're done in the room. Do you know if Jason kept a diary?"

"Not that I'm aware of. I always thought he was afraid he'd write something that would make him remember."

"Thanks for your help," Dan said.

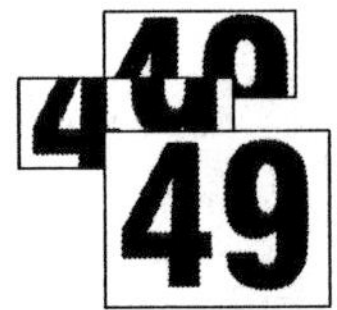

WITH THE PLANE locked on GPS and his headset in his lap, Jason found himself alone with his fears and overwhelming grief. He sat with eyes wide, staring without seeing at the bright blue sky above him.

The same thought that had afflicted him for so many years struck again with deadly force.

I must have killed her!

It didn't matter that his memory didn't allow him to know for sure. He had to be punished, but the thought of having to face a judge and jury made his stomach turn. If the faces were hostile, his guilt would probably make it impossible to remain in the courtroom. If they were sympathetic, it would mean they didn't believe the unthinkable thing he had done. Either alternative was unbearable.

Not going to trial was equally unacceptable. He couldn't live with his conscience the rest of his life. Sixty years of torture? Tears blurred his vision. *I'd rather be dead.*

The words made him shudder. The next thought came with bone-chilling logic and finality.

I'd be better off dead.

A vast expanse of azure nothingness surrounded him. He had once asked his seventh-grade science club teacher why the sky was blue. He spent the next hour finding out why. Refraction of light? Diffusion? How could it take so many words to explain such a simple phenomenon?

He bent forward and tried to look down. Behind him, ten thousand feet below, Michigan's thumb pinched off Lake Huron from the western Great Lakes. Over him, the brilliant spring sun. Some yogis spent their whole lives staring into it. How easy it would be to turn the plane around to the east, make sure he was over water and cut the engine. He could stare into that glorious ball of fire until he could no longer see. Or hear. Or feel. Or . . .

A gentle quiet settled over him. A long forgotten memory of walking with his mother along the road by their house came back with startling clarity. It was a beautiful early spring day. Green grass peeked out from below wet snow, and the wind made the hood of his jacket blow up against the back of his head. Somewhere, in one of the oaks, a male cardinal sang *Ray-doh*, his spring song. Angry with his mother for some reason, Jason stamped into a mud-puddle to try to get her wet. He succeeded. Instead of getting angry, she laughed, a lovely tinkling sound. "Shame on you," she said. "You're a regular Jecklin High."

Jason's eyes opened. Only she hadn't said 'Jecklin High.' She'd said 'Jekyll and Hyde.' She meant Jason was hiding a monster inside of him.

Jason snapped out of his reverie as the engine coughed.

The timing seemed providential.

The feeling became stronger. The motor missed again. Then it quit entirely.

A feeling of peace settled on him as the craft stalled out and began to fall back to earth. The feeling grew in intensity when he saw a vision of his mother. But as he came closer to her, he saw her hands were raised in front of her. Then he heard her shouting, "No, Jason. Go back."

Then she was gone.

Heart beating wildly, he lowered the landing gear and ailerons and pulled on the semi-circular handles of the control stick with all his strength.

He knew exactly what to do because he had faced the situation many times. The only difference was his computer joy stick never pulled back.

After a deadly game of tug-of-war, the tight spiral grew broader as the nose of the plane inched back from the perpendicular. Then, shaking violently, it finally began to move in a wider circle.

The forward drag still was beyond his control. Dark water beckoned him below.

Shoulders aching, and weak from exertion, Jason sighed as the craft leveled off and began to glide.

With the plane banking slightly, Jason stretched forward in his seat to look for a place to touch down. Land was still far away, and he didn't know if the three thousand feet of altitude would carry him there. Ditching in the water was possible but dangerous; coming down on land even more so. His only chance was to swoop in ovals and hope he had enough altitude to carry him inland.

The first swoop cost him three hundred feet of altitude and Michigan still looked continents away. White-capped water loomed closer when he shortened the westward arc.

Two more loops, and the water appeared closer still, land as far away. He tried to remember how long it had been since he last saw the shoreline below him. It seemed liked hours.

I'll never make it.

The silence surrounding him seemed unnatural. His own breathing sounded like the roll of the waves below him. Loop after loop brought him further to the east, but closer to the ground. He had less than a thousand feet of altitude when the first farmland appeared; only six hundred when he spotted a black-topped road zig-zagging along the shore.

Heart in throat, he followed it. With leaves brushing against the belly of the plane, the parapetic ribbon straightened out. It wasn't much of a target, just a raised two-lane stretch of blacktop with drainage ditches on either side.

Blood jumped in his jugulars.

The craft bounced as it touched ground, careening leftward. Pulling hard on the wheel, he steered in the direction of the slide. The rear of the fuselage swung around and the plane twisted and came to rest with the left wing dipped into the drainage ditch next to the shoulder.

Gasping for breath, he again had a vision of his mother. She was smiling.

A FLASH OF their badges got Dan and Trent past the security guards at CVG International airport. After a quick stop at Starbuck's to get Frappacinos, the two made their way to Gate 43.

"Welcome to Kentucky," Trent said. "I bet you didn't realize that the Cincinnati airport isn't in Ohio, did you?"

"Actually I did," Dan said between swigs of his drink. "It's in Covington, Kentucky."

"Wrong," Trent said with a big grin. "It's called Covington International, but it's actually in Hebron, Boone Country. Go figure."

"I don't want to figure," Dan moaned. "I've already got a headache. Don't make it worse."

"Lawrence Dumont is a real piece of work, isn't he? A real southern gentleman of the old school."

"Yeah, and a super-concerned parent. What do you make of keeping Jason under armed guard for so many years?"

Trent shrugged. "What he said. He's worried about Jason's safety. There are a lot of over-protective parents in the world. The only difference is that Lawrence has the money to carry it to an extreme."

"What about all the drugs Jason had to take?"

"Sounds to me like he needed them."

"Maybe. But he said he's been worried about Jason remembering. Maybe that's the reason for them."

"Da-a-an, I'm beginning to think you could use some medication yourself. You really are delusional."

"Sure," Dan growled. "You know, I've been thinking out Dumont's alibi. How could this Connell know Lawrence was in his hotel room all night? Lawrence says they watched a movie and had a nightcap before they went to bed. Do you suppose he could have been able to find something to put in his partner's drink if he wanted to?"

"Of course. But even if he had something to do with Melanie's death, you can be double-damned sure he wouldn't get his own hands dirty. He'd put out a contract."

"Maybe he wouldn't if he was angry enough at her. You saw the pictures. Her throat was cut viciously."

"I never thought of that."

Dan mentally scored a point with a wet finger. "You could even be right that he put out a contract, though I've never heard of a hit man slitting anyone's throat before unless they were trying to disguise a professional job."

"That's true, but I think I'd give up trying to pin anything on Lawrence. If he did it, he'd have covered his tracks with concrete before he would leave a trail."

"Maybe so. Whatever his involvement, I think I know a way to smoke him out."

"How?"

"I'm going to contact Jason Dumont and ask him to demand an autopsy on Naomi's body. I'm pretty sure Norquist will refuse, but even if he does, Jason can demand a private one. Frank won't be able to do a thing about it. Neither will Lawrence. I'd like to see his face when it gets back to him."

"Great idea."

"Thanks. What do you think about the housekeeper?"

"What about her?"

"Didn't you realize she wanted us to find something in Melanie's room? Not only that, she was making faces the whole time I was talking to Dumont. Do you suppose she knows about the diary?"

Trent shrugged. "It wouldn't surprise me. What was the newspaper you found?"

Dan opened his valise and took it out. "It's a page from the *Thief River Falls Times.* 'Dylan Hansen graduates from the University of Minnesota School of Medicine.'"

"Hmm," Trent said. "That is interesting. I wonder if Lawrence kept such close tabs on any of his female classmates. I know I didn't. If I did, my wife would have killed me." He stopped and sighed, "Look Dan, I don't want to tell you how to run your investigation, but if I were you, I'd start looking hard for this Dylan Hansen."

"I already am. See what you can find in Jason's computer. There's probably nothing to find, but we can hope. What if it isn't still working?"

"We've got a first class geek in the department."

"You're lucky. I have a bunch of third-class nerds in my outfit." He paused. "You know, this is a totally weird case. I realized from the beginning it was all a matter of who knew that Melanie would be at the hotel when she was. Excluding the possibility that she called someone when she got to Minneapolis, there really can't have been that many people who would have known."

"True," Trent said. "From my end, Lawrence knew. So did Uncle Gary. Louise, probably did, too. Beyond that, it's nearly impossible to know who else Melanie may have told about her plans."

"What about Uncle Gary? He doesn't have an alibi."

"Actually he does. His son vouches for him. I can't imagine why Gary would kill Melanie, anyway. It sounds as if he may have been helping Melanie to take Jason with her."

"Good point. It really seems more likely than ever that the killer had to be from Minnesota. I'm sure most of Naomi Marchand's family would have known about

Melanie's plans. Her cousins, too. Maybe someone didn't want Melanie to make it to the funeral."

Laughing, Trent grabbed his cheeks and pulled out on them.

"What are you doing?" Dan asked with a chuckle.

"Showing you that you're stretching, Bud. Melanie had been going back to visit her her mother for years. What difference would it make after the old lady died?"

Dan nodded. "What do you think of Jason as the murderer?"

"I seriously doubt it, but it's probably more likely than that someone murdered his mother to keep her from attending Naomi's funeral."

"Yeah? And I bet you think Oswald was alone in the Kennedy assassination, too. Don't you?"

"Nope. Johnson was on the grassy knoll."

Dan grinned and the men interlocked thumbs. "Thanks for all the help. Keep in touch."

51

MADISON DEVEREAUX, STILL dressed in her Stalkers' royal-blue-and-gold cheerleading costume, used her key to open the door to the library.

"Miss Bellamy," she called.

When she got no answer, she turned and gestured to Cameron Harrison. His flushed face and uncombed dark hair screamed youthful sexuality. "Is she gone?"

"Yes. She closed the library early to go to a meeting at Pioneer Village. Now get in here before someone sees you."

She took his arm and pulled him inside. When she closed and locked the door, he responded with a leer and reached under her skirt to pat her bottom. "Anxious, huh?"

"Stop that," she said angrily, batting his hand away. But he was right. She was anxious, but she didn't like him knowing it. The all-state hockey center had an ego to match his body, and the nagging little voice in her head that kept warning her she was being used couldn't overcome her rampant hormones.

"Well, what do we do now?" Cameron asked.

"First, I have to see what Miss Bellamy wants me to do."

"Fine. Then what?"

"Well, then we can each find a book and go up to the lounge to read," she said in a business like tone. It was lame, and she knew it. They both knew there was a very comfortable sofa there. They had used it before. More than once.

"Nah. I got a better idea. Let's go down in the basement."

Her brown eyes opened wide in surprise. Even the thought gave her a chill. "No. I hate that place. It's scary."

"That's what makes it fun. Haven't you ever messed around in a graveyard?"

Her eyes flashed. With a determined look she said, "No, and I don't intend to. There's nothing romantic about it. As for the basement, forget it. There's nothing but shelves and old books down there. Probably a lot of rats and spiders, too."

Harrison grabbed her around her waist. "Ah, c'mon. Just once. You can use the pad from Miss Bellamy's chair. It'll be fun. I promise you."

As he said it, he pulled her tightly against him, and she could feel his bulge against her pelvis.

"Absolutely not. It won't be any fun for me. Let's go up to the lounge where it's comfortable."

"Uh, uh."

She clung to him. "I hate you," she said, but she knew she hated herself as she felt her resolution crumble. "Oh, all right. But this will be the only time."

THE RAIN, WHICH had slowed by three o'clock, stopped completely by six. Wishfully taking that to be a portent, Jennifer locked up the office and left for the day.

With the sky clearing, she ramped on to Highway 394 with the convertible top down. As she drove, two endless puddles on either side of the traffic lanes continuously lapped the road. For once the weather prognosticators had been right. The Twin Cities had been hit by a cloudburst.

Luckily it was over.

Though she repeatedly told herself she was just picking up a client, Jennifer's heart beat faster at the thought of seeing Jason again as she turned onto the south 169 ramp. It beat faster still, but for a different reason, when she ploughed through wheel-well deep water at the bottom of the ramp.

Uttering a frightened cry, she gunned the engine. "Go," she whimpered, sure the engine would stop and strand her in the middle of the mini-lake.

To her relief, it kept moving. Still worried, she pumped the brakes until she convinced herself they were working. As she drove, she began to have an uneasy feeling that things weren't going to turn out the way she expected.

Her premonition got stronger as she reached the parking area at Flying Cloud. She realized she hadn't turned on her cell. As she did, the voice message screen appeared.

"Hello, Jennifer. I guess you must have already left to pick me up. I'm running late. I'll call you when I get close."

Good thing I brought a book, she thought, gathering up the advanced reading copy of Mary Ann Matson's *Jung and the Human Psyche* the publisher had sent her.

She stepped out of the car into a river gushing across the tarmac surface. Only three other cars soaked their tires in the parking lot.

Thank goodness. I need some time alone to think.

In the last few hours she had devised a strategy to help Jason deal with his ambivalent feelings about Melanie. They would go through the boxes of Melanie's belongings together. If it didn't jar his memory, at least it would help recreate some of the positive feelings he had had for his mother. One way or another, Jennifer had to get across to him that he wasn't responsible for their painful relationship.

She heard an engine and spotted a small flash of silver high above her.

Had he come already?

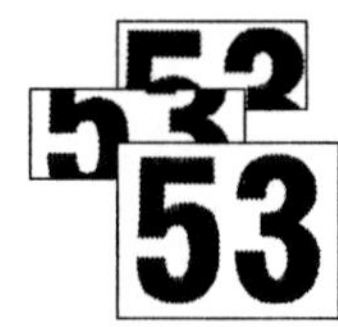

HUNCHED INTO HIS seat, Dan Arnold ground his teeth as he waited for the Northwest 737 jet to take off. An odor of jet fuel hung in the cabin, and the pilot had turned off the air-conditioning. Having to leave Ohio empty-handed was bad enough. Being stuck at O'Hare aboard a stinky jet was worse.

Utterly bored, he took the in-flight magazine from the pouch on the seat in front of him. Flipping through it, he found the crossword puzzle. He was about to take out his pen when he read the first clue, a five-letter word for frustration.

Pique!

I damned well don't need to be reminded of that, he thought as he jammed the magazine back into the seat pocket in front of him. In the process, he discovered an unopened bag of peanuts.

The first bright spot of the day.

When he couldn't tear the bag open with his fingers, he attacked it with his teeth. The bag yielded, sending the contents into his lap and onto the floor. Growling in frustration, he gathered up all he could find and stuffed them into his mouth.

After picking a couple of hairs off his tongue, he went back for the ones he had missed.

The result was as unsatisfying as his trip to Ohio had been.

For all his pains, none of the new information about Dumont's actions and Hidden Pines produced a single bit of substantive evidence. Worse, the most promising lead of all hadn't panned out. Melanie's diary, if it ever existed, had either disappeared or still remained hidden somewhere in the house. Lawrence Dumont was involved in something shady—trafficking in illegal drugs, most likely—but he no longer could be considered a viable suspect in Melanie's death. Assuming he had found a way to be in two places at the same time, he really had no motive. He wasn't the cuckolded husband striking out in a moment of rage, and he didn't stand to gain anything from her death.

Even assuming Dumont had a hidden motive and was guilty, why would he have let Jason live for so long? Any potential eye-witness, even his own son, was just too dangerous. He could remember at any time.

That just left Dylan Hansen, Dan grumped. And that bastard seemed to have dropped off the face of the earth.

Knowing he was in for a long, sleepless night, and an even worse morning, he considered getting off the plane and staying in Chicago. He hated having to face the chief, anyway. His old friend would be sympathetic enough, but he would have no choice but to tell Dan to put evidence box 665512 back into mothballs and move on.

A cabin attendant passed his seat, then stopped and smiled at him. "Hi. Sorry for the delay. Would you like some almonds?"

"Do the Cubs want to win a World Series?"

She handed him two bags.

"Thanks," he said. "Do you have any idea when we're getting out of here?"

The attendant shook her head. Dan noticed her playful eyes and her warm smile when he boarded. Was it really nearly two hours ago?

"No. There's a huge storm moving into Minneapolis and we're laying in here until we know we can land. We'll serve sandwiches after we take off."

"I can hardly wait," Dan said.

After a glance about, she reached into her apron to pull out another bag of almonds. Bending forward she whispered, "Would you like a beer? My treat?"

"Hell, yes. But this isn't First Class. Why am I getting VIP treatment?"

She reached into the pocket of her apron and pulled out his leather badge holder. Handing it to him, she said, "You dropped this."

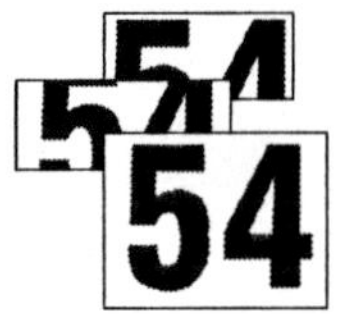

AN HOUR PASSED and Jennifer became increasingly restless as she waited in the airport's reception area for Jason's arrival. Other than the clerk at the car rentals stand, the building was deserted.

Her musings ended with what sounded like the blows of an angry giant hammering on the ceiling.

She started back toward the door, remembering her car top was down. Before she could take two steps, Jason appeared carrying a canvas bag. If he didn't look so sad, she would have laughed at the hair plastered against his forehead and dripping clothing.

"I didn't realize it was raining so hard."

"It started at Eau Claire," he said. "It's absolutely pouring, now."

She handed him a handkerchief to wipe his face. "We have to move fast. I left the top down on the car. The seats must already be drenched."

"Then we better hurry," he said. "The rain could ruin the interior."

"Just a minute."

She dropped a quarter into the newspaper box and handed a paper to him. "Put this over your head."

After buying one for herself, they ran for the parking lot.

A sheet of water awaited them. Taking one look, Jason said, "Don't go out. I'm already wet. Give me your keys, and I'll get it for you."

Jennifer took out her key chain. "That's sweet. Thanks."

She walked with him to the exit. Pushing a button on the remote on her key ring, a horn beeped. "I'll guard your bag for you," she said with a smile.

Jason dashed out, and seconds later the horn stopped. Headlights appeared twinkling from the downpour. Leaving the engine running, he got out of the car.

"Get in," he shouted. "I'll take care of my bag."

She made it to the car in three seconds. Sliding into the driver's seat, she found a deep puddle on the floor. Dropping the newspaper into it only raised the level of water over her bare toes.

Jason slid in next to her. "I must have brought the bad weather."

"No. It was raining most of the day, but the sun was shining when I came to get you. Why are you so late?"

"The plane stalled out and I had to make a forced landing near Ludington."

"Ohmygod! What happened?"

"There must have been a fuel leak. My plane couldn't be repaired now, so I had to hire a local to get me here."

"Thank goodness you're safe," she said. "You must be quite a pilot."

"I've got a lot of experience."

Conversation lapsed into silence. "Why so quiet?" Jennifer asked.

He squirmed. "I still think I murdered my mother."

The obvious pain in the words cut deeply, strengthening her resolve. "I know you do. But neither of us knows that for sure. Don't give up hope."

"I'm not," he said, beginning to shiver.

She glanced at him. "You poor thing. You must be freezing. I'll turn on the heater."

Seconds later, soothing warmth poured out of the vents at their feet.

"W-what do you sup-suppose they'll do to me if I did?"

"I'm no expert, but I don't think the court system would want to prosecute you unless the wrong person got the case. There are some who would demand the death penalty for infants."

He laughed mirthlessly.

"Now stop this," she said firmly. "I've been doing research, and I think I know what happened in your relationship to your mother. Whether or not you killed her, it wasn't your fault. You were symbiotes. It was as if you were part of her, and she was part of you."

His voice turned hostile. "Brilliant deduction. Even if that were true, why does it make me any less guilty?"

"Lottie was with another man. It was as if she were stabbing you in the heart with a knife. You struck back. You probably didn't even understand what you were doing."

"But I did," Jason said in an angry voice. "Oedipus did, too." His teeth began to chatter. "At least Lieutenant Arnold finally thinks I'm innocent. He called me while I was in Ludington and said he wants an autopsy on Naomi's body. He said he thinks it'll help draw the real murderer out from hiding."

"That sounds like a good idea."

Despite the warmth from the heater, Jason felt a chill. "I c-can hardly w-wait t-to get to the hotel so I can get out of these wet clothes."

"You're not going to the hotel yet. You're coming with me to my apartment. We're going to spend a few hours getting better acquainted with your mother while your clothes dry. I think you'll feel much better after you do."

"Y-you're the doctor."

Water began to gush onto Jennifer's windshield faster than the wipers could clear it, swallowing all vision. She slowed to a crawl, then stopped altogether. "We have to pull over, but I have no idea where I'm going."

Jason responded by cracking open his door. "I can see the side of the road. Start forward, but keep your foot on the brakes."

She did.

"Good. Now keep angling to the right. Careful. You're almost to the shoulder."

Gravel crunched.

"Stop!" Jason shouted.

Jennifer's foot slammed onto the brake pedal, but it was too late. The Audi plunged to the right and the world turned upside down.

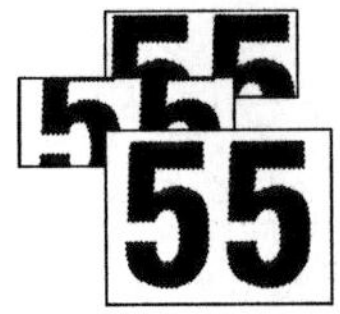

"HANG ON!" JASON screamed as he leaned away from the window.

The car continued to roll. Then it stopped violently. Despite the seat belt, Jennifer's head slammed into something.

Forcing her eyes open, she found herself squished against the driver's door with Jason sprawled against her.

"Are you all right?" he shouted.

Jennifer patted at the sting she felt on her forehead before she answered. She guessed the warm wet spot was blood. "No. But I can move my arms and legs. We have to get out of here before the airbags inflate."

"I think I can get my door open," Jason said.

Rain gushed in, as the door swung out. Jennifer choked for breath. Coughing violently, she turned her head and loosened her seatbelt. All the while, Jason did his best to shield her with his body.

"Turn off the headlights and put on the flashers," Jason commanded.

An eternity of a few seconds later, she found the right buttons.

He grabbed her arm. "Come on."

She couldn't move. Her skirt held her in place. Unable to free herself from it, she straddled the gearshift, and squeezed around the steering wheel to the passenger seat. The tartan skirt seemed to weigh a ton, and rain continued to pummel her face. Coughing and gasping, she began to lose consciousness. Before she passed out, she felt herself being lifted free. Moments later, she hung against Jason like a rag doll, fighting to catch her breath.

Finally she sputtered, "I can stand on my own."

"Good," he shouted, releasing his grip. "We have to find shelter."

"Where? I can't see a thing."

"Neither can I."

As they said it, a chain of lightning lit up the entire sky. A second bolt followed immediately on its heels, revealing a colorless landscape.

Suddenly dizzy, Jennifer fell to the ground.

Jason dropped to his knees next to her. "You must have hit your head pretty hard. You could be going into shock. We have to get help. Where's your cellular?"

"It's in my purse. I don't know what happened to it."

"We have to get you warmed up, and fast."

"Y-you're the doctor," she whimpered, stumbling to her feet. "I think I can walk."

Jason took her arm. "This way," he said. "There's a grove of pines ahead up on the hill."

"I thought taking shelter under trees was dangerous."

"No more than staying out here. Hang on to my belt. I know where we're going."

Though woozy, she kicked off her shoes and held on tightly as they began a headlong rush up the slope. Swept along by the powerful, sure-footed Jason, Jennifer was sure she was in the hands of a force of nature. Mud splashed on her skirt and against her ankles as he charged onward and upward, but her feet remained steady beneath her. Finally, unable to keep up with him, she slipped and fell to her knees.

"Jason . . ." she called out, clinging to his belt for dear life as she fought to regain her footing.

He didn't stop or answer. She didn't let go of the belt until they reached the crest of the hill. She let go, exhausted, as they finally reached level ground. Though barely able to breath, her head felt clearer.

"Made it," he wheezed, gasping for breath.

"Where are we?"

As if in answer, another lightning bolt flashed. They were standing right next to an enormous pine.

Jason pushed her toward it. "Get under the branches."

She found herself on her hands and knees on a velvety carpet that quickly changed from wet to dry. The storm continued to blow and rattle around them, but the relentless dousing had given way to an occasional droplet.

Jason squatted next to her and put an arm around her shoulders. His skin felt like ice. "How are you doing?" he asked. "I'm really worried about you."

"I'm f-fine," she stuttered, "H-how about y-you?"

"Cold, but I'm not the one who hit my head. You're not fine. I'll go look for your purse. We need to get you to the hospital."

She grabbed his arm. "No! It's t-too d-dangerous. I-I'm sure I'm f-fine."

"Don't argue. If you're going into shock, we have to warm you up. And quick. There's only one way to do it. Skin to skin contact."

"If I w-weren't t-too c-cold to b-be able to th-think, th-that would s-sound sus-suspicious to me."

"No jokes," Jason said grimly. "We still need something to retain warmth."

Her eyes opened wide. "M-my sk-skirt is d-dry inside. We can c-cover our-selves with th-that."

"Okay. Take it off."

Glad he couldn't see her embarrassed look, she got to her feet and felt for the skirt's hook. The heavy garment fell with a quiet thud. Now nearly naked from the waist down, she could barely stand the cold.

Jason's hand brushed her thigh, making her flinch. "Hurry," he said.

"O-okay. B-but I refuse to t-take off my b-bra and kn-nickers."

"Suit yourself," Jason said, "Don't peek."

"F-funny," Jennifer chattered.

His naked back brushed against her leg as he settled on the ground, making her whole body shudder. It felt like it was connected to an overcharged battery as she stretched out her hand to see which way he was lying. Then, taking a deep breath, she lowered herself next to him.

Tenser still, she inhaled and inched forward. When she touched him, she felt a jolt and pulled away. Keeping a safe distance away from him, she pulled the skirt over them.

All dizziness had disappeared.

"You're going to have to come closer than that," Jason murmured. "Haven't you ever played spoons?"

"T-that's n-none of your b-business," she retorted, gathering her courage. This time she didn't recoil when they touched, and she had an immediate sense of shared warmth. Draping her arm over his body to move closer still, the feeling of his naked pecs against her wrist and her bare legs pressed so tightly against his made her shiver. This time not from the cold.

"Still cold?" Jason asked.

"A l-little."

"You'll soon feel warmer."

That's what I'm afraid of. "A-are you sh-sure about that?"

"Trust me. Your doctor knows."

"Hmm," she said. "T-the l-last man who said 'trust me' w-wound up bent up double on his b-bed, and the last t-time a guy played doctor with me, m-my mother showed up j-just in time to stop me f-from taking my clothes off. I kinda wish she was here, now."

"You have nothing to worry about," Jason said.

Minutes later, her shivering stopped. "You asleep?" Jason whispered.

"No, but I'm getting comfortable," she murmured as she nestled her head against his back. Then, realizing what she was doing, she quickly drew away.

Realizing the situation was becoming dangerous. Jennifer cleared her throat. "How do you feel about what happened this afternoon?"

He hesitated. "I'm frightened now, but . . ."

"But what?"

"I almost let the plane crash."

"Turn around," she demanded.

He wiggled forward and rolled over to face her. Even though it was pitch black, she was sure he could see the coals burning in her eyes. "Why?"

"I didn't want to live."

"Then why didn't you call me?" she demanded.

"Sorry to put it this way, but I knew all you would do was to try to talk me out of it. I had to come to that decision myself."

"Me and my big head," she said with a bitter laugh. "I thought I meant something to you."

"Of course you do," Jason said, stroking her back. "I just didn't need you to try to stop me. Everything happened too quickly."

"The sad thing is I sort of understand what you mean," Jennifer said in a hurt voice. "Very enlightening."

As she said it, she began to roll on her side away from him.

He stopped her. "I'm really sorry, believe me. You mean everything to me."

"Until you decide to do something stupid again, you mean."

"I won't." As he said it, he reached over her back to pull her tightly against him. "I wouldn't have missed this for the world."

"Stop that!" Jennifer snarled, pushing against his chest with both hands. "This is serious. I want to know why you waited until now to tell me."

"I had to work up the courage," he said. Suddenly his lips were on hers. "Just like now."

Pulling her head away, she pushed harder against him. "You're supposed to be my doctor, remember? And I'm supposed to be yours."

He stopped abruptly. Too abruptly, Jennifer thought. "Sorry," he said. "I forgot."

"We . . . we have to remember we're supposed to be professionals, you know."

"Of course," he said, sounding embarrassed. "To be truthful, I don't think we have to worry about you going into shock anymore. When the rains stops, I'll go back to the road and try to get help. I'm still worried about you. You may have a concussion." His hand touched her gently on the forehead. "I think you may be a bit feverish, too."

She moved his hand to her cheek. "Is that feverish, too?"

"I think so. I better check some other places."

Lips met, and she tried to push him away. Then his hand moved to her breast. "No, please . . . we . . ." Her objections ended in a sigh.

Flushed, and lips tingling, she struggled to keep her distance as inexperienced fingers began to fumble with the clasps of her bra. Like a seven-year-old.

His mouth stilled her lips as she felt her bra go slack. "No . . ." she pleaded weakly as his hand moved gently down her stomach toward the place where she ached the most. She could no longer resist.

"N . . ." she got out before she felt a bolt of pleasure. Her body stiffened. Gasping, she grabbed his hand, wishing the sensation would last for an eternity. Her body relaxed into an expectant langour.

JENNIFER AWOKE TO the sound of shouting. "This is Hennepin County Deputy Sheriff Tom Nelson. Can anyone hear me?"

"We're over here," Jason called back.

A beam pierced through the branches of the tree. Footsteps rustled through the pine needles until a dark form became visible. "Anyone hurt?"

"Not seriously," Jason said, "but we can use a couple of blankets if you have any. We had to get out of our wet clothes."

"I'll be right back."

Not wanting to be caught naked, Jennifer sat up and struggled into her underwear. She shuddered at their dampness. And the cold.

Settling back under the skirt, she suddenly found herself staring into the glare of a powerful lantern. "That's too bright."

"Sorry," the deputy said, moving the beam away from her. Duckwalking under the branches of the huge tree, he said, "Here're the blankets. I'll wait for you to come out."

He tossed them the heavy olive-drab blankets and backed out. Jason passed one to Jennifer and wrapped the other one around himself. Her cheeks burned as she gathered their clothes.

"You guys okay?" Nelson asked. "If you ask me, you're lucky to be alive."

"We probably are," Jason said. "Dr. Cahill hit her head, but it doesn't seem to be too serious. Otherwise we're fine. What time is it?"

"A little after two in the morning," the deputy said. "If you're decent, I'll turn the lantern back on."

"Go ahead," Jennifer said. The wet ground felt like ice on her bare feet. *My shoes should be here somewhere.*

The deputy pointed the beam toward the road. "I called for a tow truck."

"Thanks," Jennifer said as she and Jason made their way down the slope.

"It's amazing, but your auto doesn't seem to be too badly damaged. I'll contact the Eden Prairie police to have them come and make an accident report. Contact your insurance company while you're waiting. The local police are pretty busy tonight, so I'll stick around to see if you'll need a ride home."

Eden Prairie police arrived in ten minutes. As they left, the wide lights of a wrecker lit up the road.

A grizzled young man holding a red Coke can stepped out. "What happened?"

"The shoulder must have collapsed when I drove on it."

"Yeah, looks like," he said. After taking a swig from his can he asked, "Where do you want it towed?"

"Take it to the closest VW dealer."

The wrecker left fifteen minutes later, leaving Jennifer and Jason drowsing in the backseat of Deputy Nelson's squad car as the officer went out with his lantern to look for Jennifer's purse.

The rain had nearly stopped, and he returned minutes later with it in his hand. "It was right next to the road," he said. Jennifer thanked him and pulled her blanket up around her neck. The next thing she knew, the deputy was waking them at her apartment building.

The night lay empty around them, cool and fresh. Crickets serenaded each other in full voice as Jennifer took Jason's hand and hurried up the steps to her building. She looked around anxiously as she took out her keys to unlock the security door.

It swung open. "Come on," she said.

The stairway made a right turn and continued upward with a series of similar turns all the way to the fourth floor. Jason felt a chill of déjà vu and wondered why. Even though he had been in the building only once before, he felt a familiarity with the surroundings he couldn't understand or explain.

Jennifer opened the door to the second floor and they walked halfway down the hall to her apartment. Jason opened his blanket to shield her as she fumbled the key into the lock.

Inside, four golden orbs gleamed as Jennifer opened the apartment door. "Freaky," Jason said.

"I know," Jennifer replied. The cats promptly disappeared as she hit the light switch. "Just a sec," she called.

Jason watched as she disappeared. She soon reappeared in a flannel nightgown carrying a large terry cloth robe. "Put this on."

He turned before dropping the blanket. Slipping into the garment, he said, "Looks like I'll have to spend the night. I can't take a cab dressed in your robe, pretty as it is."

"No, that'd be hard to explain," Jennifer echoed with a wistful smile.

"Something the matter?"

"I don't know how to say this, but you've really screwed up my life."

"What do you mean?"

"I've crossed the line from 'therapist' to 'the rapist.' I could even go to jail."

Jason's eyes flashed. "Don't be ridiculous. It was entirely my fault. I nearly raped you."

"Even if that were true, you're my patient. I wanted you, and that's not ethical."

"Screw ethics. Now that I trust you completely, you should be able to help me more than ever."

She hugged him tightly. "I know that's how it may seem to you, but that isn't how it works." She paused, grasping for words. "It would be like a woman coming to you when you are a doctor. She wants to get pregnant, but can't because her husband's infertile. You can't just sleep with her yourself to solve the problem."

"Of course not," Jason said. "But you can't just desert me, either. I don't have anywhere else to go."

"Don't worry," she said, hugging him more tightly. "I would never do that. We'll figure this out together. It's just too complicated for me right now."

"I really am sorry."

"Don't be. It's just that I've spent a lot of money and time getting to where I am today, and I've already helped a lot of people. I want to help a lot more, so I'm not ready to give everything up just because you're gorgeous and you caught me at a weak moment."

Jason felt the floor crumble under his feet. Choking back a sob, he said, "I really do wish I could go back to the hotel. Sleeping on the couch is probably the next best thing."

"It probably is," she said, taking his hand. "If something else happened, I wouldn't need an excuse. Please don't feel bad. I just don't know what to do about you yet. I could just kill Mike Savich for sending you to me."

Jason responded by gently rubbing the nape of her neck. "I understand. I'll sleep here."

She forced a smile and nodded. Then she gathered up their dirty clothes. "These should be fine after I wash them. Why don't you shower while I'm busy?"

"Sounds good. I wish I weren't so tired. I'd like to get a look at mother's things."

"Me too. My first appointment isn't until 10:30, so we can start tomorrow morning."

57

MARCEL DIGUS WOKE suddenly, realizing something was in the house with him.

His sleep had been uneasy. The day before, a deadly Fer-de-Lance had slithered into the dwelling of one of his tribe and bitten a woman. She died in agony within minutes, leaving four children and a husband behind.

The thought chilled him.

A second crash sounded from the kitchen. This was no snake. Some other creature was there, digging in paper.

After shoving his feet into his slippers, he noiselessly rose from his bed.

The sounds from the kitchen got louder. A wonderful morning breeze crept through the porous walls, but he immediately caught an unwelcome odor. A broom stood outside the door to the kitchen and he grabbed it. Rushing in, he confronted his expected culprit.

A striped coatimundi stopped rummaging through his garbage bag and looked up in alarm. Marcel made a run at it. The mischievous animal dropped an apple core from its mouth, bared its teeth, then beat a hasty retreat out the open back door.

"Don't you come back," Marcel shouted as he slammed the door shut. He remembered he only shut it before he went to bed. No one had locks on their doors in Kaw. The inquisitive rogue must have turned the door handle to open it. Coatis could be so bright.

With a stretch and a grudging smile, he filled a teapot with water and set it on the stove to boil. Next he opened the door of the tiny refrigerator to take out the eggs for his omelet. Instead of a cold blast, he got a mild whiff of cool air. He also got a soupcon of rotten eggs. *Remember to refill the propane tank for the refrigeration compressor,* he scolded himself. It was early for him to eat, but he knew he would never be able to go back to sleep. The postmaster wouldn't be calling Dylan Hansen about the express letter for at least another three hours.

As he broke the eggs and began to stir them with a fork, he tried to imagine an American doctor living in the wilds. French Guiana, as well as much of South America, was a very good place to disappear. Hansen was at least involved in a good cause. Other's motives weren't always as honorable.

Humming, he poured the eggs into a cast-iron skillet. After eating, he'd go back to Clancy's *Clear and Present Danger.* Then he would treat himself to an extra long swim.

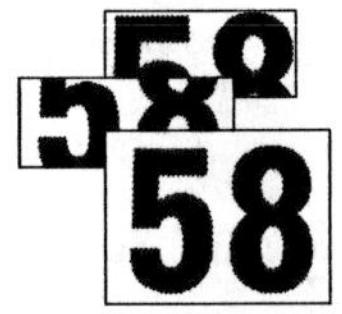

DAN ARNOLD AWOKE at 6:30 to the sound of a siren coming from somewhere on Queen Avenue. He quickly slipped into his pants and ran to the front window to see what was happening. A fire truck passed his house and disappeared down the hill toward Bassetts Creek and the former Burma-Shave plant.

His eyes burned from sleeplessnesss, and the sun beaming over the maple tree on his boulevard was giving him a headache. So did the thought of meeting Chief Davis.

Damn it all, I'm not going to give up. At least not yet.

He had to make one last visit first.

Dragging himself into the bathroom, Dan stared into the mirror and stuck out his tongue. Sure enough. It was white and furry. Tipping his head back, he examined his lovely, deep-scarlet throat. No doubt about it. Twenty-four hour flu for sure, and he had a ton of sick time to use.

Clearing his throat as he dialed, he coughed into the receiver when the dispatcher answered. She sympathized and told him to go back to bed. With a final hack, he hung up and walked to the kitchen to start his coffee maker.

Horny Hildegard moaned merrily as she brewed the coffee. He always got a kick out of it until one time a woman he had been dating called while it was at work. Before he could explain, she hung up on him and never spoke to him again.

Opening his refrigerator, he took out the half-empty Krispy Kreme box and two half-pint plastic bottles of orange juice. Meager fare, but they would have to last him for the six-hour drive ahead of him. Or at least until he found a suitable Mac and Don's.

He didn't have much of a plan except to drop in on Sheriff Norquist unannounced. The more Dan learned about Melanie's background, the angrier he became with the devious weasel's pretense of an investigation. Like it or not, Norquist would take him to Hidden Pines. Maybe he could uncover the dark secrets Lawrence Dumont was struggling to hide. Most important of all, Dan would start on the trail of Dylan Hansen.

Whether he murdered Melanie or not, Hansen had suddenly become the key player in the tragedy.

Dan squatted to open a cabinet and pull out the last item for his trip north. Hiding behind a bag of sprouting onions, the green Stanley thermos would hold the whole carafe of the Sumatran roast Hildegard was brewing. Though it had been his favorite for years, he now knew nothing would ever compare to the Kopi Luwak Lawrence Dumont had served him.

After filling the thermos with hot water, he ambled to the bathroom to shower. Pipes rattled and water spurted out from the tap, bringing an odor of rotten eggs with it.

Damned water softener, he grumbled. *Clean forgot about it.*

Luckily the water didn't leave him smelling the same way, and half an hour later, he was on his way.

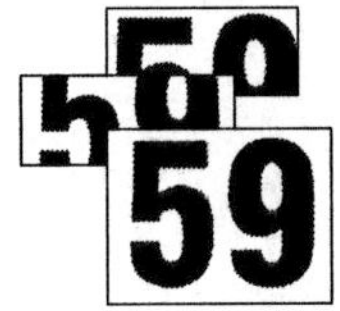

JASON AWOKE TO discover Nikko asleep on his chest. Gently moving her aside, he got to his feet and padded to the bedroom.

Bending over Jennifer's bed, he watched her sleep for a moment, then gave her shoulder a gentle shake. "Good morning."

She opened her eyes. "Good morning. What time is it?"

"Seven o'clock. If you tell me where you keep your coffee, I'll start it."

"Left cupboard, top shelf," she said with a yawn. "Did you say seven o'clock? What are you doing up already?

"I always get up early. There are too many things to do in a day. Is the cereal in a cupboard, too?"

Jennifer managed a smile. "Center right. Wait. I'll get up with you."

"You don't have to," Jason said with an evil grin. "I'll be happy to serve you breakfast in bed."

She flashed a witchy smile. "You know what I said. If you're hoping you can lure me into doing something foolish, you can forget it."

"Darn," he sighed.

Whistling "Penny Lane," Jason filled the coffee percolator with water and pulled down the coffee from its hiding place. He was about to set out the cereal on the counter top when Jennifer came up behind him and hugged him. "You sure are cheerful," she said in a playful voice. "I wonder why."

"You know why," he said, turning to face her.

"Believe it or not, this is the first time I have ever had a man stay over night in my apartment."

"Patient, you mean."

"Don't be that way. I'm sure we have a future. We just have to cure you first."

"Yeah," Jason said sadly.

She hugged him. "It won't be long. Cereal's fine, but what about waffles?"

After polishing off the last of his waffle and rinsing his plate, Jason moved to the front closet. Opening the door, he found a variety of coats and jackets covering the stack of three boxes. The top box seemed unusually light, and he laid it on top of the one beneath it. "Where do you want them?"

"By the couch," Jennifer called from the bathroom.

She was sitting on it when he returned with the last one. "I thought we looked through them already," Jason said.

"Just the one, really. I barely started on the second box, and I never even opened the third. Sit. I'll be right with you after I call the repair shop. I want to find out what happened with the car last night."

He sat and she handed him a coffee cup. A short time later she returned.

"What did the repair shop have to say?"

"I got off lucky. It should be ready tomorrow."

She sat. Pulling the tape loose from the top of one of the boxes, she reached in and removed a large stack of greeting cards. "Let's see what we have here."

She divided the cards, handing half to Jason. "It's a good thing your mother was sentimental. We wouldn't have much to go on if she threw things away." She flipped through a few of them. "Hmm. It looks like a lot of them are from her cousins."

Jason thumbed through his consignment. "These are mostly birthday cards." He stopped as he came to what seemed to be an especially thick envelope. Opening it, he found a card with a second one tucked inside it.

"This one's a valentine," he said. "Signed 'Prince Dy.' Who was that?"

Jennifer's eyes opened wide as she took the card from him. "Probably Dylan Hansen. It probably was meant to be a joke. You know, Princess Diana."

"I wonder why he sent her a card."

"She played lead with him in the class play. He must have had a sense of humor. It's signed 'Endless Love.' One of my favorite songs."

Jason bent forward. "Which box has the yearbooks?"

She pointed at one by her feet. "I think they're near the top."

He unearthed them from under the Levi jeans. Quickly turning to the index in the top one, he found the references. Dylan's senior class picture showed a young man with short-cropped hair and an awkward smile. Jason looked up to find Jennifer studying him.

"Something the matter?"

"No," she said slowly. "It just seems you look a bit like him. Your nose and eyes especially."

"Just a coincidence," Jason said, assuming a brave voice. "Mom always said how much I look like Father."

Jennifer set the cards on the floor. "Let's see what else we have here."

The next layer proved to be a nested box of tapes. "Melanie liked ABBA," said Jason.

"So do I."

"Did you know 'abba' is Hebrew for Daddy?"

"No. Ever hear 'Dancing Queen?'"

"Hasn't everyone?"

"Okay, wise guy. Do you think you can get the tapes out?"

The hardest thing was to find a grip. Dislodging one of the tapes with his thumb, he used his fist to wedge the box free and reveal large stacks of *Seventeen* and *Elle* magazines.

Jason vented a derisive snort and picked up the tape box to put it back, but Jennifer took his hand to stop him.

"Let's be sure your mother wasn't hiding something," she said in a conspiratorial tone.

A slick pile grew and slid apart as she pulled them out. Suddenly she stopped.

Curious, Jason looked down at the small, glossy-covered book in her hands. His face began to burn at the sight of the naked couple intertwined with only the title of the book to cover them.

Sexual Positions in his mother's reading material?

He felt even more uncomfortable as Jennifer flipped through the pages. "We want to be sure she hasn't hidden anything else."

He squirmed until she finally put it back into the box.

"I bet she used to hide that in her underwear drawer," she said with a steamy smile. "Shall we look through the rest of them?"

"I'm almost afraid to."

Jennifer baled out the rest of the magazines. They both breathed a sigh of relief as she came to the last one. "That was quite a shock, wasn't it?" Jason said.

"I'm sure it was for you. Children always get blown away by their parents' sexuality."

They both startled at the sound of Jennifer's telephone ringing. She answered with a worried frown. Who would be calling at eight in the morning?

Dan Arnold came on. "Sorry to bother you so early but I was wondering if you know where I can reach Jason Dumont. I'm having breakfast on my way up to Thief River Falls and I wanted to ask him some questions. He's not at his hotel room, and I keep getting his voice mail when I try to call his cell phone."

"It's in the trunk of my car. We were in a car accident."

"Oh, no. That's terrible. Are you all right?"

"We're both fine. He's right here. Hold on."

She gestured for Jason. Covering the mouthpiece, she whispered, "Dan Arnold."

Jason took the phone from her. He didn't like the idea that the lieutenant would be able to guess they'd been together all night. "Good morning."

Dan returned the greeting. "Miss Cahill told me what happened. Thank goodness you're okay, and I'm sorry to disturb you, but the reason I called is I went to see your father and uncle yesterday. I came home with more questions than answers. I hoped you might be able to help me."

Jason felt a tingle of apprehension. "What do you want to know?"

"For one thing, how long has your housekeeper been with the family?"

"Louise? I expect it's been at least twenty-five years. Father hired her before I was born. Why do you ask?"

"We didn't get a chance to talk to her ourselves. I got the feeling she and your mother were fairly close."

"I know they were. Louise and I have been, too. She practically raised me."

"Did she ever talk to you about your mother's death?"

"No more than to remind me how much Mother loved me."

Dan paused and cleared his throat. "Were you aware Melanie hadn't originally planned to take you with her to your grandmother's funeral, and that your father didn't even know you were with her until the next day?"

The words struck like a hammer blow. With a catch in his voice, Jason said, "You must be mistaken."

"Sorry. Both your father and your Uncle Gary verified that."

Jason struggled to hold back tears, though his mind was demanding to know what difference it made. "Thanks for the information. Anything else you want to ask me?"

"More than I can possibly tell you. Someone gave your mother a necklace. It has a charm bracelet-sized book on a gold chain. She was wearing it at the time she was murdered. Do you have any idea where she could have gotten it?"

"None whatsoever. My dad, I expect."

"Okay," Dan said, unhappy. "Did you ever hear her mention Dylan Hansen?"

The words struck like a lightning bolt. "No. Why do you ask that?"

"She kept a clipping about his graduating from Med school. It sounds as if they must have been pretty good friends."

Jason had to fight to keep a quaver out of his voice. "I suppose it's possible. I'm sorry I can't be more help."

"Sure," Dan said with a sigh. "I'll probably want to talk to you again when I get back from Thief River Falls."

"I can hardly wait," Jason said. "Actually, I appreciate what you're doing."

As he hung up, Jennifer stared at him with curiosity. "Bad news?"

"No. But you may be right about Dylan Hansen. Let's get back to the boxes."

JASON FELT A strange sense of promise as the tape holding the top of the third carton popped away with barely a tug. The vague anger he felt against his mother for so many years had disappeared. No matter what she had done, he was now sure he was the love of her life.

But did she love Father?

Obviously not as much as Jason had once believed. Did Father ever suspect that she might have loved someone else? If he did, he never let on to Jason. As far as he knew, his father had been genuinely devastated by her death.

Jennifer bent closer as he opened the flaps. "How sweet," she said. "Her toys."

A tall satin rabbit peeked out from the box. Jason recognized it immediately as a twin to the one Melanie kept in her bedroom at Indian Hill. He took it out and propped it up against the couch as he continued to dig.

A long green snake uncoiled itself. The stuffed toy's goofy grin reminded him of Kaa, the character in Disney's Jungle Book. He held it up next to Jennifer's face. "Sss. Care for an apple, little girl."

She broke into a low laugh. "Too late. I've already fallen."

Reaching into the box again, he pulled out a plush pink pig. After that, a Pooh Bear and a large teddy were all that were left in the box.

They looked at each other with puzzled expressions. "Did we miss something?" Jason asked.

"I don't know. It seems a bit surprising that she'd keep a box of toys."

Jason picked up the Pooh Bear. "She always loved Winnie. I bet she must have read me the story a hundred times. Did you know Milne wrote a mystery?"

"No," Jennifer said.

"*The Red House*. It's really quite good." He laid the toy back into the box with a sigh.

"Something wrong?"

"I really had hoped we would find something useful. Other than her instructional material, that is."

She laughed uneasily. "She must have been bought that before she married your father."

Jason blanched and grabbed the yearbook. Quickly referring back to the index, he opened the book to Hansen's class picture.

For an instant he had a strong sense of recognition. Then the feeling disappeared.

"We better get moving. I have to get to the office to solve my other patient's problems."

"Speaking of problems, it just occurred to me that your problem with Candy is a lot like mine. From the evidence it would seem I'm the only who could have killed Mother. That's always been the biggest reason why I think I could have done it. I've never realized we're both in the same position. Just because I left bloody footprints doesn't mean I was the only one who could have been in the bathroom with her. There was plenty of smeared blood on the floor. Whoever did it could have taken off their shoes before they stepped outside the bathroom."

"Very true," Jennifer said. "Do you want to come to my office?"

"I think I'll stop at the hotel first."

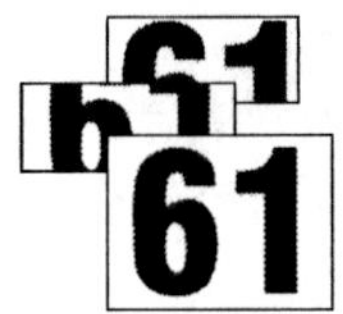

MARCEL DIGUS WIPED his forehead with his shirtsleeve as he finished off the last of the second Snickers bar. Even though he had eaten most of it before it melted, chocolate still leaked over the top of the wrapper, and he had to lick his fingers to clean off the sweet brown goo.

How much longer?

Dr. Dylan Hansen still had not shown. Only two other people besides the courier had crossed Rene Batiste's threshold that morning. One was Jeanette Malika, the aged tribal crone who lived along the river; the other, Henri Telektua. Jeanette came in every morning topped by her bright red bandana to buy bottled Evian water. Marcel noted that her daily purchases produced the closest touch to a modern environmental problem in Kaw by turning her back yard into a landfill by burying the empty bottles. Henri, the second visitor, was a free spirit, a brother who regularly defied tribal law by buying cheap Beaujolais. Marcel winked at the transgression. He liked wine himself.

A sound from the road behind him put Marcel on alert. Scrunching down, he waited for whoever was approaching to pass by. The footsteps halted and Marcel wondered if he had been spotted. Moments later, they began again and the hulking figure of Antoine LeClerc passed by.

What's he doing here?

Long strides dug into the moist soil. Six-foot-six LeClerc was a genetic freak. Standing a full foot taller than the average Frenchman, he was also the only other person in Kaw besides Marcel to hold a legal degree. A perennial candidate for a seat in the French parliament, Antoine had made it clear on his arrival twenty years before that he didn't consider himself to be a mere *Guyane Française étranger*, and that he intended to return to his native Sorbonne as soon as he got elected to governmental office.

The giant halted. With a grunt he pulled a Limoges cigarette out of his shirt pocket. After lighting it, he continued on his way.

Marcel followed him with his eyes until the man reached the doorway to Leon Batiste's store. The Indian's pulse quickened as he waited for LeClerc's return. Five hot minutes later the man emerged carrying a large manila envelope.

Suces!

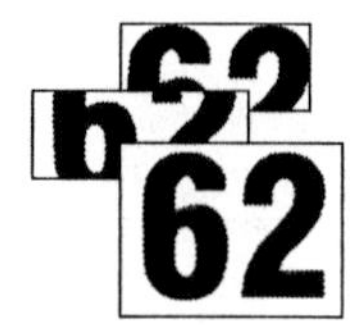

AS JASON REACHED Seventh and Hennepin, he cast a doleful eye at the sad hodgepodge of buildings surrounding him. One of the photos in his underground tour book showed what the corner looked like in the late thirties.

Hennepin, then, was the main street of a bustling metropolis. The shops were small, the streets busy with pedestrians, Model T's, and street cars. Far above where he stood, a twenty-foot-tall man contentedly blew huge smoke rings out over Hennepin Avenue to advertise Camel cigarettes. Now the only reminders of olden days were nearly indistinguishable advertising printed on weathered bricks on the sides of the remaining buildings. One read, "Rooms. $1.00 per night, $5.00 per week."

Gathering the shopping bag with Mr. Rabbit's brother closer to him, Jason crossed Hennepin toward the shiny new buildings that had taken over Seventh Street. Where Hennepin was a hodge-podge, Seventh Street was uniformly post-modern.

Reaching the International Hotel, he stopped at the desk to see if there were any messages. Having none, he took the elevator to the twentieth floor.

As he stepped out, he felt a wave of hope that his newest memories would cascade and spark even more. The feeling of foreboding he felt as he approached the room made him especially hopeful. He had no such reaction the last time.

Stopping in front of the door, he had a flash of memory. Mother used a metal key to unlock the door.

"C'mon, stump. Shake a leg."

The words came back with startling clarity. "Stump" was her nickname for him. He had forgotten it long ago—probably soon after her death.

Encouraged, Jason quickly opened the door and stepped inside.

Newly made beds and the smell of sandalwood soap greeted him, but no hoped-for flood of memories. It was just another hotel room.

When his gaze fell on the far bed, he felt a jolt. *"I get the bed by the window,"* the seven-year-old Jason said as he ran to it.

"Okay, but then I get to eat the apple in the snack bag."

Jason smiled, remembering he had thought it a fair trade because he didn't want the apple anyway.

Heartsick, he laid the stuffed rabbit on the bed where his mother would have been lying. At home, Melanie often propped herself up between Jason and the twin rabbit and pretended to be reading bedtime stories to the both of them.

Sharply-detailed memories assailed him as he moved closer to the bed he had slept in on the night of her death. He sat on the floor next to it. The present faded as he watched a long strip of soft wood lift away from the bottom of his model plane over his carving knife. He looked up when his mother turned on *Quantum Leap* as she unpacked. Young Jason laughed when Scott Bakula looked at himself in a mirror and saw a woman.

With that, the memories suddenly faded and ceased entirely. He got to his feet. Hoping to stimulate more, he took a deep breath and stepped into the bathroom.

He again caught the tangy odor of sandalwood, but felt no jolt, or even a shiver.

The soap had smelled like roses then.

That was all he remembered. The horror scene in Detective Arnold's photos did not appear. Thankfully, it was just another hotel bathroom.

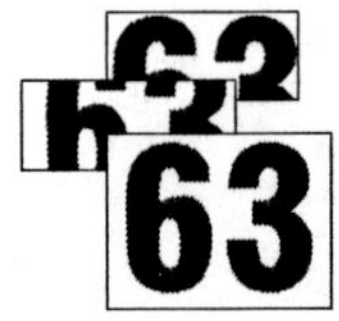

"BON JOUR, ANTOINE," MARCEL SAID, stepping out from behind his hiding place.

Startled, the Frenchman stopped in his tracks. *"Bon jour,"* he said in a nervous voice. *"Qui est la-bas?"*

"Marcel Digus. I see you have something for Dr. Dylan Hansen, *n'est-ce-pas?"*

LeClerc flinched. "That is none of your business."

"Perhaps not my business, but you see, a family member of *le bon docteur* needs to make contact with him. They have tried repeatedly to reach him at his postal box, but he has never answered any of his mail."

LeClerc moved to where the sun no longer glared in his eyes. "That may be, but it is clearly up to Doctor Hansen to decide whether he wishes to answer his mail or not."

"So you admit to picking up his mail for him."

"I admit to nothing," LeClerc said in a dismissive tone. "Now if you will excuse me . . ." He turned to start on his way.

Marcel caught him by the arm.

Even though twice Marcel's size, LeClerc halted in his tracks. Bulldogs had nasty bites. "What is it you want?"

Marcel decided to wing it. "I think I should warn you that there is an outstanding civil case against Dr. Hansen in the U.S., and I have been commissioned to serve him. Since you are his representative, I must ask for your cooperation, or I will be forced to contact the prefect in Cayenne and have *him* serve you."

When LeClerc didn't answer, Digus pressed onwards. "You are undoubtedly aware of the Hague Convention on Discovery Abroad. We have Letters Rogatory."

"*Cochon*," LeClerc exclaimed. "*Alors*, since I haven't seen Monsieur le docteur in nearly fifteen years, I may as well tell you. I do collect the mail for him, but he doesn't pick it up from me. I send everything on to a post office address in Haiti. I think it's been at least ten years since anything has arrived for him. I was given postcards that I was to send when anyone wrote to him. I have no idea where he is."

Digus took a step backward. "He isn't associated with a mission?"

"He could be. If so, I don't know which one."

"When was the last time mail arrived for *le docteur*."

"Long ago. Perhaps ten years. *Le docteur's* mother wrote to say that his bank had called about the rental fee being due for a safety deposit box where the doctor lived before coming here. Docteur Hansen wrote to me asking me to send a postcard to his mother requesting that she close the box and send the contents to Kaw. I heard back some weeks later that the bank needed the key to the box and asked where Doctor Hansen had put it. When I got no further instructions that was the last I heard from her or *le docteur*."

Digus reached into his shirt pocket and showed him the faxed copy of the photo Jennifer Cahill had sent to him. "Is this the man who hired you."

LeClerc glanced at it and shrugged. "I can't tell. The picture is too dark."

"Then could you describe him for an artist?"

"Yes."

"Would you?"

"*Pour'quoi pas?* My retainer with *le docteur* expired many years ago."

"Just how much did he pay you?"

"Five thousand U.S. dollars," LeClerc said with a blush.

"And how often did you have to act in his behalf?"

LeClerc turned redder still. "At one time, at least once or twice every month."

"It seems that you've been well-recompensed."

"The agreement was that I check the mail once a week and answer all correspondence with postcards or by typewritten letters. He also gave me a sample of his signature."

"Has he been paying for the postal box?"

"No. I've paid it for him from the retainer."

"Since you are picking up his mail, I assume you are still under contract with him."

"*Oui.* The contract actually doesn't expire for another five years."

"Aha. Then I think you should you should take time out from your busy schedule to assist us."

"Very well, but I must insist you pay me for my time."

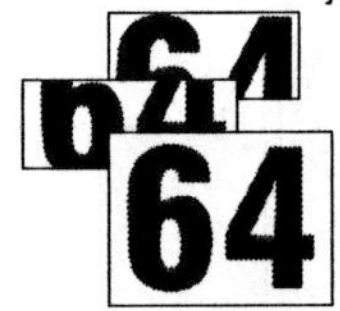

SEAN MCCULLOUGH'S IMPENETRABLE blue eyes glittered as Jennifer held up a richly detailed drawing. It showed a masked figure in combat fatigues holding a pistol in each hand, set against a backdrop of a school lunch line. Though it chilled her to the bottom of her soul, she pasted on a look of impressed admiration.

"This is really great," Jennifer said enthusiastically. "Is that you?"

McCullough, who had been crouching on his chair, hiding behind his legs, burrowed more deeply into the chair and covered his head with his arms. The knees of his black silk pants now completely obstructed Jennifer's view of his face and the front of his black tee-shirt. She had noticed the shirt when he came in for his appointment. It showed a human skull and the whole front spattered with printed blood.

Jennifer waited for an answer, but Sean remained silent.

"I bet this is for a comic book you're making, isn't it? It's so good, I'll bet you can find someone to publish it when you're done."

He drew himself in tighter against the chair.

"The only trouble is you were drawing this in math class," she said, her voice turning serious. "What's worse, it's the first class you've attended in a week."

She stopped to wait for a reaction, but Sean remained silent.

"We have an agreement, remember?"

McCullough still didn't answer. Jennifer moved closer and stared at him. "You haven't been taking your meds, either, have you?"

Prodded into response, he snapped, "That's none of your business. Leave me alone."

"It *is* my business. Yesterday's blood test says it loud and clear. I don't understand why you stopped taking them."

"I hate the way they make me feel."

Jennifer studied him for a moment. "How do the pills make you feel?"

"Like a geek. Not like myself."

"Do you like how you're feeling now?"

"What do you mean?" the teen asked, glaring around his knees.

"Are you happy with the way you feel?"

"Sure, I'm happy."

"You don't look happy to me," she persisted. "You're frowning. Last time you were smiling. You'd been doing your work in your classes. Your dad tells me you went fishing with him for the first time in ten years."

"Big deal. Who cares? All my friends told me they didn't like me the way I was acting when I was taking my meds. I'm not going to take them anymore."

"You may not have any choice. How does daily blood tests sound to you? Do you like being stuck with needles?"

"You can't do that!" Sean bellowed.

"Sure can," Jennifer lied. "You're sixteen and an unemancipated minor. Your behavior and your drawings put you in a high-risk category. You're perfectly fine when you're on your Reserpine. We want to keep you that way."

"This isn't fair. I'll get a lawyer."

"Maybe instead of thinking how you can beat the system, think about the good stuff that'll happen when you're back on the meds. You'll graduate, and your dad promised you a car when you do. You'll be on your own instead of under someone's thumb all the time. And even if you don't believe this, you'll feel a heck of a lot better."

"Not worth it. My friends won't want to have anything to do with me."

"If they're really friends, they'll stick with you. If they're not, you'll find others."

"No!"

She paused. "You only have two choices, Sean. You can either do what needs to be done voluntarily and get the bennies, or we can force you and you don't get a thing except to keep your crummy attitude. Which is it going to be?"

"Neither. I'll run away."

"Great idea," she said. "Live on the streets. Someday you might get to feeling so rotten you'll jump off a bridge, or you may get some bad dope and die that way. Or maybe you'll be lucky and just get beaten up because you have something someone else wants."

He crammed his fingers into his ears.

"Look, Sean, if you decide to kill yourself, it's pretty hard to stop you, but I want to make damned sure you don't take anyone else with you when you do. Going out in a blaze of glory is for punks. Everyone will revile your memory for the rest of their lives."

"Who cares?"

"We've talked enough. Just go back on your meds. Do we have a deal or not?"

"I don't know."

"Tell you what. I'll give you a day to think about it. In the meantime, give me your cell phone. Starting tomorrow, I'll arrange for an escort to see that you go to your classes. It won't be obvious, so you won't feel humiliated. After that . . ."

"No!" McCullough shouted, springing out of his chair with a snarl. Head lowered, he took a threatening step in her direction.

Jennifer stood her ground. After more than six years of dealing with potential violence from patients off their meds, she knew exactly what to do. Without raising her arms in protection, she stared him in his eye.

Looming like a six-foot scarecrow, the teen took another stride, chest heaving.

Mirroring the movement, Jennifer took a step backward. Her teeth rattled as the corner of the desk dug into her back.

"Sean, stop," she said in a quiet, but commanding, voice.

McCullough continued to stomp forward. Heart racing, she reached into her pocket for the aerosol bottle of pepper spray she always carried with her.

Please don't make me use this.

McCullough thrust his face into hers. As it contorted into a grin, he asked, "Whatsa matter, lady? You afraid of me?"

The question hung in the air.

Knowing that any answer could be deadly, Jennifer tightened her grip on the spray bottle. Locking eyes, she held her breath.

Seconds dragged like hours.

Then the silence ended. "What do you want?" she asked in a calm voice.

As she said it, a thought of Jason flashed in her mind . . . Could he ever have been provoked to act the same way? The silence grew deeper. With her hand hurting from the tension of her grip, and blood pounding so hard her eyes ached, she waited for Sean to make the next move.

The teen broke out laughing. "What do I want? What do you think I want? I want to be left alone."

Jennifer sprang into the breach. "This isn't the way to do it. If you feel boxed in now, the box will get a heck of a lot smaller if the legal system gets called in."

"You gonna report me?" McCullough asked in a dark voice.

Jennifer again prepared for an attack. "I'll have to let your social worker know what happened, but I won't contact the police. I definitely will, however, if you continue to threaten me."

The teen stepped back, laughing. "Just scared you. I wouldn't really have hurt you."

"Sure," she said in an ironic voice. "You're lucky it was me. Sooner or later, you'll run into someone who'll take you at your word and decide to get in the first blow. He might even make it with a gun."

After a thoughtful silence, McCullough, still glaring, reached into his pocket for his cell phone. "I don't have much choice, do I?" he said, slapping the phone in her hand.

"Believe it not, you're the winner."

McCullough turned to leave, then turned to face Jennifer. "Do you know something? You people are all hypocrites. You don't really care how I feel. You just don't want to have to deal with me on my terms, so you fill me up with drugs. That way I don't cause trouble."

"There may be some truth to that, Sean, but we run into too many people who commit crimes when they stop taking their medicine. It's the same thing as drunk driving. Getting drunk or going off meds are both willful acts, even if the damage they cause is unintentional."

"That's a lot of bull. There are a lot more people who commit crimes because they want drugs, and you know it."

She threw him a sympathetic look. "I know you don't believe this, but I really do care about you. You're very likable when you're taking your meds. And life will be a lot easier for you. We both win that way."

DAN DOWNED THE DREGS of the coffee in a single gulp as Frank Norquist appeared at his office door. Though the sheriff was smiling, Dan got a distinct feeling that he wasn't pleased to see him.

"Sorry to keep you waiting, Dan," Norquist said. "Dorrie Thompson can get her cat out of the tree herself."

Dan snickered. Not at the thought of Norquist rescuing a cat, but at Norquist himself. The sheriff could have come out of the Mix and Match story book Dan had given to three-year-old niece Trudy. To her delight, the book was cut into horizontal strips she could move to create funny monsters, like one with a dog's head, an elephant's body and a cat's feet. Frank Norquist had a handsome, if heavily joweled, face. He was clean-shaven, with every hair held in place with mousse. His legs were still muscular and athletic, but his middle panel would show a belly hanging precipitously over brown pants, and a corner of his shirt hanging out from the back of his trousers. Trudy would get a big kick out of him.

"Nice to see you again,"Norquist said, "but why didn't you let me know you were coming to visit?"

"It's not exactly a visit," Dan said in a serious voice. "I just got back from interviewing Lawrence Dumont, and I wanted to ask you a few questions about him, and Hidden Pines."

"Come on in to the office. It's more comfortable there."

"Good idea."

Dan took a moment to admire the huge wooden plaque with the Pennington County Sheriff's Department badge. The badge, with its placid lake scene, stood framed by two crossed antique shotguns and a vicious-looking four-foot-long mounted northern pike.

"Okay. So what's this about Lawrence Dumont?" Norquist asked.

"I just came back from interviewing him. I'm convinced he's hiding something."

"Really? I thought he had an iron-clad alibi."

"He does, but I think it's a distinct possibility that someone connected with Hidden Pines may know something about who murdered Melanie or may even have committed the murder themselves."

Eyes narrowing, the sheriff asked, "Why would you think that?"

"There are too many major events tied up together with Naomi Marchand's death to be totally unrelated."

Norquist snorted. "Speaking of Naomi, Jason Dumont called and asked for an exhumation. I told him there was no reason, but he insisted. He's paying for it himself, so I can't stop him. Do you have any idea why he's doing it?"

None," Dan lied. "Do you get out to Hidden Pines often?"

"I stop by there at least once a day. I deliver their permits to them and see to their security. There seems to be a ton of new paperwork every week."

Dan nodded. "Was Dylan Hansen ever connected to the clinic?"

"I have no idea," Norquist said, stiffening. "I suppose it's possible."

"Have you found his address yet?"

"The librarian is supposed to be getting it for me. I haven't heard from her."

Dan leaned forward in his chair. "Let's give her a call. It's important."

"Great idea. Margery Bellamy is also the curator of the historical society. I'm sure she knows a lot more about Hidden Pines than I do. If you want to, we can pay her a visit. It's only a few blocks away on Main Avenue. I'll drive us there."

"Thanks, but if it isn't very far away, I'd rather walk. I've had more than my share of riding today."

66

SICK OF THE CLOY of overripe lilacs, Margery Bellamy shut her office window. In the midst of her least-favorite chore, she didn't need any other annoyances. Sending out overdue book notices was busy work, pure and simple, and the chronic offenders hardly ever responded, anyway. She'd had to bar ten-year-old Teddy Field from the library until he returned a dozen books signed out to him from the year before.

The bell over the door tinkled, and she quickly got to her feet. She rolled her eyes when she saw Frank Norquist, but quickly turned her attention to the man with him.

"Hi, Marge," Norquist said in his friendliest voice. "Howya doing."

"Just great, Frank," she said in a hostile tone. "Who's this?"

"Detective-Lieutenant Arnold with the Minneapolis police. He wants to know if you found Dylan Hansen's address yet."

Margery eyed Dan appraisingly for a moment before answering. "He has a P.O. box in Kaw, a little town in French Guiana." As she said it, she secretly smiled at Frank Norquist's glare.

"Do you know if he's written to anyone lately?" Dan asked.

"As far as I know, the only person he ever wrote to was his mother. I used to ask about him when I'd bring her books. She said he was happy working with the mission. But that was years ago."

While Norquist glared, Dan grabbed his notebook and wrote the information down. "Are you sure there isn't anyone else he would have kept in touch with?"

"Nobody I can think of. As far as I know, no one has heard from him since he finished medical school. " She stopped abruptly. "Is he in some kind of trouble?"

"No. We just want to talk to him for informational purposes. Do you know if he ever was associated with Hidden Pines?"

Margery rubber-stamped another postcard before answering. "He worked there during the summers while he was in medical school. I still don't understand . . ." she said, letting her voice trail off.

Dan opened his valise and took out the newspaper clipping. Handing it to her, he said, "This was in Melanie Dumont's closet in Ohio. It seems a bit strange to me that it should turn up there, and I wondered if there was any chance she and Hansen ever were in contact when she came here to visit her mother."

With barely a look, Margery handed it back. "Not that I know about. I really don't think so. Lottie wasn't his type."

"They were in the class play together, weren't they? They must have gotten to know each other pretty well, then."

"I suppose," she said in a frosty voice. "But he was the real star. She didn't have a very good singing voice." As she said it, she glanced at Frank Norquist and blanched. His smirk made her want to scratch his eyes out.

"Do you remember anything about the play?"

"Not much. The class put it on the Friday night after school ended. Dylan was wonderful as Henry Hill. Melanie was okay as Marian. After the play, the principal gave the cast charms representing the parts they played. A lot of the boys got instruments. You may remember that 'Seventy-Six Trombones' was the big number."

"Were you in the cast?"

A flash of anger appeared in Margery's eyes. "No. I was the property manager. I got an owl. I still don't know what that had to do with the play."

"I don't either," Dan mumbled. After a brief pause, he said, "Did you ever suspect that Melanie and Dylan actually were romantically involved with each other?"

"Heavens no!" she said with a derisive snort. "I can't even imagine a more unlikely couple."

"Just curious," Dan Arnold said. "Most likely one of her cousins sent the clipping to her. Melanie probably saved it for sentimental reasons because they were in the class play together."

"That must be it," she mumbled, taking another covert look at Norquist. Realizing that the tables had turned, the creep was now covering his mouth with a hand to keep from laughing out loud. The sight made her seethe like a corked volcano.

Dan Arnold didn't seem to notice the interchange. "Frank tells me you're the head of the Pennington County Historical Society."

"I maintain the archives," she said, swelling with pride. "The actual site is at the Peder Engelstad Pioneer Village. It's one of our biggest tourist attractions. Frank can show you where it is. Do you need to go inside the building?"

"That shouldn't be necessary, thanks. I'd really like to know more about Hidden Pines Clinic."

A puckish smile momentarily touched her face. "You've probably already heard it's one of our most important business establishments. We even call ourselves, 'The City That Cares' because of it. Lawrence Dumont's grandfather started it in 1921. From the very beginning it's always been one of the foremost pain management hospitals in the world." She stopped. "It may even catch up with the Mayo Clinic some day."

"It doesn't hurt to hope," Dan said with a chuckle at his pun.

Grinning coyly, she continued. "Of course, some of the older locals think it has another face."

"Yeah?" Dan said, ears pricking. "What do you mean?"

Throwing a triumphant look at Frank Norquist, she continued. His look of amusement at her expense had given way to surprise. "You know how close we are to the Canadian border here. What you may not have known is that during Prohibition, most of the liquor in Minnesota came from Canada."

"I think I read that somewhere."

"Are you familiar with Breezy Point Resort on Big Pelican Lake in Brainerd?"

"Of course," Dan said with a nod.

"During Prohibition, wealthy people from all around the country came to vacation where they could get a cocktail when they wanted one. Pontoon planes from Canada used to come in and land on the lake two or three times a day."

Dan shrugged. He wasn't aware of that fact, but it didn't surprise him. "Are you saying the owners of Hidden Pines were rum-runners, too."

"Not at all. All I meant is that some of our most prominent families were involved in moving and selling liquid entertainment at the time."

Dan noticed Margery's glance in Frank's direction and guessed the Norquists were one of the families.

With the sheriff glaring daggers at her, she continued. "Not that I blame them. I love a glass of wine myself once in a while. Prohibition was ridiculous. Did you know that there were more alcohol-related arrests in 1932 than any other year during the ban? It ended in1933."

"I didn't," Dan said. "Did anyone here ever get caught?"

Margery's grin got wider. "Just Einar Frigstad. He was a local pharmacist. Everyone thought he was an avid fisherman because he'd go out on the river every evening with his minnow bucket and rod and reel and come back with fish. No one suspected a thing until 1931, when someone contacted the FBI in St. Paul.

"Two agents watched him for almost a week. Every evening Einar would row out to the planes. He always put what he got from them into a net with floats attached to a salt block. If anyone were around, he dumped his cargo into the river and came back later. When the salt block dissolved, the net would come back to the surface."

"Very clever," Dan mused.

"It was. Unfortunately for him, he got caught in the act with a hundred bottles of Canadian rye whiskey before he could dump his cache. He also had a couple of big walleyes in his fishing net when they caught him. It turns out he'd been buying them from the local butcher for years."

"Funny story," said Dan, "but what does that have to do with the clinic?"

Margery broke into a laugh. "He was one of he few who could dispense alcohol legally. During Prohibition, it was the same as a Class I drug. You had to have a doctor's prescription, and you bought it from a pharmacy. He used to fill the prescriptions for the clinic."

Wheels turned. "That's interesting," Dan said.

"We even have a couple of the Treasury Department's Prescription Forms for Medicinal Liquor record pads in the library. You'd be surprised how many people suffered from the grippe and bronchitis in those days."

Dan smiled. "I remember some of the older members of my family took a brandy once in a while 'for medicinal purposes.'"

"You got it. Anyway, Hidden Pines Clinic went through hundreds of prescriptions a year for alcohol. Older townspeople always used to say the patients at the clinic seemed to be in awfully good spirits. The gag used to be, 'When they left Hidden Pines, they weren't feeling any pain.'"

Dan laughed. Norquist fumed.

"They must go through thousands now, for all the analgesics. I know a lot of the locals would love to get hospice care there, but no one around here can afford it."

Margery enjoyed the look Dan gave Norquist but enjoyed Norquist's expression even more.

"Getting back to Hansen," Dan said, "when was the last time you saw him?"

Margery bundled up the postcards and slipped a rubber band around them. After pushing reflectively on her lower lip with an index finger, she said, "I think it was just a day or two before Naomi died. He returned some books."

Frank Norquist's eyes opened wider.

"What kinds of books?" Dan asked.

"A couple of novels and a book of French poetry. One of the novels was Grisham's *The Pelican Brief.* I remember he said he liked it. He told me he was leaving the next day for Miami."

Dan felt a jolt. "Miami?"

"That's what he said."

"Any idea why he was going there?" Dan asked, excitement rising.

"He was trying to line up finances to set up a clinic in French Guiana. I suppose that's why he took out the *Appolinaire.* He must have wanted to brush up on his French before he left."

A startled look came into her eyes. "Oh my," she whispered before she could catch herself. When she looked up, she didn't like Frank Norquist's sharp expression.

"Something the matter," Dan asked.

"No. I just remembered I need to pick something up from the post office before it closes."

"Is there anyone around here Dylan was friendly with?" Dan asked. "Anyone he may have stayed in contact with?"

"Sorry," Margery said, shaking her head. "I can't think of anyone."

Dan turned to Norquist. "How about you, Frank?"

"No idea," Norquist said with a knowing smile. "I think Margery may have known him a bit better than I did, anyway."

Margery's eyes narrowed. She cursed herself when she realized she was blushing.

"Okay," said Dan. "Thanks for you help. I think we better be going, Frank. Ms Bellamy needs to get back to work."

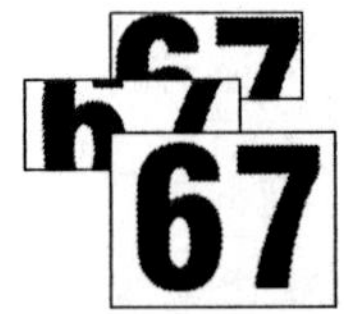

BACK ON THE STREET, Dan turned to Norquist. "Care to comment?"

Steely-eyed, the sheriff growled, "Every community has its stories. I'm surprised Margery would mention such silly rumors to you. Ridiculous woman."

"Rumors or not, it's the first I've heard about any of this."

"Okay," Norquist said with an indignant snort. "If you want to bust my chops, go right ahead. What more can I say than it never occurred to me that Hidden Pines or any of Melanie's family had the least bit to do with her murder? That's the only reason I didn't include any of the background in my report."

Guess I can't blame you for just being stupid, Dan thought. *Or maybe not.*

He had a strong feeling that stupidity wasn't the real reason Norquist had done such a lousy job. "Calm down," Dan said in a condescending voice. "I'm not blaming you, Frank. Would you mind giving me a ride to Hidden Pines?"

"How much farther is it?" Dan asked, craning to watch a ringneck pheasant dash into the ditch on his side of the car. It was the only sign of animal life he had seen in what seemed to be hours. A verdant carpet of soybeans began after they turned off the main road and preceded them all the way they had traversed.

"About another five miles," Norquist mumbled.

Dan marveled at the well-maintained road without potholes or turn-offs. Other than the crops and irrigation equipment, only an occasional harvester or soil disc evidenced that anyone ever even ventured this way. "This really is the boonies," he murmured, taking another toke from his thermos cup. Besides whatever other faults Frank Norquist had, he sure made lousy coffee.

"The clinic wants to maintain its image and its privacy," the sheriff said with a shrug. "This road gets a lot of use."

"The county must have to pay plenty for the upkeep."

"Not a cent," Norquist replied. "This is actually a private road. It's more than ten miles long and the clinic itself pays for it."

"Are you saying no one else uses the road?"

"Not legally," Norquist said. With a sly smile he added, "But then the clinic doesn't patrol. They know farmers use it to get to their fields."

"It must cost a fortune to maintain."

"It does. One of my cousins has the contract. Some people say he's worth more than the whole city put together."

"You say you do the permits for them?"

"I just process them. Sam Sherburn is Hidden Pine's attorney. He's in Minneapolis if you want to look him up."

"I'll do that," Dan said, writing the name down. "Does the county get the money from the permit processing?"

"It pays a good part of my salary. I couldn't live on what they raise in taxes."

"You say you visit Hidden Pines once a day. For security reasons?"

"Yes. They have a direct line if they have an emergency, but I try to keep an eye on the place. As Margie said, they're a huge part of the whole county's economy."

Dan nodded and turned his attention back to the landscape. Now soybeans were giving way to an occasional protruding rock and tract of scrub pine. Ahead, conifers grew larger and more numerous. "We must be getting close," he said.

"Just a couple of miles farther."

"Has anyone ever wandered off from the clinic?"

"Not that I'm aware of. The clinic's more worried about outsiders trying to get in. Patients are required to regularly leave the building for exercise as part of the rehab program, but they always have an attendant with them." Norquist paused, then resumed, chuckling. "Too bad you didn't come on Friday. They serve antelope. I always manage to pay a visit then myself. But if you're hungry, I'm sure they can find you something to eat."

Dan glanced at the sheriff's midsection. The age-old business custom of feeding cops had done marvels for Frank Norquist's girth. The words also reminded Dan of his own empty stomach. "We'll see," he said.

Driving on, Norquist's maroon Ford Victoria passed more and more dense growths of pines until Dan felt swallowed up in the continuous stands that blocked out much of the sun.

"So this is what they call 'hidden pines,' huh?"

"I s'pose they had to call it something," Norquist mumbled.

"'Hidden in the Pines' would be more to the point."

They lapsed into silence until Norquist pulled to a stop at a gate in front of a small concrete building.

The door opened and a uniformed guard came out, clipboard in hand. Norquist opened his window.

"Afternoon, Frank," the guard said. "You're around at a strange time. Too late for lunch and too early for dinner."

The sheriff threw an embarrassed grin in Dan's direction. "Professional courtesy call, Will." He introduced Dan, and the guard nodded. "Dan's reopening the investigation into the murder of Mr. Dumont's wife."

The guard's eyes darted across the clipboard. "Arnold," he said, shaking his head. "I don't see his name on the list."

Norquist looked over at Dan, then back to the guard. "Sorry. I tried to call you. I wasn't expecting him, either."

Throwing Dan a steely look, the guard raised the gate. "I see. Okay. I'll let Tess know you're on your way."

PHONE RECEIVER TO EAR, Marcel Digus listened to Jennifer Cahill's phone ring. Just as he was about to give up and try later, she answered.

"*Bon jour, Ma'mselle. C'est* Marcel Digus. *Comment ça va?*"

"*Tres bien, merci. Et vous?*"

"*Moi aussi.*"

"*Bien.* Are you calling from Cayenne?"

"*Oui.* I apologize, but I felt it was necessary."

"No apology necessary. Did our little ruse work?"

"*Perfectement.* But it seems *le bon docteur* hasn't picked up his mail for years."

"Oh no!"

"Despair not. All is not lost. I showed the picture you sent to the man who has been collecting Doctor Hansen's mail. He wasn't sure it was the same person, but he is willing to help. I know a very fine artist who should be able to draw a sketch from his description."

"Wonderful!"

". . . Provided Mssr. LeClerc is compensated for his valuable time, of course." Digus continued. "He wants one hundred and fifty Euros. I think the price is outrageous. I'm sure I can get him to accept half of that."

"Don't argue!" Jennifer shot back. "Can you find a computer and scanner to send it to me by email as soon as it's done?"

"Perhaps, but I think it would be easier if I sent it the same way we trapped Antoine—by express mail."

"Do that, too, but I'm anxious to see what the mysterious doctor looks like now." She paused. "Oh. I've sent you a check for three hundred Euros."

"*Tres gentile, mam'selle. Merci beaucoup.*"

"*De rien, mon amie.*"

"Forgive my memory," Marcel said. "He also mentioned getting a letter about a safety deposit box."

"This sounds important," Jennifer said. "Tell me about it."

After Marcel finished, she said, "Thanks for everything you've done. *Vous être magnifique.*"

AT FIRST GLANCE, the clinic, nestled among the trees, had a rustic appearance. As they drove closer, the perspective changed dramatically. Rustic quickly became glam. A fleet of Bentleys and Rolls Royces stood at the ready on a circular concrete apron that surrounded a flag pole flying the Stars and Stripes over the maroon Minnesota flag. Below these, a large green pennant with the letters "DP" drooped limply in the quiet afternoon sun. The air hung heavy with dust and the odor of dry pine needles.

Though Minneapolis was off to a wet summer, Northern Minnesota still needed several inches of rain to end its drought after an unusually early spring.

"Nice cars," Dan said, gesturing toward one of the Bentleys that had been outfitted with a handicap lift. "Where do the trucks park? Around the back?"

"No," Norquist said quickly. "They handle everything here. The sidewalk just leads to a big outdoor pool. If you want, they'll show it to you."

Dan nodded, though he noticed something that looked suspiciously like tire rubber on the edge of the walkway.

A uniformed valet appeared from the clinic as Norquist pulled to a stop. "Good afternoon, Sheriff," the young man said.

"Afternoon, Travis."

Dan got out of the car and stretched. A tall blonde woman came out of the building to meet him Dan's heart skipped a beat as his eyes moved from the unisex trousers and suit coat to her open-lipped smile and enticing eyes.

"Good afternoon," she said in a business-like tone. "You must be Lieutenant Arnold."

Dan took the pampered hand.

"I'm Tess Swanson." Taking his arm, she guided him toward the door. "Please remove your shoes when we get inside the building. We have some very comfortable slippers waiting for you."

Dan sniffed the odor of pine as he removed his shoes. Crossed fly rods, shotguns, hung with antique sporting photos showing men holding big fish and standing next to dead deer.

"Like it?" Tess asked.

"Very quaint. It looks like a hunting lodge."

"Watch," Tess said as she pushed a button on what looked like a television remote. The rear wall opened up.

Dan's mouth drooped. The quiet strains of a violin and the aroma of herbs immediately assailed his senses. In the center of a large room, a sizable circular fountain trickled mud where a middle-aged woman dressed in a towel sat with feet dangling in the fountain.

"Ever had a mud bath?" Tess asked in a mischievous tone.

"Nope. It's a bit too girly for me. I've watched women mud-wrestle, though."

Her laugh sounded like tinkling glass. "Shame on you. Actually mud baths are very relaxing. Mud provides more benefits than sitting in a Jacuzzi. It has something to do with the slow flow and viscosity. The mud is heated to 102 degrees and it's very soothing.

"We have four saunas and aromatherapy rooms and twenty-four-hour acupuncture service. We offer lessons in transcendental meditation. We just added this section to the clinic in the last six years, and we're constantly updating or adding new equipment. It's our preferred treatment area, and we hope everyone'll end up here sooner or later. Unfortunately, many of our patients have pain too severe to respond to natural cures."

Dan found his eyes being drawn deeply into hers. It made his heart race. She was the perfect person to be the clinic's spokesperson. Having an uninvited guest didn't faze her, and few men would be likely to pay the slightest attention to what she was saying when she was talking. He imagined she had a male counterpart somewhere else in the clinic with the same abilities.

"Um, what do you do for the severe cases?"

"It depends on the condition. We treat fibro-myalgia differently from disc injury problems or advanced cancer. We always try to start with a fairly heavy regimen of muscle relaxants and massage. Sometimes electro-stim alone is enough to bring some relief, though most patients have tried that themselves long before they come here."

With a press of a button, another door opened to reveal an Olympic-sized pool surrounded by exercise equipment. "This is the physical therapy area. You probably are already familiar with the exercise tracks. We have three physical therapists working on a rotating twenty-four hour schedule and continuous lifeguard service."

"Nice."

More eye contact and more teeth. "You probably can't smell the food because of the chlorine, but we have a Michelin three-star chef who superintends the kitchen. Ever had pate of hummingbird liver with truffle garnish?"

"No, and I bet you haven't had it either because there isn't any such thing."

She loosed another delightful laugh. "How did you know?"

"I just did. I'm not much of a gourmet, but I have had Kopi Luwak coffee. If you have that around here, I'd be really impressed."

"Actually we do," Tess responded. "We roast our own beans. I'll have the kitchen make some for you. Let me show you the dining area. We had duck a l'orange and a nice montrachet for lunch. I think we might have some left if you would like to try it."

"Cool," Dan said. Looking around, he asked, "Where are the wards?"

Tess's eyes flitted quickly at Norquist. "They're farther back in the building. Unfortunately, we don't allow visitors into them. Confidentiality is our biggest concern. Some of our guests would be mortified if they were to be seen and recognized."

Dan nodded.

"I can let you get a glimpse of the nursing station for one of the wards." She led him to what could have been a knothole in a fence. "Take a look."

Dan saw a large circular desk ringed by uniformed nurses and white-coated doctors. A line of computers covered the whole circumference, with another tier of monitors hanging from the ceiling.

"It looks like an intensive care unit."

"Very similar, and we do have cardiac patients. We also have world-class palliative care. Many of our patients have come here to spend their last hours with us. We're prepared for everything."

Dan shivered, remembering his father's final hours: the gaping mouth above an immense slack jaw, the short, noisy breaths fed by the plastic tube stretched from ear to ear. Pops never awoke from his coma. Dan didn't really believe the nurse when she said that his beloved father could hear him, much as he wanted to. Shaking off the memory, Dan pasted on a broad smile. "Where do you serve the Brompton's Cocktails?"

Before she could catch herself, Tess' eyes opened wide in surprise. Then, putting on another killer smile, she said, "I'm afraid I don't know what you mean. We sometimes serve something stronger than wine on special occasions with a doctor's approval. Is there something you would like?"

"Thanks, no. Ha ha. Just a joke." Time to put himself into what could be considered a compromising position, he decided. Sometimes it was the only way to learn things. "Actually I am a bit hungry. Are you in a hurry to get back, Frank?"

"Nope. Have a ball."

"I'd like that cup of coffee," Dan said, flashing a lascivious smile in Tess' direction. "And the duck. At least for now."

"I'll tell the kitchen." Tess turned to Norquist. "Why don't you do an inspection tour, Frank. I'll make sure Dan gets what he wants."

70

AT EXACTLY FIVE O'CLOCK, Jason showed up at Jennifer's office. Catching sight of him in her monitor as she was restacking the pile of files, she rushed out to meet him.

"I must have lost track of time," she said, beaming. "Do you want to come to my apartment, or should we go to your hotel? I'd like to see your room. Maybe I can help you remember, too."

"Actually, I may not need much help. But you're certainly welcome to come."

She pulled on a wide-brimmed hat that Holly Golightly could have worn in *Breakfast at Tiffany's*. Taking his arm, she said, "I bought this today. Like it?"

"It's definitely you."

"You're sweet. By the way, I got the car back. There wasn't much damage, considering."

Jason scowled. "I'm getting the idea it may not have been an accident."

"Why do you say that?"

"Just a feeling. I'm pretty sure I'm being followed again. I'm even sure someone down the hall ducked back when I went back into my room after getting something out of the soda machine."

Jennifer grasped his arm. "That sounds serious. Do you suppose someone tampered with the gas in your plane?"

"That occurred to me, too. I even called Bolton field service and talked to the grounds crew. They couldn't understand how it happened, either."

"I'll grant you that you have reason enough to worry." Pulling on his arm, she said, "Come with me. I want you to meet someone."

"Your mother?"

"No, silly. My best friend."

Marilyn was stepping out of her office when they reached the hall. "Hi, Jen." She left her key in the door to look Jason over. "My goodness. Who's this?"

"I'll give you three guesses," Jennifer said.

"You're Jason? I've heard a little about you . . . every half-hour or so for the last week." She enjoyed Jennifer's blush, then hugged him. "I've been dying to meet you."

"This is Marilyn Reid," Jennifer said. "Better get used to her sense of humor."

"It'll be a pleasure," Jason said.

"Do you need a ride home?" Marilyn asked.

"Jason and I are going to take a look at Lottie's hotel room. We're hoping I can help him remember."

"Uh, huh," Marilyn's tone added a "likely story" hint.

"Think what you like," Jennifer said primly. "It's the truth."

"Would you walk me to my car? I don't like the ramp after hours, and I don't want to ask the guard."

"Of course," Jennifer said.

The guard eyed them as they left, but the women ignored him. Marilyn's parking spot was next to Jennifer's space. All four doors of the red Achieva popped open as she pushed a button on a tiny black remote.

"Thanks for escorting me. I'll see you tomorrow, Jen."

Jennifer said, "Let's get your phone out of my trunk."

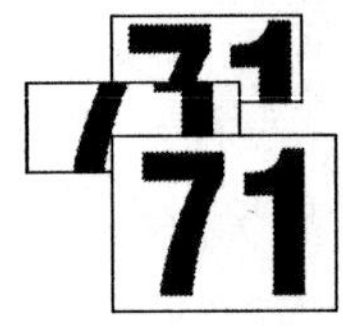

DAN FOUND TESS watching him with bemused hazel eyes as he finished the last of the duck. He'd enjoyed the meal. Nothing tasted even remotely of being reheated. He also enjoyed the astringency of the montrachet wine with its slightly greenish tinge. Everything, from the steamed baby broccoli garnished with grated truffles to the radishes with a duck on the wing carved on them, spelled class.

Obviously the chef had fixed it just for him. The evening meal—lobster or beef tenderloin in some unpronounceable wine sauce—wouldn't be ready for another hour.

As much as he had enjoyed the meal, neither the duck nor the wine pleased him half as much as what had been in the now-empty coffee carafe. It fed his newest addiction, Kopi Luwak. He knew he would be spending a good chunk of his paychecks on it from now on. He even knew of one coffee shop that offered it by the cup.

The pleasant thoughts disappeared. *How many real addicts were there at Hidden Pines?*

The librarian's light-hearted words had planted seeds that were now in full bloom. In the nearly ninety years since its founding, the list of Hidden Pines patients must have grown exponentially by repeat business, word-of-mouth and successive generations. Even more intriguing, if the clinic had begun as a playground for the super-rich, why couldn't it still be just that? Only the prices and the drugs would be different.

Then he remembered the road and tried to imagine all the equipment that must have traveled over it in those years, too.

"Would you like more coffee with your crème Brule?" Tess asked. "Jean-Paul will be more than happy to brew more for you."

Dan considered it, even wondering if he dared ask them to fill his thermos for the trip home, but decided against it. Even accepting the meal crossed professional boundaries best left unbreached. Fortunately, this was line of duty. "No, thanks. I'll have to get on the road pretty soon. I have a long drive ahead of me."

"Too bad," she said, her laugh the sound of tinkling glass. "We would be happy to put you up for the night."

The idea appealed. Dan was surprised to realize how easily she could seduce him with her laugh alone. He also suspected that she might have intended to do just that.

"We're always happy when our guests have hearty appetites," she smiled. "It shows they're on the road to recovery. How long have you been with the police?"

"Twenty-three years. I started after I graduated from St. Olaf."

"It looks as if you've kept in shape. Do you work out?"

"Twice a week," he said.

"So do I." With lowered lashes, she asked, "Does your wife work out with you?"

"That would be nice, but I'm not married."

"Oh," she said. Dan couldn't miss the note of feigned pleasure in her response. "I'm surprised. Do you enjoy working with Frank?"

For an instant, Dan imagined himself exercising with a sweating Frank. The thought sickened him. "Actually, I hadn't even spoken to him in fifteen years, and only briefly then. He seems pleasant enough, but I really don't know him very well. Does he come here often?"

"All the time," she replied, sounding bored. "What kinds of cases do you usually handle?"

"I investigate murders and cold cases. Melanie Dumont's case is both."

"How interesting," she said.

Dan maintained eye contact for several seconds before backing away.

Tess was a highly skilled temptress. The best he had ever met.

One of his colleagues, Nick Polezzio in vice, had spoken of one like her he had encountered during a sting operation. Entirely by accident, as it were.

Many wealthy businessmen didn't like the idea of hiring a prostitute in the usual way, so they would work with an escort service to arrange what seemed to be entirely chance contacts with attractive women. The favorite way to do it was for the client to furnish an itinerary, leaving it up to the woman to arrange to meet the customer somewhere along the way. To add to the feeling of spontaneity, they sometimes didn't make contact at all during a particular trip, so some amorous adventures could actually be non-commercial. The hooker's skill was such that her customer would never know one way or another.

It took nearly a month before Nick made contact.

Licking his spoon clean of the last of his crème brule, Dan met Tess's smile.

He was sure she had never lacked for anything in her adult life. Ordinary prostitution began when battle-widowed women were forced to follow the war camps to survive. Tess, on the other hand, was descended from priestesses of the Oracle of Delphi, specially trained to serve the desires of the powerful and wealthy. While the camp-followers were paid subsistence wages by their customers who had little to spend, the priestesses lived lives of luxury. Tess undoubtedly made a six-figure salary. Dan was sure Frank Norquist had succumbed to her long ago, most likely at his first opportunity.

How far would she go with Dan? There was only one way to find out for sure.

"This is great," he said. "How much does the clinic charge per day? I may want to come here some time."

"I'm afraid that would eat up your entire paycheck," she said in a playful tone, "but I'm sure we could arrange a special rate. Are you ever troubled by back pain or muscle tension in your neck and shoulders?"

"All the time." He paused meaningfully. "Do you do massages?"

Tess didn't react to his leer. "Not personally, but we have several skilled masseuses who would be happy to serve you."

As she said it, a white-coated young man appeared from nowhere to take the dishes away, and just as promptly disappeared.

Dan sat up, trying to see where the wraith had gone. "Too bad. I wouldn't want to work with anyone else but you."

"That would be fun. Maybe I could arrange something for later on this afternoon. I could arrange to have the pool to ourselves."

"I didn't bring my suit."

"Mine is in the laundry," she said with a husky laugh.

Dan shook himself back to reality. "Darn. It's too bad I have to get back to Minneapolis. I have to be in my office tomorrow morning. I should probably pay for the meal, too."

An invisible switch turned off at the words. "I understand," she said in a business-like tone. Her smile no longer was playful. "I'm sure we can find a way to bill you."

"Thanks. How many patients do you normally have?"

"Usually upwards of a hundred."

"And how long do they stay?"

"Anywhere from two weeks to several months." She got to her feet. "Is there anything else I can get you or do for you?"

"You can show me the grounds. Frank can wait a bit longer."

"Of course," she said with a low-candlepower grin. "Come with me."

Dan counted his paces as they walked the wide sidewalk along the building to the swimming pool. He still had no idea of the physical dimensions of the place, but the fenced-in pool area was at least thirty yards from the front of the building.

By the pool, a lone graying female puffing out around a green and red bikini sipped a drink under an umbrella. Beside her sat a beefy male who looked barely old enough to shave. No one else was in the pool, and the empty lifeguard chair suggested the young man was the one on duty. Inside the fence, three onion-bulb shaped air-conditioning vents turned lazily in the hot wind.

"It looks like there's more of the clinic underground," he said.

"There's a lot more. I really wish I could show you the whole facility. It's a fascinating place, and I keep finding new things all the time myself."

Looking around, Dan noticed a circular keyhole in the blank back wall and quickly turned his attention elsewhere. "Thanks for the tour," he said. "I have one last question for you. Would you see if you can find out if a man named Dylan Hansen worked here about fifteen years ago?"

"Certainly. But that's long before I came here."

"I know. Start about fifteen years ago and work backward."

Tess frowned. "I don't think our records go back that far, but I'll see what I can do."

Dan took her hand. "I really want to thank you for your help. I have a much clearer picture of the clinic, now."

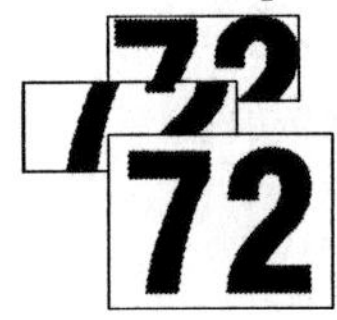

JASON SLIPPED THE plastic card into the lock slot and a green light flashed. Opening the door, he gestured for Jennifer to step in. "Getting any creepy-crawlies?" he asked.

"No," she replied. "How about you?"

"Not right this minute. I did earlier."

Jennifer slipped off her hat and set it on a rack above where Jason had hung his clothes. "Do you think anyone was following us?" she asked.

"I don't know. It isn't a very long walk."

Jennifer looked into the bathroom and shuddered.

"This is where mother slept," Jason said, gesturing toward the nearest bed.

She eyed the stuffed rabbit. "Did our long-eared friend bring any inspiration?"

"Sort of. Somehow it gave me a sense of what it was like to be with her again. I'm a little hungry. Should I order something from room service?"

"I just want a salad. I'll share it with Mr. Rabbit." She picked it up. "I like him. He's cute."

The toy had a slightly musty odor. She examined the legs, the bib overalls, then the striped tee shirt. About to put it back on the pillow, she noticed the buttoned pocket on the front of the overalls. Curious, she nearly tore the button loose to find out what was inside. Pushing a finger in, she squealed, "There's something in here!"

Jason moved next to her.

"It's a card."

They both peered closely. "'From Prince Dy with all my love. Valentine's Day, 1985,'" she read. They stared at each other. "You say there's another rabbit like it at home?" she asked.

"It's been sitting on her bed since Mother died. Father wanted to donate her things to a local charity, but I've never let him."

Jennifer's heart beat faster. "This has to mean something. We have to get it."

"I'll call Father and ask him to have Louise send it."

She put out a restraining hand. "No. I don't think it would be a good idea to ask your father." Staring into his eyes, she said, "Why don't you ask Louise directly?"

He shrugged. "I suppose I could. But why?"

"There may be some things Melanie didn't want your father to know about. Would Louise ask your father's permission before sending it?"

"If he were home she probably would. But he's at another one of his conferences. She probably wouldn't mention it to him if I asked her not to. I'll call her."

Jennifer listened as Jason dialed. When Louise answered, Jason switched to the speaker.

"Why Jason," said a delighted voice. "Where are you?"

"In Mother's hotel room. Has Father left for San Francisco yet?"

"Yesterday afternoon. His plans changed, though, and I'm not sure where he is now. I was just about to go out for the evening."

"Before you do, would you do me favor and send me Mr. Rabbit from Mother's bed?"

Louise hesitated, "I suppose I could. Why do you want it?"

"I'm hoping it'll help me remember. Just have FedEx pick it up."

"It's too late for that."

"Then take it to the airport. They have twenty-four hour express service there. Please. It's important, and I need it as soon as possible."

Louise hesitated. "Well, okay. I'm sure Mr. Dumont won't mind. Where do you want it sent?"

Jennifer broke in. "Hi, Louise. I'm working with Jason as his therapist. You can send it to my office."

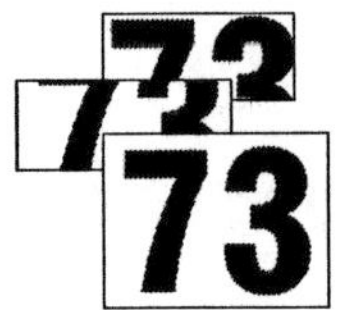

FRANK NORQUIST WASTED no time getting back from Hidden Pines, pushing sixty-five all the way.

"Got a date, Frank?" Dan asked.

"Nope," Norquist said, taking a look at his watch. "I just want to make sure you get a good start getting back to Minneapolis before it gets dark. I know the HP around here. He usually hangs out around a bend in the road a few miles south, so be sure to keep your speed down until you're through Mahnomen. If he stops you, he'll give you a ticket even though you're a cop."

"Good for him. Actually, I'm in no great hurry to get back, but thanks for the lowdown."

"How'd you like the duck?"

"Incredible. I'm no expert, but it seemed to be different from any I've had before."

"It probably was," Norquist replied, obviously anxious to show off his culinary knowledge. "Canvasback is a delicacy. I shot one once, and when it hit the ground, its stomach burst open from all the grain it had eaten." He paused. "What'd you think of Hidden Pines?"

"It's pretty spectacular, at least as much as I got to see of it. Tess is gorgeous, of course."

"For sure," Norquist said, making a face.

Dan smiled at the expression. "Does she live in town?"

"No. She has an apartment at the clinic—a god-damned New York penthouse."

How do you know? Dan wondered, the smile turning into a wide grin.

They rode back in silence. Dan dozed off and awoke at Norquist's voice. "We're at 152 West First Street. All ashore that's going ashore."

As Dan got out and started toward his car, he said, "Thanks for all the help."

"Glad to be of service," Norquist said, taking his cell phone out of his pocket. "Be sure to let me know if you find out anything."

"Sure. Going for the night?"

"No. I've got something to take care of first."

Where the heck is that book? Margery Bellamy fretted. She had been through the volumes in the 841 section twice, hoping she had misshelved it. Otherwise, someone had walked off with it.

She certainly hoped not. The *Appolinaire* was one of the most important works of nineteenth-century French poetry. Even though no one ever checked it out, she wanted to make sure it was always available.

Wait. She stopped. Eyes narrowing, she made a beeline for her office.

Snatching up the phone receiver, she dialed, so angry her fingers seemed to stick in the dial holes. The sound of Madison Devereux's voice set her off.

"It's Margery Bellamy," she blurted. "Do you remember I gave you a list of books to move to the basement?"

"Yes," came Madison's wary answer.

"Do you remember if there were any books of French poetry?"

"I don't remember. Am I in trouble?"

"Maybe. An important book is missing from the shelf. It occurred to me you may have taken it downstairs by mistake."

Madison choked back a sob. "If I did, I didn't do it on purpose."

Margery relented. "No. I'm sure it was just a mistake. When I got to work this morning, I found out you incorrectly alphabetized some of the circulation cards, though. Please be more careful in the future. Do you remember where you put the books the last time you were in the basement?"

"Um . . . they're on the second shelf from the bottom in the rack at the far end on the left when you come down the stairs."

"Okay. I think I can find them. When will you be coming in?"

"I should be there in ten or fifteen minutes."

ANXIOUS TO FIND the *Appolinaire*, but not wanting anyone to think the library was closed, Margery left the entrance unlocked and headed to the basement door.

She had first discovered it at age eight on a visit to the library with her mother. After she did, she was absolutely determined to see what lay hidden behind that door.

One day, she got her chance. Miss Dexter's third-grade class had descended unexpectedly on poor Miss Frances Shanahan. Flustered, Miss Shanahan left the door open, and while the two women busied themselves getting books for the students, Margery slipped away to investigate.

She imagined she'd find a treasure trove of forbidden books. Witchcraft maybe. Or books about sex, whatever that was. Or maybe exciting tales about dirt-poor young heroines rescuing princes imprisoned in dank dungeons. But to find out she would have to follow a dark stairway leading down to an even darker cellar.

Her adventure ended before it started. Miss Shanahan noticed her and called her to join the group sitting on the floor between the stacks.

It took more than twenty years before Margery opened that door again, this time as the new Thief River Falls librarian. The payoff wasn't worth the wait. Instead of hidden treasures she found a cellar full of obsolete books and countless folios of newspaper clippings. Frances Shanahan and her predecessors had documented every imaginable bit of local news. Engagements, weddings and death announcements, posters for upcoming class plays, and important items such as Willard Oslund killing a ten-point buck on opening day of hunting season in 1961 all found their way into the library's scrapbooks.

However trivial much of the material might seem to most people, the clippings provided grist for the historical society. For that reason, Margery constantly evaluated documents and transferred important ones to the farm whenever she had a chance.

Her feet thudded hollowly on the stone floor. Gooseflesh gathered as she found the shelf Madison had indicated. She was sure no one had even looked at the book after Dylan returned it. For years she had always thought that he took it out to improve his French before moving to South America. Now she wondered if he had meant it to be a hiding place for a special message for her.

Could there be a love letter inviting her to come with him? If so, she would regret the lost years they could have spent together for the rest of her life.

Fortunately, they still had time.

Yeah right, she thought, shaking her head at her own naiveté.

Here we are.

Squatting, her sharp eyes scanned through the dusty books. Nearly all were without jackets. One she recognized was an air raid warden's instruction book from the Second World War. Next to it, a brown, cloth-bound copy of Dale Carnegie's, *How to Win Friends and Influence People.*

She duck-walked three steps farther down the shelf and sucked in a sigh of relief when she saw *Appolinaire* reposing between books on badminton and natural healing.

Hands shaking, she pulled it free. Her heart thumped as she opened the back cover. There, in faded brown ink, was stamped NOVEMBER 1, 1990, and the painfully small signature of Dylan Hansen.

Feeling like a child opening a Christmas present, Margery took the book by its covers and held it with the pages down.

Her heart skipped a beat as a heavy envelope fell to the floor.

I was right!

Though there was barely enough light to see, she set the book on the shelf and picked up the envelope.

She recognized Dylan's handwriting immediately.

Her heart raced as she took out a single folded sheet of bond that bent under the weight of something attached to it.

From its outline she realized it was a key.

Heart tripping in anticipation, she unfolded the letter.

After a brief stop at the local McDonald's on Highway 59 South to fill his thermos, Dan started his southeasterly trek, intending to drive straight through. He changed his mind and made a detour when he saw the sign for the Thief River Falls airport. Hidden Pines might be able to hide its true identity, but its clientele couldn't. They had to have some way to get from their homes to the clinic. More than likely, most of them had flown in.

Moving at a crawl, he made several turns onto dead-end service roads until he found one that gave him a view of the entire airfield.

Stepping out, he caught a whiff of airplane fuel. A white van, intended to carry elite passengers to the terminal, stood idly next to the in-coming door.

Beyond it, seven personal Lear jets regally lolled on the apron. He quickly fetched his binoculars from the glove compartment and wrote down the numbers of the three closest.

Then, with the sun fading over the horizon to the west, he climbed back into his Taurus for the long drive back to Minneapolis.

Where the hell is this all leading?

Angrily swiping at her eyes, Margery Bellamy slipped the letter back into the book and bravely headed for the stairway.

Thank you, Dylan. I can finally get over you.

As she started up, she heard a shuffling noise at the top of the stairs. "Is that you, Madison? I didn't expect you to be here so soon."

Her answer was the click of a light switch. Then the door closed, plunging her into total darkness.

Irritation gave way to terror that rapidly turned to burning rage. "Frank? Are you up there?" she demanded. "Damn you! Turn the light back on."

Her words fell hollowly.

"All right. I can find my way in the dark. When I get upstairs, you better run."

No answer.

What could she do? Margerie knew she could find her way up the stairway, but what awaited her beyond the door? And why did Frank resort to such a childish prank? She suddenly remembered how interested he seemed when she mentioned the *Appolinaire*. What difference could it have made to him?

"Listen. I've had enough of your bullying. You can go to jail for getting an underage girl pregnant. If anything happens to me, Tammi's going to report you."

Still no response.

Hands stretched in front of her, she started forward. All she had to do was walk straight ahead. Margery knew she was pointed in the right direction before the lights went off.

Her judgment was correct. Shins collided with the bottom stair.

Holding the book in front of her as a shield, she noiselessly climbed the first step. Teetering and almost losing her balance, she bent forward and felt for the steps with her free hand and toes. By crouching, she could keep her balance.

At last her hand met the door.

Here goes.

Opening it, she was about to step up when the door swung towards her with violent force. Caught completely by surprise, she fell backwards, arms flailing.

Damn you, Frank, was her last thought as she felt her head strike something hard and darkness envelope her mind.

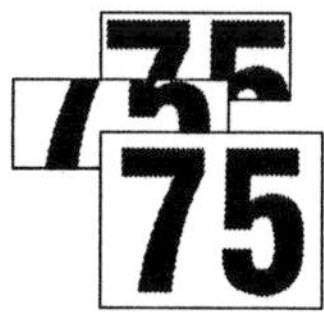

THE BELL ON the entrance to the library tinkled as Madison Devereux arrived dressed in hip-hugger jeans and a bandana top.

"Hi, Miss Bellamy," she called.

She stopped, puzzled by the silence. "Miss Bellamy?"

Noticing the door to the office was closed, she weaved her way through the book-laden chairs to open it.

"Hi," she said to an empty room.

She must be in the bathroom, Madison decided as she scanned the desk for a note with instructions for the day.

Instead of a note, she found scissors and scraps of paper. She also found an open bottle of rubber cement and a half-eaten strawberry licorice twist next to it.

She stood up straight at a noise coming from somewhere in the library.

"Miss Bellamy?"

Feeling anxious, Madison grabbed the scissors from the desk and slowly followed the side corridor around the bookshelves to the bathroom. After knocking on the door, she opened it. Empty.

She wheeled about at the sound of a footstep.

"Is that you, Miss Bellamy?" she shouted with a note of panic in her voice.

Heart pounding, she crept to the first bookshelf. Gathering up her strength, she peered around the end.

She sighed in relief.

After checking the rest of the shelves, she ran to the steps to the upstairs lounge.

"Miss Bellamy, are you up there?"

Becoming more uneasy by the second, Madison gripped the scissors tightly and started up the iron steps of the circular stairway. The sofa and stuffed chair stood empty.

That left only one place she could be. And Madison desperately didn't want to go there. Even the brief amorous session with Cameron hadn't done a thing to improve her feelings about the library's dungeon.

Her heart jumped in her throat when she saw the door to the basement ajar.

Miss Bellamy always kept it shut.

Swallowing, she reached out her hand.

The door creaked open.

"Miss Bellamy!" she cried, choking back a scream with her hand.

She found the light switch with a shaking hand. One look down into the basement, and Madison did let loose a scream. Then she raced down the stairs.

"Miss Bellamy! Are you all right?"

No answer, but she didn't see any blood on the stairway or by Margery.

Madison turned her onto her back. "Can you hear me?" she cried.

The stricken librarian didn't move. Madison cradled Margery's head in her lap. Finally working up the courage to move, she said, "I'll call 911," and raced back upstairs.

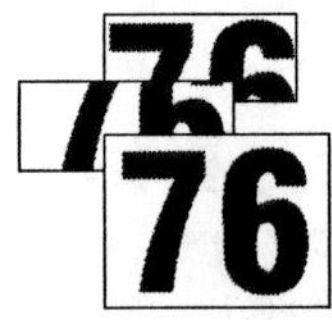

AS JENNIFER FINISHED her salad, Jason held out a slice of his jalapeno and anchovy pizza to her. "This really is good," Jason he said. "Try it."

"Thanks for the offer, but I want to save room for my cookie."

He glanced at the salad-plate-sized cookie and nodded.

The notes of "When Johnny Comes Marching Home" sounded from his shirt pocket, and Jason pulled out his cell phone.

"Hi, Dad. Louise said your travel plans changed. Where are you now?"

"St. Louis."

"What's up?"

"I was just wondering how things were going with you. You're lucky to be alive after the problem with your plane."

"Is that why you've been having me followed again?"

"What do you mean?" Lawrence said, surprise sounding genuine.

"Don't play innocent," Jason said, grinning. "I've known I've been followed for years, so I know all the tricks."

"It's not me. Believe me."

Jason laughed again. "Sure." He wondered if he should mention the mishap with Jennifer's car and decided against it. "I'm glad you called. I'm really making progress. Mr. Rabbit will help a lot."

"Mr. Rabbit?" Dumont replied in a dark voice.

Jason glanced up at Jennifer and caught her concerned look. He took the meaning. "I mean Mr. Rabbit's brother. I found one just like the one on Mom's bed in one of the boxes she left at Uncle Dean's. We're having a lot of fun going through them, looking for clues."

Before Lawrence could comment, Jason heard a garbled voice in the background, "Welcome to Lindb . . ." The phone went dead for a moment.

"Sorry," Lawrence said.

Jason sat up. "Where are you? That sounded like a flight announcement."

"I just landed. I'll be done here in a day or two, then I'll fly to Minneapolis and meet you."

"We'll be glad to see you. With any luck, I'll have the whole story by then. Cheers."

JASON HUNG UP, and Jennifer put her hand on his shoulder. "Good work."

He recoiled at her touch, and she stepped back in surprise. "Sorry. I bet he wonders who you meant when you kept saying 'we.'"

No longer smiling, Jason said, "I think he can figure that out easily enough," in an inflectionless voice. "He just doesn't know how close we are."

The abrupt stop puzzled Jennifer. "What's the matter?" she asked.

"I don't know what made me think of this right now, but I remember I was in the bedroom the whole time mother was with . . ."

"Whomever," Jennifer helped, even more puzzled by his angry tone.

Jaw set, Jason became even more animated before he continued. "Yeah. Well, I got out of bed and listened through the bathroom door. I could hear her moaning, and I was afraid someone was hurting her. I tried to open the door, but it was locked. Mother must have heard me because she said, 'I'm all right, Jason. Go back to bed.'"

Jennifer seethed. How could Melanie have continued having sex knowing her son was outside the door? Didn't she suspect that Jason might even tell Lawrence?

Her eyes opened wide at a new thought. What if she wasn't worried because she didn't intend to go back to her husband? Was her own mother's death the final liberation so she could begin life with her lover?

Jennifer took Jason's hand. "Did she say anything else?"

The pupils of his eyes dilated. "No. Mother came out and carried me back to my bed. Whoever was with her stayed inside the bathroom."

Jennifer felt a hint of alarm. "Then what happened?"

"Then she started to cry and she kissed me," he said, his breathing getting louder. "She made me promise I wouldn't get up again."

"I'm sure she did," Jennifer hissed. "That would have been an inconvenience."

He glowered at her.

"Sorry. What happened then?"

Beginning to tremble, Jason said, "All I remember is that I wrapped myself up in a ball and pulled the covers over my head. I was crying so hard I couldn't think."

"Did . . ." Jennifer began, unable to control her own tears. She gripped Jason's hand so hard that it hurt hers. "Did you . . . hear anything else?"

He yanked his hand free. Glaring, he said, "Yes. I heard them in the next bed. I kept myself from screaming, but if I had been bigger . . ."

The tone now frightened her. His expression even more. The pale face and wide eyes were familiar to her. Twice in her career she had to defend herself. Near tears, she reached into her pocket for the mace spray.

"I can understand why that made you angry."

Her grip tightened on the bottle as his face tightened into a terrifying grin. In her calmest clinical voice, she said, "I know you're upset, and that's actually a good sign. It means you're getting close to the truth."

Instead of answering, his jaw began to tremble. "Leave me alone!"

"You're frightening me, Jason," she said in a firm voice. Taking the bottle in the palm of her hand, she lifted it from her pocket. "I intend to help you but I won't let you hurt me."

His whole body stiffened.

"You know I love you and you can trust me."

Instead of relaxing, he tensed more. Finger ready on the spray trigger, she said, "I'm not your mother."

"Whore!" Jason exploded. Grabbing her left wrist, he drew back to slap her.

Terrified, she pushed the plastic plunger on the bottle.

"Bitch!" He screamed, tearing at his eyes. Then, seeming to forget his inflamed eyes, he struck out wildly.

She ducked beneath his flailing arms and dashed for the door.

Slamming the door behind her, she burst into tears at the last thing she heard. "I didn't mean to hurt you," Jason wailed. "I love you. Please come back!"

HEELS CLICKING, JENNIFER dashed for the fire escape, looking over her shoulder as she raced down the first flight. She opened the door and walked to the elevator, gripping the mace bottle tightly as the elevator door opened.

She rode to the lobby. Clear. She dashed to the lobby door and waited next to the doorman for the light to change. Seconds later it did, and she ran to the doors of the City Center

Jason wasn't waiting.

The doorman held the door open for her, but she waited for the crossing light on the walkway to turn green before coming out. When it did, she hurried across the street and entered the City Center. The building, with its enormous Atrium, was nearly deserted. It made her edgy. She wanted to find people.

With a look over her shoulder, she emerged into the dimly lit Sixth Street.

Seeing someone exiting the door behind her gave her a chill, but the young man in the green sweatshirt and beige cargo pants passed by her without a look in her direction.

She sighed in relief when she reached Hennepin Avenue. As she crossed Fifth Street to the Lumber Exchange, a shadowy figure on the other side of Hennepin seemed to be watching her and started across the street against the light.

Frightened, she ran the rest of the way to the Lumber Exchange lobby. Her heart skipped a beat when she saw the guard's desk empty.

Wide-eyed, she dashed for the stairway. She gasped for breath as she took the steps two at a time to the parking level. At the bottom, she looked back over her shoulder. Heart pounding, she cautiously opened the door. The path seemed clear to her parking space around the corner. Once again she cursed the parking ramp owner for not giving her a spot closer to the door.

After taking a deep breath, she dashed up the inclined toward her parking space.

Her lungs ached as she puffed in the hot air reeking of motor oil. The sound of a door opening made her heart thump. Uttering a cry, she took her remote car opener and pushed the unlocking button. Around the corner ahead, a horn honked.

I'm coming, baby.

Now she heard the sound of hurried footsteps behind her. Kicking off her shoes, she put on a burst of speed.

The footsteps sounded closer when she reached the car. She broke a fingernail snatching the door handle.

She dove into the seat and slammed the car door shut. Fingers fumbled for the door-lock button as she heard someone trying to open the passenger door, then the sound of a kick against it. Without taking the time to see who was trying to get in, she turned the ignition key and slammed the car into reverse. Hauling at the wheel with both hands, she swung backwards and screeched off without turning on the lights. Only at the top of the lane did she look back. A dark figure stood watching her drive away.

HEART BROKEN AND PANTING from exertion, Jason returned to the hotel room.

Jennifer had eluded him.

Sore-eyed, he walked to the bathroom sink and turned on the cold water.

What he saw in the mirror frightened him. The angry face of a seven-year-old boy stared back at him.

His mind suddenly filled with images of wild thrusts and spurting crimson. Was it a memory or what he imagined had happened? He couldn't tell.

What have I done?

Even if he hadn't killed his mother, he had as good as murdered the person he loved the most. Jennifer was gone forever.

The thought sent him to his bed for his cell phone. Punching in her speed dial number, he waited through the four rings until her voice message came on.

Despair turning to fear, he hung up and redialed.

His breath became shallower and he began to pant as he waited for Jennifer to answer. The recorded message played again. A vise tightened around his chest, and he began to shiver.

My medicine! Where's my medicine!

Shivers became shudders. Deep, bone-chilling fear sized his body.

The spark of reason burning out, Jason remembered what Mike Savich had taught him.

His aching eyes began to roll up in his head as he rushed into the bathroom to snatch up the wastebasket from under the sink. Barely able to control his fingers, he pulled out the plastic liner and gathered up the open end of the bag. He fell to the floor as he took the first deep breath and blew into the bag.

Waves of fear became a raging sea.

His reflection in the mirror seemed a blood-thirsty alien, the sound of his own breathing someone waiting to attack. His heart pounded and shudders coursed his body.

Then, as his rapid breathing continued to recycle over his fevered lips, a tightly-wound spring leaped free in his brain.

The alien in the mirror disappeared. Jason's image stared back at him with a look of amazement.

Head drenched in sweat and face afire, he took the bag away from his lips and took a normal breath. Though dizzy, a calm settled over his entire body.

The peace was short-lived. Seconds later, he began to shiver.

Certain he was in for another bout, he moved the bag to his mouth. Then he realized he was covered with goosebumps. The room was freezing. After vigorously rubbing his arms with his hands, he forgot the cold.

He calmly poured hot water into the sink. Filling his palms, he splashed the water against his face. Soothing warmth spread through his body. Finally restored, he went to his bed and gathered up the cell phone.

As he was about to push the memory button for his father's number, Jason's eyes opened wide.

Something wasn't right.

His mind flashed back to his arrival at the Minneapolis airport with his mother.

He dressed quickly and took the elevator to the lobby. The clerk, a pert Japanese woman, pointed him to the business lounge. Settling into the chair in front of the computer, he logged on to Google.

Seconds later he had the map for Lambert-St. Louis International Airport.

Scrolling down, he found Main Terminal and East Terminal.

Feeling his world was collapsing around him, he typed "Lindb . . . Terminal" into the search browser.

His heart beat faster as the words "Do You Mean Lindbergh Terminal?" in blue letters flashed at the top of the screen.

Holding his breath, he clicked on the link.

He shuddered. With more than one hundred pages of entries, all were for only one location—MSP International.

Dad was at the Minneapolis airport. He must have pushed the mute button to try to cut off the arrival announcement.

Why did he lie?

HEARTBROKEN, JASON RETURNED to his room and sat on the bed. His first inclination was to call his father and confront him. Then, changing his mind, he called Uncle Gary instead.

He brightened at the sound of a cheery greeting.

"Hi, Unc. What are you doing?"

"Why, Jason, nice of you to call. I was just going to start on my progress report notes. Speaking of progress, how are you doing?"

"I've remembered quite a bit, but I'm calling about Dad."

Gary's tone changed. "You sound unhappy. Has something happened?"

"Not exactly. Can you think of any reason why he'd be in Minneapolis and not tell me?"

"He's in Minneapolis?" Gary said in a worried tone. "Are you sure about that?"

"Yes."

"He may be on his way up to Thief River Falls. I know he's gotten some calls from the clinic, and he seemed worried about something. Maybe he didn't tell you because he didn't have any time to spend with you."

Jason nodded. "That's probably it. I need to ask you . . . was I . . . was I ever . . . violent when I was growing up."

"Hmm. Well, maybe once. You were at Grandma Grace's house and one of her neighbor's boys came over to play. She said you got into a serious argument and she had to pull you off him because you were sitting on his chest and . . ."

He stopped and Jason felt a chill. "And what?"

"She said you were choking him," Gary said slowly.

Crestfallen, Jason barely heard the words his uncle added so quickly. ". . . But boys do that when they fight, and you didn't really hurt him. I think she said you gave him a bloody nose. The next day you brought him with you to my house and everything was forgiven. You were both laughing, and we all had a good time together. He even came over to see me once or twice without you."

"We always had fun when we were together, didn't we?"

"Yes, but that's because you needed a father. I was more than happy to help."

"Do you know what caused the argument?"

"Apparently he said something about your mother you didn't like. You said something about his, and he pushed you. Mom said that's when you lit into him. She said there was more screaming than anything else. Why do you ask?"

"Something happened to me when I was little—not my mother's death—that made me very angry. It still crops up now and then and I don't know what it is."

"I'm sure it has to be related to your mother's death."

Jason's eyes lowered. "That's what I always thought, too, but now I'm not so sure. I still get mad when I think about it, and I haven't been able to bear the thought of her cheating on Dad. The anger I'm talking about is a different kind of feeling. It's more like abandonment or betrayal."

After a prolonged pause, Gary said, "That's understandable. Both your mother and father were gone a lot when you were little. I can imagine why you would have felt abandoned. I know that's how I felt when I was a child. Mother had to raise me by herself after father died."

"But you had a brother and a sister."

"Yvette and I get along great, but Lawrence and I were total opposites. He seemed to resent mother having me, and he didn't want anything to do with me. One time he ran into a tree when he was tobogganing, and he cut his head. I tried to comfort him, and he threw me into the snow and called me a queer. I'm pretty sure he still thinks I am."

Jason cringed. He never had any inkling of hard feeling between his father and uncle. "I can't imagine why he would. You've married for more than ten years and have a son. And even if you are gay or bisexual, so what? We've been out of the dark ages for quite a few years now."

Gary sighed. "He sees the world differently. I've never said anything to anyone about this before, and I don't want you to think any less of your father, but I've always been a little afraid of him. I think most people who know him are, too. He nearly killed a man who came on to him in a bar in Philadelphia. The guy had to be sent to the hospital, and Lawrence was charged with assault. It cost him more than ten thousand dollars to get the charges dropped. I'm convinced he wouldn't hesitate to do the same to me. I'm just not as vulnerable now as I was then."

Overwhelmed, Jason said, "I'm sure he wouldn't hurt you. He's always been grateful for your help. Mother was, too."

"Poor Melanie. My heart aches every time I think about her. I still remember the necklace with the little book she wore."

Jason had a fleeting memory of seeing it when he was bending forward to get her purse from the seat ahead of her on the plane.

Another thought pressed at Jason's mind. "What would happen to the business if anything happened to me?"

"Lawrence would have to produce another heir. He's the eldest, but he has to have an heir. Otherwise, the estate reverts to me because of Gary Junior. You'll have to produce an heir to maintain the inheritance. It's called primogeniture."

Wheels turned rapidly. "That must be why he's always been so concerned about my safety. What would you do with the business?"

"I'd make sure that everyone who needs them has access to the drugs. Of course, Lawrence thinks that's Socialist nonsense. He may be right. I've changed my mind about a few things myself after your grandmother left me some money."

"As far as I'm concerned, you're welcome to the business. Money doesn't interest me. To tell you the truth, I'm glad Dad is planning to get married. He can produce another heir, and I can drop out of the picture."

"I think Grandma Grace would like to hear that. Keep me posted on developments. What else is happening at your end?"

"Quite a bit," Jason said in a matter-of-fact voice. "For one thing I nearly attacked my therapist. I think I was getting too attached to her, and my psyche didn't like it."

"Is she all right?"

"Yes. She's a first-rate investigator. Did you ever hear of Dylan Hansen?"

Gary didn't answer immediately. "No-o-o. I don't think so. Who's he?"

"The police think he may have been mother's boyfriend. He moved to South America at almost the same time she was murdered. Jennifer, Dr. Cahill, has hired an investigator to try to find him."

Gary gasped. "You mean the police never investigated him before? What kind of incompetence is that?"

"They didn't even know about him until just a few days ago. Apparently the sheriff in Thief River Falls didn't do a very good investigation."

"Well, then, I hope they find him soon. He could have been the one who murdered her. Sorry to cut things off, but I have to run. Be sure to keep me posted on what's happening."

"I will," Jason said. "Good night."

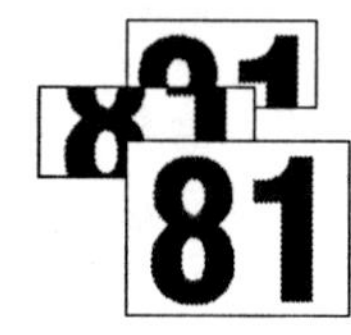

AFTER AN HOUR and a half drive, Jennifer arrived at the parking lot at her apartment building certain she hadn't been followed. Driving ten miles an hour and keeping a constant watch on her rearview mirror had reassured her, but she didn't feel secure until the door to the building complex clicked closed behind her

She absently located her mailbox key and opened the door.

With everything else she had to face in her life, Jason had created the greatest crisis of all, and she had no idea what to do about him.

Besides the personal anguish, she also had to face a professional dilemma. From the beginning she had never believed he was violent, so the possibility he had killed Melanie seemed remote, or, even if he did, it was the result of a rare psychological condition and discovering his mother with another man. She was certain he would never act that way again.

Now she wasn't so sure.

As she pulled out the assortment of ads and bills, Jennifer considered her next move.

Telling Dan Arnold what happened would only strengthen his belief in Jason's guilt. If the case ever went to trial, the attack would be evidence that Melanie's murder was not an isolated incident, but proof that Jason was still a threat to society.

If she didn't tell Dan, she would always have to live with the possibility that Jason would hurt someone else.

And yet . . .

She was sure Jason did love her, but she had somehow become a surrogate for his anger toward his mother. Given the time and proper treatment . . .

Heavy in heart and foot, she climbed the steps to the fourth floor. When neither of the cats came out to meet her when she opened the door to her apartment, she felt even more depressed.

She reached for her head to take off her hat, then remembered she had left it in the hotel room.

Finally giving in to her tears, she went to her room and fell on her bed sobbing.

BARELY ABLE TO keep his eyes open, Dan Arnold turned off I-94 ten miles southeast of Fergus Falls. An empty thermos and the long and monotonously straight trek down Highway 59 had taken its toll.

He had passed a MacDonald's on the way and wished he had stopped. Should he go back, or recline the seat and take a nap?

He decided to do neither and turned on the dome light over his head.

Gritting his teeth, Dan rummaged in his wallet for Charlie Jordan's phone number. He finally found it buried under an avalanche of coffee punch cards and credit cards.

After three rings, Charlie answered. "Hey, man, what's happening? I had given you up as dead. 'S'up?"

"I need a favor. I hope I didn't get you up."

"Nope. I'm actually still in the office."

Dan shook his head. Poor Charlie had contributed enough hours to fill two positions at the DEA and only got paid for one. A bean-counter demanding governmental accountability would rejoice; a union organizer would tear hair.

"Why don't you go home and spend some time with your wife once in a while?"

Charlie snorted. "She wouldn't like it. It would cut into the time she spends entertaining the neighbor boy. What can I do for you?"

"Have you ever heard of a pain treatment clinic called Hidden Pines in Thief River Falls, Minnesota?"

"Hold on."

Dan heard the click of keys. "Yeah. It's a huge outfit. The FDA audits them monthly and the Canadians have a man stationed at their pharmaceutical plant. Geez, they've been around forever. Why do you ask? We've never had any reason to suspect they were anything other than a legitimate operation."

"There's something going on at the clinic. They've got enough floor space for a small hospital."

"I'm sure there must be an explanation."

"They claim they're constantly upgrading their services with new equipment."

"It sounds reasonable to me."

Dan yawned. "If you knew the whole story, you'd be suspicious, too. I've met the owner of Maple Leaf Pharmaceuticals. If he had his way, you'd be out of a job."

"There's nothing illegal about that, either."

Dan snorted in exasperation. "Okay, let's go at this from another angle. Maybe you aren't allowed to tell me this, but have you had any unusually large supplies of any new drugs appearing on the street?"

After a short silence, Charlie answered in a worried tone, "As a matter of fact, we have. It's something the dealers call 'Shaz.' It's beat out crystal meth and crack cocaine because it's so much easier to come by."

"What is it?"

"It's a heroin derivative with some other ingredients we haven't been able to trace. The spectral analysis signature on it isn't like anything we know."

Dan nodded. The brave new age of technology allowed drug enforcers—and dealers, too—to tell what's in a chemical by the spikes on a computer monitor.

"What does this Shaz look like?"

"Brown powder in a gelatin capsule. Some of the street dealers we've busted say it's the best high they've ever come across. And the cheapest."

Dan wasn't surprised. Hidden Pines probably had been perfecting the recipe on their guests for years.

"Do you have any idea where it's coming from?"

"Successful drug dealers are like Al Qaida. They use the Internet and nobody knows the identity of those above them. We watch 'em, and they watch us watching 'em."

"I bet I can guess where and how it's being made."

"Yeah?" Charlie said with obvious interest. "It certainly hasn't been coming for south of the border. Our undercover people are sure of that."

"Just listen. Let's say we have a clinic that's been in operation from almost before Prohibition. It's calling itself a pain clinic but it's really a mini-Las Vegas where you can essentially get whatever you want if you have enough money. It's probably run on drugs and alcohol with a few lovely nurses thrown in since it opened. I don't know if they have slot machines, too, but it wouldn't surprise me. It probably also has been a semi-legitimate operation that made sure it had prescriptions for everything it dispensed to its patients."

"I'm with you so far."

"Good. Let's say the owners realized that the money was good, but a lot more could be made in other ways. One of the most lucrative would be even better—they could make and distribute their own drugs . . . Better still, they could always get the ingredients. Their only trouble would be that they couldn't disguise their products from the chemists."

"So far so good. Where ya going with this?"

"Be patient. This is a pharmaceuticals business that has been around for a long time. Every manufacturer has to replace equipment over the years. Does anyone keep tabs on what's done with equipment after it's retired?"

"Somehow I don't think so. I'm sure it must be sold as scrap.

"But what if it isn't scrapped. What if it gets sent across the border to the pain clinic in Minnesota?"

"I see. Very clever."

"That's only one part of the equation. Pharmaceutical companies are constantly developing new drugs and testing them with the FDA looking over their shoulder, right?"

"Yes," Charlie said with a chuckle. "And you already know how understaffed we are. I think I see where you're going with this."

"I'm sure you do. What if the drugs administered at the pain clinic aren't the drugs named in the prescription records, but actually experimental drugs the clinic is testing?"

"Everything would seem to be on the up and up."

"Yes. And the drugs prescribed could be used for ingredients in the new products. Now we have ingredients and equipment."

"The only thing missing would be the space to make the stuff."

"And they have plenty of that at Hidden Pines, believe me."

Charlie whistled. "What you're saying is they're developing drugs the FDA knows nothing about and selling it on the Internet to the drug dealers."

"I rest my case."

"I don't know off hand if all this is possible, but it sure could be. Unfortunately there's no way to know for sure. And I wouldn't be able to get a go-ahead to find out based on speculation."

"I know," Dan said, eyes narrowing. "Good old probable cause. What if you watched the trucks coming and going for a while?"

"Maybe."

"Or how about checking with the patients? I took down the registration numbers of a few of the jets parked at the airport."

"Even if they admitted to coming here to party, they obviously wouldn't know what's going on, unless . . ."

Dan sat forward. "Unless what?"

"Unless we could run a tox screen on them just after they left the clinic. Unfortunately that would be even harder to pull off than getting a warrant to raid the place."

"There has to be a way . . ."

"Sure. Find me someone at the clinic who's willing to blow the whistle."

"Funny," Dan said with a sigh.

"Cheer up. And thanks for the call, Dan. I'll start spreading the word and see what can be done."

"Be sure and keep me in the loop," Dan said before he turned off the telephone. Now wide awake and clenching his teeth, he was ready for the rest of the long trip back to Minneapolis.

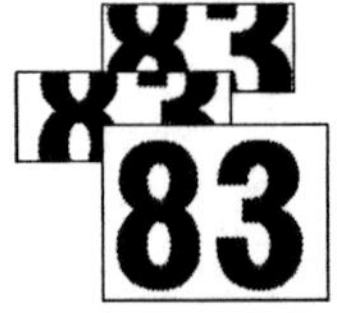

ANTOINE LECLERC ARRIVED at Marcel Digus' office at nine o'clock the next morning with dark rain clouds waiting to burst.

Marcel took a worried look at them before closing his door. While he and Natonshi DeBraak waited for Antoine to arrive, they heard a voice on Marcel's short-wave radio announce that the enormous low pressure front that covered much of the eastern half of the western hemisphere had dipped to the northernmost reaches of South America. Very colorfully but aptly put.

LeClerc deposited his umbrella next to the door and joined Marcel and Natonshi at the easel set up next to Marcel's desk.

By ten thirty the humidity was more than one-hundred percent in the office. Rain seeped under the door. Sweat polished LeClerc's massive dome and soaked his collar as he bent forward to look at the drawing.

"*Bien*. Now make his nose a bit less wide."

Using deft strokes of her crayon, Natonshi quickly removed the excess flesh, then smudged it with the tip of a petite index finger. From the corner of its cage, Anjoli the caiman watched her work with unblinking eyes.

Marcel stood aside observing in mute admiration. As far as he knew, Natonshi had never drawn from a description before, but she was doing a masterful job.

"Yes, that's him." LeClerc said.

"Finished?" Marcel asked.

"Come take a look," Natonshi purred.

Marcel swallowed hard. Natonshi, the progeny of a Maron Indian and a for-mer Dutch river captain, had olive skin, flowing curls, and wickedly enticing blue eyes.

When asked to do the drawing, she squealed, "I don't want money." The look on her face as she said it, and the sultry smiles as she flashed him as he worked, made it plain she wanted payment in another form.

And he was dangerously close to meeting her price.

"How does it look?" Natonshi asked.

Marcel looked to LeClerc for a reaction.

"*Perfectement*," LeClerc said. "That looks exactly like the man. She even has his expression right."

Marcel focused on the face. It seemed a study in earnest determination.

"You mentioned he left postcards with you," Marcel said. "It seems strange he wanted you to print rather than hand-write the messages on them."

"I suspect he wanted to disguise the fact that *le docteur* wasn't really the one who was answering." He flushed before continuing. "I didn't know that for sure, of course, or I would never have accepted the job. Having his mail forwarded to Haiti seemed suspicious, but I had no reason to suspect he was anything other than what he said he was. I still have more than a half dozen unused cards left. I never threw them away."

"*Sans blaque!*" Marcel exclaimed. "I want to see them."

"They're at my office."

Marcel glanced at his umbrella. The sound of rain beating on the roof quickly put to rest the thought of leaving his office. "I'm afraid we'll have to remain here a while longer."

"I cannot afford the time," LeClerc said. Opening his umbrella, he turned the handle on the door. A gust of wind nearly knocked him to the floor.

"It appears we are confined together for a while longer," Marcel said. "I have the latest *Paris Match* if you would like to see it."

LeClerc stared out the window. "It looks as if I will be able to read the whole issue."

JASON AWOKE AT eight o'clock and immediately called Jennifer's home number. Again he got her voice mail. He didn't know the capacity of her service, but he was sure he would soon come close to filling it.

After leaving another message, he got to his feet. The sight of her hat and uneaten cookie made him heartsick. He dressed quickly.

Anxious to get out of the room, he opened the door and started toward the elevators. Then, catching himself in mid-motion, he did an about-face and headed toward the red exit sign at the opposite end of the hallway.

As he opened the door and stepped inside, he was overwhelmed with a sense of vertigo. The stairway wound down in a dizzying square spiral and disappeared.

A confused flurry of images filled his mind. *Yes,* he cried as a vision of the chambered nautilus he had found in his mother's things stood out clearly.

I've been here before!

The realization electrified him and sent him down the spiraling stairwell on the run. He was soon out of breath and stood panting, staring down at the remaining flights.

Another memory sent him to the inside railing. Everything disappeared into a black abyss at the bottom. The sight sparked another memory, and he took off again with increased vigor. Finally, with legs wobbling and heart pounding, he covered the last steps and slumped to catch his breath.

He again peered into the dark recess at the very bottom of the handrail.

He still couldn't see a thing.

Dropping to hands and knees, he crawled to the cement newel that anchored the railing to the floor. He was pleased to see an oily accumulation of dust. Only hand brushes could clean there, and from the look of things, no one had bothered. Not for a very long time anyway. He hoped not for fifteen years.

Cautiously reaching in, the first thing he found was a balled-up candy wrapper. Some child undoubtedly had enjoyed watching it fall. Jason's smile faded as anticipation gave way to disappointment.

His fingers worked their way through large dust balls and into an increasingly tiny space until he came to the nautilus' heart. His fingers hit something sharp.

Crying out in pain, he yanked his hand free. Blood dripped from his thumb, index and middle fingers. Still, he smiled.

He had found his long-lost woodcarving knife.

Dan woke up at 8:30 in the morning. Sick of cereal and Horny Hildegard's coffee, he had opted for an omelette at his favorite feed bag. As usual, Milda's Café was packed with people when Dan arrived. An aroma of toast and bacon filled the air.

A waitress saw him and gestured for him to move to the front of the line. The black couple ahead of him good-naturedly stepped back.

Moving up, he spotted Carrie Flowers sitting alone at one of the tables.

This must be my lucky day.

He strolled to her table. "Hi, lady. Mind if I join you?"

She gestured to the seat across from him. "How are things going, Dan?"

"Lots of leads that don't seem to go anywhere. Taking a coffee break?"

"Nope. A long lunch break. I've been up since two this morning, and I still have four hours to work."

Before Dan could respond, his cell phone rang from his sport coat pocket. "Arnold."

"Lieutenant, this is Officer Ben Jameson with the Highway Patrol."

Dan's eyebrows rose. "Good morning. Got a DB for me?"

"Not exactly a body, but close. I got a call from a doctor at North Clinic in Thief River Falls. The city librarian is in critical care from a fall. It was touch and go whether or not she would survive."

"Margery Bellamy? I just talked to her yesterday."

"She was brought into the hospital at five-thirty yesterday afternoon."

"That's only twenty minutes after I left for home. Sheriff Norquist and I had been at Hidden Pines Clinic most of the afternoon. He said he had something to take care of, but it never occurred to me to ask what it was."

"She claims that Norquist knocked her down the stairs and stole a book that had a letter in it. She says she thought that Sheriff Norquist would show up at the bank this morning to try to get into a safety deposit box. I called the bank and the woman in the security box section said he had been in, but she wouldn't let him open the box because he wasn't a signatory for it. She said he'd need a court order. He said he'd get one. We'll be waiting for him when he comes back."

Dan smiled. *Good enough for the bastard.* "Outstanding. How did you get my number?"

"You gave Miss Bellamy one of your cards. We found it in her desk drawer at the library. She told us where we could find it and asked me to call you."

"I appreciate the heads up. Let me know what happens."

"Roger that."

"I have a better idea. How about giving me your phone number? Thanks," Dan said, grabbing for his pen and a napkin. "Got it. I'll be talking to you."

"Who's that?" Carrie asked as Dan put the phone back in his pocket.

"HP." He repeated what Jameson had. "To tell you the truth, I'm not at all surprised to hear that Norquist's involved in this. When they haul him in, I want to talk to him again about his connection with Hidden Pines."

"Good to see you smiling. Say, I still have half of my cinnamon roll left. It's too much for me to eat. Do you want it?"

"How about if we share?"

"Okay," she said, with a shy smile.

Their spoons met as they cut off pieces. "Do you believe in omens?" Dan asked. Carrie blushed.

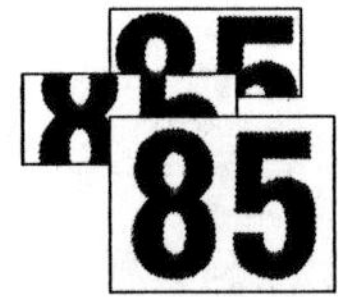

THE PHONE CALL from Jason came fifteen minutes later. Though he had barely started on his omelette, Dan jumped to his feet. "Jason Dumont says he found the murder weapon."

"What does that mean?" Carrie asked with a worried look.

"I don't know," Dan said, laying a twenty-dollar bill on the table. "But I'm meeting him at the hotel. This should be enough for both our breakfasts. Ask the waitress to put mine in a box for me. I'll pick it up from you later."

After a short but hurried drive to downtown Minneapolis, Dan had the valet at the hotel park his car. His heart pounded as Jason got up from an overstuffed chair in the lobby.

"Where is it?"

"At the bottom of the stairwell," Jason said, taking Dan by the arm. "I could hardly believe it was still there."

"Impossible. We went over every step."

"It wasn't by or on a step."

Dan noticed the blood-stained towel. "What's wrong with your hand?"

"I cut it on the knife."

"Sorry to hear that. How do you know it's the murder weapon."

"I just do. I'm not sure how."

The "B" button lit on the overhead display, and the door opened. Passing through a doorway, they found themselves at the bottom of the stairwell.

"Where is it?" Dan asked.

Jason pointed. "It's way inside. Be careful not to cut yourself."

Dan knelt. After pulling a handkerchief from his pocket and wrapping it around his hand, he cautiously reached in. After a few gropes, he found the knife. Blade up.

Looking over his shoulder, he said, "I don't want to sound unfeeling about your injury, but I sure as hell hope your blood hasn't contaminated the evidence."

"I pulled my hand out pretty quickly. I don't think I had time to bleed on it."

Firmly pinching the sides of the blade between his linen-covered fingers, Dan removed the carving tool from its hiding place. The long, hooked blade made his stomach turn. So did the dark coat of dried blood that covered the whole length of the blade and the handle. He scowled at Jason.

"Time for answers, son. Start by telling me how you knew where to find the knife."

Jason colored and averted his eyes. "I honestly don't know. I just did. A vision of a chambered nautilus brought me to Minneapolis in the first place. When I saw the stairwell, I remembered."

Dan Arnold's eyes narrowed. "Did you murder your mother?"

Scowling, Jason said, "I don't know. I had a flash of a memory at the stairwell door. When I opened it, I instantly remembered where my wood-carving knife was."

"Did you touch the handle?"

"I didn't get a chance. The blade found me first."

Dan glanced over at Jason's towel-wrapped hand. Blood had begun to soak through to the surface. "It looks like you have a bad cut. The lab tech at the station will be able to help you."

Jason nodded. "This is important, isn't it?"

"You have no idea. With any luck we may even be able to lift a print off it." He paused and stared at his shoes. "It's a shame you couldn't remember this fifteen years ago."

Jason flushed. "I know. I still can't remember very much about that night. Whatever happened between you and Carrie Flowers?"

"We had a fight," Dan said before he realized what he was saying. "What makes you ask that?"

"I just remember her asking you if you wanted a boy first. I think she was serious when she said she wanted to adopt me."

Dan turned red. "That wasn't very professional of her. It was a crime scene, for crying out loud. Things took a turn for the worse between us not long after that."

"Sorry to hear that," Jason said. "She's a very nice person."

"Yes. And I just was having breakfast with her when you called."

"I just can't help screwing up your love life, can I?"

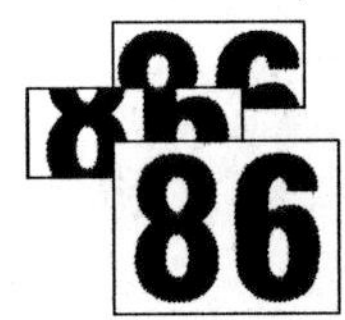

THE TRAFFIC LIGHT refused to change, and Dan took a covert look at Jason, who sat silently grasping his injured hand. The light finally turned green, and Dan eased his car around the corner to the entrance to the parking ramp. The gate swung open as he shoved his red-and-blue card into the slot. His space was just feet away from the entrance.

Quickly moving into his spot, he got out and opened the passenger door. "Last stop," he said with as much levity as he could muster. As Jason emerged from the car, Dan took him by the right arm to escort him to the elevator leading to the walkway.

The door opened when he pushed the call button. When it reopened they were on their way to the lab.

"We'll need your prints and your DNA. I'll come to get you when you're done."

Jason shrugged, and Dan pushed the large metal button on the wall to open the doors. As always, the lab reeked of something being heated or burned. No matter how the organics were analyzed before it, blood, piss, poop, semen and cloth were all subjected to the same process at the end—they went through infrared chromographic and gas spectrometric analysis. Sending a laser beam across the surface of a specimen made a tiny burn that produced smoke. A machine eagerly sucked it up and analyzed the specimen's chemical composition. The spiky patterns produced were as singular as fingerprints.

Funny how it all smelled the same at the end of the line. Just plain nasty.

A young woman with bright cherry lips, wearing a yellow-stained lab coat, came up to them. "Hello, Lieutenant. What can I do for you?"

"Ginger, this is Jason Dumont. We need his prints and DNA. He needs his hand bandaged, too. Are you busy? I can wait or come back for him."

"I'm right in the middle of a work-up, but I should be done in ten minutes I'll get Jason a cup of coffee and finish my labs. After that, I'll fix his hand and take my samples. I'll buzz you when I'm done."

Minus a little mucus from the inside of his mouth and with fresh bandages covering the three cut fingers, Jason sat on a stool in the lab waiting for Dan Arnold. The officer arrived five minutes later.

Ginger pulled Dan aside and led him through the lab door.

"I should have enough blood from the knife to do an analysis. I can type the blood immediately, but it'll take at least eighteen hours to get DNA results."

"Fair enough. Do I need to take him to the hospital?"

"I've taken care of the cuts. He says he had a tetanus shot less than a year ago, so he should be good to go."

Dan turned back toward Jason. "I see you got your repairs."

"She did a very fine job."

"Someone would like to talk to you."

"No problem," Jason said with a shrug.

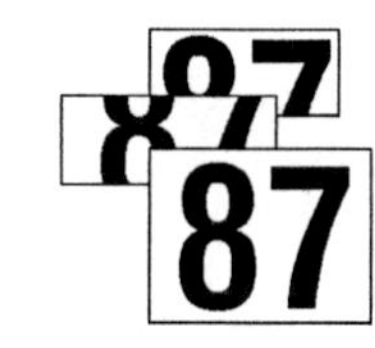

HE SOON REGRETTED his willingness. Jason didn't like Aaron Reese. The officer had an oily voice and never asked direct questions. His posture suggested a wild animal about to spring. Jason wanted to say that it wasn't necessary to beat around the bush. He was more than happy to tell him what he did—and didn't— remember.

"Let's see if I have this right," Reese said, leaning forward and tapping his pen on his teeth. "You don't remember anything after you saw your mother let someone into the room, but you do remember dropping your wood-carving knife over the edge of the railing."

"I remember I was scared to death, and I just had to get rid it. There wasn't any other way."

"What do you mean 'there wasn't any other way?'" Reese asked, bending close enough to Jason's face that Jason could smell stale tobacco on the man's breath. "Why was it so important that you get rid of the knife?"

Jason backed away. Closing his eyes, he attempted to mentally walk backward from the stairs, but every time he tried, his mind went blank. He had a strong feeling that the way he explained it wasn't the way things happened. Finally he said, "I don't know. I only wish I did."

Reese retreated and stared at him for a few seconds before continuing. "You said, 'There wasn't any other way.' There wasn't any other way to do what?"

Jason's heart pumped faster as he remembered standing at the edge of the railing watching the knife disappear into the blackness at the bottom. *It's done. Now no one will ever know.*

He muttered a cry as he opened his eyes.

"Tell me what you saw."

Jason collapsed. "I didn't see anything. I couldn't go back to the room."

"What do you mean?"

Taking a deep breath, Jason coughed and wiped tears from his eyes. "I don't know why, but I know I was afraid someone would find out what I had done."

Dan Arnold continued to study Jason through the two-way mirror. Jason sat bent across the interrogation table with his hands folded and head bowed.

Is he praying?

"I don't know what you said to him, but it sure looks like he's feeling bad about something."

Reese nodded. "For sure. A scab just got pulled off his psyche, and he's hurting."

"What do you think? Did he do it?"

"I don't know," Reese said with a shrug. "It's possible. He must have been extremely precocious, so it's certainly a possibility. My impression is that it's more likely he's covering for someone."

Dan sighed. "Yeah, that's what I've thought all along. But who? His father? He was in Miami. I don't think he'd cover for his uncle. Who else could it have been?"

"Maybe his mother."

Dan's eyebrows shot up. "Huh?"

"Think about it a moment. He's seven years old, and he finds out his mother has a boyfriend. Not only that, his mother is murdered while the boyfriend is there. Jason knows he can't do anything about his mother's infidelity, but he can at least keep his father from finding out about it. He decides the best he can do to prevent it is to destroy the evidence of what happened."

Dan cocked his head, then scowled. "Why would Jason throw the knife away if he hadn't murdered her?"

"I can think of at least one reason. What if he was worried that you could learn something from it that would lead you to find the murderer? Then the whole story would come out."

The scowl disappeared. "Yeah. Hold on. Why did he forget everything?"

"So he wouldn't have to deal with what his mother had done," Reese said, triumphantly tapping on his legal pad with his pen for emphasis. "That was his way to hang on to both parents. He had to maintain the belief they loved each other. He couldn't bring his mother back, but he could keep from remembering what she had done before she was murdered."

"What if his father actually was the one who killed her?"

"That would be an even stronger reason to get rid of the evidence."

"Hey!" Dan said, his face lighting up in a smile. Things were finally coming together. The 'why' of Jason's amnesia had always bothered him as much as the question of who had actually committed the crime.

Once again the scowl furrowed his face. "Wait a minute. Everything you've said so far is fine. I can understand him wanting to keep up the illusion that he lived in a perfect family. But why in the hell is he starting to remember now?"

Reese grinned in triumph. "There's no longer any reason to cover it up. The cat's out of the bag, as it were. His father, the police, and everyone who knew anything about his mother's murder knew about her infidelity. He realizes he doesn't have to bear the burden any longer. I'm sure he'll regain his memory quite quickly from now on."

"Yeah," Dan said, feeling a tiny part of the burden he had borne for fifteen years drop from his back. "I sure hope so."

"I do too. For Jason Dumont's sake."

"What was Melanie's boyfriend's name?"

"Dylan Hansen."

"Let's assume Hansen was the one who killed her, then."

"I'll be more than happy to do that. Why would he do it?"

"I don't know, but I think I can give you a pretty good guess. Melanie and Jason were on the way to Melanie's mother's funeral. She called Hansen to tell him to meet her at the hotel. He arrives. They get reacquainted . . ."

Dan smiled at the euphemism.

". . . . and Hansen tells her that he expects her to leave her husband and join him, that he's waited for her long enough. What if Melanie suddenly got the idea that her boyfriend may have played a role in Naomi's death and confronted him."

"That's certainly possible. For all we know, Hansen may actually have done just that. He was working at Hidden Pines when she died. Not bad, Aaron," Dan said, issuing his highest praise. "Not bad at all. I'll take it from here."

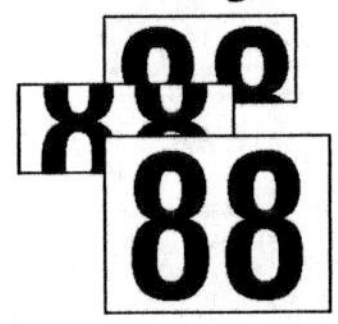

"WE'RE STILL TRYING to figure out how to continue," Dan said, reaching out his hand to pat Jason on the back. Jason jerked his shoulder away. "Why don't you come with me? I'll get you a cup of coffee, and we can go through the evidence box from the room while we're waiting to hear from the District Attorney's office."

Jason flashed a laconic smile. "You don't have any more photographs, do you?" he asked as he got to his feet.

"Yes, but none like the last ones you looked at."

Jason blew a sigh of relief. The evidence box sat unopened on top of his desk in the office.

"Is this all from the crime scene?"

"Yeah," Dan said. "What kind of coffee would you like? We've got a good Kona blend for the office staff, or I can get you something out of the machine. I think vanilla cream is the flavor of the week."

"Kona is fine. I'm really not much of a coffee connoisseur."

Dan pulled two blue-and-white plastic mugs with the black and blue logo of the Minneapolis Police out of his top desk drawer. "I'll be right back."

Jason nodded. As Dan passed the secretary's desk, he said, "Keep an eye on what's going on in my office."

"Sure," she said, looking down at the desktop level monitor. "What's up?"

"Probably nothing. I just want to see how Mr. Dumont acts when left on his own. Wait a minute or two and then tell him that the coffee is still brewing, and it'll be a while before I get back."

"Do you really think he'll fall for that?"

"One can only hope," he said. "I know he was really interested in the box."

Standing by the coffee maker, he watched four minutes tick by on his watch before filling the cups. Returning to the receptionist he asked, "Anything exciting?"

"No. He got up and took a look at the box, but he didn't open it. He just sat down again. He seems awfully restless."

"Thanks."

Dan put on a smile and reentered his office. "Sorry. I didn't think it'd take so long."

Jason took the cup. He asked, "Do you mind if I look at what's in the box?"

"Not at all. Help yourself."

Dan watched Jason closely. The first thing he took out was the yellow page ad. Jason looked up, wide-eyed.

"Does the yellow page mean something to you?"

Jason explained.

"Yes. We were going to buy a remote-controlled model airplane the next morning before we flew to Thief River Falls. I knew the one I wanted. Did you ever hear of a Pizazz 48" Ugly Stick with a Super P8 remote?"

Dan gave him a hard look. "How do you remember all that now?"

"Seeing the page reminded me. I wanted one from the first time I heard about it. Mother and Father even had an argument about who was going to get it for me."

"Really? Why?"

"Father always was the one to buy me things. Every time he went somewhere on a business trip, he'd bring me a present. He was going to buy me an Ugly Stick while he was in Miami when Grandma died, but Mother said no. She said Grandma wanted mother to buy it for me. It seemed to be important to her."

"Do you know why?"

"No."

"Keep looking."

Jason frowned as he took out the woodcarving kit. "Father bought this for me for my seventh birthday. Mother wasn't very happy, but I convinced her I could use the blades without cutting myself. I was right, too. I only nicked a finger once. I liked the curved blade because it was easiest to make small slices."

"Did you use the knife in the hotel room?"

"I was working on my plane while we watched TV. Mother didn't like shavings. She always made me work over newspaper, but I brought it with me into the bathroom."

So far so good. "Anything else?"

"I remember . . ." He stopped, face contorted.

"Yes?"

Jason shook his head. "I don't know. It reminded me of something else, but I can't quite make it out."

"Try," Dan demanded. "We have to find out how the blood got on the knife."

Jason hesitated, then reached into the box. He slowly pulled out the photo of the crime scene. He quickly went back to take out the blood-stained pajamas.

"I was wearing these. I took them off and threw them into the bathroom."

"Of course," Dan said, feeling a glimmer of hope. "That's why you left the footprints."

"No. The pajamas had feet. I hated them, but Mom made me wear them. They made me look like Ralphie in *Christmas Story*. I got frightened from all the blood and took them off."

"But you did step in the blood."

Jason stared at the photograph. "Obviously, but I had taken the pajamas off. I don't see how I could have left a trail like that."

Dan's fifteen-year-old burden began to shift ever so slightly.

"Did you go back into the bathroom?"

"I guess I must have. I don't remember."

Dan fished out his notes and read them. This time he felt a thrill when he came to the desk clerk's statement.

"The desk clerk said someone bundled up in dark clothing and a heavy cap asked for your room number. He said he thought he was trying to disguise himself, but the clerk recognized him because he had visited before. He also said he saw the same man leave about an hour and one half later."

"Carrie told me that. She thinks he's probably the one who killed mother."

"I'm sure he must have come to the room, and Melanie expected him. I think it's likely he killed her in a fight. She had defensive wounds on her arms, and I can't imagine how you could have overpowered her. But none of it explains why you didn't hear anything and how he got out of the bathroom without leaving blood on the carpet."

"I probably did know they were fighting. I don't remember. I do remember taking off the pajamas before I left the bathroom. This killer could have taken off his shoes."

"His shoes would have only been a small part of his problem. He must have gotten blood all over himself when he cut Melanie's throat. The rain gear could have hidden that."

Jason put the photo and pajamas back into the box. "Look. I want to find out what happened as much or even more than you do. Are you going to arrest me?"

Caught off guard, Dan hesitated. "I don't know yet."

"I'll make you a deal. Let me reconstruct the rest of the scene and see if it doesn't bring up some more memories. You can even send an officer with me if he keeps out of the way."

Dan began to pace. The D.A. would never take over the case with what he had. The strong evidence that someone else had been in the room would easily override the bloody footprints and Jason's discovery of the murder weapon.

"I want to know if you remember anything else."

"I promise."

Dan waited until Jason was on an elevator to the lobby before he made a stop at Aaron Reese's office.

"You really let him go?" Reese asked.

"I didn't have much choice. He's going to his hotel. Keep an eye on him."

As he was returning to his office, Ginger Halvorson, swooped down on him with mask dangling under her neck, lab coat sporting suspicious brown stains.

Dan swallowed at the sight. Chocolate, no doubt, he decided. As she drew closer, the expression on her face told him something was up.

"The DNA work on the blood found on your knife won't be done for a few hours," she said with a puckish smile, "but the blood typing is really interesting."

"Yeah? What did you find?"

"For one thing, blood on the knife that belonged to Melanie Dumont . . ."

"No great surprise there," Dan mumbled. "Why the excitement?"

Ginger's smirk grew wider. "Whoever used the knife didn't just use it on Melanie Dumont. I also found a different blood type."

Stunned, Dan could only stammer, "Y-you have to be kidding."

She responded with a devilish grin.

"If there were two victims involved, is there any way to find out how much blood came from each?"

"If there is, I'm not familiar with the procedure."

"Thanks for making my day," Dan said with a sour look. He could feel a headache itching at the inside of his skull.

"By the way . . ." she said sweetly.

"Yeah?" he growled.

"I've been studying the photos from the crime scene . . ."

"And?"

"And even though the woodcarving blade is extremely sharp, whoever slashed Melanie's throat had to be pretty strong. I don't see how a seven-year-old would have been physically capable to inflict such a deep wound."

"So you're saying I should rule Jason Dumont out as the murderer?"

"No, but I'd have to say that it's extremely doubtful."

"Thanks," Dan said, ". . . I think."

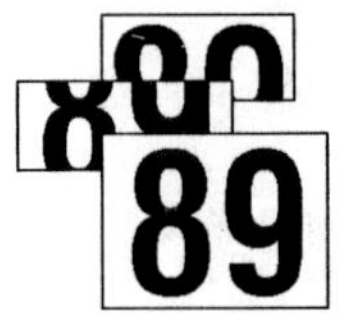

WITH EYELIDS DROOPING, Jennifer arrived at her office at 9:30 a.m. As she fumbled for her keys, she wondered where toothpicks were when she needed them. The thought of her lids curled upward like the lids of sardine cans almost made her laugh. It was the closest she came to feeling better in hours.

She had spent a long, sleepless night. The developments with Jason, the uncertainty about the impending case with Candy, and the expected delivery of Mr. Rabbit, provided more food for thought than a Sominex and a forbidden glass of Riesling could help her digest.

And now she had a hangover.

Opening the door to her office, she groaned at the sound of the busy sawyers, and the stack of files waiting for her.

Not yet! she decided, making her way to Marilyn's office.

After fifteen minutes of trouble-talk with Marilyn, Jennifer made the short trip to her office on leaden feet.

Her phone began to ring as soon as she unlocked the door, and she had to rush to get to her private office open before it switched to voice mail. She expected it was Jason. Even if she didn't want to talk to him, it was necessary.

"Hi, Jen."

The voice made her groan. Not Mike Savich!

"Did I catch you at a bad time?"

"Yes. But there hasn't been a good time lately. It's still nice to hear your voice. Are you calling from Thailand?"

"No. I'm in Columbus. We called the wedding off."

At one time, Jennifer would have been overjoyed at the words. Things had changed.

"I want to see you."

Her heart thumped. With everything else that was going on in her life, she didn't need Mike Savich to complicate things further.

"This wouldn't be a good time."

"Trouble with Jason Dumont's case?"

"That's only one problem among many."

"Sorry to hear that. I have a few days free. If you'd like, I can fly to Minneapolis to give you a hand."

Jennifer found herself stroking the bottom of her neck and quickly caught herself. Reassuming her professional demeanor, she said, "That might be a good idea. The way things stand, I could use some help."

"Then I'll come tonight. Even if we're just colleagues, it sure will be great to see you again."

She flushed. "Same here."

HARD AT WORK writing new case notes, Dan Arnold gazed out his office window to discover a pigeon staring back at him. He remembered Bill Bryson's quip. All a pigeon needed to know in its life came down to answering three questions: "Can I eat it, sit on it, or shit on it?"

Was it curiosity in its red eyes? Did it wonder why this enormous creature endlessly scratched at pieces of paper? Why not try to eat it? Or sit or shit on it? Apparently unable to find an answer, it flew off.

Despite the progress, Dan wished he could eat, sit on or shit on the Melanie Dumont murder case. Anything would be progress.

It was like his niece's Mix and Match book that somehow got made wrong. Try as would, he could never make all the rows match. The dog always ended up with bird's feet.

Only this time it wasn't just one feature that didn't match. Nothing did. Neither Jason nor Melanie's lover had a motive.

He opened his top left desk drawer to take out a yellow legal pad. At the top left line he wrote motive and top right, opportunity. Then he wrote "Gary Dumont" and "Lawrence Dumont."

He immediately crossed off Gary. The man may have had the opportunity, but no discernible motive. He also had an alibi.

His eyes moved down to Lawrence Dumont and stopped. He could have had a motive if he knew his wife had a secret lover. Opportunity? The evidence said he was in Miami when it happened, but the Hidden Pines revelations and the overwhelming probability of a connection with Frank Norquist threw a different light on everything.

Could Melanie have known something she shouldn't have, and threatened Lawrence with it?

Dan shook his head in frustration. Even if Dumont did do it, Dan could never prove it unless Jason Dumont regained his memory or Frank Norquist admitted to conspiracy.

Norquist now claimed top billing. Dan drew a double line under the sheriff's name. Playboy Frank was looking more viable all the time. No obvious motive, but his connection to Hidden Pines and his egregiously inept investigation report seemed more suspicious by the hour. The man was up to something.

The librarian was onto Frank, too.

Could Frank have been Melanie Dumont's love interest? Though he wasn't much to look at now, he could have been fifteen years ago. Melanie made frequent trips to Thief River Falls, ostensibly to see her mother. If she didn't take Jason with her, she certainly could have been trysting with the sheriff when she wasn't visiting the nursing home.

But if it were Norquist, why would he kill her? She presented no threat to him. Even if he had got caught fooling around with her, he wouldn't be the one disgraced. He wasn't married. His reputation wouldn't have suffered if anyone found out.

It might even have helped, Dan thought with a laconic smile.

The smile disappeared. *Could he have been blackmailing her?* He sneered at the idea. Blackmailers didn't kill their victims. On the other hand, the sheriff certainly wouldn't have liked it if Melanie threatened to break off the relationship. To someone of Frank's mentality, that decision belonged to him alone.

Giving up, Dan shook his head and penned two question marks by the sheriff's name before drawing a check by opportunity. Certainly it wouldn't have been that difficult for Frank to track her to the hotel.

Dylan Hansen came next on the list. The mystery man loomed larger by the minute. Motive or opportunity unknown, his involvement was certain. Dan was sure he was the man the desk clerk had seen come and go.

Dan closed his eyes. Why was the list getting longer rather than shorter?

Next came George Fox. Dan had never interviewed him, but Dan had a copy of his arrest record, on the night Melanie was murdered, in the evidence box. Dan crossed through the name with a triumphant flourish.

So where the hell does that leave us?

Nowheresville. If Frank Norquist, or anyone, for that matter, killed Melanie, why was Jason Dumont still alive? Would a murderer leave a witness, even a young one?

Dan had never heard of such a thing. Why had Jason been spared?

He tore up his worksheet in frustration. Either the murderer didn't realize Jason was around when he slit Melanie's throat, or he had some reason to keep Jason alive. Otherwise, Jason must have been the murderer.

Damn! Dan thought, slamming his fist on the desk. To hell with what the lab tech said, and to hell with what Carrie thinks, too.

Jason Dumont killed his own mother!

JENNIFER HADN'T COMPLETELY recovered from Mike Savich's call when Alexander Hunt arrived, fiddling with the controls of a miniature GameBoy. His head bobbed in time with the sounds of gunfire coming from the instrument. Jennifer could feel every bullet and actually leaped from her chair at the sound of a loud explosion.

"Did you win?"

"I just got blown up," the teenager said and slipped the game into his jeans.

"Where's your homework?

"Homework?"

"What I told you to bring with you when you came. Think."

Alexander's brow furrowed. "Oh. You mean what I'm supposed to do the next time the other kids started ragging on Mr. Domczek?"

"That's it," Jennifer said, opening the door.

"Shoot, I don't need to write it down. I can tell you what I'm going to do. I'm going to ignore them."

Jennifer gave him a stern look. "Telling me isn't enough. You were supposed to write down what you would do and why. It's called following directions."

Alexander shrugged. "Guess I forgot."

"Okay," Jennifer said with a shrug. "If we haven't got anything to talk about, let me see your Game Boy. I was thinking about getting one myself."

Grinning, Alexander fished it out of his pocket. "This one's brand new. It's got a clamshell video display."

"Cool!" she said. "Turn it on and show me."

He opened the shell and a display showed on the screen. "Let me try," Jennifer said, taking it from him.

He handed it to her. "The small buttons move the figure. You fire with the big one in the middle."

"Way cool," she said. After fingering the controls for a few seconds, she pushed the off button and opened her top file drawer.

"Hey!" Alexander exclaimed as the drawer clicked close.

"Hay is what horses eat."

Alexander reached across the desk to pull on the drawer. It refused to open.

"Gimme back my GameBoy," Alexander said with a glare. "I want it."

"I'll give it back to you when you turn in your homework," Jennifer said, taking out a yellow legal pad from her desk and handing it to him. "You've got a pen. Now do your assignment."

Alexander's mouth worked, "Bi . . ." came out before he caught himself. Glaring ice picks, he snatched the pad out of her hand.

"You can work here or in the lobby," Jennifer said, evenly.

"Here," he growled. "I don't trust you."

She looked up at the sound of someone knocking on her office door.

Answering it, she found a carrier waiting with a box. "Is Jason Dumont here?"

"Not at the moment. But I can sign for him. Is this from Indian Hill, Ohio?"

The delivery man looked. "Sure is."

She hurriedly scribbled a signature and handed the recorder back to him. After he left, she laid the box on her desk. It seemed amazingly light.

Alexander sat muttering expletives under his breath as she sat staring at the unopened parcel. Finally, unable to control her curiosity, she used scissors to cut the tape on the top of the box. Moving away a mass of tissue paper, she came upon two long pieces of fabric. Rabbit ears. Pulling them disinterred a clone of the stuffed rabbit Melanie Dumont had put into her box of toys.

The sight brought a sniffle. "Good morning, Mr. Rabbit," she murmured.

"Aren't you a little old for stuffed toys?" Alexander scoffed.

"You have your toys," she said. "I have mine. Now MYOB and do your work."

Feeling a pang of guilt, her fingers moved to the front pocket in the toy's overalls. No card from Dylan Hansen this time. The pocket was empty.

She hefted the rabbit with a frown. It seemed heavier than the one Melanie left in Minnesota. Feeling a bulge in its behind, she hastily undid the straps of the overalls and gently pulled at the trouser legs.

"You some kind of perv or sumthin?" Alexander snickered. "I'm going to tell everyone about you."

Ignoring him, she pulled off the overalls. Alexander hooted as she lifted the bottom of the shirt. Her heart jumped at the sight of the two small buttons underneath. The shape of what lay behind them made her gasp aloud.

Fingers shaking so violently she could hardly make them work, she fumbled until she worried the first one open.

"So you got a thing for rabbit's asses." Alexander brayed.

"No," she shot in return. "I see enough other asses during business hours. If you want your GameBoy back, you better finish your work and forget about me. Better still, go work in the lobby."

Glaring, Alexander got to his feet and opened the door. This time he got "Bite—" out before slamming it shut. Jennifer was sure that next time, he would hit the jackpot.

After opening the second button, she slipped a trembling finger inside the pocket. It came in contact with soft leather.

Heart thumping and barely able to control herself, she called Jason's cell phone number. It rang several times before she left a brief message. Not willing to give up, she found the number for the Empire Hotel. At last Jennifer got an answer. "Mr. Jason Dumont, please."

Her heart pounded as she waited. Finally she heard a ring. Please be there, she said, raising herself nervously on her toes.

Now nearly breathless with excitement, she listened to the phone ring until the hotel operator cut in. "Mr. Dumont doesn't seem to be in his room."

THE MINUTES DRAGGED like hours. Young Alexander had long since turned in his writing, sullenly retrieved his GameBoy, and left, slamming the door behind him. But Jason still hadn't returned her call. Jennifer's curiosity had become painful.

Once again she eyed the rabbit like a leashed terrier watching its prey. She had nearly given into temptation twice, reaching for it, but restraining herself before her fingers touched the fabric. She well knew that if they made contact, she wouldn't be able to stop herself.

At least she knew what nestled inside Mr. Rabbit's trousers. He lay facedown on her desk. The shape of the bulge in its back gave away its contents. It was a book. Hidden, thus important.

What else could it be but Melanie's diary?

After three more trips to the water fountain, she no longer could control herself. She pounced.

Fingers working furiously, she wiggled the book free. The baby-soft leather cover had begun to crack at the corners and seams. As she opened the book, she caught the faint aroma of roses. A tiny lipstick-stained card inside read, "Forever. Prince Dy."

Turning to the first page, Jennifer found an entry in small, unslanted letters:

> April 23, 1982. The most wonderful night of my life! Everyone in town must have turned out for *The Music Man*. Dylan was so handsome in his band uniform, and I looked so prim in my taffeta dress with the stiff collar under my chin. Everyone got to their feet and clapped when we were done. No one seemed to notice I had flubbed some of my lines, or that Dylan couldn't manage to sound lecherous when he sang "Marian the Librarian." He's too sweet to be Henry Hill, anyway. Mr. Townsend, the principal, gave me a big bouquet of roses when we made our curtain calls, and I gave them to Dean to put in water. I'm sure he believed me when I said I was staying overnight with Siobhan. I hated to ask her to lie for me, but she knew what we were planning to do and thought it was terribly romantic. Dylan's mother probably didn't even know he was gone. With all the painkillers she takes, she was lucky to know what day it was. Poor Mom must be twice as sick as she is.
>
> I was so scared and so excited when we got to the motel. I stayed in the car while Dylan got the room. I needed him so badly I could hardly wait to get the door open. But Dylan made me go into the bathroom to wait. Wonderfully. When he called me out he was sitting on a bed spread with rose petals holding a bottle of champagne. I'll love him until the day I die.

Excitement building, Jennifer turned pages as fast as she could. Finally, bursting to tell someone, she set the diary down and made a bee-line for Marilyn's office.

Did you bring your lunch today?" she spurted. She could feel her face glow.

"Yes," Marilyn replied. "Did you make up with Jason? You're absolutely radiant."

"No. I found Melanie Dumont's diary."

"Really?" Marilyn squeaked. "You started to read it, didn't you?"

The blush deepened. "Yes. Jason hasn't returned my calls, and I couldn't control myself."

"What's happened?"

"Quite a bit. It starts with the first time she slept with Dylan Hansen. She was really head over heels about him. She was even pregnant by him when she married Lawrence. Apparently he knew. Siobhan had told him."

"Really? Why?"

"Stop squeaking like a school girl," Jennifer said. "I feel unprofessional enough as it is."

"Sorry," Marilyn said, putting on a straight face. "Well?"

"Apparently Melanie didn't have the courage to tell him herself, so she had Siobhan tell him for her. Melanie didn't understand why he married her anyway, but she later found out that Lawrence was sterile. It's more than obvious he wanted a son, even if it wasn't biologically his."

"I'm sure he must have had a very good reason for that," Marilyn said primly.

"And I'm waiting to find out why."

"Was Dylan her first love?"

"No. In her junior year she had fallen for Frank Norquist. The guy was a complete creep then, and I don't think he's changed his spots. Melanie went to Grand Forks to watch him play football and wound up in a motel with him. Apparently she changed her mind about having sex, but he wouldn't stop. She was just thankful she didn't get pregnant."

"Erm, that *is* interesting. I want to hear more. Let's have lunch together. We can share a tuna salad sandwich while we're reading."

WITH THE COPY of the crime scene photo Dan Arnold had given him in hand, Jason returned to the hotel room to resume the painful process of recreating the fatal night. Feelings of anger and sadness had given way to a rock-solid determination to find the truth, no matter what the consequences.

But first he needed some materials.

Catching a cab, he visited a hobby store on Sixty-Sixth and Nicollet and bought a wood carving set and balsa airplane kit. The sight of the curved blade made him sick to his stomach so he kept the bag with it in the trunk as he rode back to his hotel.

His heart pounded in anticipation as he placed the airplane on the floor beside the bed where he had left it fifteen years ago. Sitting beside it, he gritted his teeth as he turned the screw clamp to tighten the blade to the knife handle. Then, with a sigh of relief, he laid it on the night table next to the bed.

The last step was to tear out another yellow page ad and lay it on the night table beside the other bed.

Done.

Trembling, he crawled under the sheets. Eyes closed, he tried to remember what happened when he heard the sound of scratching on the door. Once again his blood ran cold as he opened them and imagined his mother getting out of her bed to open the door.

As desperately as Jason tries to see the figure at the door, the visitor remains an unrecognizable silhouette.

The room again goes dark as the hall door closes.

Then, furtive whispers as the bathroom door opens and gently shuts.

Heart hammering, Jason creeps to the bathroom door and listens.

Surprise, hurt, and anger begin to roil inside his head and stomach.

The sounds stop, and Jason dashes back to his bed. He hears Mother and the stranger creep to her bed. Then he hears moans and sounds of struggle.

Furious, Jason cries, "I'll help you, Mommy!" Snatching the knife from the table, he rushes toward the bed.

"Jason, no."

The knife strikes flesh, though not the flesh he intended, and Mother cries out in pain. Realizing his mistake, he swings at the intruder. After landing one strike on the stranger's forearm, Jason is engulfed by strong arms.

A chill runs through his entire body.

Why had he told Jennifer he'd spoken to Mother through the bathroom door? Did he have to make Mother appear worse than she was to protect himself from the agony of losing his love for her to Jennifer? As much as part of him hated it, Jennifer had become as important to him as Mother had been. Had he deliberately driven Jennifer away by luring her into the words that he knew would end their relationship?

"Stop!" he said aloud, hoping to end the conflict in his head.

He forced himself to concentrate.

The intruder holds Jason with one arm. With the other, he wrests away the knife.

"Calm down," mother coos between sobs. "I understand why you're angry, and it's all my fault that this happened. But there's something you have to know."

"NO!" Jason screams.

The intruder gives Jason a gentle shake. "This is going to be hard for you to understand, but I'm your father. I love you."

Imagining he is the prisoner of a maskless Darth Vader, Jason frees an arm and pummels his enemy. "You are not!" Tears pouring down his cheeks, he screams. "Tell him, Mother."

"It's true, Jason," Mother says with a sob. "He is. His name is Dylan, and he's a doctor. We're going to South America with him to help poor people."

"No," Jason cries, breaking away with a sudden movement. Before the intruder can recapture him, he runs toward the hallway door.

"Jason, come back," mother calls.

Jason refuses to listen. As he steps into the hallway and heads toward the door to the fire escape stairway, he hears footsteps behind him.

"Come back, sweetie," Mother pleads. "We're not going to hurt you."

Panic-stricken, Jason runs down to the first landing.

"You don't have to run away. We're not mad at you and there's nowhere for you to go. Just stay where you are and I'll come and get you."

As she takes her first step, Jason breaks into a full run down the stairway.

"I'm not going to chase you," Mother calls. Sobbing, she says, "Come back when you want to, and I'll be waiting for you. I still love you. Dylan does, too."

The memory ended abruptly and Jason suddenly found himself sitting on the stairs, panting and shivering uncontrollably. Then he began to weep. Despite all he had been through, the source of all his nightmares and pain still remained buried deep in his subconscious.

Why can't I remember the rest?

BACK IN HIS ROOM, Jason paced the floor with quick, angry steps. CNN news blared from the television, but the voices never penetrated his consciousness.

Remembering his cell phone was turned off, he pushed the "ON" button. A flashing green light announced four voice messages.

"Jason, it's Jennifer. Last night was horrible. You frightened me terribly, but I still want to help you. Please give me a call."

After a beep, the second message came on. "Jason, I can understand if you don't want to see me, but Mike Savich is coming to town tonight. I'm picking him up at the airport. He's anxious to help you."

Beep. "Jason, you must call me. I'm sorry I didn't tell you before, but I found your mother's diary in Mr. Rabbit."

Jason's eyes opened wide. *Diary?*

Before he could put the cell into call mode, the last message played. "I'm sure you will be very angry with me, but I've been reading your mother's diary. Whatever you may think of her, she loved you more than you can possibly imagine. I love you too. Call me."

Stunned, Jason sat on his bed. Despite what Jennifer said, the new memories of his mother's infidelity and his attack left him inconsolable. Fifteen years of mourning ended abruptly in the worse pain ever.

He longed to be with Jennifer, but he couldn't face her. She had been right; Melanie was a horrible person. He turned off the TV, then took out his cell phone and fingered in the memory key.

Gary Dumont seemed surprised. "Well, hello, Jason. What's the matter?"

"Mother was a whore. I always knew that she must have let someone into our room, but now I know it for sure. I remember it clearly."

That brought an extended pause. "You remember?"

"Yes. Almost everything has come back." Jason sat on the bed and went through the events.

"How exciting. What happened after you ran down the fire escape?"

"I don't know. That part of my memory is still completely blocked off."

"Did you tell your psychologist friend about this?"

"Not yet. It's a long story, but we aren't friends anymore. She said she hoped Mike Savich could help me. She wants me to go to the airport with her to pick Mike up, but I don't think she can fit three people into that tiny car of hers."

"It sounds as if you'll be remembering everything soon. I'm very happy for you."

"I wish I was happy for myself."

"Oh, I forgot to tell you. I told your father the news about your recovery. He says he'll be there to meet you as soon as he can."

Dan Arnold clutched his forehead. The seed of a headache sown by the chief technician had blossomed into a man-eater. Her announcement about the two different blood types on the knife blade made his temples thump. Popping open the second Tylenol bubble of the morning from his large economy size package, he threw the caplets into his maw.

Ycch!

The swallow of the cold coffee he used to wash them down made his teeth clench. After his talk with the tech, Dan rushed to his office to call Jason Dumont. He got no response. Now an hour later, Jason still hadn't returned his call.

Dan scowled. *The lying bastard must know I'm looking for him.*

Snatching up the receiver, he was about to push the redial button when he realized the futility of another call, and he set the receiver back into the cradle and called Aaron Reese.

"Jason Dumont isn't answering his phone. Is he in his room?"

"I don't know," Reese said in a quiet voice.

"What do you mean you don't know?" Dan exploded.

"I was watching his room, and all of sudden he came out and ran for the fire escape. I waited a few seconds and started after him. I thought he must have been on the stairway, but I couldn't see or hear him. I didn't know what to do, so I started to look in the hallways as I went down. I finally gave up and went back to his room. Something come up?"

Dan put a hand to his fevered forehead. "Yeah. The bastard lied. Or he didn't tell the whole truth, anyway. At least two people were cut with the murder weapon."

"Maybe he didn't know that."

"Don't you start in on me," Dan said in a pained voice. "Keep an eye on his room."

As he hung up, he moaned to himself. *Sweet Jesus, what next?*

A glance at the evidence box brought another wave of hopelessness. Nothing added up. If Jason were guilty, why did he 'fess up to hiding the knife at all? And how could he be so convincing a liar in denying he had murdered Melanie?

There has to be an answer here somewhere.

Determined to find it, he snatched the crime-scene photograph out of the box. *I've missed something.*

Once again he was surprised by the complexity of what seemed such a simple scene. Open bathroom door, bloody footprints leading to the bed where they had found Jason Dumont. For the umpteenth time he wondered why there weren't any prints leading out of the bathroom to the hall door. The stray droplets they found in the room could have come from Melanie's visitor.

But who was this mystery man, and where was he now? Why did he leave the room if he wasn't involved in the murder?

Could he have been Lawrence Dumont?

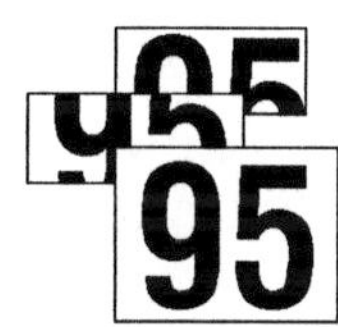

WITH WATER AND WIND still assaulting his building at two o'clock in the afternoon, Marcel Digus felt certain he was trapped forever with an irate Antoine LeClerc, sedate Anjol the caiman, and the dangerously seductive Natonshi DeBraak.

Anjol merely blinked, and Natonshi flirted with her eyes. LeClerc, on the other hand, steamed up the room with his curses and wore a path into the office floor.

"This is ridiculous," he stormed. "I'm losing a whole day's work. Contact your client. One hundred and fifty dollars isn't nearly enough."

"You know I can't do that. No one is forcing you to stay here. You're welcome to leave any time you wish."

That brought a growl.

Half an hour later, the rain began to subside. At three, Antoine LeClerc opened his umbrella and stomped out into a drizzle.

Natonshi turned to Marcel. "*Mon Dieu*, thank goodness he's gone. I thought he'd never leave."

"I was beginning to think the same thing."

"Now we're alone."

"Just for the moment," Marcel responded. "I'm taking you to school."

"Don't be silly," she said with a pout. "Everyone will be going home in just a little while. I want to stay here."

"Sorry. I promised your mother I'd take you back to your class when you were done. I'll be leaving for Cayenne, anyway. It'll take me hours to get there."

"Take me with you. I need some new clothes."

He shook his head. "Everything will be closed by the time I get there. I'm not coming back until tomorrow morning."

She stared him in the eye. "That's all right. Mother won't care."

"*Non!*"

"Oh . . ." Natonshi said stomping a sandaled foot. "*Merde!*" she shouted.

Dan was till trying to figure out what to do next. The sound of the telephone interrupted his confusion. "Arnold."

"Good morning, Dan."

The voice brought the first smile of the morning. "Good morning to you, Trent. What's new? Did Larry confess? The housekeeper decide to spill the beans?"

"No," Trent said with a chuckle. "I just wanted to tell you we finished with Jason's computer. I'm afraid there's not much to report."

"Just what I wanted to hear," Dan grumbled. "Tell me anyway."

"We found a bunch of computer games like *Zork* and *The Hitchhiker's Guide to the Galaxy*. He finished them all."

"Amazing. You bothered to call because of that?"

"Actually it is amazing. All the files were dated from 1988. He was only five years old."

"Impossible," Dan said. "No five-year-old could know what to do with a language-driven computer game, no matter how smart he was."

"You're right. We figure Melanie must have been playing the games with him. He probably dictated all the entries about flowers and plants to her, too. We found a lot of them that had been deleted."

"I'm not surprised. Melanie was a gardener."

"Uncle Gary probably had a hand in it, too."

"Woo, woo," Dan said, drawing circles in the air.

"Actually, I do have something else to tell you. I talked to Bill Connell again. When I asked him what time he and Lawrence got to the hotel, he said it was around five-thirty. He said they had something to eat in the hotel restaurant and went to their rooms. What Lawrence told us about them watching a movie and having something to drink was true. That's when he started to feel tired."

"Did Lawrence pour the drinks?"

"He doesn't remember. When I pushed him about the time he turned in, he said he really doesn't remember."

"Did he have a hangover in the morning?"

"No. He said he felt fine. Lawrence was still asleep when he woke up."

"What time was that?"

"Around nine. He turned on the TV and remembers the time from the news."

"That could have been up to twelve hours. It would be enough time for Lawrence to fly to Minneapolis and return."

"It would be a tight schedule, but certainly possible."

Dan broke into a grin and rubbed his hands together. "Now we're getting somewhere."

96

MARILYN APPEARED IN Jennifer's doorway balancing a brown bag between two cans of root beer and a handful of napkins. "Here I am," she said.

"Don't just stand there. Come in and sit down."

Marilyn sat. Handing Jennifer a napkin, she said, "I made the tuna fish with horse-radish and dill pickle, and used yogurt instead of mayonnaise. I hope that's all right."

"That's the way I make them, too," Jennifer lied.

Glancing at the intriguing leather-bound book sitting on the table, Marilyn poked at it with a finger. "This it?"

"Yes. I'm only halfway through, but it's really quite a story. Apparently Lottie . . . Melanie . . . was having an affair with Dylan Hansen the whole time she was married to Lawrence Dumont. The purported visits to see her mother were a cover story to be with him. She even paid his way through medical school."

"That had to be expensive. Lawrence must have given her a pretty sizable allowance not to have been suspicious of that."

"Apparently he didn't know anything about it. He wanted to know where every penny was spent. His mother gave her the money."

"Her mother-in-law gave her the money?" Marilyn said through a mouthful of food. Washing it down with root beer she asked, "Why'd she do that?"

"She knew how Lawrence was about money. Grace provided Melanie with the money for her wardrobe, too."

"Nice mother-in-law. Didn't you say that she left Jason a lot of money when she died, too?"

"Yup. I've actually known one or two mother-in-laws like her."

"I wonder if Grace ever suspected Melanie was having an affair."

"All Lottie said was that Grace was crazy about Jason. I told you Lottie found out Lawrence was sterile. Either Grace didn't know, or if she did, she never let on."

"I really don't get it. If he knew Lottie was cheating on him, why do you suppose he let Melanie continue to make her trips back to Minnesota?"

"She probably threatened to publicly admit to the affair and let everyone know about Lawrence's sterility if he tried to stop her. Apparently she knew the estate would revert to his brother if it ever came out."

Marilyn made a sour face. "That doesn't make her sound very nice, does it? Didn't you say she left poor Jason behind when she went to see Dylan?"

"Yes. I'm absolutely furious with her for treating him that way. I guess she wanted to keep him from getting hurt. From what she writes, she never loved anyone other than Dylan. Lawrence Dumont was just a means to get her mother the medical care she needed. When Naomi died, Melanie was free. I'm sure she was planning to run away with Dylan the night she was murdered."

"Some people might even say she got what she deserved," Marilyn said in a detached voice. "It sounds as if Lawrence had a motive for killing her."

"He had an alibi."

"That makes me even more suspicious."

"Then add George Fox to your list. He has an alibi, too. He was in jail."

Marilyn made a face. "That's different. What did Melanie think of Mr. Moneybags?"

"She admired him. All she really knew about him was that he was a top executive with a huge pharmaceuticals firm who owned a pain clinic in her home town that seemed to be taking good care of her mother. Lawrence was generous with her and Jason, and she enjoyed the company parties and rubbing shoulders with Cincinnati's upper crust, even though was still just a Minnesota farm girl at heart."

Marilyn glowered. "I'm liking her less all the time. Stop talking and eat your sandwich."

Taking a nibble, Jennifer asked, "Is this really tuna fish?"

"Yes. It's sushi, of course. Isn't that what you use?"

"No. But it's good. I'm not complaining."

"Getting back to Melanie, what did her rich husband get out of this bargain?" Marilyn asked.

"Everything he wanted, apparently: an uncomplaining wife, an adoring son and an heir to the Dumont name and its fortune. He would have lost everything if he didn't have a son. I already mentioned the estate had some kind of primogeniture inheritance clause. Since he couldn't father a child himself, he was lucky in a way she was sleeping with Dylan. Melanie mentions in several places how happy she was that Jason and Lawrence were close. She always made sure she told Jason how wonderful his father was. Only Jason never realized Lawrence wasn't the person she was talking about."

97

AT A LOSS TO know what to do next, Dan went to the office's supply cabinet and took out a handful of three-by-five note cards. Filling them in, he would provide a time line of what happened at the International Hotel from their arrival to the time the troops arrived on the crime scene.

With great patience he printed each of the events Jason had described writing in the estimated times various things happened.

Soon he had more than twenty cards neatly arranged on his desk top. The time line began with Melanie and Jason's arrival at the hotel at the left side, and ended with Dan's arrival at the right.

Between them lay a vast space, and even the filled-in areas had blanks.

Why did Jason take off his pajamas to run to the stairway to hide the knife? Did he run out naked, or did he stop to put on his clothes first? Why did he go back into the bathroom if he already knew Melanie was dead?

The last question seemed to be the easiest to answer. Jason was a seven-year-old, unable to comprehend his mother's murder. Whether or not he was wearing clothes when he disposed of the knife wouldn't matter unless someone saw him.

He scowled. Perhaps that actually was an important clue like the dog that didn't bark at night, though even if he were dressed, he was certain someone would have noticed a little boy out in the hallway in the middle of the night.

His phone rang, and he answered, expecting Aaron Reese to report on his vigil at Jason's hotel.

He was surprised to realize it was Tess. "Hello, Ms. Swanson. This is a nice surprise. Were you able to find Dylan Hansen's employment record with Hidden Pines?"

"Yes," Tess said in a serious voice. "I'm afraid it isn't very good."

"How so?"

"He worked for us during the summers of 1988, 1989, and from early June to November in 1989. We fired him on suspicion of stealing drugs."

Dan sat up straighter in his chair. "That's a serious charge. Why didn't the clinic report him to the police?"

"We couldn't prove anything. And we never had any evidence he was using drugs himself. According to our records, he voluntarily submitted to a blood test. The drugs just seemed to mysteriously disappear when he was working."

"Why would he have taken them? Did the clinic think he was a dealer?"

"No," Tess said with a hint of amusement. "The staff thought he stole them for his mother."

The words struck like a bolt of lightning. Tess couldn't be considered a reliable source, but her accusation shed unexpected light on Dylan Hansen's character. "Yeah?"

"People who knew her say she had been using drugs from her early teens. She was only sixteen when Dylan was born."

"Was Hansen working the night Naomi Marchand died?"

"I have his record here. What's the date?"

"November 5th, 1990."

"Let's see. Yes. That was the last night he worked for us. The night supervisor told him not to come back."

Dan's mind raced as he wondered if there was any way to verify her story. If Melanie suddenly suspected Dylan was involved in Naomi's death, the relationship could have turned sour quickly. And if he was a dealer, it might even explain how he got through medical school. "Where did you get this information?"

"Most of it comes from his employment record, but I also checked with some people who were working here at the time."

"Would you please fax me a copy? It could be very important evidence."

"Of course," Tess said without hesitation. "Give me your number."

When he hung up, Dan returned to the checkerboard that was developing on his desktop. After serious study he moved one of the cards to mark the time the desk clerk saw Melanie's purported visitor leave the hotel.

He silently cursed. It was all very logical, but it didn't tell him a thing.

Jennifer's voice cracked. "I'm all talked out," she said. "Do you want to take over for a while?"

"Sure. Where are you?"

"I was just about to start Saturday, October 8th. Five years before she was murdered."

Marilyn wiped her fingers on the napkin before picking up the diary. Taking a deep breath, she began to read aloud:

> One of the worst nights of my life.
> Saturday Night. Dylan met me at the Starlite. It was pouring and he was an hour late and in a terrible mood when he got to the motel. I never liked the place and told him so many times. He said he didn't want to risk running into someone who knew us. Even though his clothes were wet, I jumped off the bed and landed in his arms like I always did.

> I still can't believe what happened next. He broke my heart by throwing me to the floor. The rage in his eyes frightened me, and for a moment I really worried he would hurt me.

Marilyn looked up at Jennifer, who was equally wide-eyed, then quickly returned to reading.

> Dylan bent over me and I felt myself cowering. I could barely speak. "What did I do?" was all I could gasp.
>
> He raised his hand and began to shout. "I gave up Harvard Medical School to be with you. Instead of a top surgeon, I'm a lousy bottle washer with Hidden Pines Pain Clinic. I hate the place. It should be burned to the ground and the ruins sown with salt. I'd give anything for us to be able to get your mother out of there, but the only way she'll ever leave is to die. I can't wait any longer. I want you and Jason with me now."
>
> I tried to answer, but before I could, he turned around and left.

The last words came out in a barely audible voice. "Wow. Has this Dylan shown any violence before?"

"No," Jennifer said. "Everything else has been about how much Melanie and Dylan had loved each other, and how he treated her like she was a princess."

"Do you suppose . . ."

"That Dylan could have killed Naomi? It certainly sounds as if it's possible. He may even have killed Melanie, too, if she figured out what happened."

"There's a lot of things I don't understand," Marilyn said. "For one thing, if Melanie was sure Lawrence knew about her affair, why didn't she try to find some way to escape?"

"Where would she have gone?" Jennifer replied. "Naomi was a hostage at Hidden Pines Clinic, and Lawrence would never have let her take Jason with her. I'm sure she must have felt trapped. Lawrence probably felt the same way."

"And they both wanted to keep Jason. The poor kid. Lawrence must have realized that Naomi's death would end his hold on Melanie. He obviously didn't know she was taking Jason with her. Otherwise he would have made sure she didn't."

"Then how did she do it?" Jennifer stopped and rolled her eyes. "I'm getting a headache."

Marilyn nodded. "Me too. Ohmygosh. Look at the time. I have to get back to the office. Promise you'll call me if you turn up anything important?"

SHOES OFF AND feet on her desk, Jennifer was on the last pages of the diary when her cell phone rang.

"Are you Jennifer Cahill," a soft voice asked.

"Yes. Who are you?"

"My name is Tammi Wheeler. I'm a friend of Margery Bellamy. She told me you were trying to help Melanie Dumont's son. She gave me your phone number."

"I appreciate the call. Do you have information about Melanie?"

"No. I'm calling because Margery is in critical care. The doctor's didn't know if she was going to live when she was admitted."

Jennifer's eyes opened wide. "What happened?"

"She fell or got pushed down the basement stairs at the library. I don't think it was an accident. I'm pretty sure I know who did it."

"Who?"

"Sheriff Norquist. Margery hates him, and he feels the same way about her. She knows what Frank did. It's probably the reason he tried to kill her."

"Go on."

"It's a long story, but I had Frank Norquist's baby. I was only fifteen at the time. I got home late from a school dance one night. I met Frank in the hallway. He had been at Emery's all night and had had too much to drink.

"He was fumbling to get his key into the lock so I offered to help him. I had a bit of a crush on him and when he asked me if I wanted to come in and have some lemonade, I said sure. We were no more in the apartment when he grabbed me and started to take off my clothes."

Jennifer suddenly remembered Tom Buchanan in *The Great Gatsby*. He viewed women as an entitlement that came with power, too. Not surprisingly, both Frank and Tom were captains of their football teams. And accomplished bullies as well.

Tammi giggled uncomfortably.

"I told him to stop, but I sorta didn't want him to, too. He carried me to his bed. I told him to use a condom, but he said he didn't have any. We had unprotected sex. I had no idea I would get pregnant. When I told him, he denied everything. I knew what would happen if my parents found out, and I was scared."

Even though it was a familiar story, Jennifer still seethed. "I'm sure you were."

"I went to Dylan Hansen. I'd look in on his mother three days a week when he was at medical school. He was working at the Hidden Pines Clinic that summer.."

She stopped and began to sob.

"I think I know what happened then," Jennifer said in a sympathetic voice. "You asked him for an abortion. Dylan refused and confronted Frank."

Tammi sniffled. "Yes. He told Frank to come over to his mother's house. When Dylan told him about me, Frank denied it. Dylan said a blood test would prove who was telling the truth. That's when they got into an argument, and Frank threatened to kill Dylan if anything ever got out. Dylan's mother was listening and told Frank that if anything ever happened to her son, she would tell the whole world what happened."

"Dylan was supposed to have moved to South America," Jennifer said. "He answered all her letters, so his mother must have believed he was all right."

"I know. And when she died seven years later, Frank must have thought he was safe. He didn't know Margery knew what happened."

"How did Margery find out?"

"I was working in the library, and she noticed that I was getting bigger. I told her the whole thing."

"Did you have the baby?"

"Margery gave me money to go to St. Paul, and the Catholic Diocese found me a place to stay until Clark was born. He's eighteen years old now, and he'll be starting college this fall. Margery kept in touch with me the whole time, and even gave me money once in a while. I sure pray she recovers."

"So do I," Jennifer said. Her mind raced. Norquist might well have wanted to keep Margery quiet, but he'd also have a strong motive to want Dylan Hansen dead, too.

She felt a chill.

What if Dylan Hansen had been the intended victim instead of Lottie?

If so, Norquist would be the prime suspect. Since there was no time limit on punishment for statutory rape in Minnesota, Norquist could still go to jail. "I'm really pleased you told me this. I'm sure Lieutenant Arnold will want to hear about it, too. Would you be willing to repeat your story to him if he contacts you?"

"After what Frank did to Margery, I'll be happy to."

"How's Margery doing?"

The doctors think she's going to make it."

"How's Margery?"

"They think she's going to make it."

EXPECTING A CALL from Aaron or Jason, Dan was surprised to hear Jennifer Cahill's voice.

"Good morning. What can I do for you?"

"A young woman named Tammi Wheeler just called me."

Dan listened with interest to her account of the phone call. "Good old Frank. Does she want to do something about it?"

"Maybe. The important thing is that Norquist threatened Dylan when confronted."

"You're right," Dan said. "It is."

"What if Melanie wasn't the intended victim? What if it was Dylan Hansen?"

The words made Dan's hair stand on end. "That never even occurred to me, but it certainly makes sense. I never could come up with a motive for Melanie's murder, but I sure can come up with reasons why someone would want to kill Hansen."

"Thank you," Jennifer said triumphantly. "I also think it's likely that whoever killed Melanie played a role in Naomi's death. I'm sure the murderer counted on Melanie coming to her mother's funeral."

"And also must have known that if Melanie showed up, Dylan would too. But how would Frank Norquist know about Melanie's affair?"

"He was worried about Dylan Hansen," Jennifer said, waving her hand. "What would you have done?"

"I'd keep an eye on him, I suppose."

"Do you think he could have followed Dylan to where he was meeting Melanie?"

"Yes," he said, writing as fast as he could. "Thanks for calling. I really appreciate the insight."

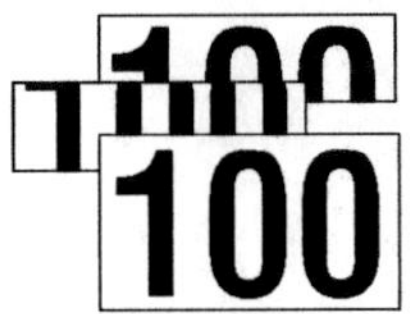

A RIVER OF NEW possibilities coursed uncontrollably through Dan's mind. *Was Dylan Hansen murderer or the intended victim?*

Excitement turned to dismay. He couldn't have been the victim. Once again his niece's cat had a cat's head and body but this time it came up with elephant's legs. Assuming it had been Hansen in Melanie's room, had she been murdered after he left? And why did he drop off the face of the earth if he knew who did it?

Did Melanie have a second visitor that night, or did Dylan Hansen murder her?

Frustrated, he rubbed his forehead. No longer did the cat have elephant feet. They were stomping on the top of his head.

A knock on his door came as a welcome relief.

"Come in."

Sandy Burns, the dispatcher, opened the door and peeked in. "Carrie Flowers just called. She wants you to meet her at the Fourth Precinct. She says someone there wants to talk to you."

As he neared the station, Dan rejected the busy parking area behind the building in favor of a spot under a tree on the street. After turning on his flashers, he took off for the station door on the run. The officer at the desk recognized him and pushed the buzzer to open the door into the operations area.

Ignoring surprised looks from the precinct denizens, he knocked on Carrie Flowers' door.

She greeted him without a smile. She stepped aside to reveal Jason Dumont sitting behind her.

Dan thought he looked terrible.

"I'm glad to see you," Jason said. "I ditched whoever you sent after me. I knew you would be looking for me, but I was afraid to come back to your office."

"I'm sure you were," Dan said in an even voice. "Especially since we found two different blood types on the knife blade."

"I knew you would," Jason replied. "That's why I came here. I honestly didn't remember what happened. I wasn't trying to deceive you."

"I'm sure you weren't," Dan lied. "Let's hear the rest of the story."

"I still don't have it all myself," Jason said. Bending forward, he began to relate his newest recollections.

When he related his attack on his mother, Dan interrupted. "The coroner's report said there were defensive wounds on your mother's arms. He thought they came when she tried to fend off her attacker."

Nodding, Jason resumed telling his story.

When he finished, Dan said, "So you obviously didn't kill this man who was in the room. If you did, you could never have disposed of the body. Unless . . ."

"Unless what?" Carrie asked in an angry voice.

"Unless your mother helped you."

"Brilliant," Carrie growled. "What did she do with the body? Did you find another one you're not telling me about?"

Glaring, Dan shot back. "Then what happened to him? Jason?"

"All I know is that the next thing I remember is returning to the room and seeing mother in the bathroom."

Dan quickly took his notebook from his pocket and jotted something in it. "But there wasn't anyone else in the room when you returned?"

"No."

"What happened next?"

"I ran in to see if I could help her. I got scared and grabbed the knife. I was full of blood, so I took off my pajamas. I ran to the fire escape. When I came back to the room, I must have thought I might still be able to help mother, so I went back into the bathroom. When I knew she was dead, I hid under my bed. I was sure that if I had come back earlier, I could have saved mother's life."

"You couldn't have," Carrie said, putting comforting arms around Jason's neck. "You would only have been killed yourself."

Jason began to sob, and Carrie glared at Dan.

"She's right," Dan conceded. "But getting back to what happened, do you remember anything more about the stranger?"

Carrie handed a Kleenex to Jason. After blowing his nose, he said, "I remember he was tall. Sort of like my father. At first I thought it could have been Uncle Gary. When I finally got a look at him, I knew it wasn't."

"Can you describe him?" Dan asked eagerly.

"Yes. I can even show you his picture. He was in mother's yearbook."

"What's his name?"

"Dylan Hansen."

"Bingo!" Dan said, jumping to his feet. "We already have the picture of him Jennifer Cahill sent to me. I'll get copies to the police websites. He'll be on all the news networks by tonight."

"Good, but I may be able to come up with something even better," Jason said.

"What do you mean?" Dan asked, excited.

"I've still got a big blank to fill in. If you both come back with me to my room, I may be able to find the missing pieces. You were both there with me after it happened." He said, "And you're the one who comforted me."

"Let's go," she said before Dan could respond.

Dan took the ticket the parking ramp machine spat at him, and waited for the gate arm to rise. "I haven't been here since the night your mother was murdered," he said. "Half of the floor was torn up at the time."

"I know," Jason said, earnestly craning his neck.

How would he know that? Dan wondered as he searched for a parking space. He finally found one on the third level.

Jason was the first one out of the car. Looking back down the ramp he said, "The door at the bottom of the fire escape stairway leads directly into this ramp, doesn't it?"

"It sure does," Dan replied. "Why do you ask?"

"I want to take a look at it. There's something familiar about this place."

Dan's pulse quickened and Carrie flashed him a hopeful look. "Go for it. But the door to the hotel is locked. We'll have to open it from inside."

"That's all right," said Jason. "I want to take a look at it from this side first."

"Be my guest."

They took the elevator to the first level. The fire escape door was only a few feet away.

Jason studied the door for a moment, then moved to it, turned and put his back against it. He stood wide-eyed and staring for a moment, then closed his eyes. Opening them, he shouted, "I was here! I'm sure of it!"

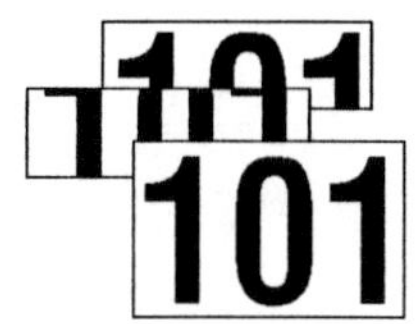

JENNIFER SLOWED AS she approached the corner of Forty-fourth and Halifax and made a left. Candy Lane lived high on a hill in a brooding mansion. A stairway through a tiered retaining wall with brightly-colored pansies, impatiens and petunias led to it. She had passed many others like it. The "old" area of Edina was built in the forties and fifties and most of the houses were Tudors and lavishly turned-out Dutch Colonials.

Jennifer parked Marilyn's Achieva across the street and turned off the ignition. Candy knew Jennifer's Audi, and would have been suspicious if she spotted it. She wouldn't recognize Jennifer, either. The Minnesota Twins jacket and matching baseball cap made her indistinguishable from any of the other nameless workers who passed out flyers in the neighborhood.

Getting caught wasn't the problem. Catching Candy wearing her Converse shoes was. But the trial was still several weeks away, and Jennifer was certain Candy would make a mistake, sooner or later.

And Tim Vincent would be happy to help when she did. Just like Mark was. She had a terrible feeling she was using Tim, too.

Calling him wasn't easy, but necessary. Carefully avoiding personal matters, she found out that the phone number for the mysterious call she received the morning Candy poisoned herself came from a disposable cellular. Untraceable.

He also explained the difference between the rules of evidence in a Civil Court as opposed to a Criminal Court. Charging Candy with a crime could lead to a search warrant. Otherwise Jennifer would have to rely on a "disclosure and spoilage" writ that would allow the possibility of the evidence getting "lost," damaged, or the substitution of another pair of shoes for the incriminating footwear.

Nothing to do except sit back and wait.

She had nearly finished the newspaper she brought with her when Candy suddenly emerged from a car and dashed toward the stairs to the house in a pair of red tennis shoes. Jennifer recognized them immediately, and her heart leapt.

Both Candy and the car were gone in a flash. Confused about what to do next, Jennifer got out of the car and crossed the street.

As she did, she saw a layer of mud at the base of the step. Undoubtedly overflow from the recent rain. In it were two perfect shoe prints. Bending forward she saw the distinctive diagonal mark they had noticed from the print in Jennifer's office.

Though barely able to talk, she took out her cell phone.

Tim Vincent and two Edina police officers arrived half an hour later. Vincent unslung a canvas bag from his shoulder and squatted. "Mud's still wet, huh?"

"Yes. Can you take an impression from that?"

"Nope. It has to be dry."

"Then how . . . ?"

"Relax," Vincent said opening the bag. "I've got a hair dryer"

Jennifer broke out laughing. "You're kidding, aren't you?"

"Of course," Vincent said, pulling out a small black object. "Would you guys get the portable generator, please?"

Grinning, he turned back to an open-mouthed Jennifer. "I can tell without taking impression that you caught a break. There's no doubt this is a match to the print we found in your office."

Getting to his feet, he held the hair dryer out to Jennifer. "Hold this."

Mouth still agape, she took it from him as he removed his cell phone from his pocket. "We have a go," he said. "I'll send you a photo of the prints. You can show them to the judge to get a search warrant."

The two officers quickly returned carrying a small engine on four-by-fours. They set it on the ground near the prints. Vincent pulled the starter cord. With a puff of smoke, the engine jumped to life, sounding like a power lawn mower.

Once it was smoothly running, Vincent plugged the hair-dryer cord into the end of a second cord that unrolled from inside the generator. The whine of the dryer joined the buzz of the generator.

"Voila," he said, moving the dryer over the surface of the mud.

At first, nothing happened, but in no time, the mud began to solidify.

Minutes later the dirt dried, and he poured a grayish liquid into the footprint.

Candy Lane appeared on the stairway. When she saw Jennifer, her eyes narrowed. "What are you doing here?" she demanded. "You're not supposed to come within a hundred yards of me."

"I'm just standing on the sidewalk," Jennifer said, casually. "You're the one who came too close to me."

"We're taking an impression of your shoe print," Vincent said. Eyeing her red tennis shoes, he said, "It looks like you may still be wearing the ones that left the impression. Take them off."

"I will not. I don't have to," she said, crossing her arms in front of her chest. She turned to go up the stairway when one of the Edina police raced up the steps after her. Snaring her around her waist, he lifted her back down the stairs.

"Leave me alone," Candy screamed as she kicked against his legs with her heels.

"Let's just go and sit in the car," the officer said in a calm voice.

As Candy was led away, she turned and threw a venomous look at Jennifer. "I'll get you for this," she hissed.

102

JASON DANCED EXCITEDLY as he waited for the elevator door to the open. All the thoughts hadn't yet straightened themselves out yet, but at least he understood the buzz of emotions playing in his mind.

The elevator door opened. When it did, he raced out with Dan and Carrie.

"Where you going?" Dan called.

"I'm not sure."

He led them to the fire escape door. "Follow me in, Lieutenant."

Opening the fire escape door, Jason ran down to the first landing. "Just wait at the railing," he called over his shoulder.

Looking up, he saw Dan at the top looking down at him. "Good. Now start down as if you're chasing me."

Quick footsteps rang out, and Jason rushed down two more flights. "Now stop and go back up the stairs."

Dan soon again appeared at the top of the stairway. "What now?"

"Go back out the door."

Jason squeezed his eyes closed and listened for the door to shut.

What do I do now?

Mother was gone. He knew he would have to go back to the room sooner or later. But as much as he wanted to, his feet remained rooted in place.

Finally they worked, and he started back up. He found it harder to breathe as he climbed, but at last he could see the top just two flights ahead of him. Starting up the last flight, the sound of the door opening stopped him in his tracks.

Had Mommy come back to get him? About to call out, he saw a dark figure appear at the top of the stairs. Moments later, loud footsteps echoed on the stairway.

That's not Mom! It's someone scary and he's coming this way!

His heart thudded. What can I do?

RUN!

He had only one direction to escape from whomever was thumping so heavily down the stairs above him. Uttering a soft cry, he turned around and dashed down.

Flight after flight the thumps continued to pursue him two flights behind. Jason's lungs ached for air and he nearly cried out when he felt something sharp stick him in the bottom of his left foot.

He stopped. The thumps got louder and he again started to run. Limping.

Nearly exhausted, he covered his mouth with a hand to silence his labored breathing. Finally, unable to go any farther, he stopped and took three gasping breaths. In the interval, the figure on the steps moved several steps closer. The spectre was gasping, too. The sounds seemed familiar somehow.

For a moment Jason considered stopping and letting the figure catch up with him.

Then he remembered what the dark figure looked like.

Gathering up the last of his strength he began to run. The stairway suddenly ended and he could see a doorway ahead. With heart pounding and the footsteps crashing behind him, he opened the door.

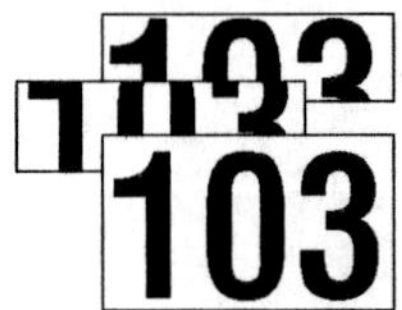

103

JASON STOOD NEXT to the open door, pointing.

"It was just like this the last time I was here. There were bits of concrete and dust everywhere. I could barely get the door open."

"I don't understand why the man who was behind you didn't see you when he came into the garage."

"There was a trash bin next to the door and I hid behind it just as the door opened. I didn't know who it was, but he sure was big."

Dan nodded. "I have a feeling it was a good thing you hid. So he came through the door holding a large black bag. What happened then?"

"He started to walk up the ramp. I heard a noise coming from the outside, and he stopped and turned around."

"What kind of noise?"

"An engine. It was a truck. I could see its headlights through the plastic that was covering the entrance. When he realized someone was coming, the man headed straight to one of the holes and dumped the bag inside of it. Then he took off toward the stairway leading to the lobby. When I was sure he couldn't see me, I ran to the stairway door and opened it."

Dan frowned. "It was locked. How did you get back in."

"I told you there was debris on the floor. Something must have kept the door from locking."

"Then what?"

"Then I climbed back up the stairs to the room. I saw mother in the bathroom and ran in to help her. When I started to walk in the blood, I got scared and took off my pajamas. That's when I ran back and dropped the knife. I still wanted to help mother, but when she didn't move when I took her hand, I ran under my bed and hid."

Dan nodded. Turning to Carrie, he said, "The cement trucks were still here when we arrived. They were pouring cement. The bag must be buried under the floor."

104

HEADLIGHTS FROM AN automobile flashed and brakes squealed as it ended its descent at the bottom of the exit ramp.

Rob Connors, wearing dusty bib overalls and a hard hat, glanced over at it.

"You want to know why we were working here fifteen years ago?" he asked in a loud voice. He pointed a beefy fingers toward the spiral where the vehicle had just disappeared. "There's your reason. Whoever constructed the building screwed up.

The concrete was crumbling and the cars were actually sliding on the debris. The ceiling was too low, too. Cars were always scraping against the ceiling."

"Look, I don't mind," Dan Arnold said. "And you were working here from the third of November until the second of December?"

"I don't remember exactly," Connors said, his bug eyes glittering like bits of obsidian. "That sounds about right. Look. I don't mind coming down here, but I have no idea what you want. We had all our permits, and everything met code, so we didn't do anything illegal. And that was fifteen years ago. Why're you worried about it now?"

Dan patted him on the shoulder. "Relax. You didn't do anything wrong. We just needed to ask you a question or two about how your crews operated. It sounds as if you had some fairly deep holes when you were working."

"We actually had to lower this floor three feet. We tore it up section by section so the ramp could stay open."

"That must have been quite a job," Dan said, glancing at Carrie. "What did your crews do with the broken concrete after they got done with it?"

"We ran it through the crusher, enriched it and reused it," Connor said with obvious impatience. "That way we didn't need to use so much new 'crete."

Dan nodded. "How about the trash?"

A faint look of concern crept across Connor's face. "We had a dumpster."

"Did you keep it locked at night?"

Eyes squinted. "Of course. Why?"

"I used to work construction when I was younger," Dan said. "Sometimes we threw the trash into the excavations."

"None of my crews would've done that," Connor said in a defensive voice. "This is a high-visibility public place. Disposing of trash that way is illegal, and I didn't want any bad publicity for the company. If anyone had done that, I would have fired him."

"So, the men threw their trash into . . ."

"We used twenty gallon trash bags."

"And you're sure these bags were thrown into the dumpster?"

Connor's face turned purple. "I couldn't watch them twenty-four hours a day. Even if one or two got thrown into the digs, it wouldn't have made much of a difference. The 'crete was more than three feet thick."

"What'd happen to the trash that was bagged after the dumpster was locked?"

"It would have been left out until the next day."

"At the time, we met a cement truck when we got to the International. Why was it there at one in the morning?"

"We were working around the clock to get a bonus. Every day we finished before the deadline was worth twenty thousand dollars to us. I made sure someone was there most of the time."

"That's all we needed to know," Dan said. "Thanks for your help."

Connor shrugged and threw him a puzzled look. "You brought me here just to ask me that?"

"Yes. Actually you've been very helpful."

Dan and Carrie watched Connor stomp off to his truck and drive off.

Dan grabbed his cell phone. "Okay, Matt, bring in the magnetic imager."

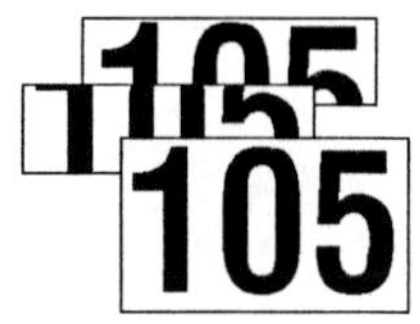

"WE'VE GOT ANOTHER one, Lieutenant," the plainclothesman called as he set an orange marker on the floor.

Dan Arnold marked the position on his rough map. That made seven bags so far. Too many. His chances of getting approval to dig were declining by the minute, even though Jason Dumont was sure he saw the figure drop a trash bag into one of the construction holes.

An auto slowed, and Dan waved him on. He did the same to shoo away the attendant, who had been rubbernecking. Luckily it was well past rush hour and most of the cars had already left for the day.

He studied the five blaze-orange markers. He had, at most, one shot. And it was a blind one. Cadaver gas detectors worked on dirt, but not concrete.

Jason and Carrie stood to the side, talking. Dan gestured to them. "We're coming up with too many bags," he said in a worried tone. "I've got a better idea. Show me where you were hiding, Jason."

Jason moved to a spot near the fire escape door and squatted on his haunches. "There was a trash bin here, and I hid behind it."

"Good," Dan said. "Now pretend you're a statue."

With that, he headed for the nearest marker. Turning around, he said, "Is this the place?"

"No. It was farther back and more to the right."

Dan took six steps. "Here?"

"It could be, but I think it may have been even farther back . . . Yeah, there."

"Good." Dan called out to Carrie, "Come over here. I need your body."

She came grinning.

"Stand here," Dan said.

She did. "Now I'm going to go to each of the other markers. I want to make sure we have the right one."

One by one, Dan stood on the markers. Each time, Jason shouted an emphatic, "No." After coming to the last one, Dan took out his cell phone and hit the call button. "Hi, Jack. We're ready for the compressor and jackhammer."

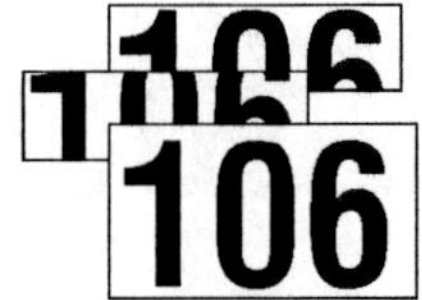

106

CHIPS, CHUNKS, DUST, and an occasional spark flew as three men worked in tandem with hammer blades centered on a yellow chalk line. Dan, Carrie and Jason stood nearby with their mouths and noses covered by linen masks and ears stuffed with rubber plugs. The floor vibrated under their feet. Unable to talk, they communicated by expressions and gestures.

Suddenly a sizable chunk jiggled free. Dan held up his hand. "Stop!" he shouted.

They did, and the quiet was deafening.

"Let's see what we've got here." A flashlight jumped to life and illuminated the hole. His pulse quickened at the sight of something dark just peeking out of the concrete. Uttering a cry, he dropped to the floor on his stomach and reached in.

His fingers met plastic!

"Grab this," he called out. He handed the flashlight over his shoulder. Someone took it. "I need the box cutter."

"Right here," Carrie answered.

Dan reached back and Carrie slapped it into his hand like a nurse assisting a surgeon. "Now shine the flashlight down here."

Even with Dan's body in the way, scattered bits of light splashed inside the opening. Some landed on top of a black plastic bag.

"We got it!" he shouted. Inching forward, he reached down with knife in hand. The plastic was brittle and crackled as the blade easily cut through it. Dan gripped the blade with his mouth, pirate-style, then pulled the plastic apart.

"Hand me the flashlight."

His heart hammered as strands of brown hair appeared. "We've hit pay dirt."

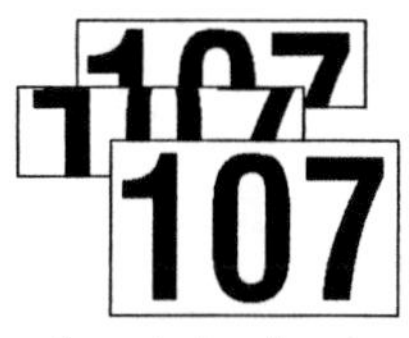

DAN WATCHED AS Investigator Mark Phillips emerged from the pit in the ramp floor with hammer and chisel in hand. Heat and exertion had turned his face deep carmine. It also left him sweat-stained from the cleft in his chin to the steer's head on his belt buckle.

"That's it for now," he wheezed. "I'll get my camera and take some snaps."

"How long before you can attempt an identification of the corpse?" Dan asked. "I've been waiting fifteen years for this and I don't want to wait much longer."

"It'll be a while. We're going to have to enlarge the hole quite a bit to get it out."

"Too long. I need to know what all's inside of it now. A flashlight won't work."

"No," Phillips said, "but I have something that will. I'll be right back."

Dan stood at the edge of the hole impatiently beaming his flashlight into the opening he had made in the bag. No matter where he stood, he couldn't see a thing.

Shortly, Phillips returned carrying what looked like a small black valise. "Hold this so I can open it."

Puzzled, Dan cradled it in his hands. Phillips opened it, revealing an intriguing piece of equipment. A coiled piece of what looked like electrical cable stretched out from a black piece of plastic resembling the eyepiece end of a plastic telescope. A metal cylinder stuck out of the plastic at a right angle.

"What the hell is this?"

"Bend over," Phillips said with an evil grin.

"Huh?"

"You ever had a colonoscopy?"

"Yeah. I'll never forget it. Hey, wait a minute . . ."

"Relax. We're not going to use it that way, but it's the same thing. It's called a Borescope. The black part is the eyepiece and there's a fiber-optic light at the end of the flexible cable. You may have a bit of trouble finding a way to fit yourself into the hole in the concrete, but once you do, this baby will let you see everything in the bag."

"Cool. Any ideas how I'm going to get down close enough?"

Phillips grinned. "Do you mind standing on your head?"

"I don't know. I haven't tried it in thirty years. Why?"

"I have an idea."

Lying belly-down on a stretcher with the investigator holding his feet and his eye to the seeing end of an endoscope, Dan could imagine Carrie ready to explode from holding her hand over her mouth to keep from laughing aloud. He didn't blame her. It had to be a funny sight.

It took a moment to learn how to operate the equipment, but he soon could see the innards of the plastic bag. The picture from the eyepiece was bright enough, but the field of vision extremely limited. At his pushing, the fiber-optic lens snaked forward across the top of the skull with its bits of skin and hair. Dan guessed the body had mummified. Pushing the cable forward, he came to the victim's doubled-up legs.

Dan blinked, beginning to feel the effects of the blood rushing to his head. He gave it a shake.

The victim was lying in a fetal position. Had he been buried alive?

Taking a deep breath to ward off vertigo, Dan pulled the peek-cord back.

"Jesus!" he exclaimed, nearly diving headfirst off the litter when he saw an empty eye-socket staring back at him.

"You all right?" Phillips called.

"I'm fine. Just do your job and hang on to my feet."

Feeling dizzy again, he slowly maneuvered the cord forward, moving down toward the victim's ribs. On the way he thought he caught a glint of light. Gently pulling back, he repeated the motion. Yes. Something seemed to be hanging around the corpse's neck. He eased forward, lost sight of it and pulled back to start anew. After sliding his body slightly to change the position of the lens, he retraced his steps.

"Yes!" he cried as he saw what he was looking for, a necklace with an amulet dangling over the empty rib cage.

His vision blurred, this time more severely. His head now throbbed and he could hardly breathe.

No! I'm too close.

Rheumy-eyed and dizzy, he inched the scope forward. At last the amulet hanging from the chain came clearly into view.

It was a miniature trombone.

The sight made him dizzier than he had been before. "Pull me up," he shouted.

Blood thumped in his head as he sprawled face down on the floor. After several deep breaths, he pushed himself to his feet.

Turning to Jason he said, "We've found Dylan Hansen. What can you tell me about this mysterious dark figure that threw him into the hole?"

"I told you all I remember. He was tall and wearing rain gear."

Dan suddenly remembered the phone call from the HP officer. Stepping aside, he pushed a button.

"This is Matson."

"Greetings, officer. This is Lieutenant Arnold. Do you have Frank Norquist in custody?"

"No. He never came back. The dispatcher with the sheriff's officer has been trying to raise him all day, but he isn't answering."

"It looks as if things may have gotten too hot for him. Be sure to let me know if you find him."

"I sure will."

Dan turned to Jason. "Have you ever seen pictures of Frank Norquist?"

"Just the one in Mother's yearbook."

"Could he have been the one you saw?"

"It's suppose it's possible. He was a football player. I expect he may have been big."

"Oh, he was. For sure. He's even bigger now. And he's on the loose."

108

IT WAS FULL dark when the taxi boat glided into the parogue at Cayenne, Marcel Digus grabbed the handlebars of his motor bike. The boat landed with a light bump, and Marcel pushed the bike up the short incline to the street.

Even though he had been there many times, he always felt a bit overwhelmed when he came to the big city. He still wasn't used to seeing street lights, automobiles, telephone and electric lines, or buildings with more than one story.

Marcel jammed his foot down on the starter, and the motor bike's engine jumped to life.

Cautiously crawling forward, he came to the first traffic sign and turned left. A large sign announced Place de Palmistes. He rolled to a stop and parked in front of the shop with a sign advertising Services de Typographie et Photographie, happy; the eight-hour trip was over, but it had left him and the Vespa splashed with mud.

As expected, the shop door was locked, but Marcel knew that the owner was still there. He never went home before midnight. Unmarried, Pierre Hugo surfed the net until he finally couldn't keep his eyes open.

Marcel rang the doorbell. Seconds later, a man in a white shirt came to the door. He looked out the window and then unlocked the door. "Allo, Marcel. Why so late?"

"I have something I need emailed," Marcel said.

Pierre Hugo took the drawing from him with a grunt. Marcel caught the odor of Beaujolais on the man's breath. "*Ou va t'il?*"

"To the US. Here's the address."

Pierre stuck out his lower lip and nodded. "*Pas mal du tout.* Who did this masterpiece?"

Marcel colored. "A friend."

Pierre noticed the mud. "It must be important if you came all the way from Kaw after a hurricane."

"It is," Marcel said, laying a twenty-Euro note on the counter. "May I use your phone to call my client?"

"Be my guest."

The Local Irish Pub was crowded and customarily noisy for a Friday evening, with three tables in the Sanctuary section filled. It made for cramped quarters. Jennifer, sitting cheek to jowl with Marilyn, had to scrunch up her shoulders to finish the last piece of her shepherd's pie. Marilyn's elbows took up much of the table as she worked on her Curry House chicken.

"Do you think you can find a place to put some dessert?" Jennifer asked. "I mean in your stomach, not on the table."

"Yes. And you have to have some, too. My treat. I don't understand why you think you have to reward me for offering to drive you to the airport. I want to meet this Mike Savich, too."

"It isn't a reward, it's a celebration. Candy Lane got what was coming to her."

"Are you sure?"

"She's under house arrest with a locator on her ankle."

"That doesn't necessarily mean anything. Kids can get out of them. From what you've told me about Candy, I don't think it would even slow her down."

"Forget Candy. How does Whiskey Kissed Chocolate cake sound to you?"

"Too good to be true."

Jennifer gestured to their waiter.

"Good choice," he said as he wrote the order onto his pad. "Let me take your dishes."

A surprised Marilyn hurriedly scooped up the last of the rice with her spoon as he pulled her plate away.

They turned at the gale of giggles from the next table. A victimized bride-to-be sat blushing at the sight of the flimsy negligee she was pulling out of her gift box.

Jennifer watched with a wistful smile. She had seen many wedding parties in her life, but she enjoyed the sight less and less with the passage of time. Each year the brides seemed to look younger. This one looked younger than some of her patients.

"What's going on?" Marilyn asked.

"The bride's opening her presents. If those women have any more wine, they'll have to be rolled out of here."

"You're not jealous, are you?" Marilyn chided.

"Of course not. Whatever gave you that idea?"

"You look wistful."

"I do not. Just wishful. I just wish for once I could pick out the right man."

"What about Mike Savich? He changed his mind about going to Thailand to get married because of you."

"I never said that! More to the point, he never said that."

"You don't really think he's coming to Minneapolis just to see Jason, do you?"

Jennifer snorted. "You've got the wildest imagination! Please keep it under control. I don't want you dropping any wide hints around Mike."

"Trust me. Seriously though, you don't sound terribly happy. Anything the matter?"

"To tell the truth, I'm not as thrilled about seeing him as I thought I'd be. I'm glad you're coming with me. I don't want to face him alone."

"Jason, huh."

"Yeah."

"If that's the case, then maybe you should forgive him. After all, it was the seven-year-old in him who tried to hit you. Jason the adult would never do such a thing."

Jennifer's eyes grew wide at the words. "I guess I must have been so shocked when he threatened me I was just a psychologist dealing with a violent patient. I never looked at it from a seven-year-old's perspective. Some therapist I am." She grabbed for her purse and took out her cell phone. When she turned it on, she found the message light flashing.

"*Bon soir, Ma'mselle. C'est* Marcel Digus," said a cheerful voice. "I wanted you to know that I am sending you a scan of the drawing of the mysterious *docteur.* I think you will be pleased with it."

Jennifer threw the cell back into her purse and jumped to her feet. Hurriedly digging into her purse for her billfold, she handed two twenties to Marilyn. "This should be enough to cover everything. I have to get back to the office."

"What's the big rush? Stay here and finish your dessert."

"The man in South America emailed the drawing of Dylan Hansen. I have to see it."

"Oh. Then I'll have the waiter box up our cake and I'll take them with me. Just run along. If the guard is around I'll have him walk me to my car. Otherwise I'll meet you in the lobby."

"Deal," Jennifer said. "Thanks too much."

THE GUARD SAT at his desk. Before he could go into his routine, Jennifer hastened into the elevator. As the door shut, she wished she wasn't so quick to brush him off. She was feeling edgy.

If your body tells you something is wrong, there probably is a reason.

Paying heed to her sensibilities, she hugged the wall as she tiptoed to the turn in the hallway leading to her office.

The sound of labored breathing stopped her in her tracks.

Uncertain if she should continue on, she sighed in relief when she caught sight of a reflection in the window. The cleaning woman was swabbing the floor with wide sweeps of her mop.

Jennifer put her shoes on and started forward. *"Buenos noches,"* she said.

The woman returned her greeting without looking up from the floor. "Watch your step, *par favor."*

Jennifer stepped gingerly through the thin layer of liquid soap to her office door. Fingers shook with anticipation as she set the key into the lock and turned it. Barely hesitating long enough to turn on her lights, she dashed to her inner office door and made a bee-line for her computer.

She tapped her foot in anticipation as she waited for the start-up screen to appear. When it did, she hurriedly clicked on the e-mail icon.

The mail counter indicated forty new messages. She clicked on the one labeled "Drawing." Her heart pounded as she opened the jpeg enclosure.

The machine took its merry time, but finally an image appeared on the screen.

Dan's cellphone vibrated. Rushing to the door of the hotel to escape the din of the jackhammers, he answered just as his voicemail message began.

"This is Trish, Dan," his assistant said. "You just got an email from Jennifer Cahill. She said the attachment is a drawing from some lawyer in South America. Should I send an officer over with it?"

Dylan Hansen? "No. Just forward it to my Gmail address, and I'll pick it up here at the hotel."

Leaving a curious Carrie and Jason behind, he rushed to the check-in desk. When he flashed his badge, the clerk nervously handed him a slip of paper. "You'll need this to log on. The computer is just around the corner to the left."

He found an IMAC computer sitting on a large desk.

His fingers flew as he logged on to his mail account and found Jennifer's message. His pulse raced as he waited for the image to appear on the screen.

When it did, Dan's eyes opened. "Oh, jeez!"

Without logging off, he rushed back to the parking ramp. Carrie stood alone.

"Where's Jason?" Dan shouted.

"He just got a call from Jennifer Cahill. He's on his way to her office."

"Oh shit," he cried. Heart pounding, he ran for a quiet place beyond the ramp. Jennifer's phone rang three times and went dead.

Fighting his rising concern, he tried another number.

"Damn!"

Fingers shaking, he dialed 911. "This is Lieutenant Dan Arnold. Send a squad to the Lumber Exchange immediately. I'm on my way there myself."

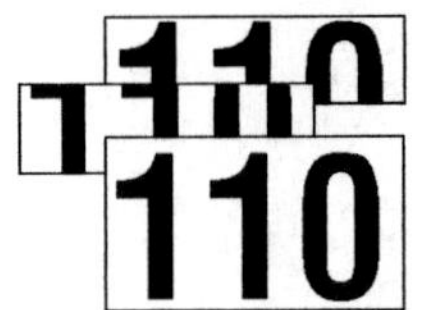

JENNIFER FELT A wave of uneasiness as she stepped out of the elevator. Anxiety grew deeper with each step.

This time I'm going to wait for him.

She was tapping her foot and looking at her watch when he appeared two minutes later.

"Good evening, Miss Cahill. What can I do for you?"

Barely able to speak, she said, "I'd like you to escort me to my car, please."

"This must be my lucky day. Two beautiful women in less than an hour."

"Marilyn is here?"

"I walked her to her car five minutes ago."

Forcing a smile, she took the man's arm. A glance at her watch told her that Mike's plane would land at eight o'clock. That left only an hour to get to the airport and find a place to park.

"You're working late on a Friday night," the guard said as he opened the door leading into the ramp.

"Yeah," she responded.

That ended the conversation. Opening the door to the ramp, Jennifer was surprised to see so many cars still in the ramp. Then she remembered it had a weekend special for parking for revelers at Block E.

"Here we are," the guard said as they came to Marilyn's car.

"Thanks."

"My pleasure," the guard said. Suddenly a beeper echoed. The guard pulled a small black box from a leather carrier next to his holster. "That's an alarm. I have to get back upstairs."

She watched him leave, then turned back to the car. *Marilyn must have heard me. Where is she?*

The garage suddenly seemed eerily quiet and Jennifer considered turning around and heading back to the building.

Then she heard a rustle ahead of her.

"Marilyn?"

Blood pounded in her ears at the silence.

She took a step forward, then froze, not knowing to take another step forward and look in Marilyn's car or turn to flee.

"Marilyn, please say something."

Taking another short step forward, she looked through the back window and saw the raised headrests. She reached out for the door handle and stopped in mid-motion. It was covered with a dark wet stain.

"Jennifer!"

She spun around in terror at the voice.

"It's Jason. What's the matter?"

Her eyes widened. "Stay away from me."

"Don't be silly. I'm worried about you."

Her hand inched downward to her bottle of mace. As he stepped forward, she said. "Jason, stop."

"Sure. Just get into your car and drive away if that's what you want to do. I don't want to hurt you. I know I frightened you and I'm sorry."

She took another step backward. As she did, she got a view of the front seats in Marilyn's car.

"Marilyn," she screamed at the sight of her friend slumped in the passenger side seat.

She screamed again as a dark figure appeared holding a pistol with a silencer. "I made a mistake," said an unhappy voice. "I thought she was you. I didn't want to hurt anyone, but I had no choice."

Jason stepped forward, eyes wide in disbelief. "Uncle Gary?"

"None of this should ever have happened," Gary Dumont said. "You should have died in the hotel room with your mother."

Jennifer watched as his finger tightened on the trigger in slow motion.

A white blur flashed behind him. The gun flew up, and Gary screamed as something slammed into his back.

Jennifer and Jason stood dumfounded at the sight of Candy Lane with a baseball bat in her hand.

"How did you get away from your house?" Jennifer asked.

With a superior grin, she said, "It was easy. Removing the ankle bracelet was child's play. I came here to break the headlights and knock the mirror off your car. But when I saw him kill your friend, I couldn't let him hurt you. I hate you so much I can't imagine life without you."

Gary groaned and started to reach for the gun. Jason kicked it away, then planted a foot on Gary's neck. "Don't move."

Sirens sounded outside the ramp, and a car with flashing red and blue lights stopped next to them.

"I'm glad I got here in time," said Dan Arnold.

Epilogue

A UNIFORMED OFFICER cuffed Gary and pulled him to his feet. As a second officer held out cuffs for Candy Lane, Jennifer moved next to her. "You don't have to do that. I'll see she gets home. She saved my life."

Jennifer watched, heart in throat, as one of two EMTs stepped back from Marilyn's open car door shaking his head. "Call the coroner," the man said.

"Oh no," Jennifer said with a sob.

Jason took two threatening steps toward Gary, shaking in rage. "You planned this whole thing from beginning to end, didn't you?" he growled. "You killed my mother and now another innocent victim. It wouldn't have done you a bit of good. I remember everything now. I remember what happened the last time I visited you before Mother and I flew to Minneapolis. You didn't mean to kill mother. You wanted to kill me."

"I had no choice," Gary said with a sob. "I was sure Lawrence would kill me if he suspected what had happened to you. I made you promise you wouldn't tell anyone, but I knew sooner or later it would come out. I couldn't let myself be arrested."

"You knew Melanie was pregnant when she married Lawrence," Jennifer said. "You found out that Lawrence was sterile and couldn't produce an heir. The estate would ultimately revert to him."

"Why didn't he just remarry and produce another heir in case something happened to Jason?" Dan asked.

"Father knew Gary would demand a DNA test on the offspring," Jason said. "It would prove he wasn't my father."

"Yes," Gary said.

"But why did you come to Minneapolis?"

"Sheriff Norquist told Lawrence about finding out about Dylan Hansen's safety deposit box," Gary said. "I knew about it when my contact in French Guiana forwarded the letter from Hansen's mother. I never told Lawrence about it because I knew Hansen and his mother were both dead and couldn't cause any trouble."

He stopped. "But then you told me Dr. Cahill had hired a private investigator to find him and I realized I was in serious danger if the man I used to answer Dylan's mail could remember me. That made it imperative to take care of her, too. That's when things got out of hand."

"Why is Father in Thief River Falls?"

"Lawrence said Sheriff Norquist called him and told him about finding the key in a letter Hansen left for the town librarian. I told Lawrence he had to personally make sure no one ever opened the box. It would shut Hidden Pines down, and the family would lose everything."

"Is he there now?" Jason asked.

"I'm sure he is. He said he wouldn't come back until everything was taken care of. We both had an interest in safeguarding the inheritance."

"I loved you," Jason said. "You loved me and mother. How could you have done what you did to me?"

"I couldn't help myself. When you resisted, I knew you would eventually tell, even though you promised me you'd keep the secret. There was only one sure way to keep you from telling Lawrence. I never intended to hurt Melanie. It was a complete accident."

Jason glared at him. "Now I know why I've always hated to be touched. I should have known it was you when you mentioned seeing her wearing the necklace. The night she was murdered was the first time I ever saw it. She had a gold allergy. So do I."

Dan pointed an accusing finger at Gary Dumont. "Now it all makes sense. You knew you would have a chance to catch Jason in an unguarded moment when Melanie brought him to Minneapolis. You probably even orchestrated everything to make sure Jason was with her."

Gary Dumont nodded once again.

"Were you responsible for Naomi's death, too?" Dan asked in a growl.

"No. But I think Lawrence and Sheriff Norquist may have had a hand in it."

"Why did you kill Dylan?"

"It was an accident, too. I saw Dylan Hansen in the lobby, but I didn't have any idea who he was. I intended to lure Melanie out of the room and do what I had to do while she was gone. That's why I stole her luggage. I waited until I was sure Jason would have been asleep, and then I was going to call her. She was supposed to come down to the front desk and identify her bags and leave Jason alone in the room. I never dreamed things would turn out the way they did."

"You . . . you must have seen me running out of the room with mother after me," Jason said. "Mother left the door unlocked and you let yourself in."

"Yes. I had no idea what was going on, but it seemed perfect. I would hide until everyone was asleep and . . ."

"Kill Jason then," Dan said, seething. *This bastard is even more ruthless than Lawrence.*

"Yes," Gary said, "but when I got in, Dylan Hansen was in the bathroom. I had no idea he was there, and I nearly had a heart attack when I heard, 'Back already?' He must have been in the shower became he came out of the bathroom in a towel and saw me. I shot him and was dragging him into the bathroom when Melanie showed up. I had left the gun on the floor by the closet. She saw what I was doing and tried to attack me. Jason's knife was on the sink . . ."

Jason roared in rage and swung out wildly at Gary.

Dan caught him. "We have to know what happened. I can imagine how angry you must be, but I've suffered a lot at his hands over the years, too."

Jason turned his back on Gary and refused to turn around to look at him.

Dan pressed onward. "Why didn't you just leave both the bodies behind?"

"I still had to account for Jason. I got blood on my clothes and there was blood on the bathroom floor. I had brought a trash bag with me to carry Jason's body from the room. I threw my clothes and Hansen's body into it. Luckily, I was close to Hansen's size so I got into his clothes to wait for Jason to come back. I intended to leave his body with Melanie's and have Hansen take the blame. I had his wallet, so I knew who he was."

"Why did you change your plans?" Dan asked.

"The phone rang. Of course I didn't answer it. The answering machine came on. Security was on its way to the room. I knew I couldn't wait."

"So you took the bag and left. You didn't realize it, but you chased Jason all the way down the stairway to the parking ramp. When the paving crew showed up, you ditched the body into one of the holes and took off. Then what happened?"

"I went back through the lobby into the hotel."

"And the desk clerk saw you. Why did you try to establish Hansen's identity in South America?"

"I wanted to make sure people thought he was still alive. I visited Kaw on an expedition to find botanicals for Maple Leaf. It seemed the perfect place to have Hansen reappear and so I took out a postal box. I hired someone to answer his mail."

"You had me fooled," Dan said. "I never even suspected you. I suspected Lawrence and tried to keep track of his movements. You were on sabbatical leave, so you could come and go as you pleased without suspicion from anyone."

"Were you in the garage last night?" Jennifer asked.

"Yes. I wanted to see where you parked. I expected you would show up with Jason."

Jason turned and wiped at his eyes. "You nicked the fuel line in my airplane, didn't you?"

"I hired someone to do it. Everything could have ended when you were flying to Minneapolis."

Jason took a step forward, glaring. "I don't know how I felt when I lost my mother, but I've never felt so betrayed before. I can't even begin to tell you how much I hate you. I'd give anything to be able to choke you to death."

"You had better ask for protective confinement when you're in prison," Dan said, "otherwise you'll end up like Jeffrey Daumer. Cons don't like child molesters."

He gestured for an officer. "Take him away. I can't even stand to look at him."

Jason watched, steely-eyed, as Gary Dumont, head hanging, was led away.

"This isn't right. Father is as guilty in his own way as Gary is. He can't get off."

"He won't. The DEA is going to raid Hidden Pines. He's the owner. And I'm sure Frank Norquist will be more than happy to turn state's evidence against him if he thinks he can get a reduced sentence."

Jennifer put her forehead against Jason's chest and began to sob. "Marilyn's dead. She didn't even know any of you. I don't even understand why your uncle killed her."

"He must have thought she was you," Dan said. "She probably was going to put something into her car on the passenger side. Your car was next to it, so Gary probably thought you were going to open your driver's door." He turned to Jason. "Did you tell him you were going to the airport with Ms Cahill?"

"Yes."

"Ohmygod!" Jennifer said.

"What's the matter?" Jason asked.

"Mike Savich is waiting for me at the airport. I don't know if I'm fit to drive, though."

10:30 News Report, KKAQ Radio, Thief River Falls

Pennington County Sheriff Francis Grantham Norquist was arrested this afternoon at Northwest Medical Center while attempting to tamper with the life support system of Margery Bellamy. Ms. Bellamy, Thief River Falls head librarian, had been admitted to the Medical Center intensive care unit after falling down the basement stairs in the library building. Though Bellamy declined comment, Eric Klein, spokesman for the Minnesota Bureau of Criminal Apprehension, stated that there was strong evidence that Ms Bellamy's fall was not accidental. Klein stated that the Bureau was investigating a person of interest in the matter. Ms. Bellamy's condition has been upgraded from "critical," to "serious but stable." Friends are requested to contact the Medical Center before sending cards or flowers.